# Dark Country
## Songs of Love & Murder

Darren E Laws

# Dark Country

*Song of Love and Murder*

*The second Georgina O'Neil Novel*

Darren E Laws

Fiction aimed at the heart
and the head...

Published by Caffeine Nights Publishing 2014

Published in Great Britain by Caffeine Nights Publishing

www.caffeine-nights.com

British Library Cataloguing in Publication Data.

A CIP catalogue record for this book is available from the British Library

ISBN: 978-1-907565-10-6

Cover design by

Mark (Wills) Williams

Everything else by

Default, Luck and Accident

# Darren E Laws

Born in East London, Darren's first writing success came in the mid 1990's, winning first place in a short story competition for a BBC Radio 4 arts program. The thrill of hearing his words read on Radio 4 drove him to write a series of short stories with a dark and quirky nature before progressing to lengthier works. Darren then crafted his first novel 'Turtle Island', a crime thriller, which was picked up by an American publisher.

Darren also has another novel, 'Tripping', a surreal black comedy described as chick-noir, published.

Dark Country is the second Georgina O'Neil novel. A third novel in the series is being written.

To Natalie

Always
Brave beyond words

## ACKNOWLEDGEMENTS

Thank you Sarah Able for editing this book with me. It was such a rewarding experience and the book is so much better for your sharp eye and mind.

Thank you Will for the brilliant cover!

Thank you Natalie for your patience.

# Prologue

## Hello Darkness, my Old Friend

Portmorion, Maryland
November 2002

The echo of darkness hung in the air with only the constant throb in her temple as company. Georgina placed the phone down and contemplated the long night ahead. Time would slow, insomnia's effect would prove Einstein wrong in this other realm of physics. Tick-tock. She could see the vapor trails of her breath and realized that somewhere, somehow the seasons had changed since she was last at home. Though nothing else had. There were still the unopened boxes which had remained obediently dormant in her absence. She had long since forgotten the contents, the only betrayal a black permanent marker designating the final destination, bathroom, sitting room, bedroom ... This was home, yet she felt like a tourist. The clock in the bedroom shouted the passing of each second, taunting the emptiness of her life. She reflected on the past six months and smiled at the knowledge of making a good friend in Leroy. He was at the end of the phone over eight hundred miles away, the closest friend she had. Rather than spending a night looking at the ceiling waiting for dawn to break, Georgina headed along the corridor to the sitting room. There was no TV, she was hardly ever home, so what was the point. 3:37 a.m. Time had slowed to the point where it appeared to be moving backwards. She settled onto the sofa grabbing a novel from a bookcase filled with books, this was not an act of discerning choice, it was a random action buffered by the fact that she knew she wanted to read every book collected on the shelves. Books she had read were passed on to friends, acquaintances or occasionally and purposely left in public places, more so if she enjoyed the book. As the words of the book eased her mind, the shutters of sleep approached and her eyes grew heavier until the mental images of the fiction world she was reading were replaced by the "will-o'-the-wisp" images of sleep dancing before her. Fleeting, taunting images like a boxer's jab which she couldn't control. Memories of why Georgina chose to fight sleep where possible. Sometimes she lost the fight and sleep would come even though it wasn't wanted. On good nights, if sleep came, there would be no dreams or none that she would remember, just a brief encounter with blackness. Georgina would wake refreshed and happy. This wasn't to be the case tonight. Tick-tock, tick-tock.

Georgina woke with a noise in her head and as the reality of being awake filtered through, she realized that the alien sound which woke her was actually emanating from her throat ... a scream came from deep within her. Starting from the pit of her stomach working its way up through her chest and throat, ending in a piercing shriek. Cold air rushed against her skin which felt clammy to the touch. Beads of sweat matted her hair, sticking it to her forehead. She had no idea how long she had been asleep, only that daylight was creeping through a tiny crack in the curtains. Who needs an alarm clock?

*The Teenarosa Motel, Talinha, Texas*
*Saturday July 26, 1958*

*Jonah Fintall banged on the dust-laden window once more. Small microbes of dirt bounced back into the dry atmosphere. He turned to his left where Officer Mike Reynolds was standing impatiently fighting off the sweat from streaming down his forehead into his eyes. His complexion was ruddy but seemed to go hand-in-hand with his overweight stature.*

*"See, it's like I told you, she's not answering." Jonah pressed his face closer to the glass and peered through the grimy film to the room inside. "I can see her in the bed, she hasn't moved all morning." His homely Texan accent bounced off the window.*

*Officer Reynolds wiped the sweat from his face using a handkerchief that was already soaking wet. "It's not a crime to ignore fans, Mr. Fintall."*

*"I know, I know. But what about the girl?"*

*"The girl?"*

*"Yeah, her daughter. She booked in with her two nights ago. A little one, no more than three or four, I'd say."*

*The police officer looked at the motel manager and then at the door. "You got a key?"*

"Spare keys to all the rooms." Fintall searched in his pocket and removed a solitary key, which he handed to Reynolds.

Officer Reynolds' puffy fingers grabbed the key and placed it in the lock. "You better be right, Mr. Fintall." He banged loudly on the door and waited a full minute. Jonah Fintall was still looking through the window. Room 11 remained silent.

"Any movement?" Reynolds asked. Hoping for some activity inside the motel room.

Jonah shook his head. "I don't like the look of this. Had a suicide here three, maybe four years ago. Had to throw away a whole bunch of bedding. Blood just wouldn't shift, no matter how much you scrubbed."

Reynolds turned the key in the lock and slowly turned the door handle. The door sprang free. The smell of dry air and death poured through the opening. Reynolds stepped back and placed his back against the door frame, his head tilted upward trying to find a clean cool stream of air. "Mrs. Dark ... Mrs. Dark, are you okay in there?"

No answer. Just the constant buzzing of blowflies.

Reynolds steadied himself and wrapped his chubby fingers around the grip of his regular issue pistol, flicking the holding strap off his holster and withdrawing the weapon in one easy movement. Jonah Fintall moved away from the policeman but remained peering through the window. Reynolds turned and weapon drawn entered the motel room.

"Mrs. Dark ... Mrs. Dark?" Sweat finally breached his eyebrows and ran into his eyes. Officer Mike Reynolds blinked. The salt concentrate in his sweat stung. His hand trembled slightly but Reynolds breathed deeply a couple of times to regain his composure. "Mrs. Dark?"

No reply. The buzzing of the flies grew more intense.

The officer drew closer to the bed. The outline of a woman's body was clear through the linen sheet. The odor of decay in the hot room was evident. Reynolds leaned forward and tapped the woman's foot with the muzzle of his gun. There was no response. He turned and looked at Jonah Fintall who was now standing in the open doorway, watching the proceedings. Reynolds could not hide the desperate look of fear etched on his face. He walked around the side of the bed until he could see a mop of tousled blonde hair protruding from beneath the sheet. By the side of the bed on the cabinet was an empty medicine bottle with a few white pills scattered, some of which were on the floor. Reynolds trod on something, which cracked under the weight of his heavy boot. He looked down to find some more tablets. "Mrs. Dark?"

The door to the bathroom was closed. Reynolds moved closer to the body in the bed. He reached forward, fingers outstretched, until they grasped the bed sheet. Reynolds pulled the sheet down. Amy Dark did not react; she did not move or give any signs of life. Her eyes were closed as though asleep, her features soft, showing no troubles or angst in her sleep.

"Mrs. Dark?" Reynolds voice was soft as though he didn't want to disturb her; maybe it was the fear of waking the dead. His hand moved forward closer to her shoulder. "Mrs. Dark, its Officer Mike Reynolds from the Talinha County Police."

He made contact with her body, first his fingers, then his hand as he gently rocked her body. Her body moved as one as though she were a mannequin. The cold, unforgiving feel of her body registered in Reynolds' brain. Amy Dark was in the throes of rigor mortis.

Reynolds turned his head to face Jonah Fintall. "She's dead."

Fintall's face briefly lit up. "This place will be a shrine," he whispered.

Reynolds pulled the sheet back exposing the body of Amy Dark. She was wearing a nightgown. "This don't make sense, who dresses for bed and then commits suicide."

"I could open it up as a bona fide tourist attraction."

Reynolds looked at the motel manager with disbelief.

There was a muted sob from behind Officer Reynolds. At first he thought it had come from the body. He had heard of such things, gasses escaping corpses in low groans or moans. But this was a definite cry. The cry of a young child.

"The girl," Fintall said, as he entered the room. The smell of corruption slowed his pace. As he passed by the body of Amy Dark, Jonah Fintall glanced briefly at her. There was nothing dignified about her death, it was obvious her bowels and bladder had passed excrement and urine on her death as the body's muscles relaxed. It was not how he would have liked to remember the Queen of Country and Western music.

The cry came again.

Reynolds turned to the bathroom door. "I'm coming, honey. Just hold on."

Officer Reynolds placed his gun back in the holster and secured the safety strap. He edged toward the door with more confidence than when he entered the motel room and walked straight into the bathroom.

*"Poor little m ..."*

The sound of the gun firing was like an explosion in the room. Fortunately Reynolds knew little of it before his spinal cord was severed by the bullet snuffing his life like a candle. Reynolds fell to the ground, never to get up, just the brief realization of a hot stinging sensation. Fintall had no desire or curiosity to hang around; on hearing the shot he turned and ran for all his life was worth. His whole body felt saturated with sweat and much to his shame, urine. Fear had relinquished his body's automatic hold over his bladder and for the first time since he was a boy, Jonah Fintall had wet himself. As he ran he felt spurts of hot piss drenching his legs and trousers, his bowels threatened betrayal but nothing was going to stop him from running. Nothing, except the second shot which he heard in its entirety. The blast knocked him sideways, punching the wind from his stomach. Fintall's legs wobbled unsteadily but he kept on running. He could see his small office and living quarters only yards away. Soon he would be safe. He had a gun in the office. Soon he would have the gun in his hand and be on equal terms with his assailant. He never heard the third shot as his head split like a ripe banana filled with minced meat. Jonah Fintall managed to run three more steps before his legs finally stopped receiving signals from his brain, the brain that was now lying in segments in the dust forced through the large exit wound in his forehead.

*Fortune's End Trailer Park, Wink Winkler, Texas*
*Wednesday July 26, 1978*

*"Ssh now, baby, hush."*

Caroline Dark walked back and forth across the mobile home. She had seven steps each way before being confronted by a wall or a room divider. The baby continued to cry. The wail from its tiny lungs filled the confines of the small trailer.

*"Come on Susan, give your momma, some peace. Hush now."*

Caroline was drained and close to breaking point. Six weeks on the road, living out of a coach, instead of a string of low rent motels and hotels had taken a toll on Caroline Dark's health. She wished now that she had never listened to her boyfriend, Bobby Oates. The very idea of touring with a young baby in tow was little short of mad. And where was Bobby now? Caroline sighed ... she wished she knew. It had been two weeks since he had last been in touch. Two painfully long weeks of endless shows and upping sticks and moving on to the next state or town. "The surest fastest way to make bucks." She wished she had never listened to him. If it were not for the support of her band and the two roadies then the tour would have finished when Bobby left. Caroline sat down on the quilted seating at the end of the trailer and looked out of the window. At least she was home now for a night or two. Home, such as it was, was a cheap trailer sited in the cheapest trailer park in Texas. This was her night off, her one free night before another string of shows taking her through Texas to Louisiana. Caroline's reflection stared back, so haggard and unfamiliar was her face, that for a moment, she thought someone was outside staring in at her. Her eyes were heavy and ringed with dark circles, blackened by interrupted nights of lost sleep as Susan started to cut her first tooth. Caroline's skin was dry, flaking in places, dehydrated by the harsh sun and wind that had been battering Texas for the past few days. Her hair was in equally poor condition and thankfully hidden under a Stetson when she performed.

Susan continued to cry.

"For Christ's sake, shut up," Caroline whispered, exhausted by her life.

The baby was not planned, nothing much was planned in Caroline's life. Nothing much, except this two-bit tour that was supposed to bring her enough money to take a year or two out and do nothing except raise little Susan and maybe write a song or two for a new album when she was ready to come back. Bobby had the money and Bobby was gone, whether he would have it when he returned was a moot question and one Caroline was keen to ask. On the small table in front of Caroline was a bottle of beer, the lid was off and a glass sat with the sticky residue of a drink at the bottom.

There was a knock at the door.

Susan continued to cry.

"Come in, it's open." Caroline raised her voice so it could be heard above the baby.

The door swung inwards and for a moment the visitor was obscured. He walked into view silhouetted under the light above his head.

"Detective Gary Morris, ma'am. Lawton PD Comanche County." A man, aged no more than twenty-five, held up a leather wallet with *a shiny badge and an ID card. Caroline was too far away to see the photo. She was more concerned with hiding the plastic bag of marijuana on the table. She scooped it off and placed it under her legs, hidden by the table. Susan continued to cry, but her sobs were quieter now. Her little body shook every now and then.*

*"Don't get up, ma'am. I ... I ..." Morris looked around the confines of the small trailer. "You are, erm, Caroline Dark?"*

*Caroline laughed. "Well, at least I know you're not a fan. What is it, detective, has my baby been keeping the neighbors awake?"*

*"No ma'am, nothing like that." Morris looked distinctly uncomfortable.*

*Caroline sensed that he had no desire to be in the same room as her. "Comanche County, where the heck is that? Never heard of no Comanche County before."*

*"No ma'am, it's not in Texas."*

*Neither was Morris's accent. "I am sorry to have to ask you but did you know a Mr. Robert Oates, ma'am?"*

*And now he was talking using past tense. Caroline had seen enough movies to realize that when police talked in past tense it was usually with good reason. She could feel a burning in the pit of her stomach, which was threatening to rise. Caroline nodded affirmation. As she held the baby close to her chest she could feel the tiny heart of her child beating through the thin fabric of her blouse, the pattern synchronizing with her own until there was just one heart beating.*

*"I am afraid to tell you, ma'am, that we have a body at the morgue that we believe to be that of Bobby Oates. We found your address in his pocket but need a formal identification."*

*Caroline did not hear much beyond the word 'body'. She could see his lips moving but the detective's words began to sound muffled as though someone had placed their hands over her ears and was pressing down tightly. Her heart now beat out of rhythm with Susan's. A sudden rush of acid began to rise from her stomach. She held Susan tighter and just as suddenly there was the feeling of cold air as perspiration drenched her body. The fan swirling hot air above her head quickly cooled off the water breaking through her skin.*

*"We really do need you to come up to Lawton to give a positive ID." Morris's words broke through to Caroline's ears. The blockage of sound clearing as quickly as it came and with it the sense that she was going to faint passed.*

*Caroline nodded.*

*"I have a car waiting." The detective gestured outside.*

Morris's car was air-conditioned, though it didn't quite hide the heavy metallic musk that seemed to hang in the air. Caroline noticed the police radio tucked under the parcel shelf. Every now and then there was a garbled message that crackled through the speaker. Susan was lying in her travel cot, now wide-awake and absorbed by the novelty of the journey.

"How far did you say it was, detective, only I have a concert tomorrow evening in Lubbock. The Cactus Theater, you know it?"

"Like I said, I ain't from around these parts. Anyways, you'll be back in time." Morris looked in the rear view at his passenger.

His eyes looked black in the dark confines of the vehicle, making the whites stand out even more, giving them an intensity that was piercing. Caroline could not hold his gaze, not even in the mirror. She looked away. Morris engaged drive and pulled away, kicking up dust in the tire tracks.

"Maybe I should have told some of the band members, in case…"

"Like I said, we won't be long and I'll return you back home, no worries, ma'am."

The car headed northeast into the blackness of the coming night. Caroline watched silently as the miles went by. She read the road signs but didn't once see a sign for Lawton. It wasn't in Texas, was all she knew. That indicated at least a five-hour drive and even then she was fairly familiar with the surrounding towns. The car was now firmly in the Dust Bowl countryside with nothing much for company except a few rocks. Morris was quiet, apart from once offering Caroline a cigarette. Her mind was firmly rooted on Bobby Oates.

"How did he die?"

"That's what the autopsy will find."

"You must have some idea though."

The car began to slow down and Morris turned left off the asphalt onto a dirt-track road. Caroline bounced heavily on the back seat of the car.

"I'd put the belt on, ma'am. These roads can get a little scary." The amber tip of Morris's cigarette bounced with equal enthusiasm between his lips. For the first time during the ride now, Caroline started to feel uneasy about the journey and the policeman driving her.

She asked again. "How did Bobby die?"

The car headlights exposed a collection of wooden buildings that looked abandoned and Gary Morris killed the lights. Now he drove in darkness.

"Oh, it was quite painless ... mostly."

Caroline's right hand moved to the door handle, while her left hand slowly gripped Susan's cot. She pulled back on the handle and the door popped open.

"You thinking of going somewhere?" Morris asked coolly. His foot hit the gas pedal and the car accelerated.

"Who are you?"

"I am a friend of your mother's."

Caroline's heart quickened. "I have no mother."

"I know."

Caroline was paralyzed on the seat. Fear gripped her limbs like a vice, rooting her to the spot. "Who are you?"

Morris slammed his foot down hard on the brakes. Underneath the car came the sound of hard mud and stones pinging up under the chassis. The car shuddered and slid, sending waves of dirt into the dark air. Caroline struggled with the door. She was half falling out; her tenure only held by a strong grip on the seat belt that she should have been wearing. The car eventually halted, throwing Caroline forward. Her head glanced off the seat in front and she bounced back into her seat. Susan remained safe in her cot. Caroline sat dazed, unable to comprehend what was happening. She heard a door open and the sound of footsteps. The next thing she knew she was being pulled from the back of the car and dragged along the ground.

From somewhere deep within, her voice screamed out across the open prairie.

"Scream all you want, honey, but nobody will hear you." Morris dropped her to the ground. "Now, you stay here while I get things nice 'n' cozy."

Caroline heard the jingle of keys and a door opening and then a stream of light bathed the wooden decking she was lying on. As she turned to get her bearing Morris's hands roughly grabbed her hair pulling her into the wooden building.

"Now, don't you worry about little Susan. She'll be alright, we won't be long." Morris powerfully dragged Caroline, almost lifting her from the floor by her hair. He threw her forcibly away from *where he was standing. Caroline's head banged off something hard and unforgiving. She passed out.*

When she woke, Caroline was lying on a bed. The room was like any motel room but strangely familiar. There was the sound of Susan crying from a room behind a door opposite. Caroline's eyes darted around the room trying to make sense of what was happening, of what had happened. There was a smell of decay in the air. Stale, trapped air. Gary Morris was sitting in a chair in the corner of the room.

"You are with us now." He smiled. It wasn't the mad smile of the clearly insane but the smile of someone who looked genuinely concerned, and that worried Caroline even more.

Caroline tried to sit up in the bed but found it impossible. Her head throbbed with the pain. With a great effort she put her hand to the back of her head and felt a huge bump but to her relief no sign of broken skin or blood. "My head."

"Don't worry, that's just the drugs."

Caroline noticed the bitter taste in her mouth. A mixture of copper and salt.

"It won't last long. By the end you'll even begin to enjoy the sensation." Morris leaned forward into the dim light of the table lamp set on the nightstand. His raw white face was exposed making his eyes appear darker. He had the essence of a predator and was relishing the situation. "You look so much like your mother, especially now."

And the reason the room seemed so familiar to Caroline was suddenly confirmed to her. This was the room Caroline's mother, Amy Dark, was murdered in. This was the same bed that she was lying in when she died and though she did not know it they were the same sheets, a sick memento purchased from a memorabilia auction house. Everything was perfectly reproduced. Caroline's arm dropped limply by her side.

"Won't be long now. Let's just get you into the right position." Morris stood and walked over to the bedside and joined Caroline. He lifted her arm. Caroline could not stop him. She no longer had control over her limbs. Gary Morris pulled the sheet back to reveal the damp stain spreading through the bedding. "Good, it's almost time."

Caroline wanted to speak, she wanted to scream and fight back but everything was so difficult. He was right, Gary Morris was right; the feeling spreading through her body now was sublime. For the first time in a long, long while, Caroline was at last feeling an overwhelming sense of peace. The anger, the fear, the injustice all dissipated.

"Now you can sleep." Morris's hand covered Caroline's face and his finger and thumb closed her eyelids, shutting out the world. "Sleep like your mama slept. You'll thank me for this. For closing this world of pain."

And with that action came the darkness and peace Caroline had secretly longed for, but in the sober reality of day would never be brave enough to take alone.

# Part One
## Dark

# Chapter 1 Ghosts

The ice was inches thick across the pond. The grass surrounding it was brittle to walk on and crunched under foot. Ducks skidded on the glass surface confused at the sudden hardness of the water. The air was cold and biting and somehow seemed to mute the ambient noise of traffic from the freeway not more than half a mile away. Susan Dark stopped walking, her breath visible in the cold air. She looked around. Everything was calm. Winter had a vice-like grip on the madness of the world and had slowed everything, people included, down to a slow bearable pace. The only reason to rush was to stay warm but if you wrapped up in enough layers you could take it easy all day and enjoy the silence.

Susan watched the world gently slipping into stasis. The season had stopped nature's clock, everything had become frozen in time, in slumber, awaiting the coming spring and the end of a gentle hibernation in peace. She sat on a wooden bench that had become covered in light snow, wiping the seat before she sat. The park would be full during the summer, filled with sun worshipers taking lunch breaks and time off from the melee of work just to catch life away from the office. Government buildings would be vacated while staff flocked to the green grass in search of relaxation, if only for an hour. Some of the most powerful and yet unknown people would be mingling with colleagues, laughing and joking with safe anonymity. But for the next few months there would be more wildlife than human life in the park. Susan liked these quiet months, where she would meet no one but the occasional seasoned jogger. With no one around to see her or more importantly hear her, Susan sang the first few lines from one of her mother's biggest hits, "Lonesome, as I am". The poignancy of the song never failed to hit Susan, and her voice quivered with emotion whenever she sang it. Her mother's legacy to her was financial security, as "fans" bought her back catalog in huge amounts making Caroline Dark another in a long line of recording artists who sold many more records after she died than when she was alive. Making Caroline Dark a carbon copy of her mother, Amy Dark but with better royalty rights to bequeath. Susan's voice moved across the frozen lake in a haunting melody that entertained only the ducks and geese. Her voice faltered over the line "My heart waits for you to come home." It wasn't a difficult line to sing in terms of technique, it barely touched Susan's vocal range, but it was emotionally difficult to sing. Her eyes filled with tears, they always did.

"Never have I felt so alone." She fought with her vocal chords willing them not to give in to the sadness deep within her heart. Her voice hovered in the air like winter fog with only the sound of the ducks, geese and other birds an accompaniment to her solo voice. Susan hung her head, lost for a moment of personal grief. Her tears hit the snow under her feet, the salt from them melting the snow as though it was acid burning through the surface. These waves of melancholy haunted Susan whenever she sang a song by her mother or grandmother. She held no pretense about their deaths, Susan only knew her mother for a few short months. Her grandmother, Amy Dark, was nothing more than a celluloid memory. An image captured on film at her concerts and her one brief moment in the limelight as the star of a movie, *State of Confusion*, a light-hearted romantic comedy about a country and western singer finding love. This was to be the first in a series of movies, sadly cut short by her murder. She often found herself thinking of them when she was in the middle of cutting an album and looking for inspiration needing to tap into her emotions when writing a new song. Or when, like today, she had to go into the studio to do a cover of one of their records. Susan wiped her eyes and stood. She walked back to the recording studio, through the park and out onto the main street. All the while she was humming the bars to the chorus of "Lonesome, as I am" and the sense of melancholy was replaced with a sense of oneness with her mother and grandmother. Susan held no real religious conviction but somehow felt that she would not be alone in the studio. She often felt her mother's presence and was told on many occasions about the striking similarities not only in looks but also in sound.

The peace of the park was soon replaced by the buzzing noise of the city, traffic and people going about their daily activities as Susan made her way to the studio.

Portmorion, Maryland

Georgina O'Neil stopped running to regain her breath and looked out toward the sea; forty feet below where she stood was the harbor.

Fishing vessels vied for space on the cramped quay and fishermen walked back and forth to large wooden sheds, their daily catch was stored by the side of the boats on the dock awaiting processing before being transported to shops, supermarkets and local markets. Georgina made a point of stopping today and watching the overwhelming beauty of the sea and of nature in full winter bloom. Snow clung to flat surfaces but had been blown away from exposed places. The winter promised to be harsh, but nothing short of a full force gale would stop her daily run when she was at home. The white caps on the sea told a story of bad weather further out, hence the queue of seafaring vessels and stranded fishermen. The wind shifted direction cutting into Georgina's face, whipping at her with a stinging sensation. The tip of her nose, cold and red, almost numb from the elements. Georgina jogged on the spot determined to keep her muscles warm, the last thing she wanted was to seize up and pull a muscle or tendon on her way home. She took a last look at the picturesque scene in front of her before turning to her left and finishing the last mile along the coast road, and then the downhill stretch to her house. Georgina's feet bounced off the ground, her body felt light and comfortable with the exercise, she could run like this for another hour with ease but time was her enemy today. She had to get home, shower and get ready for work. Her house came into view and Georgina's speed increased slightly. The prospects of a warm shower now the overwhelming desire. Her door key was placed around her neck like a winner's medal, attached to a blue ribbon. Georgina grabbed the ribbon and pulled the key from between her sweatshirt and tee shirt. Her front door was weathered and needed a fresh coat of paint as it lost the battle to the salty air, sun, rain and snow. She stopped by the door, her breath fairly labored, and found the lock. Twisting the key, she was greeted with a sense of home and of how her job had impacted on her private life. The cardboard boxes which she had been meaning to empty ever since she had moved in over three years ago remained untouched but life had shuffled along. She was okay with things as they were, she was in no hurry. That was the good thing about home, the good thing about Portmorion, nobody was in a hurry. Today was unique in many respects for Georgina. The culmination of an enquiry on a previous case in Missouri was due, it just so happened to coincide with her yearly review. Georgina knew promotion was not going to be on the agenda. She'd shower, dress and drive to Headquarters at Washington DC for a 2:30 p.m. appointment without the knowledge that her fate had been sealed long ago while sitting in the living room of a police officer on Turtle Island. Her fate had been dictated by the events of her two journeys to that little anomaly of an island and by decisions she made which she knew at the time went against her better judgment. The past would be waiting in the office for her arrival. Georgina stripped as she walked to the bathroom and the waiting shower. Her sweats were bundled unceremoniously into the laundry basket that was close to overflowing. Georgina turned the shower on. Strong jets of water were forced out of the showerhead by the powerful pump and the room began to mist as the heat from the water clung to cold surfaces. Goosebumps prickled Georgina's skin as tiny hairs searched for heat to trap. She stood under the stream, closing her eyes as she was consumed by water. She felt safe standing in a vacuum of water, it was the same when she was running, there was very little from the outside world that could touch her. Her fingers rubbed soap into bubbles and she massaged her face. Her fingertips felt the fine line of a scar across her forehead. The mark was not obtrusive, a small ridge but a permanent reminder for the most part hidden under her fringe. She purposely grew her hair an extra half-inch longer to cosmetically conceal a memory that was more painful than the wound itself.

Studio 9 ached for a revamp. The technology was new but the studio was old and wore its history with pride. The walls were decorated with images of a bygone era, pictures of its colorful and rich past. Somewhere along the corridor, Susan Dark would pass photographs of her mother and her grandmother, pictures of them sitting in the very same recording studio where she was recording her new album. Doing exactly what she would be doing, singing in a box with a pair of cans over her head playing her backing track while she cut a vocal. Today would be stranger than most though, today she would be singing with her dead mother and grandmother for the first time. No ghostly apparition just the wonders of modern digital technology as Caroline and Amy Dark rose from the grave to sing once more. The weirder part would be when they come to shoot the video to accompany the song. Magically, Susan would be reunited with them as video technicians splice old film of her mother and grandmother and merge it seamlessly with new footage of Susan sitting with them, laughing with them, talking and singing with them. All the things she longed to do, all the things most women of her age were able to do. Today though was the song "Lonesome, as I am", written and recorded by her grandmother in 1951 and recorded by her mother in 1977. Now half a century from when Amy Dark sat alone in her kitchen and scribbled the words onto a scrap piece of paper, Susan would be singing a solo verse and backing vocals in a family reunion that only one generation of the Dark family would ever know about. Susan felt strangely apprehensive, as though she was under the scrutiny of her family's history. The weight of expectation placed upon her shoulders had risen inexorably since news of the recording had leaked in the trade press. *Country Music Week* magazine was the first to break the story after a careless record executive at her label was overheard talking too loudly at a convention. Susan all but walked away from the project … all but. Had it not been for her serious cash flow situation, she could have easily left the record company, had it not been for her serious cash flow situation she could have retained her artistic integrity and turned down the huge cash advance for the *Dark Family Album*, as the record title was going to be. There were three family traits in the Dark family and Susan had inherited two of them, a wonderful singing voice and a terrible ability to finance her affairs properly. The third was that her mother and grandmother had both had their successful singing careers cut short through violence. Susan had no desire to inherit the third family trait.

She made her way along the corridor until she came to one of the studio's recording rooms. She could see Gil Frolan, the record producer sitting inside the mixing room. The air was thick with smoke, nicotine painted the surface of everything from the faders on the mixing desk to the yellowed wall tiles. Frolan was sucking hard on his twenty-third cigarette of the day and it wasn't even midday yet.

"C'mon in, babe."

When Frolan spoke it looked as though his lungs had caught fire. Smoke poured out of his mouth like a factory chimney in the industrial age. Susan dreaded to think what the condition of the man's lungs were like, his skin was ravaged by the effects of smoking. Hundreds of lines etched his eyes and mouth from the repeated action of sucking in deeply on the long white sticks of tobacco. His long silver hair was wiry and tinged with brown streaks that on first inspection looked like highlights until you drew closer and could smell the rank odor of stale tobacco. The brown streaks, a physical imprint of over sixty years addiction to a nicotine craving that manifested itself with a continual chain of cigarettes permanently placed between his parched lips, only the tips of his fingers matched his hair and teeth in discoloration.

Susan smiled. Frolan was the Country & Western history man. The man who had produced all the greats during the past fifty years and at seventy-five still had the magic touch to produce hit records. He had worked with both her mother and grandmother. He knew things about them she never would.

# Chapter 2 Demons

Every now and then the windows would mist over and Leroy LaPortiere would turn the hot air heaters on in the car and watch as the semi-opaque fog of chilled air was chased away toward the top of the windshield. Washington DC could be bitter in the winter. Life outside the Missouri police force was not what he had hoped, even with a reasonable compensation payment and invalidity pension. He stretched his legs. Sitting in the confines of the car on a freezing cold day did little to help stave off the pain in his right thigh. His fingers massaged the wound on his leg. Now all that was left was scar tissue and an indentation where the muscle would never recover. The bullet had passed clean through, it all sounds so clinical when they say that in the movies. The bullet had missed the bone and by luck, the femoral artery but what it hadn't missed was a large expanse of muscle, which it ungraciously tore out of his body as it gouged its way through. He watched the front door of the house. He had been watching it for hours, from before the sun rose. A little before dawn, lights inside the house indicated life, hope. Leroy moved his fingers toward the hot air coming through the vents. Snow continued to fall in a light flurry laying a white carpet on the sidewalk. There was a fresh set of tracks laid as a man walking a dog passed by the house. Leroy took his sight from the door for a second and in that second it opened. The movement caught his eye and he was just in time to see her leave the house. Leroy opened the car door and the blast of winter cut into his face. He followed from a discreet distance. The meeting would have to look accidental, though he wanted to call out. Call to her, shout her name. The name he had called so many times, the name he had whispered to her when they were making love. His lips parted and the name escaped in a whisper of frosty air.

"Lia."

Georgina didn't know whether it was the ride in the elevator that made her feel nauseous or the prospect of the next hour being grilled by her superiors in the presence of her father. Truth was she had felt a sickness inside her ever since events on Turtle Island. She had hoped for some peace of mind and the chance to return to a little normality but it was six weeks since the case came to its violent conclusion and the dreams still haunted her sleep, the memories still haunted her waking day and the aftermath now threatened her career. She allowed herself a silent laugh when she thought about the term *career* to describe her employment. The elevator doors opened and the smell of Fahrenheit aftershave assaulted Georgina's nostrils. It was the brand of aftershave Director Ebbley wore. A gift. Not from his wife but a younger person, a daughter ... a lover. Georgina shuddered, *a lover*? She very much doubted it. Somewhere in the air too would be the scent of her father, Assistant Director Wynan O'Neil. Here, today, though that meant nothing except maybe the guarantee of a fair hearing. The door ahead of her was austere, a portent and a metaphor. She knocked and waited.

The door handle turned and the door was opened inwards where Georgina was greeted by a Monica Lewinski clone; at least she thought it was a clone.

"Come in, Agent O'Neil."

Georgina's hand was clasped by something that felt neither dead nor alive. A clammy half-state handshake. Limp and cool, insincere and dismissive. The woman would remain silent throughout the meeting but scribble notes furiously in shorthand. Sitting behind a conference table was Director Harold Ebbley, her father, Assistant Director Wynan O'Neil, and a hairless man with intense green eyes, made all the more so by the lack of any eyebrows or eyelashes. He was the only man that stood when Georgina entered the room. He walked around the table and offered his hand.

"Special Agent Lakeland Farmer." His hand was warm and his grip firm but not tight. "I am here to act as an impartial witness to the hearing." He pulled a chair from the table and gestured with his hand for Georgina to sit. As she sat the door opened and a fourth man entered. A man Georgina knew and one of the last people she expected to see at the hearing.

"Sorry I'm late. Delays at the airport. You know what it's like these days." He swept what little hair he had over the bald expanse of head.

Captain Norman Frusco made his excuses and sat next to her father. He was holding a pile of files bound with string. As he placed them down on the table she could clearly see the Missouri Police emblem on the top one. Frusco barely hinted at recognition as he looked at Georgina. Ebbley coughed and cleared his throat.

"Right gentlemen, let's get this enquiry underway."

Susan left her voice hanging in the air, there was a time when she swore that she would never follow in her mother's footsteps but some things are gifts that you can't ignore and she had natural pitch. Her singing was effortless when she was relaxed, but on days like these, she had to work at it. Gil Frolan sat listening to the latest vocal she had laid down. Susan watched through the window awaiting any instructions, hardly daring to enter the mixing room for the sake of her voice in the smoggy atmosphere.

Gil leaned forward on the mixing desk and pressed a button linking the room with the studio. "Can we go over the last verse once more Susan, honey?"

She moved close to the microphone and spoke softly. "Sure, Gil."

The playback of the backing track started in her headphones. There were no other instructions from Gil; Susan knew that all she had to do was sing her level best. That was all. Her mother's voice started to sing like a sweet lullaby in her ear then her grandmother's voice faded into the mix. Susan took a breath. The words to the song were imprinted in her mind, almost as natural to her as the breath in her lungs.

If the marrow in his bones could freeze, Leroy was sure his was close to frozen. He was far from the balmier climate of Missouri and felt as removed from his home as was possible. He had watched Lia all morning. Watched and followed. Two qualities in his old job that were requisite but now as a private citizen made him nothing more than a stalker. A sad and cold stalker. He stomped his feet and instantly regretted it as pain reverberated through his toes. In his mind, Leroy had a visual image of his toes shattering like glass, breaking away from his feet. Seeing her so close was unbearable, he imagined her perfume floating on the cold breeze to him. A fragrant greeting that would be followed by a welcomed hello and the embrace of a lover. Leroy watched Lia cross the busy street. Cabs, busses and cars played the equivalent of human pinball seeking out pedestrian ball bearings. She made it across safely despite the traffic lights being against her. Leroy watched her. He watched her and he longed for reconciliation. She entered MacCaully's Coffee Shop and sat at a table by the window. The lights changed and Leroy started to cross the road. A man sat at the table with Lia. Leroy's step slowed down. The man at the table leaned forward and kissed Lia. A kiss that seemed to last forever. Long slow and passionate. The world slowed down. Leroy was standing at the window of the coffee shop invisible to his ex-girlfriend, yet feeling exposed and raw. It felt as though he had been eviscerated.

Norman Frusco had been talking for nearly an hour. Georgina felt herself drifting off. She desperately wanted to be in another place not in a stuffy room with a heating system overcompensating for the falling snow and temperatures outside the sealed windows, listening to her career being put through a shredder. At times she found herself studying the snow drifting down from the sky. Every single snowflake is unique, the structure and make-up complex and often more individual than a lot of human beings she had met. Certainly more so than many she had worked with. Every now and then she would look at her father and feel a deep and profound sadness. She had failed to meet his expectations … she had failed to meet her own. Her cell phone rang; the sound in the sterile atmosphere was like a bomb going off and drew critical eyes from the board, interrupting Frusco mid-flow. Georgina looked at the phone sitting on the desk and wished that she had, as she had intended, turned it off.

Director Ebbley did not hide the disdain in his voice. "Maybe this would be a good time to take a break. Let's adjourn for fifteen minutes."

The phone rang again. Georgina looked at the display screen. It simply read: Leroy.

Leroy waited in his car. His heart felt as cold as the metal fire hydrant on the sidewalk that was covered in snow. Seeing Lia again was a mistake. He knew it was a mistake before he got on the plane from Missouri. Knuckles rapped on the side window, breaking Leroy from his sense of melancholy. He looked at the long slender white fingers, the knuckles were glowing with a healthy looking red tint, fingernails cut short and buffed, though he noticed one nail was chewed as far as it were possible without drawing blood. Leroy pressed a button and the window lowered. Georgina poked her head through the opening.

"Hiya, big man." Her face told Leroy she was pleased to see him and the notion pleased him.

Leroy smiled back.

Georgina felt comforted knowing she had a friend. His smiling face was a welcoming sight.

"Get your cute white ass in here and I'll take you for lunch."

"My cute white ass?" She opened the door and sat on the passenger's seat.

The last time she had been in a car with Leroy they were hurtling through a pitch-dark night trying to save the life of a family. She wondered if the scars of those days would ever leave them. Today, on a snowy day in Washington DC she knew they might as well be back in the dark on that fateful night; demons had hooked themselves into the very hearts of both Georgina and Leroy. Maybe they were the demons that were exorcised from the corrupted souls on Turtle Island. Transient monsters looking for a home, somewhere where they could nourish and feed until the time was ripe. Georgina leaned forward and her lips locked onto Leroy's. For a moment she wanted the kiss to last a lifetime … and so did he.

She was glad to be out of the stuffy confines of the recording studio. The air-conditioning only served to make her voice dry. A cab would take Susan across town to her hotel. It was a little after three and her work for the day was complete, ahead lay a long afternoon and evening to fill. She had a deep desire to get hammered and laid, though not necessarily in that order but she knew she couldn't get drunk and the chances of getting laid were even more remote. She stopped off at a newspaper vendor and rifled through some local publications in the hope of averting another dreadfully dull evening alone.

Washington DC was fast becoming a white canvas. The definition and outline of buildings was blurring as the hard edges were eroded with layers of snow.

"You gonna buy that or are you just another tourist who thinks this is the public library?"

Susan looked at the magazine she was holding in her hand. *Country Music Week.* The front cover had some angelic pubescent fifteen-year-old from Wyoming smiling sublimely through a shimmering haze of summer sunshine. Just to the left of the picture Susan noticed her name and a story subheading. 'The Dark Mystery'.

"Yeah, I'll have this one." She handed over ten bucks and walked away. The voice in the background shouted "Hey, lady, here's your change."

# Chapter 3 Falling

"It is therefore the findings of this panel that negligence on behalf of FBI Agent Georgina O'Neil did act as a contributory factor to the deaths of Korjca Piekarsca and the subsequent events on Turtle Island." Director Ebbley dispatched the summary with the detachment of the disinterested, though his eyes never once wavered from Georgina's.

Georgina felt a cold trickle of sweat run down the small of her back, a refugee seeking sanctuary against the inevitable.

"We cannot ignore the manner in which the case was handled. You showed an uncharacteristic incompetence and failed to ask for support or back up at every opportunity."

Georgina looked over her shoulder at the door. She might as well just stand up and walk through it. She noticed the seat where her father presided for the entire three days of the hearing was empty. Norman Frusco had disappeared, though the pile of brown folders still sat on the desk close to Director Ebbley.

"To your benefit you did show a tenacious and intuitive approach to the situation and it is duly noted that the safe outcome for Jo-Lynn Montoya and her son were in great part due to the actions of yourself and detective LaPorter."

"LaPortiere." Georgina corrected the director then wished she had kept her mouth shut.

Ebbley stood. The chair behind him scraped against the hard floor. He leaned forward across the desk until he was inches away from Georgina's face. "That is the sort of attention to detail that was sadly lacking in your field work, Miss O'Neil."

Georgina had the sense of falling and there was nothing she could do at this point to stop herself. She was falling and she knew that when she hit the ground it was going to hurt.

Susan sprawled on the bed. Her diminutive frame was all but swallowed by the queen-size bed. Such a big bed, such a small person and so alone. She reached out and grabbed the magazine from the duvet and rolled onto her back. Page thirty-eight. She remembered the page and eagerly scanned through the magazine until the picture of her mother caught her attention.

*A Dark Mystery.*

Susan thought she was about to read the sort of tabloid journalism that only achieved indignation from the accused and reverence from the gossip hungry vultures who kept gutter mags going. She reached above her head and dimmed the overhead light, shielding the glaring light from her tired eyes and turned on the bedside lamp on the nightstand. The walnut nightstand was highly polished and though she hadn't checked she knew there would be a Gideons' Bible inside the top drawer. She also knew that in the second drawer there would be a pay card offering the services of the local cable company porn channels. Such a variety of things to do for the lonely and the stranded. She plumped the pillow up and leaned back against the headboard of the bed. A cold bottle of Bud was peppered with condensation looking as though it had just run the four minute mile in a sweat house. It would take five or six bottles of Bud to get Susan somewhere comfortable in her mind. She lifted the bottle to her lips and took a swig. She had all night. As she read the article her eyes kept glancing back to the byline for the author's name, "Fisher Sutherland". The name meant nothing to her but this man, this stranger, knew more about her mother and grandmother than she did. The notion unsettled her. An outsider had taken more time in his life to learn about her immediate family that she had. The article kept mentioning Sutherland's soon to be published biography on the Dark family, *A Dark Legacy*. She read the article three times and each time, new grains of knowledge embedded in her mind, little snippets of information about her family. By the third reading she was feeling tired. A glance to her side would have shown the true reason for her lethargy but she knew the cause as she levered the cap of a fourth bottle of Bud. She closed her eyes just briefly, it felt so good. The world was shut out for a brief moment. Susan pulled the duvet cover back and sank beneath the embrace of the garish patterned cover.

Georgina woke ... something was beeping. Her arms felt odd. It was as though she was a marionette and someone else was operating her limbs. There was a tingling feeling in her hands. Georgina opened her eyes. The world was soft and out of focus. There was a low whooshing noise in her ears, like white noise or sea breaking against a low flat sandy beach. She opened her mouth, it felt dry. The back of her throat was raw, as though it had been scrubbed with a file. There was the beep again; a soft sound, inoffensive but now it sounded regular, hypnotic. For a moment the world was colorless, everything was white, then the colors started to bleed through, rich saturated hues and with the color came focus and the sound in her ears clarified. She could feel a warm feeling now in her left hand; she looked down and focused on a huge brown hand engulfing hers.

"Hi." The voice was familiar and belonged to Leroy. "Glad to see you're back with us." Leroy's smile was reassuring or at least was meant to be. Leroy let go of her hand and stood. Georgina tried to follow the large ex-detective but the effort of lifting her head was overpowering.

"I'll get your father. He's waiting outside."

Georgina could hear the door open and the soft shuffle of shoe leather on the vinyl flooring. A face loomed over her.

"Baby." Wynan O'Neil bent forward and kissed Georgina's forehead. Georgina could feel the coldness of his lips and nose pressing against her skin but could sense the warmth in his heart and voice. "You had us worried for a while."

She tried to focus on her father's face but it was as though she was viewing the world through a layer of Vaseline. Georgina blinked but there was no improvement. "How long is a while?" Her voice croaked.

"Four long days." Leroy's voice came from the side of the bed.

Georgina turned her head to the large brown blur next to her. "Four days?"

Leroy smiled though she could not make out his features. He gripped her hand once more. Georgina's face asked her next question without her even opening her lips.

"The docs are still doing tests, honey. Blood work, ECGs, they're waiting for the results to come back on the lab work and a CAT scan." Wynan tried to sound positive.

The vast bank of machinery behind her continued running, checking her, monitoring her, scanning her body for telltale signs of another imminent breakdown. For the first time Georgina became aware of pads attached to her chest and temple. She felt tired, drained by the exertion, the hypnotic beep, beep, beep of her heart rhythm relayed though the monitor was somehow comforting. She closed her eyes.

The waiting room was warm; outside winter still gripped Washington DC. Schools had been closed as boiler systems faltered against the burden of extra work. Children made the most of the free time, building snowmen, playing on frozen lakes and wishing for an endless season. Leroy took his jacket off, folded it and placed it behind his neck for a makeshift pillow. The wall was no mattress but would make do; he had spent many more hours in circumstances far less comfortable on surveillance. Three hours had passed since Georgina had regained consciousness and then fallen back to sleep. Time stood still, dragging its feet like a petulant child in a candy store.

"She seems so fragile."

Leroy didn't know how long his eyes had been closed but was aware that at some point he had fallen asleep. Wynan O'Neil was standing in front of him looking a little more gray than usual.

"Is everything okay?" Leroy's voice betrayed the befuddled condition of his tired mind.

"I wish I knew. D'you mind?" Wynan gestured to the vacant seat next to Leroy.

"No, not at all. Sit down."

Wynan sat. "I got you a coffee. Don't know how you take it but I figured you could do with a little sugar for energy." He passed Leroy one of the two vending cups he was holding.

Outside the confines of the small waiting room the hospital buzzed with activity. White coats moved in a frenzied blur, green smocks flashed passed the window, some pushing patients dressed in blue gowns, other patients being wheeled on gurneys to waiting lifts and operating theatres filled with experts in their chosen fields. The air, even in the waiting room, was coated with an antiseptic hue so thick it was almost visible.

Leroy sipped from the coffee. "Busy night."

"The last time I was in hospital was with Georgina's mother. This seems so … reminiscent. I vowed then that I never wanted to go into a hospital again. A hard task in my line of work but I managed it, until now." Wynan shifted on his seat, as though the sense of discomfort was consuming him.

"Is that what you think this is, a replay of what happened to Georgina's mother?"

"Medical history. There is a weakness, a defect. I was warned, all those years ago. The headaches, the irrationality, the changes of mood, the inability to function properly …"

Leroy was unsure whether Wynan was referring to Georgina or her mother but he wasn't going to push. Wynan looked into a space ahead of him; it contained the future and the past.

"You think this is a tumor, like Georgina's mother?"

Wynan's head dropped further. Bad memories swirled inside his head like phantoms. "We'll know soon."

# Chapter 4 Six Days Later

The grass was lush. A green so vivid it was startling. There was a breathtaking silence and the feeling of warmth seeping through the sun. This was not the sort of day for a funeral but sorrowful faces gathered round a rectangular hole in the ground. Georgina recognized everyone, every weeping distraught face. Her father stood over the pit, a clutch of damp earth in his hand. She could see the whites of his fingernails muddied with the soil. Leaning close into his side was Cally, Wynan O'Neil's wife and Georgina's stepmother. To the side of Cally was a stroller, an infant was strapped in, also dressed in black. And Georgina thought, *how strange*?

The color robbed the child, for it was no more than a baby, of its sex. No pretty pinks, no pale blues. Black is not a summer color. Georgina watched as the soil was cast down to the grave. Inside the freshly dug earth was a casket. Georgina tried to tear her eyes away from her father and the new nuclear family. She could sense a deeper sorrow and it struck her with the pain of an aching heart that she was the cause of so much grief. She was the missing part of the jigsaw that she was actually inside the wooden box, looking up through the closed lid but the thought did not distress her, in a way it brought relief. She watched as Wynan released the clump of soil, she saw it break and scatter as it made its way down to her. Georgina woke.

She had been asleep, though she never knew how long. Georgina opened her eyes as though she had just had a nap.

"I'll get the doctor."

She recognized Leroy's voice. The feeling of pressure around her hand drew her eyes across the bed and to the concerned face of her father.

"Hello, honey. Good to have you back."

Wynan's grip tightened, his thumb ran over the back of her hand.

Everything that was not said in those minutes after she had woken was somehow known. Somehow she was also aware of things that Wynan did not even know yet.

# Chapter 5 Meeting the Future

"I'm trying to find Fisher Sutherland, he's one of your writers, I believe?" Susan Dark twiddled a pen dexterously between her finger and thumb while she waited to be put through to the journalist who penned the article on her mother and grandmother. She hummed while waiting, unaware or unconcerned of being heard. The link between her phone and the office was a distance of over three hundred miles and the static void in-between was apparently almost impenetrable but Sutherland's voice came through crystal clear, as though he was standing right next to her, or at least in the room next to her.

"Fisher Sutherland."

Susan was not sure what she expected but the voice of the reporter was clearly something she had not envisaged. The accent was harsh, almost guttural and most surprisingly British.

"It's err … Susan Dark." Susan let her introduction hang in the air for a small beat before continuing. "I want to speak with you."

"Wow, this is an honor. I didn't think you would want to speak to me so soon. I mean I only contacted your management last week."

"I'm sorry? You … you must be mistaken, I am contacting you with regard to the article in *Country Music Week* and your forthcoming book."

"Yeah." Sutherland's voice was sure, matter-of-fact. It was as though he was saying why else would you be contacting me. "I spoke with …"

Susan could hear paper being rustled as though Sutherland was skimming through pages looking for his contact's name.

"Stevie Anderson."

It did not surprise Susan to learn that her manager had not passed on a simple, albeit important, message. Stevie was up to his ass with the IRS and more intent on finding a million selling crossover act à la Shania Twain than being messenger boy to his minnow acts, even if they *eventually* sold a million.

"Now I guess Mr. Anderson never got around to telling you what I wanted then."

Susan waited unsure of the reporter's question or indeed even if it was a question or what it sounded like, a rhetorical statement. But she hedged her guesses and answered anyway. "Nope."

"Now you got me wondering what you want though. And being as I am, by my very nature curious, I won't tell you until you divulge first." Sutherland had a London accent that Susan at first found harsh but the more she listened to the man speak the more she appreciated it. She found herself thumbing through the magazine looking to see if there was a picture of the journalist. Sure enough there was a small photo of Sutherland by his byline. She had not paid attention to the picture when she had read and re-read the article. Her mind was consumed by other things but now this link, this vocal thread through the air connected with something dormant deep inside. She found herself studying the image closely while listening to his voice. Her concentration was such that she could almost see his lips moving.

"So, what do you want?"

This time it was a clearly defined question.

"I want to meet with you."

"Hmmm … sounds good. Where are you?"

"I'm in Washington for three more days recording, then I have a two week break before starting a small tour in the southern States."

"Three days …" To Susan's ears she heard the British journalist say "free daze." The clipped tones of his accent put blocked edges onto words that should have flowed. Sutherland mulled over Susan's itinerary. "Tell you what, I'll meet you the day after tomorrow. D'you know Fabian's Bar, off Whitenall Avenue. It's on the corner of 53rd and West."

"Sure," Susan said confidently but did not have a clue if such a place existed. She knew she would find it easy enough with the aid of a cab ride.

"Well, I'll meet you inside the saloon bar at 12:30."

"That's 12:30, Wednesday inside Fabian's Bar." Susan scribbled hastily on a pad next to the phone. "Could you bring all the research material you have on my mother and grandmother with you?"

"No problems. And what do I get?"

Susan looked at the photo and hoped that the handsome man staring back at her had not been digitally enhanced. "Exclusivity." Susan could not see Fisher Sutherland smiling.

She sat for a while trying to regain her breath. This was hard. Although the room was large and well-ventilated, beads of sweat formed around Georgina's temple. Her hand slowly moved toward her head. It took immense concentration to perform the simple act.

Perspiration was brushed away by her fingers, fingers that felt as though they belonged to someone else. They touched the top of her head and the alien feeling of skin and stubble greeted the restricted nerve endings in her fingers. Though the receptors in her fingers were still a little muggy she could feel where the folds of skin had been sewn together after the operation. A tramline of stitching would eventually fade with her hair hiding any scarring but for now she could feel where the surgeons had entered her head and performed surgery on her brain. She felt a little like Frankenstein's monster. She breathed hard and once again rose to her feet, leaning heavily on a walker that was more often seen used by the elderly and infirm. She laughed blackly to herself, who was she kidding? She was infirm. She was more fragile than a newborn baby and well-aware of the irony of having to learn to walk and talk again. Skills that she had taken for granted for longer than she could remember were now a challenge. She thought hard and slowly placed her left leg forward and shifted her body weight as she locked the leg.

Physiotherapy nurse, Jane Patterson, watched patiently as her patient struggled with basic motor functions.

"Okay, Georgina, just two more steps and we'll call it a day."

Two steps, it sounded like a marathon. Georgina looked at the nurse aware that her face probably gave away her feelings. She closed her eyes and concentrated determined to get the words right. "Jussssst two?" She tried a smile. Her lips rose at the corners and for a brief second there was a flash of life in her eyes. Georgina moved her right leg forward and once again shifted her weight. The movement looked painful to the casual observer but even more painful to Leroy LaPortiere who was watching through the reinforced window panel in the doors to the therapy room. His hands were clenched tight watching his friend's struggle, he felt useless. He had felt that way since she slipped into the brief coma, since the eight-hour operation to remove a tumor growing inside her brain, since watching the person who woke from that operation and discovering someone who had changed dramatically. Leroy's sense of frustration was matched by Georgina's father but came nowhere near to her own. The FBI was no longer an option. The disciplinary hearing was cancelled the moment Georgina's body hit the floor. Other things, more basic matters now had priority in Georgina O'Neil's life, and right at this moment, putting her left foot forward for that final step was as huge and complicated a hurdle as she wanted to face.

# Chapter 6 New Beginnings

Tuesday April 8, 2003

The blushing, almost shy approach of spring was covering the grass in a blanket of daisies. Georgina looked out of her kitchen window. Vibrant color stung her eyes as the pale hues of winter were receding for another year. She wondered whether she would be allowed to adopt the same sense of optimism that Mother Nature unfailingly took every year. There were flower buds developing, awaiting the first rush of warm air blown in from the warmer western climates. She had woken with a song in her head as she did on many days and hummed to herself as she rinsed the dinner plates from the previous evening. Two dinner plates, two cups, two glasses still stained with the remnants of red wine. She liked the idea of washing for an extra person. It was something that had been missing from her life for so long. Romance was finally catching up with her. It still had a lot of work to do before it reached the dizzy heights obtained by most of the world's populace but Georgina enjoyed the company of a man living with her, even if they had not progressed to actual physical contact yet. Both of them had been hurt one way or the other and both were more than prepared to give it as long as it took before committing themselves to something stronger than a goodnight kiss, even if they did share the same roof. She dried her hands on a dish towel and threw it on the drainer. She walked out of the kitchen down to her bedroom. Her leg trailed slightly but to most observers they would not detect any real impediment. Georgina had surprised the doctors with her resilience. She had surprised her doctors but not her father or Leroy. Five months had passed since her operation. Five months of learning, convalescence and a rugged determination to fight every inch of damage her condition had inflicted. As she passed a closed door on her right, Georgina rapped with her knuckles on the door.

"It's time, Leroy." She heard a murmur from within the room and smiled to herself once more. She continued humming. Occasionally a line from the song made its way through her memory. This in itself was a reason for joy as her brain began to repair and reopen paths that had been closed, albeit temporarily.

"Don't leave me now I need your help …"

The door to Leroy's room opened. "Mornin'. You say something?"

"Just singing, Leroy. Just singing."

"I liked you better when you were grumpy." Leroy rubbed his eyes. His mind not alert or fresh to the new day yet.

"Been in my head all morning, ever since I woke up. Think I even dreamed about that song."

"Yeah well, country and western has never been my forte. Bout time you dreamed of Marvin Gaye or Missy Elliott."

"Strange though, I never did listen to Susan Dark before but since she's been missing she's been appearing to me in all sorts of places. Seems I can't even turn the radio or TV on without hearing about her."

Leroy strolled across the hall to the bathroom. "Yeah well that ain't hardly surprising considering the coverage she's got. Bet it will be like Elvis, she'll turn up after her records sell an extra few million."

"Evlvis is dead." Georgina flushed red from the neck to her rapidly growing hair and quickly corrected her verbal mistake. "Elvis."

"Wait and see."

Georgina collected the mail from her mailbox. She instantly recognized the large white envelope from the community hospital. Her follow up appointment was due with the tumor specialist. Three other envelopes were delivered with it. Two were addressed to Leroy. One was official, bearing the state crest; the second was covered in advertising offering Leroy a platinum MasterCard from some bank she had never heard of. She picked the envelopes up and headed back to the kitchen. A wall of steam greeted her from a kettle that was past boiling point. Georgina killed the gas burner and waited for the steam to stop pouring out of the spout before filling two waiting mugs of dried coffee granules, sugar and milk. She sat on the stool and ripped open her appointment from Dr. Zackny's administration team.

"Anything interesting in the mail?"

Georgina looked up to find Leroy standing at the door. "Zackny wants another look inside the old kaboodle."

"When?"

"This Thursday, 9:45 a.m."

"I'll drive you down. You want company?"

Georgina folded the sheet of paper. "Yeah, that would be nice."

"It's gonna be okay, you know." Leroy wanted to believe that as much as Georgina, maybe more so.

Georgina ran her hand through her growing hair. "Yeah … of course it is." She smiled. "You have a letter. Official looking."

Leroy took the envelope and looked at the franked mark and the state crest.

"So, you applied?" Georgina's voice was light. Not questioning or having a hint of criticism.

"It's what I do."

"I remember."

"Besides, they may have turned me down." Leroy's finger slid under the gap of sealed paper and tugged at the gummed restraint until the paper tore. He flipped open the letter headed 'The Washington Department of Professional Regulation' and speed-read the paragraphs until he found the wording 'license application granted'. The letter was signed by the Honorable, Robert J Davenport.

"Looks like I have to go to town Thursday too."

The smile on Leroy's face told Georgina all she needed to know. "Congratulations, Leroy. Or should I say, Private Detective LaPortiere."

The drive to the community hospital was a refreshing change of pace after weeks of convalescing at home. The city seemed extra loud. Leroy had taken the long route avoiding passing the FBI building where Georgina had worked for so long and where her father still held an office. She said nothing but noted his kindness. She knew she held deep feelings for the man driving her to the hospital, his friendship through the last few months had played a monumental part in her recovery but Leroy was holding back from committing himself to anything more than a platonic goodnight kiss. Georgina knew that Lia still held a part of his heart and while she did then she could not expect Leroy to move on or beyond the point where he was.

"Are you ready?" a hand reached out and touched Georgina's shoulder.

Georgina looked at Dr. Zackny. He was tanned and relaxed-looking, full of confidence and radiated optimism. Georgina was not ready. She did not want to know the results of the scan. It was a secret she could happily live without it ever being exposed. The tumor had been removed; her head bore the scars to that trauma. If it were regenerating then she knew there would not be a second operation, only palliative care.

"Am I rerady?" Georgina whispered, the battle with her speech still being fought and occasionally lost. "Ready." She corrected herself.

Leroy squeezed her hand and hugged Georgina close. He felt a single sob leave her body, convulsed in a painful wrench of betrayal. "Don't worry, Georgina."

"I'm scared."

Georgina stood and walked with the doctor through double doors that had 'radiation warning' signs emblazoned on them. The CAT scanner waited through a glass-paneled wall.

Leroy had an hour to kill and as much as he loved Georgina knew that the time would be eaten up with nothing but worry if he just sat around. He stood and walked out of the hospital and headed for City Hall and his waiting detective's license. The car whizzed through the early morning traffic and within minutes he was filling a parking meter with change. There was a spring in his step that hadn't been there for months as he bounded up the stone steps. Inside he was greeted with austere serenity. The building oozed officiousness and brought about the correct amount of gravity to the patrons inside. LaPortiere had experienced a similar feeling inside jails, police stations, libraries and hospitals. He briefly thought about Georgina, she would be lying perfectly still inside the CAT scanner, a different interior but one that held an equal solemnity. A small reception desk was housed at the far end of the entrance hall. Its occupant protected in a toughened glass and wood booth similar to a movie theater kiosk but up a notch in terms of ornate grandeur. Leroy strolled to the booth. The receptionist looked up from a computer screen where she was typing in details conveyed to her over the phone that was undoubtedly connected to the headset she was wearing. She held her hand up to ward off Leroy's approach and returned just as quickly to the keyboard. She mouthed "just a moment," and smiled. Her fingers deftly traversed the keyboard with lightning speed and precision as she entered information into a database.

Leroy waited. He searched inside his jacket pocket for the letter from the Department of Professional Regulation and placed it under the small gap, which allowed brief contact with the outside world for the receptionist wrapped in her elaborate cocoon. The receptionist wore a brass badge with her name emblazoned with black lettering: Linda Hoffman. She took the letter and read through it without breaking contact with her telephone conversation.

*"... Yes, there are parking facilities but there is a two hour time limit ... renewable ... uh-huh."* Her fingers continued to type furiously. *"Not before nine in the morning ... until five."* She looked up to Leroy to re-acknowledge his presence but this time rolled her eyes until the whites filled the sockets. *"Yes, Senator Taylor ... no ... look forward to it ... bye."* She pressed a button on the console to where her headset was plugged. "I'm sorry, Mr ..."

"LaPortiere, Leroy LaPortiere."

"I am sorry to have kept you waiting Mr. LaPortiere. I hope you will appreciate some enquiries are more demanding than others." She smiled and Leroy instantly forgave her his brief wait. "You need the third floor, the Nixon Room."

"The Nixon Room?"

"All of our departmental offices are housed in rooms named after presidents, even impeached ones."

"I'd love to know what is in the Clinton Room." Leroy returned the smile.

"You need to see ..." she quickly scanned through a list of names. "Alberta Cordell. She is the secretary to the governing license registrar. I will ring ahead to tell her to expect you." The receptionist gave Leroy the letter back. "Take the elevator to the third, head out of the lift and turn right then it is the third door along." Her finger hit the switch on her console once more and immediately the phone rang.

Leroy headed toward the lift.


"The scan should tell us all we need to know, Miss O'Neil, but your medical insurance company is happy to pick up the tab for extra testing. Best to be safe." Doctor Zackny's face had lines etched into it from his well-practiced smiles. The past hour had dragged, forty-five minutes of which had been spent inside the claustrophobic environment of the CAT scanner with nothing to look at or do except keep as still as possible. She wanted to tune out but could not settle her mind enough to relax, so she spent the entire procedure staring at the curved lining of the scanner wondering about all the previous occupants of the chamber. It was a huge relief to be out.

At that present time Georgina never cared about the results, all she really wanted to do was get outside the building and take a huge gulp of air. By the time she had dressed and made her way to the room, Leroy was back. He was waiting on one of the huge brown leather sofas that occupied the suite. She was nonetheless relieved to see a familiar and caring face.

"You got your ticket."

Leroy opened a calfskin wallet. "Back in business."

"I knew you could never retire." Georgina sat on the sofa and took the wallet from Leroy. "Private Investigator's License, A00098976574, Leroy Reginald LaPortiere ... Reginald?"

Leroy's skin darkened as he blushed. "My grandfather's name."

"Not a bad picture though."

Leroy didn't know if Georgina was still mocking him and made a grab for the wallet. "Gimme that."

She pulled it back just out of his reach and for a second they touched. His hand brushed against her breast. She felt soft. Leroy felt a frisson of excitement and the silence that followed the touch spoke volumes. "I was being serious." Georgina broke the brief silence. "It is a good pic ... ture." She noticed the coffee and bagel on the coffee table in front of her. "Mine?"

"Thought you might be hungry. Had I known you were gonna be so damned cheeky ..." Leroy smiled.

Georgina looked at the photo on the license once more. "You look cool." She handed him the wallet back. "All you need now is a case."

"Already have one."

"How? But you haven't even advertised."

"That singer who went missing."

"Susan Dark?"

"Her manager, Stevie Anderson. He's going ape shit because the police aren't doing enough to find his prodigy, so he contacted a buddy of mine down in Missouri and my name was passed on."

"But don't she come from Nashville or somewhere like that."

"Seems not all country and western singers actually like the country. She comes from Washington. That's where Mr. Anderson has an office."

"So, who was this buddy?"

Leroy fished an envelope out of his jacket. It was a plain white envelope. Georgina remembered handing it to Leroy during the week. Georgina pulled the letter out and read it. She noticed the signature straight away. Norman Frusco.

"You are still in touch with Frusco?"

Leroy shrugged, he didn't know why but he felt as though he were a child caught mixing with the wrong crowd. "He was proved innocent of any impropriety on Turtle Island and believe it or not he asked to be kept updated with your condition. I think the old bastard really cares."

"Says here that Anderson actually contacted Barbara Dace. She'll want in on any investigation. You know what reporters are like. So, Frusco's still screwing Dace."

Leroy shrugged again. "Seems so." Then he laughed. "It's pathetic, there he is pushing retirement and he's getting more action than both of us put together."

"Why didn't you tell me about this? The letter is a week old."

"I wanted the ticket first. Can't investigate without it. I wanted to know that if I was going to do this it was going to be legit. I can't retire, I'm too young and while I would love to go sail off round the world, I ain't ready yet." Leroy looked at Georgina as though wanting confirmation that he was doing the right thing.

The door to the waiting room opened. Dr. Zackny was holding a cappuccino in one hand and an appointment card in the other.

"The results will be ready in a week or so. I am making them a priority." Dr. Zackny handed the appointment card to Georgina. "See you in a week."

For the next seven days time slowed inexorably. Georgina tried to concentrate on anything but the pending results but couldn't escape the nagging fear which never seemed far away. Leroy also busied himself. Making tentative calls to get his first investigation underway but he also knew he would not be able to fully concentrate until he knew the results of Georgina's tests. He drew a line through each day on the calendar in the kitchen and as the time drew nearer for the journey back to the hospital the fear and restlessness heightened for both of them.

Thursday April 17

The journey back to the hospital was accompanied by a talk radio jock who between playing the odd song from Susan Dark had opened up the phone lines to discuss the singer's disappearance. Georgina was happy for the distraction and Leroy made mental notes of snippets of information that were useful. Before long Leroy was parking in the hospital parking lot.

Leroy sat next to Georgina in Dr. Zackny's office. Zackny was holding her open folder reading through the results. He did not need to remind himself of the results but went through with the facade as though it was expected.

As Georgina tried to read his face she felt her stomach turn. Zackny gave nothing away, his face lined but stoical.

"D'you mind scooting up a bit," Zackny said to Leroy.

Leroy moved to the other side of Georgina. He felt her hand clasp his; it was warm, slightly sweaty. Zackny occupied Leroy's place on the sofa.

"Phew, haven't sat all day." Was the cheery disposition a precursor to bad news?

Georgina's grip tightened.

"We have some good news." Zackny's features broke into what could almost be described as a smile. Georgina felt a rush of cold run through her body, a wave of release and allowed herself a smile. "The tumor is still in recession. The surgery while invasive managed to remove ninety-five percent of the growth, the rest, which as you know was in too delicate an area, has responded very well to the chemotherapy and radiotherapy. Now, we can't be sure that things will always continue on this course but with continued monitoring you can begin to look forward with some renewed optimism, Miss O'Neil. We will want to see you again in three weeks, if progress continues then we may even be able to double the time before your next visit."

Zackny sipped from his coffee cup. "Have you experienced any headaches since the operation?"

Georgina shook her head. "No."

"Dizziness?"

Another shake of the head.

"Excessive tiredness or slurring of the speech."

Leroy looked at Georgina.

"No tiredness but some speech problems, just mild stuff, sometimes I struggle for the right word or mix up a word."

Zackny scribbled on the note board he was carrying. "Okay. I am going to prescribe a painkiller in case you get a headache. Now, take only one of these and I want you to contact me straight away if you do get a headache and we'll get you in for a checkup. This really is good news, Miss O'Neil. Excellent progress." Dr. Zackny stood "Oh and Mr. LaPortiere, I want you to keep a close eye on Miss O'Neil. Whatever you are both doing is working. I want it to continue."

# Chapter 7 Getting Connected

The music had been going around in her head for days; it never stopped. Even when she slept she would drift off to a lullaby from Susan Dark. The journey back home in the car was filled with relief. A pressure valve somewhere had been released and most of her anxiety had escaped with a few well-chosen sentences from her doctor.

"You're quiet?"

Georgina looked at Leroy. "Oh, you know. Lots of things going around in this head of mine."

"Like for instance?"

"Susan Dark. Don't you think it is strange that she has been haunting me and then you are going to be working the case?"

"Her name has been in the media a lot, I guess you picked up on it." Leroy steered the car through a left turn and headed out of town. The sign markers directed the car to Portmorion. "You know, I could do with some help, an assistant if you like. Your help would be invaluable."

"I don't know." Georgina watched the approaching countryside. The quiet solitude of the land and in the far distance she knew the sea would be turning tide, with surfers waiting for the rip tide and the easterly breeze.

"As a consultant only."

"What no action … no fair." Georgina smiled.

"You heard the doctor," Leroy said. "I really mean it. You'd be a great asset."

"Pity you can't persuade my old employers."

Trees lined the road, towering above the car forming a living tunnel that temporarily reduced the daylight. Leroy took off his sunglasses and briefly looked at Georgina.

"I am serious."

"I know. I'll think about it."

"Might help you get rid of her singing in your head."

"I never did like country." Georgina shifted in her seat and pulled the seat belt away from her chest. "So, what is your next move?"

"I'm gonna see Mr. Stevie Anderson tomorrow. We've got a two o'clock appointment."

"We?"

The car slowed to a halt outside Georgina's house. The sound of the doors thudding shut alerted a neighbor's dog who barked a greeting. The limp in Georgina's left leg was more pronounced and she felt tired. She hoped Leroy didn't notice but he did. Halfway to Georgina's front door, a greeting coming from the owner of the house next door stopped them.

"Miss O'Neil ... Miss O'Neil."

Georgina recognized the voice belonging to the elderly woman next door and stopped. "What is it, Mary?"

The old lady arrived at her door breathless. "You've had a delivery. Got the right address but the name's wrong, a Mr. LaPorter or something."

"LaPortiere," Georgina corrected her.

"Yes, that's it." The old lady smiled, pleased that she had half-remembered the name. "A big package too."

"Good, it's arrived," Leroy said adding to the mystery.

"What's arrived?"

"A gift for you."

Now filled with curiosity Georgina began to follow the old lady back to her house.

"It is too heavy for Tom; otherwise I would have had him bring it round."

Georgina followed the old woman into the house with Leroy a couple of steps behind. He noticed Georgina trailing her left leg and almost as his eyes became aware of it, Georgina appeared to consciously adjust her stride.

The house had a lived-in smell to it, history of a family blended and aromatically fused with years of life. Georgina immediately knew they kept animals even without the knowledge of Cato's barking. Cato was a mongrel of a dog, a real cross breed of races that mixed a little spaniel with some terrier and maybe even a collie some way down the line. Cato also left behind his own distinct aroma that no matter how many baths Mary gave him refused to go away. An African Grey Parrot sat perfectly still and perfectly disinterested in the intruders into his home. He rested on a wiry, willowy branch of wood that was growing from a large pot in the corner of the sitting room. Cato came racing in through the back, barking excitedly not showing the ice-cool demeanor of the bird.

"Don't you mind Cato. He's all bark." The elderly lady bent down and ruffled the dog's thick coat. "Aren't ya, boy."

Sitting on the dining table was a huge brown cardboard box with the word fragile printed on the side and a huge 'Intel' logo next to it.

"It came about two. A nice young fella, built like a weightlifter with a real cute ass." There was a twinkle in Mary's eye as she recalled the delivery guy. "There are times when I wish I was thirty years younger." Mary laughed. It was a genuine and deep laugh, wholly good-natured but with a little devilment.

"And there are times when I wish you were too." An old man entered the room, his warm smile greeting his neighbor. "How are ya, Georgie?"

"Not too bad Mr. Paxton, not too bad."

"And is this here your beau?" Tom Paxton smiled again. The devilment was shared with his wife.

"Tom Paxton, you should know better at your age asking a young fine lady questions like that." Mary mock scolded her husband.

Georgina could feel the flush of blood reddening her face. Leroy stepped forward.

"Been here a whole lot of weeks and I feel rude not to have introduced myself before now. My name is Leroy LaPortiere. I am a friend of Georgina. We worked together and she kindly helped me out when I needed somewhere to stay."

"Nice to meet you, Leroy." Tom offered his hand. "I'm Tom and this here is Mary. My one and only."

"Cos no one else will have ya."

"Ain't that the truth."

Leroy nodded his hellos to the old couple, who seemed as happily at ease with each other as with everything else in their world.

"See ya got yerself a compooter," Tom said, his accent betraying his Hicksville upbringing. "What ya got there, an Intel Pentium M processor?"

Leroy shook his head. "Hell if I know. I just went to a store and asked for the latest model."

Georgina moved toward the box, more than curious now. "Why have you bought me a computer?"

"Communication, research and fun. Besides, as my assistant you'll need it."

"If you need help setting it up, just ask my Tom," Mary offered.

Georgina turned and looked at the old couple. In her mind she was saying, *are you kidding me?* and her expression must have been saying something similar.

"Follow me," Tom said. He turned and walked out through the door leading to the hall. Two doors down, he opened another door and hit a light switch. The room was illuminated, casting light on an L-shaped desk with a monitor on each of the two ends. Directly under the monitors were two workstations.

"I got them linked on a network. Mary uses this one here to write on and to scan and design some desktop publishing. I use the other for some basic programming. You know, C++, cobal, Java, just basic script."

"Tom's underplaying his skills as usual," Mary said. "He used to be a software development programmer for a computer games company before he retired. You heard of 'Blood River', 'House of Death' or 'Chimera'? Tom worked on them all."

The framed posters on the walls were more than decoration. On closer inspection they proved to be some of the top selling computer games of the late 1990's. Garish, graphic images of blood spattered zombies toting rifles and blasting innocent bystanders, vampires biting the necks of busty cartoon nubile nymphs, and high-octane sports cars racing through busy malls told the story of Tom Paxton's work. Leroy moved into the room, determined not to let his jaw drop completely to the floor but he was clearly impressed.

"I know squat about computers."

"Well son," Tom said "this is more like painting with code. Hell, it's like being back in school."

"So, you still do some of this?"

"Been working on my own game for the past two years, should be finished just before I am." Tom's voice had a seriousness about it that Leroy did not dare question.

"Don't you go listening to this old morbid man. He's been telling me he's dying for the past forty years." Mary sat on one of the two office chairs in the room. The weight weary on her legs and a relieved sigh escaped her lips.

Georgina stood by the door looking at the high-tech enclave. "We're all dying ... to one degree or another."

The silence that greeted Georgina's comment told her that she had overstepped the mark and allowed her own plight to consume her with a greater degree of self-pity. It was the first time Leroy had seen such a public display of emotion outside the hospital.

Georgina consciously rubbed the scar underneath the thickening growth of hair. Leroy walked to the door and joined Georgina.

"I'll erm … I'll pick up the computer. Maybe you could pop in later tonight to help us get this thing up and running." Leroy took hold of Georgina's arm and guided her out of the room. "You okay?"

"I'm sorry, Leroy. Guess I am just tired."

Georgina looked tired. The adventures of the day had taken a toll on her. Dark circles pushed her eyes back further into her head, coupled with the weight she had lost, making her look increasingly gaunt.

"I just need to rest. I'll be alright … honest." She gave Leroy a reassuring smile but he didn't buy it.

"You got a headache."

"No, it's just been a long day."

Darkness was falling when Tom Paxton knocked on the door. Mary stood by his side. She was holding a freshly baked apple and apricot pie, the smell of which was greeting Georgina before she had opened the door. Leroy had spent the early part of the evening unpacking the computer and setting up an office complete with phone access while Georgina slept. He was just assembling the final pieces of the beech desk unit when the knock at the door came. The floor was littered with cardboard boxes and styrofoam. White clusters of styrofoam converged in small packs charged with static and clinging to any surface available.

"How's it goin, bud?" Tom asked, watching Leroy tighten a tiny screw into the underside of the work desk.

"Just about got it done." Leroy's reply came in strangulated gasps as he tightened the screw making sure it would not free itself.

The computer was waiting to be put in place and booted up. The rattle of beer bottles caught Leroy's attention.

"Thought you might like one of these to keep you goin' for a while." Tom broke a bottle from a cardboard six-pack and tossed it to Leroy. Leroy smiled.

"Remind me why we never introduced ourselves before now." He twisted the top of the beer and it made a refreshing sound of carbonated fizz. Before long, Tom was under the desk running cables and wire to sockets and computer ports. Leroy sat drinking beer. The smell of food soon poured from the kitchen along with the sound of talking and the occasional dirty laugh. Georgina and Mary were cooking up a storm and drinking a river of wine as they chatted about everything from men, work, sex and babies to world politics, art and religion. Some conversations managed to broach all the subjects. These mostly brought the biggest sound of hilarity from the kitchen.

Tom scrambled from under the desk and got easily to his feet with a youthful spring for a man approaching his twilight years.

"Right, let's fire it up and see what we've got." Tom hit the silver switch located at the top of the computer base and pressed the monitor button.

A healthy report of noise from deep within the computer followed some beeps. Leroy had a look of anticipation etched on his face as he watched the computer take its first breaths of life. Light flicked from the monitor and the operating system logo briefly flashed on the screen for a second.

"Welcome to the twenty-first century." Tom smiled and slapped Leroy's back.

"Dinner's ready." The cry came from the kitchen and Leroy felt a pang of disappointment, the sort of feeling he had not experienced since childhood.

"Come on, the dang thing will still be here waiting for us after grub."

It was all Leroy could do to stop himself saying, *yes, dad.* The two men walked to the kitchen.

Leroy rolled in the bed, his sleep hindered by a racing mind that refused to settle all night. He opened his eyes and stared at the ceiling for a while, wondering what Lia would be doing. His mind wandered to his ex-girlfriend, today of all days he needed to be focused but Lia haunted him like a succubus. Erotic images of her flashed through his mind, stirring his heart in more ways than just the emotive. His hand found his early morning erection as the images battled with both his early morning horniness and the longing for some female company. His mind avoided the indelicacy of his plight, it would not question the fact that here he was, a thirty-six-year-old man whose only sexual pleasure for the past six months came only from his hand and a mind that teased him with his past. Sex with Lia was good ... no, sex with Lia was fantastic but he traded her for a job whose only rewards were treachery, danger and a world filled with liars, killers and general human waste. He fantasized about Lia, naked straddling his body, her mouth around him, swallowing his cock, taking him deep into her, first her mouth and then inside her. He could clearly remember how she felt, the urban musk of her body during sex, how she tasted. As he became harder and his hand more frenzied, the image of Lia changed. Her face morphed like it was subject to some computer manipulation. Lia became Georgina. He grew even harder, nearing the point of no return. His head turned toward the wall, knowing that Georgina was inside the room next door, lying in her bed, sleeping.

Friday April 18

The alarm was soft, a background encroachment designed solely to lure Georgina from her sleep. The room was still draped in a cloak of darkness that she fought to become accustomed to. She rummaged inside her wardrobe for her sports gear. She finally located her tracksuit bottoms and sweatshirt at the back of the unit where they had lain dormant since her illness. She dressed by the light of her bedside lamp, tied the laces to her Nike Air running shoes and left the house silently, making sure she didn't wake Leroy. The sky was shifting hues as the sun began its slow march. Georgina was realistic about her level of mobility and fitness, hence the early morning start. She knew there would not be many prying eyes to watch her struggle with her basic motor skills. Left foot in front of right ad infinitum or until the pain or sheer struggle mentally exhausted her. There would be no running, not just yet. Only a brisk walk that she hoped would not look too pathetic to any casual observers. The early morning darkness would also cover the tears of frustration that dogged her every step.

She felt hunted.

By the time Georgina had made it to the coast road the morning sun had risen. Salty sea mist breezed in from the shore and settled just off the beaches allowing the powerful heat of the day to start burning it away. The walk to the sea front was extremely difficult but her arrival at her destination brought a sense of accomplishment. It had taken a little over an hour, in times past she would have run the whole way and covered the same labored steps in fifteen to twenty minutes. She sat on the sea wall and looked out across the bay and the Atlantic Ocean. The endless, tireless sea, unremitting in its endeavors to breach the sandy beaches and stretch its tendrils further ashore. Fishing boats bobbed in the bay, rocked silently by the changing tides.

"Maybe one day I'll get that boat."

The voice startled Georgina, though she instantly recognized Leroy's deep honeyed voice. She turned to find him close behind her dressed in sweats.

"I'd like to live out there," Georgina said. Her eyes fixed back on the ocean. "It's so peaceful. It's like time doesn't exist."

Leroy's hand rested on her shoulder. She felt him draw near until he was right behind her, a solid wall of caring humanity. She leaned back resting into his chest, her head nestling into his breastbone. Sweat ran from Leroy's forehead, down the length of his nose where it dripped down onto Georgina's tee shirt.

"Man, I ain't fit." A throbbing pain from the scar in his thigh reminded Leroy just why he wasn't fit. The doctors said he would carry a limp for the rest of his life but he proved them wrong. Intensive physiotherapy and yoga had helped but the battle was won as much in his mind. He caught his breath. Georgina could feel Leroy's heart thumping from the physical exertion. His arms moved around her shoulders and locked across her chest.

"Are you alright, babe?"

He had never used a familiar term of endearment before but now somehow seemed to be the right time. Georgina looked out at the sea.

"Yeah, I'm fine."

Stevie Anderson flicked through his appointment diary. There was only one meeting scheduled for the day, a two-thirty with Mr. LaPortiere. Anderson's office was a little matted, dulled by years of hard work, with little time for redecoration or replacing the furnishings. Hell, they were still functional, a bit like Anderson himself. The shine, the gloss, the edges had been roughened a little but basically Anderson was the same man he was forty years ago, surprisingly fit for a man in his profession, Anderson prided himself on his physique. At six feet two inches, his stature was broad and upright, free from arthritis or rheumatoid pain. At seventy-two years of age he quite easily passed for someone fifteen years younger. The fact that he sat bolt upright and never slouched took another five years of his age. Exercise had kept his body healthy and his mind alert. Many men his age had already kissed goodbye to their sex lives but Anderson always had a nubile waif, at least thirty years his junior, somewhere in the background, one of the many perks of working in the record industry. Singing nymphet wannabes were lured to his office in the hope of becoming another Phoenix Delta or Susan Dark. They were all worth procuring in his eyes, the talented and the not so talented. Waiting at his home would be a thirty-six-year-old from Arkansas whose major talent lay in the sack, not that Anderson would ever be so cruel as to tell her that, well not until he grew bored with her, which he would; eventually. He always did. Her stage name was Misty Blue which did little to hide her trailer park background or her real name of Lori Deane. Anderson's groin twitched just thinking about her.

"How'd I look?" Leroy felt nervous. The palms of his hands were still sweating a little, even after a long cooling shower.

Georgina studied Leroy. He was dressed in his finest handmade dark charcoal suit. The white shirt looked crisp and fresh against his black complexion; the neck was open with no tie in evidence. She wanted to say he looked 'hot' but decided on "Fine, you look just fine." Georgina hoped that Leroy did not notice the slight slur in her speech. It was a little after one in the afternoon and she felt tired. The early morning exercise had finally taken its toll. Georgina sat in her favorite chair with her legs curled up, drawn into her side, resting just under her buttocks. She had a pair of baggy gray pants on that nobody but Leroy would ever see her wearing. She liked the fact that she could slob out in front of him and not worry. She liked the fact and she hated it too.

"Damn, I feel like I am back at school or the academy."

"It's a job, Leroy. It's right to give the correct impression."

"Yeah, I s'pose. Well, you gonna wish me luck?"

Georgina was too tired to stand. She beckoned Leroy over by nodding her head back in a jerking motion. He drew down close to her.

"Turn around."

Leroy straightened and turned puzzled.

"You got a great ass, Leroy." Georgina pulled her hand back and playfully slapped Leroy's butt. "You look great. Good luck."

The drive to Anderson's office was short. Leroy bounded up the steps to the third floor office, choosing to bypass the elevator. The frosted glass on the entrance door was discreet almost austere, not a hint of brashness, simple gold leaf lettering announcing S. Anderson

Music Management. Leroy turned the handle and entered. He was greeted by a receptionist, a gangly effeminate man, thin by anyone's standards, he could have leapt from the pages of the darker reaches of history and the concentration camps of Germany. Paul Pennell pushed his rakish fingers through a mop of thick black hair that looked too heavy sitting on his head and spindly neck. The black polo neck jumper hid a jaunty Adam's apple that bobbed almost obscenely when he talked.

"Ah, Mr. LaPortiere. I will tell Mr. Anderson you are here." Pennell's accent was New York with a hint of Jersey and more than a dash of camp theatrics. He leaned forward and pressed on the intercom. "Your two-thirty is here."

"Thanks, Paul." Anderson's voice crackled through the speaker, metallic and distorted.

"You can go right on in." Paul Pennell smiled.

If Leroy were gay he would have realized that Pennell was hitting on him. As Leroy passed, Pennell watched Leroy's ass and smiled. Anderson was sitting behind his desk. What Leroy was not expecting to find though was the sight of Barbara Dace, the dogged middle-aged anchor for MRTV sitting opposite in one of two seats. Her short gray hair had grown a little since he last saw her but it was still cut expensively and flatteringly to enhance her features. Leroy could easily see what attracted his ex-boss, Captain Norman Frusco, into having an affair with the woman. There was no sign of John Keller her trusty cameraman. Leroy thought they always operated together, like Batman and Robin.

"Barbara." Leroy nodded and smiled.

"Mr. LaPortiere, good to meet you finally. Miss Dace has been telling me all about you." Anderson reached forward and shook Leroy's hand. His grip was over tight and meant to make sure he was not easily forgotten.

Leroy studied this gray rigid block of a man and felt for a moment that he was in an office with possibly two of the most attractive elder citizens of America.

Anderson sat.

"Take a seat." Barbara playfully patted the seat of the chair next to her. As Leroy sat, Barbara leaned to her side and said, "Norman sends his regards."

"Let's get down to business." Anderson started. "There is nothing complicated, in a nutshell, Mr. LaPortiere, Susan Dark has disappeared. It could be nothing more than succumbing to nerves prior to the release of her album."

"But Susan Dark has released three albums before, why get a case of nerves now?" Barbara interjected, cutting Anderson short.

"Who knows? Maybe because a lot is expected from this record. She is singing with her mother and grandmother."

The question mark on Barbara's face prompted Anderson to explain and as he spoke, Leroy realized that there was a whole history to learn before he could even start the case. "We have used modern technology to fuse old tracks by Amy and Caroline together and Susan has recorded new verses and choruses. It's her best work. We have even shot three videos, cost a dammed fortune to splice and edit, lots of blue and green screen work but it's worth it. Susan hugs her mother at one point. When Susan saw the result she cried."

"Doesn't sound as though this was work she wanted to walk away from?" Leroy spoke.

"She got all uppity and went strange just after that article in *Country Music Week* magazine." Anderson tossed a copy of the article across the desk for both Barbara and Leroy to look at. As Leroy read, he got the feeling that this case was going to be anything but straightforward.

"This was meant to be her breakthrough album. I have got some pre-release copies for you both along with all the footage from the video shoot. It may be helpful." Anderson opened a drawer in his desk and placed two lots of CD's on the desk.

Barbara leaned forward and picked up her copies. She studied the album first.

"'This side right of wrong.'" She scanned the track listing "'You've left, but I'm right', 'Lonesome, as I am' ..." She looked at the picture on the CD cover. An arty black and white shot. A picture that steered away from the typical Country and Western genre. Susan Dark was standing against a backdrop of wrecked cars piled high on top of each other, the only color in the picture was from the ominous clouds overhead, rays of light had been colored yellow, casting down on Susan. "I feel like I need therapy just holding this," Barbara said.

"You know the country scene, Ms. Dace, they just love maudlin."

Leroy opened the CD and pulled out the booklet that accompanied it. Eight pages including mocked-up photos of the Dark family reunion, the resemblance of the women in the pictures was uncanny. They looked more like sisters than three generations of progeny.

"The police are being as helpful as a crock of shit. Pardon the expression, Ms. Dace," Anderson continued. "They say that Susan checked out of the hotel and that no sign or evidence of a crime could be found. She is, to quote them, *'One of a quarter of a million people who go walkabout every year. We neither have the time nor the resource to investigate every missing person, even if they are famous.'* The official line is that she is an adult and capable of making her own decisions and that maybe one of those decisions is that she wants to be alone and unless any evidence that could relate this matter to a crime could be found then all they can do is add her to a very long list." Anderson was shaking his head. "I have put together all the information I know about the movements of Susan during the last three days I had contact with her. Everything is in here." Anderson handed Leroy a bright yellow folder. "Places she was seen, her hotel, the recording studio, the video shoot. Plus a list of all the people she may have contacted during that time. It's not comprehensive but … it's a start."

Leroy flicked through the folder. "Hmmm, you sure you need me. This is quite impressive."

"Thanks for the compliment but I have other fish to fry. This whole business is impacting too deeply on me already. The main proviso is that you share any information with Ms. Dace. If the worst happens it is in the interest of everyone that we generate a lot of media coverage."

The frown on Leroy's face showed all too clearly his disgust at the predatory nature of the music manager.

"It's easy to be sanctimonious Mr. LaPortiere but like it or not I have invested a lot of time effort and money into this project and like it or not with the right coverage the media and the public alike will lap this story up. I am in the business of management and I will manage this situation the best way for Susan Dark and her career."

"Even if she is dead." Leroy wished he had bitten his tongue but felt better for speaking.

"If, she is dead, God forbid, then I have a duty to provide her fan base with information and product. I am sure you will no doubt still cash your check from Anderson Music Management." Anderson's smile grated with Leroy.

The coffee bar was like one of a thousand that had sprung up across America in the 1990's. It had all the suburban cheesiness of a situation comedy movie set and the warmth and heart of an operating theater. Barbara Dace sat holding a cup of latte, dying for a cigarette. The nicotine patch on her arm had long given up the struggle with her habit. The patch could not infuse enough nicotine to satisfy Barbara's hunger.

"I hate these politically correct non-smoking zones." She gulped the coffee hoping for some caffeine release to combat the craving. "They're so sterile it's like a Martha Stewart cloning farm, makes me want to puke, or maybe that's just the coffee. D'you think they actually put any coffee in this?"

Leroy was sitting opposite her, the folder open on the table. "So, what's the deal with you and Anderson?"

"We go way back. He was a friend." She smiled, fond memories of her youth returned to briefly light up her eyes. "This is just a quid pro quo situation. We both get what we want. So, where are you gonna start?"

"With this." Leroy lifted the folder. "Some background checks first, then a little legwork. Go over those last few days Susan was around."

"You think she's dead?"

"I ain't thinking nothing at the minute."

"Keep me clued in, Leroy."

"Sure, it's in the contract."

"How's Georgina?"

"She's a fighter. She's getting there. You can come and see her if you want."

"No, I gotta get back to Missouri tonight. John's filming a toxic dumping scandal and I am supposed to be with him."

Leroy nodded. "I'll keep you posted."

"I'll be back up at the end of the week. Maybe catch up with Georgina then?"

"Sure, she'd like that."

On the drive back to Georgina's house, Leroy called ahead on his cell phone and asked Georgina to do a little research on the Internet to see what she could come up with regarding Susan Dark and her family. The phone betrayed Georgina's tiredness accentuating the slur in her voice. Leroy hung up feeling that maybe he was asking a little too much too soon.

She sat at the desk staring at the blank screen, waiting for the web page to load. Deep within her head were the beginnings of a headache. She recognized the signs all too well. The monitor appeared bright, overtly vivid and Georgina could not find a switch to control the amount of light spewing from it. The search engine's main page appeared; in the center of the screen was a small empty box. Georgina typed the name Susan Dark in the box and hit the search button. The computer raced away eager to please its new owner, searching a world full of servers, networks and code for anything that contained the words 'Susan Dark' or anything closely related. Within seconds the page changed and was replaced with a list of related sites. Georgina looked at the top of the page and saw that this was page one of twenty-two thousand pages. She hovered the mouse over the first link on the top of the page and clicked.

The sight of Georgina's door was a welcome one. Leroy felt a buzz of excitement; it was the rush of adrenaline that had been missing from his life for what seemed so long. He turned the key in the door and entered the house. All was quiet. The computer was silent, monitor turned off staring back at the world through a soulless black eye that reflected Leroy's image. There was a nice neat stack of freshly printed-paper awaiting Leroy's arrival. He took the stack of print-outs and added them to the folder given to him by Stevie Anderson earlier in the day. There would be a lot of reading before bed. Leroy walked down the hall to Georgina's bedroom. The door was ajar. Georgina never fully closed it. Leroy pushed lightly against the door and poked his head through the small gap. Georgina was nothing more than a mound hiding under a duvet cover; on the nightstand by the bed was a half-filled glass of water. Leroy watched her for a few seconds, waiting for the tiniest of movements from her to reassure him that everything was okay. He walked back to the sitting room and poured himself a neat malt before settling down in a chair to read.

Darkness fell upon the house. At some stage Leroy turned the side lamp on to give enough light to read. He was conscious of disturbing Georgina but as he flicked through the mass of information that she had downloaded from the Internet he became restless for her interpretation of some of the stories that he had read. Twice he went to her room and twice he had returned without waking her. On the second occasion he took a stack of paper from the printer and started writing down questions and comments. The biggest surprise to Leroy was Anderson's link with Susan's family. He had managed both her mother and grandmother, which until now had not once been mentioned, certainly not by Stevie Anderson. This was particularly unsettling to Leroy. Georgina had circled various names on articles but one in particular caught Leroy's eye. It was a name that struck a chord "Fisher Sutherland" as Leroy racked his brain he remembered why. Sutherland was the journalist who covered the "Dark Mystery" story for *Country Music Week* magazine. Georgina had printed a forthcoming titles page from Amazon and noted that Sutherland was about to publish a biography on the Dark family's tragedies. Fisher Sutherland was someone Leroy wanted to speak with. Georgina had already compiled a list of names, phone numbers and contact addresses, Leroy quickly scanned down the list and found Sutherland's name and details. From the little he had read Leroy knew that Sutherland would be the best person to talk to about Susan. Under the contact number for Sutherland was a new number penciled in the page border. Leroy lifted the phone and dialed the number. The phone rang for a while before an answering machine kicked in.

"Fisher Sutherland. Talk."

Leroy was taken aback by the short gruff message and took a few seconds to compose his thoughts, seconds which seemed like hours. "Hi, err, I am … you don't know me but I am Leroy LaPortiere. I am investigating the disappearance of Susan Dark. I would appreciate a call. Thanks. Sorry, my number is 555 0142."

Leroy settled back in the chair with Sutherland's article and reread it. He wondered whether the disappearance of a third generation of the Dark family could be *just* coincidence.

The forest was dense. Trees reached in a never-ending grasp for the sky, shutting out daylight even on the clearest day. The cabin had stood in the deepest, darkest part of the forest for over fifty years. Built with little expense spared at the time and still a secret from prying eyes to all but those paid handsomely to work on the project. Nobody ever heard the felling of a tree or the violent cutting teeth of a chainsaw. Wildlife had soon got used to the constant hammering of nails and the high-pitched squeal of drills. They barely batted an eye to the encroachment of man on their peaceful environment. The whole project took five solid months from start to finish and it stood the test of time. Hidden from view above by the dense forestation and verdant undergrowth it was the perfect retreat. A hunter's lair. Power was supplied by a generator, making life inside the domain more comfortable as the years moved on.

Saturday April 19

Leroy heard Georgina leave the house early in the morning. The daily routine was beginning. He was not sure whether Georgina was battling for fitness or against her illness, whichever it was he could see the determination that suggested that she was not going to stop until she was somewhere near her normal self. Leroy knew that Georgina never accepted half-measures, especially when it came to herself. He showered and gave Georgina a half hour head start before lacing his trainers and hitting the road. There was a fine drizzle in the air but the rain seemed to be heading out to sea. As Leroy reached the top of Ocean Drive, he paused to catch his breath and look down on Portmorion Bay. Fishing boats were anchored with leisure boats along the jetty. He could see sea traffic dotted around the horizon, many beginning to return from a night's haul, filled to the gunnels with fish for the market. At least once a week he or Georgina would buy from the market. Georgina kept threatening to take Leroy sea fishing. She promised to hire out a boat one day and surprise him. Leroy smiled at the idea. Georgina was making progress, by this time the previous day Leroy had already caught up with her. He scanned the coastal road and could just make out her slow shuffling figure a couple of hundred yards away. He would rest a while longer by the dry stone wall overlooking the bay, and while catching his breath give Georgina a much-needed boost in her confidence. While he sat on the wall he wondered about Susan Dark, about where she was, if she still alive. If indeed she had even been kidnapped. There had been no ransom note, no demand for money or anything else. Maybe she just wanted the quite life. He thought early retirement would open a world of opportunities but he found himself in a small dark room with only one door out and that led him back into the only world he could really understand. Leroy also realized that Georgina was in that room with him.

The cabin had bore witness to the passing of time and had remained stoically youthful in the face of adverse weather and the comings and goings of man. Rooms were added over time and the subterranean basement which was gouged out of the ground at the time of its construction took on a new identity over the years. Now it was awaiting a final dressing to make things just perfect. Photographs helped.

"I know but do you have a forwarding address or phone number ..." Leroy hung onto the phone impatiently, drumming his fingers against the desk.

Georgina swung around in her office chair. "Quit that, you're driving me crazy."

"Huh?" Leroy looked up.

"The infernal drummerring." Her eyes darted at Leroy's fingers, which ceased mid-drum. Georgina silently cursed her tongue for not obeying the message sent from her brain. She turned hoping Leroy would not have noticed her slight slurring. She returned her attention to the case file.

"You do; listen I don't care if it is Timbuktu." Leroy could not help but allow the sarcasm to filter through his voice. He started to jot down an address on a piece of paper in front of him. The velum watermarked paper that was really only meant for his letterhead. He scribbled furiously, hoping he would be able to read his own writing back when the conversation on the phone had ended. "And a phone number? Well, how about an email address?" Leroy cricked his neck. He had been on the phone to the *Country Music Week* magazine for over half an hour and in that time had been passed to five different people, all of whom he was assured would be able to help him locate Fisher Sutherland. "You do, good ... but you can't give it to me."

Across the room, Georgina picked up the phone extension and cut in on the conversation. "Miss, my name is Agent Georgina O'Neil of the FBI, badge number ND1111474501. Now, we can either release the information my colleague is requesting or I can get a warrant issued and just about bring a halt to the entire production of the magazine for the next three days while we conduct unnecessary searches for information." Georgina listened to hushed silence for a brief moment and then a voice on the other end of the line spoke apologetically.

"I have just found the information you need, including a contact telephone number."

Georgina smiled and placed the handset back down.

She needed to scream. She was suffering and felt confined yet isolated. There was nothing but darkness.

Georgina wondered about Susan Dark. She wondered how it was possible for a young woman to disappear and for no one to care. Well, no one but for a few fans and a manager concerned about losing a meal ticket. There was no family left. No boyfriend or girlfriend. Nothing traceable working backwards in her life beyond the point of her time in the studio and the hotel room she mysteriously checked out of. To all purposes she had vanished and no one really seemed to care. The doorbell rang, startling Georgina out of her train of thought. She looked down the hall to the pale blue wooden door. Just beyond the frosted panel of glass she could make out the figure of her father. Georgina's eyes lit up and a smile lifted her face from the gathering cloud.

"I'll get it, you continue working." She said to Leroy who was listening to the engaged tone of Fisher Sutherland's phone. At least he knew Sutherland was at home.

Georgina opened the door and was greeted by her father and Cally. Cally was three years younger than Georgina. While the past year had not been kind to Georgina in terms of health and stress, it was not these factors which made any real difference. Cally just had that annoyingly youthful look. Georgina knew it was one of the factors that drew her father's attention.

"Georgie." Wynan O'Neil stepped forward and embraced his daughter, swallowing her up in his arms. For a brief moment, with her eyes closed and the fresh aroma of her father's aftershave, she felt like a child. She wanted to stay in his arms longer but Wynan made the first move backwards. Georgina let go. Cally leaned forward and just about made contact with Georgina's face as she planted a weak but sociable kiss on her cheek.

"What brings you guys here?" Georgina's face was once again radiant with welcoming happiness.

Wynan stepped into the house and Cally followed. "We have some news."

"Some very good news." Cally spoke for the first time. Her voice was soft yet strong.

Georgina closed the door and followed her father and stepmother down the hall into the sitting room.

Georgina could honestly say she was not shocked when she heard the news.

"We're having a baby." Wynan was holding Cally's hand tightly as he spoke. For a second Georgina could almost believe she was the parent watching her offspring deliver the "good" news.

Later in the evening Georgina was in the kitchen pouring coffee when her father walked in and closed the door. Leroy was keeping Cally entertained in the sitting room with stories of his police work in Missouri.

"You seem quiet." Wynan still had a little of the Irish accent he had brought with him fifty years ago when his mother and father emigrated.

"Oh, you know. I've a lot on my mind." She hoped her father did not interpret her reply with physical connotations about her illness, though the subtext to her comment was also true. She turned to face her father. "I am happy for you both … really." Her hand reached out and grasped her father's arm and squeezed. "It'll be funny adjusting to life with a little brother or sister."

"Are you sure you are okay?"

About what, she thought. Her imminent sibling or was the enquiry aimed at her current state of health. "Yeah, sure." She gave her father a reassuring hug but the thought could not escape her mind that the two women her father most cared about in the world both had something growing in them. How ironic that one should mean life and the other death.

"That's my girl." Wynan pulled back and looked at his daughter. "You look tired."

"Been a long day."

Leroy looked at her bed, the glass of water was there, she wasn't; another day had arrived. In the midst of the revelations of the previous evening Georgina had become distant, especially so after her father and Cally had left. Leroy had continued to work quietly but Georgina had slipped away to bed without saying goodnight. When he had finally noticed her gone it was too late. Leroy looked in as he passed and saw her sleeping. He wanted to slip in beside her but chose the comfort of a hot bath and an empty bed.

Sunday 20 April

The road was getting easier to run. While her pace was nothing special, Georgina noticed that over the past couple of days she had at least developed something near a normal running pattern. She didn't have to think so hard about making her legs work the way they should. This gave her time to think about Leroy's case. She had always used running to clear her mind of the junk of life and concentrate on important matters, usually work related. One foot forward and then the other, one foot forward and then the other; her breathing came in sharp rapid but rhythmical bouts. The whole process became a mantra that helped her drift off into her own private space inside her head. She began thinking about Susan Dark again. Susan haunted her and she didn't know why. Georgina didn't relate to Susan in age, she was 10 years older, nor in stature but it wasn't the physical similarities that drew her to this woman, it was the fact that she could fall off the face of the world and not many people would notice or even care. There was a symbiotic link growing. Georgina liked that; it would help her help Susan, that's if it wasn't too late. She dismissed such thoughts quickly and returned to thinking about the Darks and their sad history. She wondered whether Susan's disappearance was linked to her mother and grandmother's murders. Then the thought hit her like a thunderbolt. It was the question they should have been asking from the very beginning … her pace quickened.

She arrived at the door breathless. There was a pulsating sensation in her temple but Georgina ignored it. She was too excited. Leroy was not at home. He must have been out on the run behind her somewhere. Through the excitement, Georgina registered that she was getting faster, that she was improving. She went straight to the study; sweat still dripping down her forehead. She used the cuff of her sleeve to wipe away the excess and sat down in front of the computer. Reaching forward she grabbed Leroy's notes and files on the case and flipped through them. She went straight to the back, to the few scant notes relating to Susan's mother and grandmother. Her eyes scanned the pages eating up the words until they rested on the information she needed and then cursed herself for overlooking an obvious and vital piece of information. Nobody had ever been convicted for either of the murders. Georgina knew that they did not have one missing person case to solve but two murders to solve first. For the first time in six months she had allowed herself to become excited but more importantly they now had a place to start, even if it was over forty years ago.

# Chapter 8 Paris, Texas

Wednesday May 14, 2003

The flight bothered Georgina; all flights bothered Georgina, physically and mentally. She was unaware of the fact that she had been holding Leroy's hand tightly for the past hour. This flight though was smooth and trouble free, not a hitch, a glitch or a bump, yet still she clung to his hand as though he was the only parachute on board.

"You really are scared of flying, aren't you?" Leroy said.

Georgina looked a little paler than usual. "It's not the flying … it's the crashing and dying, consumed in a ball of burning oxygen that actually bothers me." She looked comfortingly at the sick bag restrained behind the elasticized netting of the seat in front of her. Georgina took the folder out of her folio case and started to reread the contents once more, mostly to distract her mind from her phobia.

"This British guy, Fishzerr …"

"Sutherland, Fisher Sutherland." Leroy corrected her.

"What makes you so certain he'll be there?"

"The man's a journo … he's like a rat. I could sense his nose twitching even as we spoke."

"Long way to come for a hunch."

"Fisher Sutherland is going to get an epilogue for his book and if he is lucky a scoop, making him just one step ahead of the rest of the pack."

"Two steps." Barbara Dace turned. She was sitting in the seat in front of Leroy.

"Okay, two steps." Leroy conceded. "Even so, Sutherland is about the closest thing we have right now to somebody that has a unique overview of the whole Dark mystery."

"Mystery, did you really just say mystery?" Georgina said in mocking tones. "You make us sound like the Scooby gang or something." Georgina could not help but laugh at the notion.

"You know what I mean," Leroy said, trying to sound affronted.

She had slept but she wasn't sure now if she was awake or dreaming.

The room had to be perfect. Some things were replicas, some items were originals, stored away in various places just waiting for the day when they would be woken from their slumber and brought back into the world of the living for a few days. He had worked meticulously from photos, knowing full well that memory was never enough. The smell of freshly cut and sawn timber still hung in the confines of the cabin but at last the structural building work had been completed three days ahead of schedule. In many, many ways that was a good thing, it eased the pressure, took away the notion or necessity to facilitate last minute changes of plan and this was planned. It had been planned to the last detail for over twenty years. In many respects it was like the times before but each time was slightly different. This was the very last time. There would be no more after this one. It was a lifetime's work coming to fulfillment.

Fisher Sutherland sat alone in his motel room watching eastern European porn on a cable channel. His laptop computer was sitting on the dressing table by the window. The window was closed and the air conditioning cooled the air to something a little more bearable. He was munching his way through a chicken burger while watching a nubile Russian teenage girl employ every available orifice in her body to what he considered good use. The images on the TV whetted his appetite for something other than chicken burger between his teeth. Sutherland swigged from a cold bottle of beer and decided to search out the nightlife in Wink Winkler. He knew there were some good bars around; many that played live music and many that had live entertainment of a different variety. Tonight, he didn't want to be alone, no matter how good the porn channel and anyhow he always thought porn channels were better when watched with female company.

Time was held captive there was nothing but a vague sense of reality and dreams. She felt isolated but could not gauge whether she was cold or hot, awake or asleep and the strange thing was that she did not care. She enjoyed the sense of peace. Her mind tried to settle on one thought, she wanted to focus on a solitary issue but as she did she began to drift off once more. It was as though she was a ghostly spirit caught on a breeze. Just before drifting off into unconsciousness the notion occurred to Susan Dark that she might be dead, the corners of her mouth raised slightly, trying to form a smile.

Barbara Dace showered and then rang Norman Frusco. The motel was better than average and she was quite an expert on bad motels. The water was hot, the air conditioning was cool and the bed sheets crisp, white and clean, the one downside for Barbara was that her lover was only two states away but tonight that might well have been the other side of the earth. Her conversations with Norman could last for hours and the excitement she felt made her feel ridiculous and love-struck. For a while she could forget that she was a woman in her late fifties and in the twilight of her career. There was no getting away from it; Norman made her feel good and it had been a long time since any man had made her feel anything except cynical and bitter. She felt so good she could quite easily dismiss the fact that she was the other woman this time. On the bed, next to her opened case was a small stack of papers and notes that Leroy La Portiere and Georgina O'Neil had vetted. Her cameraman, John Keller was on standby awaiting her call to fly from Missouri at a moment's notice. Now she was running her own production company it paid to be more sensible with finances. Dace knew there was a story here in Texas though and her exclusivity to the hunt for Susan Dark guaranteed a big payday.

Thursday May 15

When Georgina awoke everything was dark. The blackness was total and consuming. So thick was its hold that Georgina felt the night was actually stealing the air from the room. She sat with her eyes open staring into the void, occasionally blinking and when she blinked the thin covering of skin across her eyes did not yield any further darkness. Eventually the stealthy approach of daylight crept into the room and with it shape, substance and focus. Georgina spent those hours thinking about her father, Cally and the new life growing inside her stepmother. The knock at the door pulled her back into Texas and the search for a missing person.

Leroy waited outside the room. He knocked again, unsure of whether Georgina had heard him.

"Wait a moment." Her voice called out. She walked to the door, still dressed in her pajamas and unfazed by the notion of Leroy seeing her at not exactly her best. Georgina rubbed some encrusted sleep from the corner of her eye and hoped that her breath was not too disgusting. She turned the handle of the door.

"Morning, sleepyhead." Leroy was a morning person. For a brief moment Georgina hated that. She wanted to be coaxed into the day. The journey had taken a toll on her and as much as she wanted to give the impression of getting back to fitness to everyone else she could not fool her body or her brain into anything other than a slow but progressive start.

"You wanna come with us to interview this Sutherland character?" Leroy said.

"Us" meant Barbara Dace was tagging along.

"Sure. Give me a half hour to shower and get some breakfast."

"I'll give you fifteen minutes and breakfast is my treat."

She said she was eighteen but in the harsh light of day the girl looked no more than fourteen. She fit the bill to a tee though. She was exactly what he was looking for. The girl was ripe. She had that fresh look he found so appealing, barely any make-up, and a small and svelte body. He slid out of the bed, hoping not to wake her. His mind raced to remember her name, he wasn't even sure if she had told him. For some reason he kept thinking of France. Was she French? Sutherland's foot hit something cold. As his eyes focused he realized it was a used condom. At least he had the presence of mind to wear a rubber. The girl rolled over, her body exposed to the dull light in the room but it was still light enough for him to see the bruises along her ribs and stomach. God, did he do that? Sutherland racked his brain, he could not remember. Her small boyish chest rose slightly as she breathed. There were no marks around her face, just a plain but natural beauty; Fisher Sutherland could see what attracted him to her. He lifted his foot and peeled the condom away and carried it gingerly between finger and thumb to the bathroom. Though it was filled with his swimmers, Sutherland still felt a slight revulsion at holding it, a cold clamminess had replaced the heat of passion when he was wearing it. He let it fall from his grasp and plop unceremoniously into the toilet. There was a small splashing sound as it hit the water. Sutherland looked down and could see that the condom actually landed in a mixture of water and vomit. He couldn't remember being sick, then again he couldn't remember much. A memory flashed in his mind, a tiny segment, a replay highlighting some of the previous night but in a very condensed form. At least ten memories fought for his attention. For the moment he went with the one where he was fucking her. Sutherland looked in the bathroom mirror and smiled, the memory an instant aphrodisiac. He felt a stirring and twitching sensation in his penis and looked back at the bed and a young, naked and vulnerable girl who was still locked in a deep drug and booze induced coma. As he walked back into the room the sight of her naked and vulnerable body made him become more aroused. The notion of fucking her while she was in a drug-hazed state hardened him. He pulled the rest of the sheet off the bed and gently turned her onto her back. It was as though she was sleeping the sleep of the innocent, she did not stir apart from a tiny murmur that escaped her lips.

She could feel a moving sensation, a constant rocking. It was as though she was on a boat. Slowly she was being rocked back to consciousness. Her body, which had been shut down, began to stir. Sensations began to filter through and her mind began to clear as dreams raced away and reality forced its way into her. She awoke. A weight was bearing down on her pinning her to the mattress, a rough hand, the palm smelling of stale tobacco and alcohol, forced over her mouth covering her nose making it almost impossible to breathe. Her eyes opened and stared wildly ahead, fixating on the person on her … inside her.

She could feel the acids in her stomach mixing and blending an uneasy cocktail of what she had consumed. She knew she was going to be sick again. She could feel the vomit in her stomach rising and there was nothing she could do. She tried to scream but his hand covered her mouth so perfectly and still his body moved inside her. There was nothing she could do.

Sutherland was so turned on, he could not stop. This time he could not even wait to put a condom on. He wanted to feel her, not some latex simulation. He put his hand over her mouth, should she wake and scream. He didn't want to alert neighboring guests and he was sure she would find the experience equally exciting once her mind cleared.

Her eyes widened, she knew what was coming and there was nothing she could do to stop it.

His eyes widened, his pupils briefly dilated, the black opening outward, eating the pale blue coloring of his eyes. He was moments away from coming, the rush inside his body unstoppable.

She tried to stop it but it was too late.

Sutherland pulled back harder on her mouth and for a split second he noticed that she was awake but it was too late he was too consumed by his own passion to care. Suddenly hot acrid smelling liquid was being pushed through his fingers. She tried to cough but she could not breathe. Vomit poured through her nostrils onto Sutherland's hand, the heat of it intense. He felt her breathe in, then her whole body went rigid. Almost immediately he pulled his hand away and she finally breathed in, filling her lungs with puke and she went limp.

Sutherland pulled his hand away, any sense of eroticism instantly gone as he was awash with the contents of her stomach. Fisher went limp.

# Chapter 9 Motel Babylon

Three Hours Later
Carlton McCabe's Diner
Three Miles from the Teenarosa Motel

"He's an hour late, I don't think he's gonna show." Barbara Dace was staring at her fourth cup of coffee. Her appetite for caffeine was as diminished as her will for waiting any longer. She pushed her empty breakfast plate away.

Georgina remained silent, almost distant. Dace had noticed that she wasn't in a talkative mood and kept her comments aimed for the most part at Leroy.

"He'll be here," Leroy said.

"Why?"

"Because he is like you, a journalist and he can smell a good story like a dog smells a bitch in heat."

"Thanks for that charming analogy."

Leroy smiled. "You got awful frazzled since you quit the nicotine."

"I've always been stressed. It was only the cigarettes that hid it."

"Sounds like BS to me."

"Four cups of coffee don't help much," Georgina spoke.

Leroy and Barbara fell silent for a moment and looked at Georgina, who was watching a car pulling into the drive.

"Besides, I think this is him now," she said.

Barbara leaned forward, craning her neck to the left to watch the car. "What makes you so sure this is him?"

Georgina looked around the deserted diner. "He looks British."

"He *looks* British?" Leroy said.

"That and he was driving on the wrong side of the road when he pulled in here."

The fact that he was late, the fact that he was sweating profusely, the fact that he had just disposed of the body of a young girl he had just killed all played a part in his erratic driving but none of these things were accidents. He sat for a moment in the car. Sutherland wiped a bead of sweat from his forehead with the cuff of his jacket and at the same time took the opportunity to have a quick sniff under his arms to see if sweat had turned to stink. He could smell nothing other than the twenty-four-hour protection deodorant he had sprayed profusely over his body after he had spent thirty minutes in the shower scrubbing under his nails, washing and rewashing his hair and body. Sutherland remained calm during the time immediately after the girl had choked to death. He had a well-rehearsed plan of how to dispose of the body. The solution was perfect. Now, a little after three hours later, Fisher Sutherland felt confident that she would not be found until he wanted her to be found.

"What's he doing?" Barbara said.

"Sniffing his armpits," Georgina replied. She continued watching the man, barely disguising her amusement and bemusement.

"Strange I though the Brits had bad teeth and it was the French that left something to be desired on the personal odor front." Leroy pushed back in his seat and finished his coffee. He gathered his papers and documents in readiness for the meeting with the journalist.

"Well, they say the Brits are European these days so maybe he has adopted a little entente uncordial," Barbara said.

Fisher Sutherland opened the door of the Ford and walked the thirty paces across the gravel path to the diner. The crunch of the stones under his foot assured Sutherland that he was attached to the earth and not experiencing some hallucinatory event due to lack of sleep, drugs or too much alcohol consumption. He quickly looked at the fingers on both of his hands, checking for signs of vomit, he was certain he had meticulously scrubbed them, washing away trace elements, elements that could link him with the dead young girl lying naked in his bed. The image of her puke covered face flashed in his mind, a game played by his brain, one that was to return to tease him on many more occasions often prompted by nothing more than a smell or a sound. For now though, Sutherland closed his eyes briefly and shook his head as though trying to rid himself of an irritation, a small pinball inside his head rolling around touching off stimuli, awakening memory with image and sound. He was within feet of the door.

"The guy looks pretty fried to me," Dace said watching the journalist's every step.

"Maybe he don't travel well," Georgina said.

"Well, as long as he's playing with a full set of cards I don't care what condition he's in," Leroy said. "He is the most knowledgeable person we can find at the moment. He's the *only* person we can find at the moment who knows anything about this unfortunate family."

She was in a box. Her whole life had been spent living up to the expectations of strangers. The only equivalent person she could think of were the sons of royalty. Being born a prince, your whole life was already to some extent preordained and thus it seemed inevitable that Susan Dark would follow in the footsteps of her mother and her mother before. There was a lot to be said for tradition and it was usually said by those who did not have to endure the straight-jacketed lifestyle of living under a spotlight. At times Susan felt that she was a tiny germ in a microcosm and that every time she looked up she could see the lenses of microscopes peering down on her. The unflinching eyes of the press watching for a slip, a stumble, waiting to see if she would follow the path of her alcoholic, drug-taking mother or if she had inherited the noble Presbyterian virtues of her grandmother, a native of Nova Scotia, lured to the big time and the big city lights with dreams of fame. No matter how true and noble the virtue, temptation was a weaving dancer, provocative and alluring even to the most staid of creatures.

"We are, none of us, innocent." Susan's lips moved. She felt warm and cozy and for now unquestioning. A song ran through her mind, a lullaby her mother used to sing, she was sure.

"Hush little baby don't you cry, mama's gonna sing you a lullaby. Hush little darlin' go to sleep …"

"Hi, Fisher Sutherland." Fisher held out his hand and hoped that it was not sweating. He was amazed at how steady it was … considering.

Georgina looked up at the man offering his hand and shook it. He was handsome, though slightly rough around the edges. Possibly early fifties though it was hard to tell. His hair was short but plentiful. There was no sign of premature balding or gray. The color was a light brown and complemented by his steely blue eyes. His face had at least a day's beard growth, though this only added to his appeal in her eyes. His hand was warm and relatively soft, this was definitely a city boy not a manual worker. His suit was made of a light linen material in a brown color that almost perfectly matched his hair; under the jacket he wore a plaid blue shirt opened to his breastbone revealing a white tee shirt underneath. Fisher placed a copy of his book on the table.

"A gift. It's an advanced reading copy or something, so my publisher tells me, but everything in there is in the final print."

Georgina opened the book and was surprised to see that Sutherland had signed it. She wondered just how conceited this British journalist was.

"Pay no minds to the signature," Sutherland said. "I was er … practicing. My agent has lined up a whole book tour." He let the excuse trail away. "May I sit?"

Barbara Dace shifted along on the bench seat making room for Sutherland's medium built frame.

"You want a drink or a coffee or something?" Leroy asked.

"Yeah, sure, love a beer."

"So would I but they don't have a license."

"Coffee would be fine then." Sutherland replied.

Leroy caught the attention of a waitress and signaled for another coffee to be brought over. "So, what can you tell us, Mr. Sutherland?"

"I can do better than tell you. Thought you might like a guided tour starting at the Teenarosa Motel, July 26, 1958."

The Teenarosa Motel

The Teenarosa Motel looked exactly the same as it did the day it was opened over fifty years ago. It stood in the middle of nowhere with nothing but the highway for company. Red dirt and sand washed the area, making it look like the fiery Dante-esque inferno during the hot summer days, and a lonely, cold as hell, dark as pitch sanctuary from the night. The road traffic roared past, not even blinking. There were better places to be. Sutherland's leg continually bounced against Georgina's thigh for the better part of the journey. She was not sure if this was a reaction to the road surface or something else. Sutherland smiled at her. Leroy was driving, Barbara sat next him. She was reading Sutherland's book. Her eyes skim reading looking for juicy tidbits. The index was fairly comprehensive and she found herself skipping back and forth. Three generations of one family murdered and disappeared and police apathy prevailed. Barbara wondered if they were dealing with someone who was very smart or whether it was just a case of overworked and under-resourced cops burying a time and man hungry situation.

"The owner back in 1958 was a Jonah Fintall, he died trying to escape from Amy Dark's murderer. His son Elijah took over the running of the motel and as far as I know he still runs it today." Sutherland's accent was crisp and sharp in the dry heat of the day. "Elijah's set up a shrine to Amy Dark, right after her death and has made a pretty penny renting out the room in its *untouched* state." Fisher used air quotes when he said untouched. He continued. "He also has a line of tacky souvenirs, not to mention a website retailing various ghoulish mementos, such as photographs of the murder scene, fragments of the bedding along with a certificate of authentication. You pay more for the soiled ones."

"Charming." Barbara cut in. "Listen Leroy, I think I am going to get John down here to shoot some footage."

Leroy was tired of sitting in the car, in the heat. He wanted to get out and stretch his legs and have a poke around, maybe talk with Elijah Fintall. "No problems Barbara, just don't air a thing until …"

"I know the score, Leroy."

Georgina opened the door of the car and was blasted by some Texan sun. She took the car's air-con for granted and was surprised at the ferocity of the heat. "Leroy, coming for a chat with Mr. Elijah?"

"Be right behind you."

"I'll tag along if you don't mind?" Fisher Sutherland said, not really leaving his statement open to debate. Georgina had no powers of state behind her anymore. She didn't even have a gumshoe license.

"Yeah, sure."

"Might make an interesting epilogue to the book."

Elijah Fintall, sixty-two years of age and one hundred and sixty pounds overweight. His heart was in a state of premature decay though he knew nothing about that yet. He had signs. No erections for fifteen years, though for ten of those years it really didn't matter and now a wonder drug in the shape of a little blue pill put the smile back on his face. His doctor would not prescribe Viagra. His doctor knew nothing about the fact that when he wanted a little lead in his pencil, he popped a bluey. The Internet was a wondrous invention, first he found his wife, and to be frank, bought her and then he found a tablet that gave him the best wood he had ever had in his life and it lasted for hours. May-Li, his wife didn't know about his secret but she had her suspicions. Elijah rubbed his hands together as he watched the two detectives and two journalists approach, even with the coach load of Japanese tourists on one of his famous "Amy Dark" pilgrimages he still had room in his motel for another eight customers. He sat behind the low counter with his feet resting on the bar of the stool that begrudgingly bore his bulky frame, though not as begrudgingly as May-Li.

"May-Li, honey?" Elijah called over his shoulder and waited … impatiently.

"May-Li, get your chinky little ass outta here."

"Yes, Lijah." The "E" was always lost whenever she pronounced his name. At first he thought it was cute, now it plain drove him crazy. She had endured five years of marriage to this overweight barbarian, spending most nights lying awake listening to her husband snoring, waiting for him to catch his breath. Occasionally he would stop breathing and there would be blessed silence and then he would go and spoil it all by catching his breath and the snores would continue. Elijah had delivered on all of his promises though and as much as she hated feeling his fat, sweaty body pressing into hers, a deal was a deal.

The door to the office opened. Leroy and Georgina were the first to walk through, quickly followed by Barbara and Fisher. Elijah's face opened outward in a fat, grimacing smile. His yellowed teeth and rotten gums were briefly exposed and when he spoke a waft of halitosis attacked anyone close enough. Georgina, involuntarily but perceptibly moved back a pace.

"Howdy, folks, what can my wife and I be doing for you on this fine day?"

Georgina wondered at how his teeth managed to stay in his mouth as he talked. They seemed to be attached more through memory than any obvious amount of gum tissue.

Leroy opened his wallet and flashed his detective's license. "We want some information about Amy Dark."

"You want information it's gonna cost you money."

"I somehow knew he was going to say that," Barbara whispered to Fisher Sutherland.

"I thought you four were going to hire a room." Elijah's hand was fondling his wife's buttocks. He was oblivious to the fact that May-Li was embarrassed.

Leroy kept his wallet in his hand. "Well, how much does a room cost?"

"Forty bucks."

Leroy's hand started to count through some bills.

"Each," Elijah added.

Leroy threw him eighty dollars. "Imagine we are sharing." He gave Elijah a cold stare.

"That's fine. So, what do ya want to know?"

Barbara stepped forward. "Everything."

Georgina studied the reception room. There were pictures of Amy Dark on the walls and on the counter there was a rack with Amy Dark CD's and tapes. There was a signed gold disc hanging next to a picture of her motel room, number 11. Georgina moved closer to the disc, an expert would have noticed the record was a fake almost immediately but Georgina was no expert, well not on Amy Dark anyway. An eagle-eyed fan might have noticed the thumb print on the gold paint covering the record where an over-anxious Elijah Fintall could not wait until the paint had dried before faking the signature and mounting the items together in a cheap wooden frame, which he painted black. Elijah studied Fisher Sutherland for a long moment.

"Have we met before?"

Before Fisher could reply the answer came to Fintall. "You're that English hack, doing the biography on the Darks. Damn, I thought we had met."

"So Mr. Fintall, I think it's time you took us for your tour," Leroy said.

With that Fintall slapped May-Li's butt real hard. An audible slap resounded in the room and May-Li could not hide the fact that her eyes were watering. "Best bit of chinky ass in the whole goddam USA. Best thing I ever bought." Fintall laughed. "Oh yeah, she's bought and paid for, aren't ya honey?"

Bought and paid for, the notion disgusted Barbara. She could not contemplate such a thing. Fisher Sutherland could, though his wallet or imagination had never stretched to buying a woman for life, a night or maybe two, if she was special, was the furthest he could think into the future where women was concerned. Not even the mother of his child enjoyed more than three days of his company at a stretch.

Elijah Fintall lumbered his frame from the stool, as he stretched his legs toward the ground he broke wind. A loud fart reverberated from his butt cheeks.

"Get out an' walk." Elijah showed no embarrassment; instead he waved his hand and fanned the putrid smell that accompanied the fart. "Phew, that one's a doozy." As he stood he pulled the seat of his pants away from his overlarge posterior. He grabbed a key fob hanging on the wall. "Room 11, here we come."

Day or night, it was difficult to tell, sometimes it was easier than others. There would be clues, for instance, she could hear the early morning bird song or the late evening trill as indigenous birds sung to their hearts' content and prepared to sleep. The sense of isolation was at times overwhelming but yet at others brought a serene peace and tranquility, it allowed her to think.

The door opened. Inside, the room was like a movie set or a moment trapped in time. A bed was unmade; the sheets pushed back and crumpled, sitting on the bed was a life size mannequin sporting a blonde wig, wearing a light summer dress that was opened to the waist. The dummy wore a fifties style bra with French knickers. A glass tumbler was filled with liquid, sitting on the nightstand. White tablets, probably aspirin, had been strategically arranged. The bathroom door just behind the bed was slightly ajar; a small figure was peering between the gap; a child of no more than three. Georgina had seen enough crime scenes in her life to recognize a clumsy half-assed reenactment when she saw one. The room had a musty smell, the result of too much heat and not enough ventilation, though it could easily have been emanating from Elijah Fintall. Fisher Sutherland followed Georgina inside the room.

"And this room is exactly the way it was found in 1958?" Leroy asked Fintall.

"On my pappy's casket." Fintall placed his hand over his large breast.

"Bullshit, it is," Leroy said.

"Well, as damned near as anyway," Fintall conceded.

Barbara Dace took a few snaps with a digital camera. Sutherland whispered to Georgina.

"The killer had stayed with Amy Dark for hours. Nobody is sure why, it seems like he was waiting to be found and when he was, he shot the witnesses, leaving Caroline Dark as the sole survivor.

Although she wasn't found for a further three days, abandoned in a department store. She was too young to recall anything from that day."

"Amy Dark wasn't shot though."

Sutherland shook his head. "Drugged with a poisonous cocktail. I don't think forensics even bothered working out the ingredients. I couldn't find out anyway."

Georgina walked into the bathroom.

"Miss, I don't usually allow tourists to go walkabout." Elijah moved forward quickly and grabbed Georgina's arm.

"Hey." Leroy pulled at Elijah Fintall. "Let the lady go." For a brief moment Elijah foolishly thought about tussling with the large black detective but he relinquished his grip.

"But maybe for an extra fifty, she can have access to the whole damn suite."

"Fifty?" Barbara said, disgusted by the fat man's avarice.

"It's a bargain, pay the man, Leroy," Georgina said.

Leroy reluctantly opened his wallet again and fished for fifty bucks. Elijah all but salivated. Georgina made her way into the bathroom. The once white tiles were thick and darkened with dust and nearly fifty years of grime. Rather than being disgusted, Georgina found herself excited by the prospect of extracting evidence that may have survived half a century. She fished in her handbag, pulling out a transparent cellophane bag. Inside the bag was a pair of latex gloves. She snapped on the gloves. The small bathroom was feeling crowded with Leroy, Barbara, Fisher Sutherland and Elijah vying for space with Georgina. The old enamel bath was lined with a ring of scum; Georgina presumed they were body fats that had adhered to the surface. The once brilliant chrome faucet was now dull and matted, a rust iron trail led to the drain. Georgina hitched her skirt to mid-thigh and crouched down on her haunches, then kneeled on the bathroom floor. It was not very elegant looking but she was not concerned with appearances at the moment. She kneeled lower and looked under the bath. The pipe work was exposed with the P trap sitting in a cut recess in the floor. Georgina smiled.

# Chapter 10 Silence like a Cancer Grows

*The Teenarosa Motel, Talinha, Texas*
*Saturday March 27, 1954*

*Joseph Wills sat alone for an hour in the dark, spending most of the time asking himself a plethora of questions, most of which had to do with the lady sitting inside motel room number 11. Any other man ... most other men, would not have to face such questions, they would never be posed by a society that thought itself cultured, adult and righteous. But Joseph Wills had a disadvantage over most of American society, something which would not affect the majority of the population and certainly not the residents of a town like Talinha in the mid-point of the twentieth century; for Joseph Wills was a black man having an affair, an extremely passionate sexual affair, with a homegrown celebrity who not only was white but also a virtue of the Christian right wing of small town America. Joseph continued to sit and ponder. They had kept their meetings a secret for seven months, the last four of which had been highly sexually charged. He would wait until the cover of darkness and then make his move. Amy Dark would close both curtains if the coast was clear or leave them half drawn if she suspected their night might be interrupted. Joseph kept an eye out for anyone who may or may not be a reporter. The slightest whiff of scandal would kill them both. As night fell, the light inside the motel room was lit. Occasionally, Joseph would catch a glimpse of Amy walking back and forth across the room. He felt an aching desire to be with her in the room, both of them tearing at each other's clothes until they were naked and sweating, locked together in an embrace that felt so very intense. She appeared at the window and briefly looked out into the blackness, her eyes searching for him, her heart thumping hard with a burning sensation running down her stomach and deeper inside. Amy Dark pulled the curtains closed.*

Georgina pulled at the P trap fitting, twisting her hand while maintaining a firm grip on the pipe. It twisted one way then she twisted it in the opposite direction.

"What you doing? You gonna bust that?" Georgina was getting tired of hearing Elijah's whining voice.

"Give Mr. Fintall another twenty bucks and a further thirty to leave us in peace, Leroy?"

"Another fifty? I'm going to need an overdraft at this rate. Fifty bucks and you leave right, you leave us alone to do what we gotta?" Leroy held the fifty in front of Elijah.

Fifty bucks would pay for an extra consignment of Viagra. Elijah's puffy hand reached out, his stubby fingers grasping the air close to the money.

"I need your promise," Leroy said.

Elijah grabbed the money and left the room.

"Let me try that?" Leroy said. He joined Georgina at the side of the bath.

"Put on some protection, I don't want us to contaminate any evidence," Georgina said.

Leroy pulled a pair of latex gloves over his large hands. "I'm more concerned about contaminating myself. God knows what sort of shit is in here."

Georgina looked at the toilet bowl and shuddered, not relishing their next search. "Believe me, Leroy, this is a walk in the park."

Leroy gripped the pipework and pulled hard while twisting the trap. The P trap suddenly gave way to sheer force and came free in his hand. Georgina opened the transparent plastic bag.

"Put the whole damn trap in here." She waited for Leroy to place the P trap in the bag before sealing the top.

"Now, Leroy, how squeamish are you?" Georgina looked at the toilet bowl.

Georgina still had friends at the Academy and Leroy could draw on a few favors if necessary but all the physical evidence could be shipped to laboratories and processed without raising too many eyebrows. If the worst came to the worst Barbara Dace's boyfriend and Leroy's old boss, Norman Frusco, would help. Georgina began to feel tired on the journey back to their motel and fell silent. She had started to read Fisher Sutherland's book on the Dark family and had become engrossed. The author sat beside her for the duration of the trip, lost in his own thoughts and as hard as he tried to think about the events in the motel room in Talinha, his mind kept returning to the events in his own room the previous evening. Barbara Dace talked incessantly on the cell phone to her lead cameraman, John Keller. She knew something was happening, her gut instinct, which rarely betrayed her, was on hyper alert. She reminded herself to thank Norman properly when she returned to Missouri. Though Leroy's eyes were fixed on the road ahead, his mind was a whirr with information. He wanted the samples from the Teenarosa Motel tested and the results returned but knew it would be a matter of days before any news would come through, after all who in their right mind would be in a rush to process nearly fifty-year-old evidence of a closed case? They would regroup back in Georgina's motel room and go through the day's events. Fisher Sutherland was harder to shake off than a fourteen-day cold and somehow managed to gatecrash the party. All Georgina wanted to do now though was sleep but she gracefully played host to a murder party.

*Saturday March 27, 1954*

*"I'm pregnant." Amy Dark let the words hang in the air for a moment allowing them to sink into Joseph Wills' consciousness.*

*"But, how can this be?" Wills was staggered. "We woz using protection."*

*"I know, I know. You tell me?"*

*"Are you sure?"*

*"My monthly friend has not paid a visit for the past three months now."*

*"Three?"*

*Amy Dark walked to Joseph. She took hold of his hand and placed it on her stomach and he could feel the slightest bump. A firmness in her abdomen that was never there before. His hands felt the beginning of life.*

*"What do you want to do?" Joseph asked, fearing the answer no matter what that answer was. But Amy was silent.*

*"I mean; there are places …"*

*Amy's look told Joseph all he needed to know.*

*"The baby's going to be part black."*

*Amy looked at Joseph but did not answer.*

*"I mean, that is something that you can't hide. People will ask questions. Some will hate you." The words slipped out of Joseph's mouth but the passage was not an easy one. He knew about hate. He knew all about color hate and people's prejudices, people who considered themselves God-fearing, church-going, ordinary, decent white folk. The motel room suddenly felt very small and yet somehow Joseph Wills felt very lost as he stood inside it. Amy however seemed too calm.*

Thursday May 15, 2003

The mini bar was empty. Georgina wanted an ice-cold coke with plenty of ice. The icemaker outside the room could deliver the ice but the small refrigerator inside was bare. Leroy, Barbara and Fisher Sutherland finally left her room after another three hours of deliberating. A UPS truck arrived to courier the samples back to the labs at Quantico. She addressed them for the personal attention of Darrell Garside, one of the few remaining ex-colleagues that Georgina could always trust. Leroy wrapped a second set of samples and sent them to Missouri for the attention of Norman Frusco. The P trap had proven fruitful, bearing at least a dozen hairs and though they were dried with the passing of time, the dark conditions had preserved them for the best part of nearly fifty years. Georgina left her motel room and wandered across the small concourse to the reception in the hunt for a soft drink. Halfway across, Georgina was having second thoughts about the ice in the drink. The reception area was empty but behind a set of doors came the sound of talking and the familiar clink of glasses. She pushed on the door and entered a licensed bar area. There were plenty of faces she had never seen before, including a uniformed cop. She wondered if she imagined the room going quiet or whether it had actually happened; if it had, it was only momentary. The room was dark with discreet lighting and a polished floor. Tables and chairs skirted the wall with a large bar area on the far wall. The room doubled as a breakfast area for guests but at night it became the only place for a hundred miles where you could buy a beer or spirits right through the long night. Georgina walked to the bar. A female bartender smiled. "What's your poison?"

The notion for a soft drink was suddenly dispelled. Georgina looked along the optics-lined row. Her eyes stopped on a Scottish Malt Whisky. "I'll have a double Laphroaig."

"A good choice."

Georgina turned and faced Fisher Sutherland. "I thought you had gone back to your motel."

"I have." Fisher lifted his glass in a mock toast. "I decided to book in here for the night, it's not like I have anyone waiting for me and anyhow, I will be on hand for your next incursion into the dark country."

"The dark country?"

"The blood spattered lands of Texas. Well, maybe not blood spattered but just a little of the gruesome history." Sutherland's eyes caught the light in the darkened room and for a brief moment Georgina thought she saw a hint of enjoyment in them. "So, are you going to let me buy you a drink?"

Georgina shrugged. It had been a long time since a man had bought her a drink or even paid her any attention. "If you tell me everything you know about the Dark family?"

Sutherland snorted through his nostrils. The sound was like a laugh. "That could take all night."

In the darkened atmosphere of the room, Fisher Sutherland passed as attractive. Georgina was in no mood to mix business with pleasure when she left her motel room but she felt her heart quicken a little. "I have all night."

"Insomniac, huh?"

Georgina knew the answer. Sleep was not the friend it once was. In sleep, Georgina had no control. It was not the dreams that frightened her, nor was it the fear of the invader inside her head; the dark growth that was lurking. No, it was the silence and the consummate void. Georgina had spent the last three nights waiting for Susan Dark to come back to her dreams, she had waited for her voice to sing to her once more but there were no more songs. Susan had stopped singing. Waves of smoke drifted across the floor and Georgina coughed. "Do you mind if we do this back at my motel room?"

Sutherland called the bartender and opened his wallet. "I'll have a bottle of Laphroaig."

There was a mellow serenade of crickets to accompany Georgina and Fisher back to her motel room. Georgina didn't know yet if she wanted to spend the rest of the night interrogating Sutherland for every last drop of information about the Dark dynasty or fucking him. She felt like she needed to lose control, it would just be sex.

As they approached the motel room door though Leroy LaPortiere emerged from the shadows. He had a look on his face that Georgina instantly recognized.

"All hell's gonna break loose. The police have found a body. Might be Susan."

Georgina felt her blood run cold. Any thoughts of passion were dispelled within the grace of a sentence. Fisher Sutherland's blood ran cold too but for a different reason.

"I was in the motel lobby talking with Dace when the sheriff got the call on her radio, caused quite a stir. Barbara's followed her and gonna call us when she finds anything," Leroy said.

"Fisher and I were erm … we were going to …"

"I was going to tell Georgina about Caroline Dark. A little background info." Fisher Sutherland stepped in.

Leroy looked at Fisher then he looked at Georgina. "Cool, you won't mind if I crash the party then."

"No, sure, yep, that'll be fine." Georgina didn't know why but she felt as though her parents had caught her doing something wicked.

"Hey and a fine whisky too," Leroy said noticing the bottle.

"So you don't know anything about this body?" Sutherland asked.

"The sheriff was doing a routine visit when the call came through. All we heard was the crackle of the radio and a voice saying a young female has been found out off the road somewhere."

"Shouldn't you, I meant wouldn't you, want to be out there finding out." Sutherland did not want to give up on his evening alone with Georgina.

"Nah, it's cool. If it is Susan, it's case closed anyway. Barbara still gets her scoop for network." Leroy could see the flesh on Georgina's arms rising in thousands of goosebumps. "Let's get inside and have a warming drink."

Georgina opened her motel room door.

# Chapter 11 Body of Proof

Thursday May 15, 2003

The body was found a mile off the roadside. She was stripped naked and left to the ravages of the Texan sun. Her fingers had been severed at the last joint (post mortem) while all body hair had been shaved including the head. The teeth on the upper jaw had been filed with an industrial instrument of some kind, while the lower jaw had been removed by something, though the nature of the instrument would never be known. Accelerated decomposition had begun in the fierce heat leading to body gases expanding the outer dermis. There was evidence of the body being subject to interest by the local wildlife with irregular bite marks and signs of gnawing around the trunk, groin and shins with the left breast totally degenerated.

"She could be anybody." Harker Brown knelt in the dusty soil. A halogen arc lamp had been erected overhead to illuminate the scene of crime adding to the high nighttime temperature, which was still in the mid-seventies fahrenheit. Sweat dripped from Brown's forehead onto his regulation pants. "This area is secure so we can move the body and ship her back to the lab."

Sheriff Mary T Rankin shifted the dry soil back and forth with her feet. "This dirt is our only witness, make sure our crime scene boys go over it with a fine tooth comb, Harker?"

"As always, Mary." Harker looked toward the mobile support unit for help from one of his team. Moving the body was going to be a delicate operation. He'd seen one split open like an overripe fruit once and was in no hurry to repeat the experience. "Any missing persons added to your board of late?"

"Fourteen."

"Well, I guess that might narrow down our field of search a bit."

"Maybe." Mary looked across the dark open plain. "Hell of a way to end such a young life, hell of a way."

"Who is the woman?" Harker asked.

"TV reporter."

"Christ that was quick."

"She followed me out here. I was at the Teenarosa Motel."

"You talked to her?"

"That's my next job. Careful with the young girl now, Harker; life has played this girl a mighty bad deal of the cards. It's up to us now to settle her soul." The sheriff nodded her hat toward the crime scene's officer and walked toward the figure of Barbara Dace.

"What do you think you were playing at?"

"Last time I checked, Leroy, you were not my father." The word "father" slurred slightly in Georgina's mouth and she cursed herself. She knew she was tired and was in no mood for an argument with Leroy. Fisher Sutherland was in the bathroom, preening himself, making ready for what he hoped would be the inevitable.

"Look at you. You're tired, you need rest, not … not …"

Georgina gave Leroy a withering look. "How would you know what I need?"

It was Leroy's turn to feel hurt and he could not disguise the fact that Georgina's words were like body blows to him.

"I'm sorry, Leroy, that was not fair."

"It's you I am looking out for."

Georgina learned forward and kissed Leroy's face. "I know. But I am a big girl. Sometimes I need to make a mistake. It gets lonely."

Leroy sighed. "I know."

"Anyway, you big lunk, it looks as though whatever is happening with Barbara has put paid to any romantic notions I may … or may not have had."

Leroy was about to speak when his cell phone rang, the trill of the ring obtrusive and urgent. "Yeah." Leroy answered. He mouthed to Georgina. "It's Barbara." Leroy mumbled and grunted and occasionally nodded though to little effect as far as the conversation on the phone was concerned then he closed the cell phone. Georgina looked at him with resigned expectation. Dark rings formed under her eyes and Leroy was not sure if her skin had not sallowed in color.

"Barbara's made a useful friend."

The door to the bathroom opened. Fisher Sutherland emerged looking refreshed. His hair was slightly damp and Georgina noticed water droplets on his shirt. She wasn't sure what it was that she found so appealing about him, whether it was something as simple as the accent or the fact that there was a level of intelligence about him, it was true he was not unattractive but he was not from the same mold of man she was usually attracted to. Maybe, she thought, her perception of men had been altered by the trauma in her life, or maybe she was just desperate for some male company without strings and he was there, the right place at the right time. It was true that Leroy was there, too, but Georgina figured that with him she could not have an easy relationship, a one night stand, a quick and pointless but truly gratuitous fuck without consequences or expectations. She looked at Fisher Sutherland and he became more attractive, yes, she figured she could spend a night with him.

"So, what's all the excitement?" Sutherland sensed an atmosphere between Georgina and the black detective.

Leroy poured the whisky from the bottle into three glasses. He was determined to outstay his welcome tonight.

The room in the cabin was complete. He felt an overwhelming sense of achievement and knew that in her heart of hearts that she would be pleased when she saw it. He felt she would feel honored. The room was an exact facsimile, everything was as it should be; everything was now perfect. She would understand. He washed his hands in the sink, pouring the water from a white cast iron jug. His hands felt rough; they no longer had the softness of the city. The once manicured nails were dirty and broken with honest labor. Soon it would be time to show her past to her. To glory in the revelations of her history and watch her face as slowly the pennies dropped and Susan Dark realized maybe for the first time in her life exactly who she was.

*Friday July 25, 1958*

*Joseph watched from afar. It seemed like he had spent all of his life watching from a distance. The child, his baby, was a ghost to him. Amy Dark was right, the press would vilify her for her illegitimate child and to protect her career she cut Joseph out of her life and the life of her baby. For three and a half years, Amy had toured Europe and Asia at the behest of her manager, Stevie Anderson and his silent partner, Randolph Thorne, but home was calling and try as she might Amy Dark could not resist the pull of her spiritual Texan homeland. Stevie Anderson had called and talked about a comeback album. The studio time was booked and Gil Frolan was lined up to produce as soon as he finished work with Frankie MacFarlane. Joseph moved closer to the window, he could see his child walking excitedly across the room pushing a toy dog which had large caster wheels attached to the legs. Any hint of the child's African-*

*American genetics was far from evident. Joseph's own skin color*
*was dusky brown and he was surprised to see how little of his genes*
*had transferred. He pressed closer to the glass, determined to get a*
*better view. He wanted to hold his child, hold her for the first time.*
*He had to knock on the door and demand to see her. Consumed by*
*anguish, longing and loss, Joseph made a decision.*

Friday May 16, 2003

"I am so pissed with you right now … but … thanks." Georgina
kissed Leroy on the cheek. Georgina was standing outside Leroy's
motel room.

Leroy answered the door wearing his boxer shorts and a white tee
shirt. It was obvious that Georgina had woken him from a deep
slumber. She on the other hand was wide awake. Her forehead had a
little perspiration, the result of a two-mile jog before the sun became
too hot to run.

"You look wrecked."

"Thanks. Your British pal drinks like a fish." Leroy walked back
into the room, preferring the darkened shade to the bright day
outside. Georgina followed him in.

"You weren't doing too bad the last I checked."

"Well, you done the right thing by going to bed early."

"And you saved me from doing the wrong thing by my going to
bed early … I do appreciate you looking out for me but …"

Leroy sat on the bed. "But sometimes you have to make mistakes.
But why with him?"

"Because he was available. Don't you feel lonely, Leroy?"

"You know I miss Lia. Takes a long time to move on."

Georgina sat on the bed next to Leroy. She had thought long and
hard during the night and more so during her early morning run.

"You know that if we … I'm not sure how to say this, without it
sounding strange. What I am trying to say is that if we, you know,
slept together, then part of what makes us such special friends might
die … and I guess I am scared of that happening."

Leroy looked at Georgina. Her hand rested on his bare thigh.

"So?" Leroy said.

"So, sometimes you have to make a decision."

Georgina leaned closer to Leroy. Her hand soft against his leg. He
could feel the warmth of her touch; it was a feeling that had been

missing from his life for such a long time. There was a repeated and persistent knocking at the door and the moment vanished.

Barbara Dace knocked on the door with an urgency that was fed by excitement. Standing under the shade of the roof, Sheriff Mary T Rankin surveyed the vista. She breathed deeply.

"There's a whole bunch of trouble in our little world."

Barbara turned around to face the sheriff. "Sorry?"

"Can't you just feel the pain, there's pain everywhere." The sheriff's face was a little red as though she had exerted herself but the truth was that she was in the middle of a hot flush. She had avoided any real form of mid-life crisis and gone straight into the menopause.

Barbara nodded. "I've seen too much pain lately."

"I know. I can see it in your aura." Rankin waved her hand in front of Barbara. It appeared as though she was parting clouds or wafting fog away from the reporter's face. "A hell of a lot of pain."

The motel door opened and Georgina's face lifted when she saw Barbara. "Leroy's in the shower."

Barbara gave what Georgina interpreted as a knowing nod. "This is Sheriff Mary T Rankin." Barbara introduced the Texan law officer.

Mary stood a little more upright, resplendent in full-uniform and statutory shades. "Here to help you, ma'am, for a little quid pro quo." Rankin breezed past Georgina and entered Leroy's motel room. Barbara shrugged and followed.

He shivered at the ease of it all; everyone was playing the game as though he had scripted it, the predictability of the police, the dogged but useless investigation by the detective and his ailing sidekick. Management played its part too by keeping the story out of the media. Though pretty soon that would all change, blood would be spilled for just a little of what he had planned. Tonight he would make a fire in the cabin and eat a ready meal from the microwave; tomorrow he would go over everything once more, just to be sure. He would check and double check the photos, making sure that everything was as it should be, nothing was to be out of place, nothing was to be missing and now he had Susan, nothing could be. He would bathe her and dress her, then arrange her just so. The excitement and anticipation made him sexually excited. Soon the fun would really begin.

# Chapter 12 Dust and the Desert Girl

The Talinha County Police Records Archive
Friday May 16, 2003

Georgina didn't know what to make of the sheriff. She knew instantly that she liked her but she was a little concerned by her slightly eccentric behavior or as Leroy had put it when he cornered Georgina leaving the motel.

"She's a fruitcake."

"I know she's a little off the highway but she can give us access to information we can't hope to get elsewhere."

"At a price."

Georgina stopped walking, allowing Barbara, John Keller, Fisher Sutherland and the sheriff to continue ahead of them. "Not much of a price, besides the cases could be linked."

Leroy paused for a second. His shoes were covered with the dry sandy dust of Talinha. The sun continued to slow bake him, reminding him of a hot Missouri summer day, only the heat was dryer. The only sound was a low buzzing from an electric pylon and the faint chatter of Barbara and the sheriff. "It's a distraction and one that Stevie Anderson won't be paying for."

Georgina had the taste of copper in her mouth all morning as though she had been sucking pennies. For a minute she struggled to think of what she was going to say. It was as though she had forgotten how to talk then just as quickly the words formed automatically. "Since *whem* has this been about money."

"Are you okay?"

"Don't fuss, I'm fine." Georgina dismissed her word stumble with the wave of her hand.

"You know it's never been about the money but Anderson legitimizes our being here."

"Listen, we spend a day, two at the worst, helping sheriff holy hands overcome a severe staff shortage and who knows we might even do *sssome* good." Georgina smiled.

As much as Leroy enjoyed seeing her smile, he could also tell when Georgina was faking her condition. He was hoping she would slow down and rest but knew it was not her way.

"The desert girl?"

"Definitely not Susan. She's too short plus our records don't mention any body tattoos, Jane Doe has a seven of clubs tattooed on her inner left thigh about two inches from her pubis."

"Ouch, brings tears to my eyes thinking about it."

"We have fourteen possible candidates. One of the deputies is contacting the parents of local missing children fitting the description, height and approximate age."

Georgina looked up at the huge industrial warehouse in front of her. The corrugated steel paneled building looked innocuous situated in the heart of a business park two miles out of Talinha main town but it was the archive storage facility for every recorded crime in Talinha as well as other towns in Texas for the past ninety years.

"I hope they have a good filing system," Leroy said.

The security at the gate was impressive. Georgina was certain that there was no way they would ever have gained entry to the facility without the help of Sheriff Rankin. Rankin spent five minutes organizing day passes for Georgina, Leroy, Barbara, John and Fisher. She was on first name terms with almost every security guard they encountered and was known by almost everyone there. Once inside the large warehouse they were confronted with a hive of activity, with workers dressed in color-coded coveralls, the color depicting their task or section. Georgina soon figured that yellow was retrieval, orange incoming storage and blue uniforms were responsible for electronic copying of all media.

"Somewhere in here," Sheriff Rankin said, "is every piece of information that was collected on the assassination of JFK. Well, every piece garnered by the Dallas PD."

Rows of shelving ran in vertical columns over twenty feet in height, each shelf was crammed with identical brown boxes. Each box was the same height and width. The storage facility had the sort of uniformity only dreamed of by Nazis and possibly white supremacists. In between the aisles ran forklift trucks and mobile platform lifts. The platform lift was operated from a cradle that rose on hydraulic arms that enabled the operator easy access to any given file within a matter of seconds. Barbara Dace watched the process impressed with the efficiency of it all.

"Our section is right down this way." The sheriff led the party along an endless aisle of boxes. The smell in the air was primarily of cardboard, though the air filtration and conditioning process removed and replaced the air to keep a constant environment that made degradation of paper documents almost null and void. "We are lucky that the location of this archive is right on our doorstep, other folk in Texas have to rely on our internal courier service to transport documents, though they guarantee that every PD can have any document supplied within eight hours from order to delivery."

They continued walking. At the bottom of the row the sheriff turned left and continued down another aisle until she reached halfway. "Our records start here."

She placed her hand on a cardboard box. "At the beginning of 1915." At the bottom of the aisle was a small hydraulic platform on wheels with a yellow suited worker waiting instruction. Sheriff Mary T Rankin beckoned the man forward and slowly the electric platform silently made its way toward them. "Of course large items of evidence are stored in another area of this facility but easily located thanks to a remarkable software cross referencing program and the invention of bar coding."

Georgina looked at Leroy; any preconceived notions about working with a back county organization with little or no concept of orderliness, regulation or method had been shattered. The fact was that the archive could teach most police forces a lesson, though the price Sheriff Mary T Rankin paid for such order was in men on the ground and the ability to continue to carry out her role in the community to a degree that she wanted to. She and the people of Talinha had become a victim of politics and bureaucracy. Georgina looked at the boxes for any hint of a clue as to their contents but the only clue was the town name imprinted on each box and the year clearly stamped in large bold lettering. A bar code held all the vital information, that and a series of what appeared to be random numbers. Leroy knew the filing system back at his old PD was decrepit compared with this and wondered what sort of an impact a facility such as this would have on the prosecution rate. The hydraulic platform stopped a foot from the sheriff and the yellow-suited worker had a name badge clearly identifying him as Jez Brown. The bespectacled archivist jumped from the platform.

"Mary." His Texan accent betrayed his roots within the space of a word, the name of the sheriff.

"Hiya, Jez."

"What can we do for you today?"

"We're taking a trip back to 1958 and the Teenarosa Motel."

*July 25, 1958*

*Joseph knocked on the door. He felt fear, anxiety and excitement mixing in a cocktail of emotions as he stood waiting for Amy Dark to answer. He clenched his fists, making the knuckles prominent then opened his hands allowing the blood to circulate through them. He thanked God that Amy was a creature of habit and when he learned that she was about to record a new album in Texas knew automatically that she would opt for somewhere familiar, somewhere away from it all, even if the motel did bear memories of some pain. Joseph also knew the motel and this room in particular also held many, many more memories that she wanted to hold close. Amy Dark opened the door; the smile on her face instantly erased as though a wiper blade had swished across her face. She felt the bottom of her stomach fall and continue to fall, her feet threatened to betray her grip with gravity.*

*"Amy."*

*"Oh my ... Joseph." She stepped forward and pulled the door to her back, cutting the view inside the room from Joseph. "You ... you should have written to me first. It's not good you being here like this."*

*"I did write. I have written every day for the past two years." Joseph put his hand in his pocket and pulled out a crumpled piece of paper. "This is tomorrow's letter. I wrote it because I never thought I would have the nerve to see you again."*

*"Maybe you should have sent the letter instead."*

*"And where would it end up." Joseph's eyes showed the pain he felt in his heart. "In the pile hidden away from you with all the others?"*

*"Who is it, honey?" The voice came through the door soft and enquiring but like a sledgehammer to Joseph.*

*"Now is not a good time, Joseph," Amy said. She pulled the door tighter to her back. "It's alright, honey, it's just a fan."*

*"A fan?" Joseph could not hide his incredulity, the words dripped from his mouth as though they were acid. "A fan." He pushed against the door but Amy blocked his attempt. "I want to see my daughter."*

*"You don't have a daughter."*

*"She is mine," Joseph said, his voice determined but low.*

*"We can't meet like this, Joseph. Meet me tomorrow."*

*"Where?"*

*"Here, at ten thirty."*

*"And what about lover boy in there."*

*"Don't worry, I will be on my own. You have to go now."*

*"Tomorrow." Joseph stepped back turned and headed into the darkness.*

*Amy watched her ex-lover become consumed by darkness. Her heart was racing but not in the way it used to pound for Joseph. Her life had changed disproportionately and he was the catalyst that had provoked the revolution. She opened the door and walked back into her new life.*

Friday May 16, 2003

"The records show that Caroline Dark was adopted by various foster families in Texas after her mother was killed." Georgina was sitting in a bare room that was furnished with a table, four chairs, a computer with scanner and a color photocopier. Although very clinical the room had balanced fluorescent lighting, soft ambient music and an endless supply of filtered coffee. Barbara, Leroy and the sheriff were also reading through material from the box marked 1958, RDOH 39997471243TXTA.

"She had no other family," Leroy said as a matter of fact without referring to the papers in front of him. "Well, that's what Fisher Sutherland's book says anyway." He looked up to find the sheriff, Barbara and Georgina looking at him. "So, I managed to read a few chapters before lights out last night."

"Nice one," Fisher said smiling.

"Well, ain't you just a regular country boy," the sheriff said.

The sheriff's radio crackled and a voice that sounded like it belonged to a different constellation made its uneasy way through the small speaker on her shoulder. "Go again, Luke. I missed the half of that."

The voice repeated this time slightly clearer. "We might have an ID on the Jane Doe."

"Go ahead, don't keep me suspended in pantyhose."

"Paris Thorne."

"Go again, Luke. I thought you said Paris Thorne there for a minute."

The radio crackled again. "Affirmative. Paris Thorne."

"Good lord. What makes you think that?"

"Harker found some I.D. when making a sweep of the area. We have a driving license and what looks like a membership card to one of those swanky nightclubs, some place in New York."

Barbara Dace pulled herself away from the mounds of paperwork in front of her. She was the only other person in the room that knew the significance of the dead girl's name. American socialites and good-time party girls were the stuff that pages of celebrity magazines were made of and to her shame the source of filler material on slow news days. Paris Thorne, eighteen years of age, was branded by the media as a "wild child", constantly photographed with beautiful people, often dressed in haute couture, wearing revealing gowns originally designed for much older anorexic women but suiting her boyish body to a tee. Pictured drunk, rumors of drug taking and the assurance that she was no longer daddy's blue-eyed virgin girl, Paris was the continual thorn in the side of her multi-millionaire father and would-be Presidential runner, Randolph Thorne, media owner and newspaper magnate.

*Tuesday October 13, 1959*

*He remembered that fateful day in July 1958 with such clarity. Joseph remembered returning the following day at 10.30 a.m. as arranged and finding the motel room with Amy Dark's body and his daughter missing and the bodies of Officer Reynolds and Jonah Fintall. Joseph Wills could feel the warm summer rain splashing on his face, as he was led away with his hands cuffed behind his back and the coolness of the steel of his manacles cutting into his wrists where an over-zealous detective took pleasure in snapping the cuffs as tight as he could manage. Joseph looked as his wrists and rubbed the wrist bone as though easing away the pain. His cell was just that, a cell. Spartan to the extreme, without access to any home comfort. The wardens took great pleasure in denying Joseph any of the privileges afforded his white cell mates save for his final meal and even then Joseph knew they had pissed in his coffee, coughed up lumpy globules of mucus into his burger and maybe even worse. The meal sat untouched and cold, though not much colder than when it was served. Joseph waited for the arrival of the priest, he looked at the clock on the wall, the one concession granted by the governor of the prison. How kind, Joseph thought, he could watch the last few remaining hours of his life eaten away in a vacuum of despair. He was not even afforded the luxury of a lengthened spell on death row. His case rushed through by a totally Caucasian penal and judicial system. Fifteen minutes to go and not a hope of a reprieve, there would be no massed group of white folk protesting his innocence, there would be no senator hoping to buy the votes of the wealthy proclaiming a miscarriage of justice, nor would there be any family weeping into the massed cameras of the American media. Tonight at one minute past midnight Joseph Wills was going to be executed, put to death by electrocution and nobody would care at all, nobody except Joseph. He had cried for every night during his stay on death row and only he knew the tears were for Amy Dark and his daughter, Caroline. He had cried for them, for his loss and for the fact that he knew he would never see them again.*

# Chapter 13 Life and Death and Somewhere In Between

Friday May 16, 2003

The headache began at a little after three in the afternoon. It was the first debilitating headache Georgina could remember since the day she blacked out at Headquarters. Leroy noticed her becoming more silent, less involved in conversation. At first he thought she was deep in research but the closer he studied Georgina the more he saw she was drifting into a world of her own, a quiet space but it was not a place of thought and contemplation but an escape from the world in which she was suffering albeit silently. The brightness of the archival viewing room was not helping. Sheriff Mary T Rankin beckoned Leroy closer.

"I do not care what you choose to believe or not believe, I only know and have belief in my own particular gifts and I see that your friend is in an awful lot of pain."

Leroy could see that Georgina was pale, introverted and quiet, much more so than usual. He knew he had pushed her too hard too fast. Only months after major treatment from a debilitating disease and to help pursue his own selfish notions, his own personal escape from the pain of losing someone so close to him in his life and he had overstepped the boundaries of friendship for his own personal good. He looked at Georgina and wondered what price pursuing his selfish distraction would have on the one true friend left in his life.

"And I sense you are also in a dark place."

Leroy felt angry at the sheriff's intrusion but the clinical side of his nature was confused at why he felt such anger toward her when clearly she was a trained observer who could see what was more obvious to an outsider than someone as close as him.

"I need her insight and experience." Leroy paused for a second, taking a long look at the sheriff. "And Barbara tells me you need mine."

"We are a small town police force with more than enough petty problems consuming our day. If Paris Thorne is lying dead in the mortuary then the answer is yes, I could do with the help and experience that your friend has indicated that you have."

"Then maybe, we should keep out personal insight and work on the reasons we are both here."

"You know, Leroy, I am not your enemy," Mary Rankin said. Her hand reached forward and touched Leroy's arm. Even through the boundary of his black leather jacket she could feel his pain. It was a different pain from the physical one she could see enveloping Georgina but it was there all the same.

Georgina skipped through the documents to the court proceedings file. The folder was brown and insignificant in appearance as these things usually are. The anonymity of the casing always belied the information inside. She opened the folder, tugging at the blue ribbon that was neatly tied around the bland manila exterior, unaware that she was the first person in a half century to break the seal.

"Leroy?" Georgina was calling his name as her eyes read feverishly through the report. Her heart thumped a little louder in her chest matching the rhythm of the pounding in her head.

*Tuesday October 13, 1959*

*It was eight minutes to midnight; in a little over ten minutes all signs of life would have left Joseph Wills' body. It seemed strange to him, knowing the precise time at which he was going to die but Joseph did not feel privileged to be the holder of such information, even though it was knowledge that many people would like to have access to. He could hear footsteps walking up the bare corridor to his cell and knew it would be the priest doing a little overtime for God in the last-minute hope of catching another of the fallen. It was never too late to convert the evil doers and offer them a seat in the kingdom of heaven at the right hand of God. Joseph shook his head, wondering if God gave dispensation for the wrongly accused, for those cut down in their prime or before. The footsteps grew nearer and so very soon Joseph would be prepared for the chair. Along with the priest was the prison barber ready to shave his head clean of hair, just to make sure the electrodes had a good clean contact. The prison authorities wanted no repeat of the Frank Gillam affair, Governor Stiles was in an election year and his office gave strict orders that all executions had to be fatally efficient. Gillam had taken twenty-eight minutes to die in the chair, the doctor still registering a heartbeat in Gillam's cooked body after nearly twenty-six minutes of direct current passing through it. The smell of*

*Gillam's body took three weeks to clear the execution room. Fortunately press observers were not permitted to record pictorially, so no photographs of his twisted face were ever documented but those who saw Frank Gillam post mortem would never forget that every tooth in his mouth had been ground to pulp as his body contorted under the current passing through him, nor the fact that when the hood was removed that his eyeballs had melted leaving dark black hollows filled with sickening smoke. No, there was to be no repeat of the Gillam affair, Joseph Wills had to be put to death quickly. Joseph looked at the clock; he had six and a half minutes of life left, six and a half minutes of breathing, of thought, of being. The footsteps arrived at their destination and the door to Joseph's cell was opened. The priest was there, Bible in hand, the barber was there, ready with his clippers and a razor, the prison governor was there, barely containing the malevolent smile that forced his lips into a grimace.*

Friday May 16, 2003

"Well ain't that just the meat and potatoes," Sheriff Mary T Rankin said. She was leaning over Georgina with one hand pressed on the table offering support, reading the court proceedings file over Georgina's shoulder. She placed her other hand on Georgina's back, near the nape of her neck. Georgina felt a surge of heat radiating from the sheriff's hand but it was pleasant and calming. The continual thumping inside her head diminished as the heat surfed through her neck, it felt as though it was directly targeting the built-up pressure inside Georgina's brain and dissipating it. Georgina's vision sharpened and the light that was hurting her eyes suddenly became bearable. She wondered if she was imagining the experience or whether her headache had naturally come to the end of its course, having burned itself out. Either way Georgina was grateful.

"You see," Georgina began. "Joseph Wills, though never declared the natural father of Caroline Dark was an obvious prime suspect. But I believe he was nothing more than an easy victim, someone who was convenient to lay the blame for Amy Dark's murder. All the evidence was insubstantial except for the presence of his fingerprints in the room."

"By his own admission he had broken in and searched for documentation to prove he was the father of Caroline Dark."

"Yeah, but where does this information get us? We could find out that Caroline and Amy were both killed by the same man or different killers. The fact is that neither her mother nor grandmother's fate may have diddly squat to do with Susan's disappearance." Even the heat radiating from the sheriff's fingers could not dissipate the weariness in her mind. Georgina physically slumped in her chair, defeated by exhaustion and crushed by fatigue.

"We need a break," Leroy said. "Can we book these files out? I think fresh minds will tackle these conundrums tomorrow."

Georgina closed her eyes; the warmth on her neck was soothing. Within seconds she was in a deep sleep. She drifted off into a calm slumber with the sheriff's magical healing fingers massaging away her pain. The feeling of the sheriff's fingers pressing, manipulating, coercing and erasing Georgina's pain lasted long after Mary T Rankin had stepped away. The room fell silent with no one daring to breathe for fear of waking Georgina.

"It's okay," the sheriff said. "She'll wake soon, when she's ready."

*Tuesday October 13, 1959*

*The walk from the cell to the execution room was short with barely time to think about anything but the fact that it would be the last time Joseph would walk anywhere. It seemed perverse but somehow Joseph wanted to savor those last few yards. The corridor was lit with yellowed tungsten light bulbs that struggled with the darkness in a perpetual battle. Joseph made a point of breathing long and deeply, filling his lungs with the stale air. Inside the prison even the air was confined with little chance of escaping. The priest walked two steps ahead, reading from Psalm 23.*

*"Yea though I walk through the valley of the shadow of death," Joseph said to himself and for a moment allowed a little black humor to lighten the moment. He wanted to tell the priest to stop, not to waste his time, that if there was a God, it would appear that he had abandoned Joseph in his darkest hour. Joseph turned a corner. The priest's monotonous voice stopped and he stepped to one side. The view, now unrestricted afforded Joseph a first glimpse of the machine that would stop his heart beating, though the very sight of the electric chair nearly accomplished this feat on its own. Joseph could feel a warm comforting feeling as his bladder betrayed his fear and he knew now why he was made to wear a diaper for the*

*carnival of death. His steps shortened and yet he still walked freely toward the chair. It all seemed very surreal, any minute Joseph thought he would wake up which was of course ironic. Joseph smiled as he was gently seated and had the leather arm and leg restraints secured. The door was closed and Joseph faced a long purple velvet curtain, behind the curtain sat various dignitaries, reporters, and most importantly Amy Dark's killer. When the curtain was pulled open, Joseph knew instantly who had killed Amy Dark. He knew who had taken the life of the only woman he had ever loved. He knew and there wasn't a damned thing he could do about it.*

Saturday May 17, 2003

Georgina woke. The room was dark and she knew straight away that she was not where she had been when she fell asleep. She did not even remember falling asleep, let alone returning to her motel room. She was lying in her bed. The faint hum of the air conditioning unit was the only noise disturbing the silence. Georgina sat up. The pounding inside her head had completely gone and she remembered the sheriff.

"She really put the voodoo on you." It was Leroy's voice, coming from the other side of the room. "Wow, you went out like a light. It was as though you had been hypnotized."

"What time is it?"

Leroy stood from the chair and switched on the vanity light above the mirror on the wall by the dressing table. He knew it would be there, Georgina's room was a replica of his own. He studied his watch. "A little after ten." He pulled the curtains back in the room and a shaft of bright light lit up the drab interior. "In the morning. You have an appointment in Talinha County Morgue with Sheriff Rankin. I am gonna sit here and do some more research on the Darks, see if I can dig up anything new."

Paris Thorne lay on the cold stainless steel table, though naked her body did not register the coolness of the sterile trestle. There was no modesty sheet provided; dignity it is assumed passes away with the soul. The forensic surgeon finished the last of the large and unsightly sutures that pulled the two halves of the girl's chest cavity back together. Georgina watched silently, Sheriff Rankin could not keep physical or mental detachment once she laid eyes on the sight of the body. Somehow when she was in the desert the body had become nothing more than just one more statistic, maybe it was the harsh surroundings, maybe it was the fact that Mary Rankin had not ventured too close to the body, other than for a cursory look before moving on to examine the surrounding area but here in the realms of sanity and quietness, the body, her Jane Doe had a personal empathy that touched the sheriff. Sarah Allen, the Chief Medical Examiner for Talinha County, Texas, wiped the blood from her latex surgical gloves on the smock she was wearing before removing them and throwing them into a bin marked for incineration. She walked toward Georgina and the sheriff.

"This will all be in my report but she died from asphyxiation through inhalation of her own vomit, she also had a crushed larynx and windpipe. There is evidence of sex both pre and post mortem, the fingers were removed after she was killed, as was the lower jaw. Household bleach was poured into the victim's vagina, anus and throat destroying any chance of obtaining any sperm or worthwhile DNA."

Georgina noted the use of the word victim, she had heard it used many times before by medical examiners, disassociation is sometimes the only way to remain focused and unattached. This was lesson number one at training school. Georgina looked at the sheriff who looked like she must have missed school that day.

"But," Medical Examiner Allen continued. "It would seem our killer is not so smart. The girl's stomach contents provided an undigested sperm sample. My mother always taught me to spit but our girl here may have enough evidence to catch her killer. We are running the sample through all DNA databases at the moment, if he is in there we will know within the next couple of hours."

"I want to catch this bastard," Sheriff Rankin said.

"Did the body have any fingerprints?" Georgina asked.

Sarah Allen smiled, though there was not a hint of humor. "Three, two partials and an index fingerprint on the girl's right inner thigh. If he has a record he will be on CODIS or IAFIS. I'd say grab a coffee and head to our relatives' room, we'll keep you in touch as soon as we know anything?"

Mary Rankin could not help but walk over to the body. She placed a hand on what was left of the girl's face and said, "You know and you're trying to tell us, aren't you sweetie."

*Tuesday October 13, 1959*

*They like to say that death by electrocution is quick and relatively painless. Joseph Wills knew otherwise as wave upon wave of electricity surged through his body. Just moments before the switch was thrown the prison barber shaved Joseph's head, a patch on each arm and cleared the hair from his calves to make certain the electrodes had a good contact. The execution was delayed for a full minute after Kevin O'Dowd accidentally slipped with the razor and drew blood from Joseph's scalp. Joseph felt the blood collect above his eyebrow before dropping onto his lap.*

*"Why not finish the job and slit my throat," Joseph said.*

*The cut was washed and Joseph felt the sting of an astringent used to stem the flow of blood, yet somehow that tingle felt sublime to Joseph in his last few moments on earth.*

*"Open your mouth, Joseph?"*

*Joseph recognized Wilbur Hennessy's voice. Wilbur was one of the few humane souls in the prison who had not been turned by the everyday darkness that prevailed within the walls. Joseph obediently obliged and tasted the bitterness of a leather strap.*

*"Bite down."*

*Joseph followed the order and wondered with much disgust about how many other men's mouths had the strap been placed in and then the truth was told to him in the form of electricity. The lights above his head dimmed as the hungry machine consumed power and redirected it through every muscle in Joseph's writhing body. The constraints stretched but there was no fear of them not holding onto their occupant. Joseph could smell the stench of burning and realized that it was his body being fried in the intense voltage. The smell seemed to linger for ages in his nostrils before any sense of reason began to fail him. He felt his front teeth break as they were convulsed deeper into the strap and then briefly all pain subsided, the light above his head grew stronger. Joseph tried to breathe but his heart had stopped. The room turned very dark.*

# Chapter 14 Lost and Alone

Saturday May 17, 2003

Sheriff Mary T Rankin insisted on driving Georgina back to her motel. The roads seemed eerily quiet with hardly another car passing them in either direction for the entire journey.

"The bleach … find out what brand. I am sure the lab boys can come up with a make. I know bleach can be generic but most brands these days like to use their own patented formula. That might just give you a lead, you should be able to narrow down how many bottles were purchased on that day and from which stores, say in a fifty mile radius."

The sheriff nodded taking in everything Georgina said.

"The fact that we didn't get a hit on the DNA means one of two things. Either our killer is new to the area or he has never been caught. It frightens me to think of the latter because there may be other bodies. This MO is unique with the bleach as a signature. I am certain that this was not a crime of passion or passion gone wrong, this has been thought out, maybe carried out before, if it has then your brilliant archival system will turn something up of a similar nature."

Rankin turned her head briefly and looked at Georgina. "That's if he's local." The sheriff put a CD in her car stereo and Susan Dark began to sing. Her haunting voice filled the car and reminded Georgina the true reason why she was in Texas.

"You a fan?"

"I love country," the sheriff replied.

*I'm lost, I'm lost and alone,* Susan sang and the words rang true in so many ways.

Fisher Sutherland took the opportunity of being alone for a day to take a drive into the country. He needed head space, time to plan. Time to be alone and collect his thoughts…

Susan wondered to herself in the moments after she woke whether this was what being born was like, or whether she had died and was experiencing reincarnation but she had the unique perspective of memory, something babies, to the best of her knowledge, did not have. Susan felt herself awakening from a long sleep though in many ways it was not a sleep. There were profound instances of acute recall. It was as though she had suffered a paralysis and had been observing life as a spectator. Her life had up to this point been a map, something plotted sometimes beyond her control and then suddenly it had taken a sharp detour and now here she was at a crossroads. It was the noise of something heavy being scraped along a wooden floor that pulled her from the dormant state. The noise was grating and sounded like something very heavy being moved. She lifted her arm. At first the limb felt heavy, as though it belonged to someone else or maybe that someone else was controlling it. The movement of her arm triggered a sensor, a small infrared beam, and the lighting in the room flickered into a spasm before settling and illuminating everything around her. Susan's eyes flickered like the strobing light and slowly adjusted. She lifted her head forward and scanned the room. She was quite alone. The noise continued above her. As her heart rhythm increased the blood returned to Susan's limbs, first her arms and then her legs.

The email was from Stevie Anderson, Susan's manager. Leroy's hand hovered briefly over the mouse before clicking on the document to open it. As much of a technophobe as he was, Leroy, could not help but be impressed with the wireless connection on his laptop computer, he read the short missive and his new found liking for the technology suddenly waned.

*Leroy,*

*Looking forward to a progress update but feel it's fair to inform you that a decision has been made to launch Susan's album and DVD. As her manager, I feel it would be foolish not to take advantage of the current situation to not only increase potential sales but also highlight her predicament and hopefully render a positive outcome with the increased publicity. The launch date has been set for May 23. I will be holding a press conference at 9:00 a.m. in the conference rooms at Radiate Records at which time your employment with me will terminate. Please don't see this as failure on your behalf, I will of course reimburse and compensate you for your work.*

*Regards,*
*Stevie Anderson.*

This was a first for Leroy, being fired by email. He double-checked the date on his fake Rolex watch. May 17. He had six days.

Georgina waited until the sheriff had pulled away before heading toward the motel reception and claiming her key. Twilight had given way to night as the black sky extinguished the rose plume of a summer's evening. She was tired of the arid atmosphere of Texas and looked upward for a hint of rain, something to dampen the increasing thirst of the desert. Inside the motel lobby the fizzing blue light of the fly catcher flared white with the bodies of suicidal insects, was it the attraction of the cobalt light or merely a decision by the insects to leave the planet in search of somewhere damper, a fly nirvana where it was hot but also wet. Georgina rang the bell and waited for Tyrone to retrieve her keys and hopefully any mail. The forensic results from the FBI were due. Tyrone was not in a hurry; rushing, he found, only made you sweat more. Hell, people in Texas even talked slow. Standing at five feet and four inches, Tyrone was at least ninety pounds overweight, a victim of never having rushed anywhere in his life. His shirt was impossibly white, his hair groomed to perfection and his teeth when he smiled, which he seemed to do permanently, were capped porcelain veneers, the sort of smile that cost more than a night manager at a middle of nowhere motel could possibly earn legally.

"How are you this evening, Ms. O'Neil?" He showed his ten thousand-dollar smile.

"Fine, Tyrone," Georgina said and *fine* just about summed it up.

Tyrone turned and lifted Georgina's key from the pigeonhole behind him and scooped up her mail from the small portal. "And you have a message."

Tyrone's hands were puffy but as he handed over the various envelopes, keys and paper, Georgina smelled expensive hand lotion. It was imported European hand lotion not the sort that you picked off the shelf of the local Walmart for three bucks. Georgina took the keys and post and opened the hastily scrawled message. She didn't recognize the handwriting but it was so illegible an octogenarian with dyslexia could have written it. She did her best to interpret the writing, the message was from Fisher Sutherland. She could just make out his signature and cell phone number. There were two envelopes, one plain manila the other was secured in a tamper proof heat-sealed plastic bag with a Bureau crest on the front. The contents of the bag were the DNA results she had been waiting for and by the weight of the package the strands of hairs and scrapings of body fats from the P trap from Amy Dark's room in the Teenarosa Motel had produced comprehensive results. Georgina only hoped that there would be something in there to point them on the right road to finding Susan Dark before it was too late. There was a sense of claustrophobia enveloping Georgina, the world was squeezing in around her, she wanted to breathe and for once she felt helpless and hopeless. Doctors would have diagnosed depression and put her on some happy pills, friends would have said it was a phase she was going through, family would have said it was to be expected after being diagnosed with such a debilitating illness. Georgina knew in her heart that it was all of these things and none of them. Susan Dark's voice came to her, singing sweetly about loss and tragedy and Georgina knew time was running out but it was not too late … there was still hope.

Barbara Dace cursed the gearbox of her car as her foot slipped prematurely off the clutch and the teeth inside the box objected in a grunt of clashing metal. She depressed her foot once more and this time moved the gearshift into fifth. John Keller, her cameraman, winced at the howling mechanical protestation. She was the first to network the discovery of Paris Thorne's body and ahead of the jackal pack by an hour in terms of a scoop and days in terms of information. The sheriff was a worthy ally to have in her corner, by throwing a news ban on other networks from getting too close, leaving Barbara in a very privileged position, though it also helped immensely that Randolph Thorne, Paris's father, also owned the network Barbara worked for. Barbara pressed hard on the gas pedal and the Chrysler responded, picking up speed on the open road. In the near distance the hue of the evening sky was glowing brightly as they drew closer to the city. The bright lights of the conurbation fought darkness, pushing it backward, up toward the moon.

"Man, my heart is buzzing."

"Keep your eye on the speed, Barbs, you don't want another ticket."

"This is an interview with one of the most powerful men in the industry, John."

"I know who Randolph Thorne is. Just watch out for the cops."

Stevie Anderson took a few seconds each day to look in the mirror and assess exactly who he was. Usually this happened late at night at home in the bathroom after a long day in the office. Relaxation music poured through the speakers like thick cream. A little known fact about Stevie "Mr. Country" Anderson was that he did not have one single country and western CD in his collection. C&W was work, it paid for his lifestyle, it was not his life. The gentle strains of synthesizers and harps mixed with oceanic callings of whales peppered the tranquil atmosphere. The figure of a tall, broadly built man with perfect posture, a year round tan and eyes that retained the sparkle of youth or at least a man much younger than his seventy-two years stared back. The sound from outside of a police car with sirens blaring briefly interrupted the moment of peace. Anderson felt his heart quicken a little but as the noise faded into the background a sense of calm returned. Standing by the sink was a small blue triangular pill and a tumbler filled with water. He looked at his watch; Lori would be home within the hour. He popped the pill with a gulp of water and felt his heart rate quicken once more though this time it was a different stimulation.

# Chapter 15 A Meeting with Destiny

Saturday May 17, 2003

"The results confirm that Caroline Dark's father can't have been Joseph Wills. There were also fourteen other DNA samples, nine of which we cannot find a match for." Georgina had wanted an early night. Opening the sealed test results from the FBI lab had put paid to that. She didn't tell Leroy about the note from her father that was stapled to the results. Handwritten, the note was an affirmation of the bond between father and daughter, something that could be written but never said by her father to her face. Georgina would not say that the note had reduced her to tears for thirty minutes before she could regain her composure and confront Leroy with the newfound information. The note simply said *I love you gee-gee*.

"Who were the other four strikes?" Leroy was holding a glass of milk. He had decided not to tell Georgina of their impending unemployment, at least not for a couple more days.

Georgina sat on his bed. The motel room appeared to have shrunk. The corners of the room were eating away at the free space, consuming the light. "We have Jonah Fintall, the original manager killed at the scene, so I think we can rule him out from being a suspect. We also have his seed, Elijah. He was 17 at the time of Amy Dark's murder but that would also put him in the frame for killing his father and Officer Reynolds the dead cop at the SOC. It doesn't seem likely, no evidence pointed towards him and he was away at University at the time. Two other matches are Amy Dark and Caroline Dark."

"That leaves one unknown," Leroy said.

"But a few suspects in the frame. Gil Frolan and Stevie Anderson for starters."

"Susan's record producer and manager."

"Frolan was also Amy and Caroline's producer."

Leroy put the glass of milk on the floor and rubbed his face. His broad hands covered his features as they massaged away the tension of the day. "You think he might have anything to do with it?"

Georgina lay back on the bed and stared at the ceiling. Her voice came in a weary gasp. "I don't know … I mean, why kill the golden goose?"

"I guess you're right, it don't make sense."

"Does it have to be neat tidy and precise? Maybe the murders are not even connected to each other let alone Susan's kidnapping." As Georgina was saying it the notion filled her with dread, she didn't want to contemplate a whole string of unrelated coincidences. "Christ, I need a massage." She tilted her head to her shoulder and heard an audible click at the base of her neck.

"What else was in the report?" Leroy stood and walked over to where Georgina was lying on the bed, now with her eyes closed. He sat down next to her and lifted her so that her head, neck and shoulders were lying on his lap. He pressed his fingers into the bunched up muscles in her neck.

"The lab is … ooh, that feels good … down a bit … yeah … you got it …the lab is running checks on other databases, military, medical, etc. Dad says he'll be in touch if anything comes up." Georgina could feel sleep rushing up to meet her like anesthesia. Leroy continued working on her shoulders and neck enjoying the warmth of her skin and the softness of her skin.

Randolph Thorne waited in the lounge of the Excelsior Hotel, his minders were waiting discreetly in the shadows. The paid goon squad was well-versed with trying to appear inconspicuous, though with the average weight of the four men coming in at two hundred and fifty-two pounds it was not always a task completed with ease. Randolph was a hard man, known throughout the world of business and commerce as someone not to fuck with. A man who didn't achieve the position he had in the world, as leader of a multi-media empire, without having crushed many a person be it rival, foe or even friend. Tonight, he was a man in grief, and worse and far more dangerous, a father in pain looking for revenge. He was not the sort of person prone to public displays of sorrow; Thorne maintained the innate ability to control emotion no matter how pressed. Even for acts of cold-blooded vengeance, Randolph Thorne could remain icily detached and wait for years with the patience of Job before extracting retribution but tonight his only daughter was lying on a mortuary slab growing as cold as the steel under her body, tonight there was fire in his blood and it was not the result of the whisky coursing through his system. Ice melted in his glass from the heat of his hands as he cradled the finest Scotch the hotel stocked. Thorne looked up to see Barbara Dace enter the lobby with her cameraman in tow. He knew Dace and trusted her as much as any one of his employees, which was not much. Thorne was canny enough to know she was a hunter, he hoped she had the smarts to realize he was the ultimate huntsman and never the prey.

"Jesus, John, I think I'm going to pee myself."

"There's an image I don't want to take with me to bed tonight." Keller jogged to keep up with Barbara Dace. For a woman reticent of meeting a media magnate she put on a bold front.

Barbara asked the concierge if Randolph Thorne was waiting in the lounge as arranged, after viewing her ID he pointed the way to the hotel's resting area. She could see Thorne glancing toward her, then the big man stood, rising like a colossus and from the shadows emerged four henchmen sticking to his side like limpet mines and just as deadly. As she made her way toward Thorne, John Keller followed struggling with his camera bag. As used as he was to carrying the portable equipment, Keller knew he could blame his lifestyle and addiction to tobacco, fatty food and alcohol for his general lack of fitness. Whenever he arrived at a destination puffing hard with sweat cascading down his face he was confronted with his own mortality, yet still he would live in denial of his life of excess.

Thorne's hand was warm and hard like granite with the grip as solid. He shook Barbara's hand with little enthusiasm but she could see the determination in his face. This was not going to be an interview it was going to be an interrogation and she was not going to be in the privileged position of asking the questions.

"Sit." Thorne barked.

The bodyguards formed a formidable human wall, blocking John Keller's path.

"Okay, I get it. It's a private meeting."

One of the guards stepped forward. "Mr. Thorne has arranged an open tab for you at the bar. Knock yourself out."

Keller didn't need telling twice and headed straight for the bar. Barbara sat, hoping she did not look as flustered as she felt.

"I am not going to beat around the bush, Ms. Dace, my daughter, as hard as it may be for you to believe, was the one true thing I had in my life. Yes, she was reckless … she was a free spirit." Thorne already realized that he was speaking of his flesh and blood in the past tense and it felt as though his soul was being gutted from him with a scythe. "The world knows of her misdemeanors." For a brief second he allowed himself a smile, as though a private memory had flitted through his mind like a colorful butterfly. "But …" He paused, lost again for a moment. "They never knew her, not truly. In fact, hardly at all."

"Mr. Thorne?" Barbara interjected but Thorne waved her interruption down with a gesture from those large solid hands.

He continued. "I don't need to reiterate that everything I say here is off the record, Miss Dace."

Barbara nodded affirmation. Thorne exuded power in a physical sense and something more ethereal that Barbara had found with a few other men of power she had met.

"I am about to strike a very lucrative deal for you, Ms. Dace."

"But?"

Thorne looked at Dace.

She shrugged. "There is always a but."

"I just need to be assured of your total discretion." Thorne reached inside his jacket and produced a folded document, which he handed to Barbara Dace.

She took the paper and unfolded it. "This is a contract?"

"Your own network news show." Thorne's lips parted in what Barbara assumed was a smile though there was more than a hint of malevolence.

"As I said earlier, but?"

"I want the heads up on anything you find about the …" Thorne paused as he searched for the word to describe the killer of his only daughter "… person who killed Paris." Thorne breathed the word "person" with utter disdain. He continued. "I know you are working closely with the sheriff and a couple of detectives, I want to know everything you find out."

"And for that I get a network show?" Barbara opened her handbag and fished around inside for a packet of cigarettes but all she found was a box of nicotine patches and a lighter. Thorne's large hands offered Barbara the poison she was looking for in the shape of a king size filtered low tar cigarette. "I'm giving up." She took the cigarette.

"I told you I need a heads-up. I want to be one step ahead of the sheriff when it comes to arresting this … person. Ten minutes that's all I need."

The flare of her lighter exposed Barbara's features as she inhaled.

"Let's just say that I don't think our justice system will exert the punishment that is deserved or if it does eventually, then this low-life sorry son-of-a-bitch will probably have spent ten to fifteen on death row before the appeals process even begins. I think Paris deserves better."

"You're going to kill him."

"If it were your daughter wouldn't you?"

Barbara looked at the contract.

"What time is it?"

"A little after eleven." Leroy was lying on the bed next to Georgina, both of them victims to fatigue. "I better get back to my room."

Georgina wanted to say: *stay*.

"We've got another long day tomorrow. We're going back to the archives at Talinha to view the police files on the Caroline Dark murder."

"She sang to me again."

Leroy shifted his legs to the edge of the bed and was about to stand.

"Susan. She's alive, at least for now. I don't know why, I can just feel it. It's as though she is trying to contact me. God, that sounds mad. I think I have been hanging around the sheriff too long." Georgina managed a stifled laugh and sat up. Sleep still invaded her mind.

Leroy picked up the forensic results from the FBI lab. "D'you mind if I have a look through these before I get some shut-eye tonight."

Georgina shrugged. "Knock yourself out." She watched Leroy leave the motel room with a sad heart. The man occupied space in her life.

# Chapter 16 Alibi and Lies

The Talinha County Police Records Archive
Sunday May 18, 2003

Sheriff Mary T Rankin was waiting in her car. The air conditioning was working overtime forcing the heat out of the small compartment with a wall of icy air. The impressive Archive building shimmered in a heat haze. Movement to the left of the building on the main road caught her eye as a Ford sedan cut through the mirage of heat. The car pulled up behind the sheriff's vehicle and waited. Rankin checked her mirror, glancing at the occupant of the Ford. Fisher Sutherland.

In the distance a plume of red dust was being thrown into the air by the tires of Leroy LaPortiere's rental, little over fifty yards behind Barbara Dace and John Keller followed in a silver Subaru four-wheel drive. Georgina sat in the passenger seat comfortable with Leroy's driving. She read through the forensic report once more hoping to glean a microbe of important information.

"Damn country is nothing but a dust bowl." Leroy squirted water on the windshield and wiped away the fog of road dust.

"We're just in the Dust Bowl part," Georgina said without looking up. When Leroy knocked on her motel room door earlier in the morning she had been in a deep sleep. Georgina didn't know whether to put this down to the two whiskey chasers followed by her medication or the fact that she fell asleep after an hour's slow masturbation. She had enjoyed Leroy's touch earlier in the evening; she missed the touch of a man, an intimate touch. She felt invigorated and ready for the day.

The archive building was clearly visible on a flat skyline that only fought with the earth and the sky. Leroy accelerated toward the building and hopefully a conclusion to some questions that had been nagging at him all night. In the distance he could see Sheriff Mary T Rankin chatting amiably with Fisher Sutherland.

Susan Dark's voice filled the confines of the Subaru. Her sweet, sometimes husky voice wrung out lyrics with heartfelt emotion. John Keller swigged from a coke can. For the past twenty-five minutes the car had been set on cruise control with little else to do but look at the back of Leroy's rental, the arrival of the archive could not come quick enough for the cameraman.

"I gotta ask."

"I know you do," Barbara replied.

Susan Dark continued singing while Barbara thought about Thorne's proposition, given the same circumstances she knew that she would do exactly what Thorne was intending. Barbara knew she would happily kill the murderer of anyone she loved.

"So?"

Barbara opened her clutch bag and pulled out a folded document. "I may have just boosted our pension plan. Read it later." She wondered why she felt so empty having finally achieved what she had been striving for, for so very long.

John took a hand from the steering wheel and slipped the contract in his pocket. Barbara touched his arm affectionately. "Thorne has offered me an anchor on network. You are an integral part of my life, John, and before I sign I want to know whether you will come with me."

Keller took his eyes off the road for a second to look at Barbara. She seemed tired almost as tired as he felt. "Looks like we got us a desk job."

Finally she smiled.

*Wednesday July 26, 1978*

*Caroline Dark drove back from the local mart having stocked up on tinned foods, baby formula and beer. She wanted something stronger but her budget wouldn't allow. She could almost laugh at the irony of being a well-established country singer with many albums to her name and a list of fully booked venues still to play, she could nearly laugh at that were it not for the fact that she hadn't seen Bobby Oates, her so-called "significant other" for two weeks. He had fled and cleaned out the bank account. She looked in the rear view at the bundle wrapped in a blanket, secured in her travel cot on the back seat. Susan Dark was sleeping. The motion of the car had a soporific effect, which Caroline had used on many occasions to get her baby daughter to sleep.*

*"Your daddy's a lying, cheating bastard." Now Caroline did smile. "Hey, honey buns, looks like I have the title of my next single."*

*Caroline swung the big 64 Caddy into the Fortune's End Trailer Park, driving past endless hard luck stories and working class miscreants. As she drove down the alley to her home she noticed a Gran Torino reverse and turn toward her. The car swept by without stopping though Caroline's was the only trailer at the end of the road. She parked and took the shopping in before reaching in and taking Susan as gently as she could. Tonight she needed sleep. She prayed to God for a full night without interruptions. She prayed to God every day and every night.*

Sunday May 18, 2003

The files on the "78" case were sealed and had remained unopened since the case was closed unsolved in 1995.

"We are but dust, only our memories and generosity live on like shadows." Georgina wiped away a thin layer of dust from the top of the cardboard box.

There were no evident signs as to the content, just a barcode and human faith that the subject matter inside related to the needs and desires of the request. There were three boxes in total.

The sheriff duly signed for them and took the small contingent of detectives and media folk to the viewing room. Sheriff Rankin led the way choosing to walk with Leroy. Fisher Sutherland walked two paces behind deliberately having teamed up with Georgina.

"You look a little fresher today. Not that I thought you looked a dog before, far from it."

"Is that a British compliment?" Georgina said enjoying teasing the journalist.

"From me, love, you better believe it." Sutherland smiled.

Georgina liked his smile, whether it was the light in the archive or just that she hadn't seen him smile before, but his whole face softened. His eyes briefly lost their world-weary look as they opened and become more receptive.

"I can't help thinking we may have had some unfinished business from the other evening. I was wondering if dinner might be acceptable."

"Dinner is always acceptable, Mr. Sutherland."

He smiled again and for a moment had forgotten about the waif of a girl who had died at his hands. She was not even a memory. She no longer existed in so many ways. "So, is dinner acceptable tonight?"

"I'd say it was a necessity."

The sheriff broke the seals on the boxes and lifted the lids on each of them. Trapped air escaped as though gasping for breath. It was evident to everyone that this was not the opening of the Ark of the Covenant; in fact it was as disappointing as the files from the Amy Dark case. Leroy dug in and retrieved a pile of papers from the first box. They were PD files.

"Grab a bunch, people. I want names and addresses where possible, anything that strikes you as unusual I want flagged straight away."

Sheriff Rankin sat next to Georgina; both held fat folders of stuffed paper. The thing that struck Georgina almost immediately was that there were no evidence bags.

"This is all we have for all of these years of investigation?"

"This is only a missing person's case, darlin'. There never was enough evidence to bring charges. The police had their suspicions but nothing more than hearsay really. If we had a body then maybe we would have had more evidence."

"Didn't help much with Amy Dark," Leroy said as he opened his black leather briefcase, inside was his laptop computer. He fired it up and clicked on the case folder, which was basically his notes and a list of names linked to all three cases. The list was short, depressingly short. As he read he added notes.

Barbara Dace took the only folder in the third box. Before sitting she walked over to Sheriff Rankin. "I want permission to film a little material, nothing too elaborate just a few shots of Georgina and Leroy reading. It probably won't get used but its filler if we need it."

The sheriff looked up. "Sure, but no filming outside this room and no filming any documents."

"D'you have the blood groups of each of the girls?" Sutherland asked.

"Why'd you ask?" Leroy said.

"Something I was curious about when I was doing research for my book. I checked with county records and they only had Amy Dark. It was always suspected that Caroline had a bit of chit-chat in her."

Leroy looked confused.

"You know, chit-chat. No offence meant. It was always suspected that Amy had an affair with the guy who was executed for her murder. So, who the hell did Joseph piss off enough to frame him for murder?" Sutherland said.

"Good question. It's one I have been asking myself now for days," Georgina said.

"Why, don't you think Joseph is guilty?" Sutherland said. "Even if Joseph Wills was hurting at being dumped and not allowed to see his daughter, he could not have killed Amy."

"Why?" Georgina wasn't sure who asked the question first because it came simultaneously from three of the five people in the room.

"Because Officer Reynolds and the hotel manager, Jonah Fintall, were both shot fleeing the scene of crime, possibly the morning after. There were not the same forensic investigations we have today. There were no liver temperature readings to estimate time of death but the scene of crime pathologist estimated that Amy had been dead at least four hours before Reynolds and Fintall broke in. Whoever it was had taken Caroline Dark. The police wanted a scapegoat and Joseph Wills fitted the bill." Sutherland spoke with the authority of a man who had done his research.

"And it couldn't be Joseph Wills because?" the sheriff asked.

"Because, if we assume Fintall and Reynolds both died late morning, Reynolds last called in to his PD at 8:35 for back-up, then how did Wills manage to get rid of the weapon that shot both Fintall and Reynolds dead and why would he hide 'his daughter' and then return to the scene of the crime? A thorough search of the motel and its surrounding area never turned up the weapon that killed them." Sutherland smiled, pleased with his background knowledge.

Georgina flipped through her notebook. "Wills was arrested on the statement of a motel guest, Arron Hinkle, as being observed waiting outside Ms. Dark's motel room for a full two hours the previous night and being sighted in the morning. His fingerprints, found on the door handle, corroborate this."

"Don't forget the DNA collected from the waste pipe," Leroy said.

"That proves he was inside the room, maybe even had a bath with Amy Dark, it does not constitute a timeline nor confirm guilt to her murder." Sutherland said.

"So, we assume Joseph Wills was there the previous night but left for home straight after seeing Amy Dark, probably via bus, as he didn't drive," Georgina said "and then returned the following morning ... but why?"

"We need to run a check on local bus companies, see if any were operating and if they have records," Leroy said.

"Wills was arrested the following day having returned for some reason. He was a patsy," Sutherland said.

John Keller remained seated while he filmed the scene unfolding before him in the viewing room. His camera was a silent intruder that most people sensed the minute it was pointed in their direction. Fisher Sutherland turned his head. Keller picked up on this conscious movement and tried his best to obtain a full facial shot of the British writer.

Barbara scribbled notes furiously, cursing her diminishing shorthand vocabulary. "So, who is the link between Amy Dark's murder and Caroline Dark's murder?"

"Disappearance." Sheriff Rankin interrupted.

"And Susan's abduction?" Georgina added.

"The manager, Stevie Anderson. He has means, motive and opportunity, though it could be career suicide." Leroy offered.

"Elvis Presley, John Lennon, Jim Morrison, Jimi Hendrix and Karen Carpenter."

Everyone turned toward Fisher Sutherland.

"They all sold more records, tee shirts and merchandise after they died." Sutherland smiled.

"Who else?" Sheriff Rankin asked, ignoring Sutherland's comments for the moment.

"Gil Frolan, the record producer. He was studio man for all three ladies. His career could have been enhanced by the boosted sales of a dead legend." Leroy referred to his notebook.

"Still sounds like you're clutching at straws," Sheriff Rankin said.

"We need something better than we have. Susan Dark is somewhere, she may be dead, she may be alive but she ain't got many people rootin' for her." Leroy closed his notebook and returned his focus to the folder extracted from the Caroline Dark file.

*Wednesday July 26, 1978*

*"For heaven's sake, honey, go to sleep."*

*Caroline Dark's voice was strained to breaking and she wasn't far behind. The trailer was getting smaller by the hour and somehow her baby, Susan Dark, was managing to fill it with her constant crying, her continuous wanting and her unyielding presence. Caroline dipped her finger in the bottle of beer and offered it to the mouth of her daughter. Susan sucked and for a moment was blissfully quiet. Caroline took a large swig straight from the bottle using her free hand. She knew the respite would be all too brief and for once cursed the strong lungs of the Dark family.*

*"Where are you, Bobby Oates?" She looked at Susan. "Where's your daddy?"*

*It was as though Susan sensed the desperation of her mother's situation and felt unease over her plight. Susan screwed her face into a tight unyielding mass of angst and cried.*

*The light in the trailer was at best tepid, a pathetic attempt to hold back the night, it only added to the prevailing air of depression. It was as though when Bobby left with all of her money, her hopes and her future, he also took the radiance, leaving her with nothing but the darkness. Caroline looked around the living space, it could hardly be called a room, everything looked tired, there was no gloss, even the shine on her one gold selling disc had tarnished. Susan continued working her lungs to maximum distress. Her screams threatened to peel the paint off the walls, Caroline's hand gripped the bottle of beer tighter and tighter. There was a knock at the door.*

*Susan continued to cry.*

*"Come in, it's open." Caroline raised her voice so it could be heard above the baby.*

*The door swung inwards and for a moment the visitor was obscured. He walked into view under the light above his head.*

*"Detective Gary Morris, ma'am. Lawton PD."*

"Ssh! … don't worry, don't worry about a thing, everything will be over soon."

Susan moved her head forward; lifting it from the pillow she was resting on. The voice was disembodied but strangely warm and comforting in tone. There was nothing to see though, the room, if it were a room, was dark. Susan had lain awake for hours but neither light nor clarity of mind would prevail. Every now and then she would feel a sudden rush of warm euphoria and with it came sleep and the retreat of reality or was it the retreat of dream and the beginning of reality? Susan was no longer sure. But for now she had the voice to focus on. A voice, the instrument of her trade. Balanced between bliss and sleep, Susan's moments of lucidity were few and far between, the prevailing sense of overwhelming sleepiness pummeled her desire to question, now she was waking albeit slowly and the feeling of splendid isolation was evaporating.

"I've waited all of your life for this moment." The voice again.

She was no longer floating in space, Susan could feel the weight of gravity pinning her to the ground, no, it was something softer than that. It was a mattress. The sound of her voice singing filled the air.

Sunday May 18, 2003

The documents and folders lay scattered on the table amongst the dead coffee cups. The information within them absorbed, copied and noted. Georgina was aching for some fieldwork and she knew Leroy would be twitchy. Armed with the scant knowledge culled from the folders on Caroline Dark's abduction, Fisher Sutherland led Leroy to the Fortune's End Trailer Park in Wink Winkler but Georgina's fieldwork was taking her in the opposite direction sitting as a passenger in Sheriff Mary T Rankin's car. While Dace and Keller regrouped at their motel.

"We had a lucky break with the bleach used on the Thorne girl, seems it was a unique brand. The chemical composition narrowed our search down to two brands. We ran checks on the local stores that sold the bleach in question and hit fourteen stores in a fifty-mile radius."

The car Rankin was driving successfully managed to hit every pothole and ride every bump with the nauseating sensation of a cheap roller coaster. "I then phoned each store to get a breakdown of sales for the past week and for the period twelve and twenty-four hours before and after Paris Thorne was murdered." Rankin took one hand off the wheel of the car and reached over onto the back seat to retrieve a folder. "Hold it straight a moment?" She twisted further taking her eyes of the road and let go of the wheel altogether.

Georgina leaned sideways and grabbed the wheel. The car barely strayed half a foot off its course. Ahead lay a road the Romans would have been proud of, long and straight and seemingly going nowhere but to a remote destination somewhere beyond infinity.

"Ah, got it." The sheriff returned to the wheel and handed Georgina the file. "Twelve stores sold the bleach in the week before the murder and immediately after."

Georgina flipped open the report.

"But here's where it gets interesting. Only five sold bottles of that brand in the twenty-four hours after Paris's death and two stores sold bottles in the twelve hours after the estimated time of death." Rankin allowed herself a smile. "And one of those reported selling a bottle to a complete stranger who quote, *was acting kinda weird.*"

"The Twenty-Four Drugstore," Georgina said, reading the name from the report sheet.

"Two-For." The sheriff corrected Georgina. "It's one of those places where if you buy two you get one for free. Maybe's you don't get them out where you live right now but a whole chain of them have sprouted up like mushrooms on a damp day this past year or so right across the county."

"Good, there's more chance of the store having some security video. So how far to the *Two-For*?"

"Bout seventy miles."

The road stretched out ahead, a long strip of black tar that ended somewhere in the distance.

Leroy gratefully pulled his Chrysler to a halt. The Fortune's End Trailer Park could not have been more aptly named. Mobile homes appeared to be growing out of the ground, trailers lay like abused spouses cowering from the next beating nature would give them, trees grew twisted like sick old men bent over in search of a supportive arm to help keep them standing.

"Fortune's End … huh, more like hell on earth." Leroy looked at the scene of desolation in front of him. It always amazed him to find areas of abject poverty in this country. It always shocked him to find a sub-culture barely making a living in the heartlands of America, a socio-deprived underclass whose main goal in life was just to survive another day.

"Its fuckin' lovely innit. Welcome to America." Sutherland laughed. Something about the laugh cut through to the bone with Leroy. "I'll bet the President don't get out here much." Sutherland laughed again, seemingly amused by his own laconic wit.

"Well, come on then?" Sutherland turned and started walking down the dirt track road, heading toward the trailer at the end of the lane.

The building was not so much a ghost as a decomposing soul. Single level, with weeds threatening to suffocate what little life was left in the building either that or drag it down back under the harsh red, unforgiving soil.

"You'd think some entrepreneur would have turned this into a shrine." Sutherland said.

"Yeah, I guess Wink Winkler doesn't have an Elijah Fintall handy. It makes you wonder what sort of impact your life has in the grand scheme of things." Leroy looked at the rotten window frames hanging from the front of the dwelling like decayed teeth.

The door squealed in protest as Fisher Sutherland pulled the fly screen open and pushed against the flimsy door it protected. "I was in here last year, don't think a soul's been here since," Sutherland said.

Inside the trailer conditions did not improve. Leroy followed Sutherland, the floorboards made unhealthy protests threatening to crack with each step he took.

"Man, this place should be condemned."

Sutherland picked up a notice board from the dust-covered table and turned it toward the tall black detective.

"It is. I pulled the board off the door last time I was here. This place has got woodworm, dry rot, damp rot and a whole lot of pests that make me shudder just thinking about it." Sutherland tossed the demolition notice to Leroy. "The entire park is being flattened."

Leroy looked out of the broken window and for the first time realized that the entire park was deserted.

"Everyone was paid off. Seems that Caroline Dark has some inheritance to pass on to Susan. What do you reckon this shack of shit is worth?" Sutherland said.

"Prime real estate like this, gotta be two hundred, maybe even two hundred and fifty." said Leroy.

"Thousand?" Sutherland asked incredulously.

"Nah, I was just thinking in terms of dollars," Leroy replied.

"I've checked it out," Sutherland said. "Seems the least that has been paid out is ninety thousand."

"That's a lot of moola for a pile of rotten wood." Leroy pressed his fingers into what was left of the frame that used to hold the window casing and watched them sink deeply into the wood. He turned and scanned the room, looking at the table and chairs where Caroline once sat. The room was beyond the services of a cleaner, dust sat equally comfortable with the roaches and decay. "So how did Caroline Dark get to own this?"

"Misfortune if you ask me," Sutherland said. He walked the few short steps to the bedroom and pushed open the door. The bed was stripped of everything including the mattress. "It was one of the few things passed on by mommy," Sutherland continued. "Stevie Anderson was joint executor of the will and when Caroline was old enough told her about this place and the few thousand dollars her mother left."

Leroy stared at the journalist, his eyes were inquisitive and Sutherland was astute enough to recognize the look.

"I thought it was too dull for the book," Sutherland said.

"Anything else you'd like to tell me before we spend a few more fruitless days looking up our own asses for clues." Leroy looked at the demolition notice once more. At the bottom of the board were land regulation details and the phone number for a law practice that represented the prospective landowners, H&J Drilling. Leroy scribbled the phone number down along with the name H&J. "Where's all the correspondence for this place?"

"Now, that I don't know. I think it must have been redirected to the will executor?"

Everything was leading back to Stevie Anderson. Leroy had the feeling he was being used and it was a feeling he didn't like.

The sign read *Two-For*. Georgina was just pleased to be out of the car. It was a small town store in a small town, the sort of one-horse town where the horse has been put out to the glue factory. Shops lined both sides of the road, all of them with just one exception small independent traders. The town of Girvan was safe from the encroaching arms of new century consumerism, the only sign of global capitalism was the *Two-For* drugstore. There was a feeling of tightness in Georgina's head, it was as though her brain had been shrink-wrapped, with the sensation came a slight blurring of her long distance vision. She rubbed her eyes and tried to focus on the mass of color at the end of the street but the sound of a marching band gave her all the clues she needed.

Sheriff Rankin stopped before the entrance to the store and looked toward the cacophony of music and marching feet. An old lady with skin the texture of a walnut and just as brown waited by the door looking at the parade.

"They're marchin' for Jesus … hallelujah, praise be."

Georgina wondered about the futility of marching for someone who died over two thousand years ago but admired the optimism. As she entered the store Georgina's vision cleared enough for her to notice the surveillance cameras mounted on the wall and a small black dome sitting anonymously in the center of the ceiling. This

Orwellian wonderland was just about the worst place in town to commit or be party to a crime. She hoped that in true fascistic style the store kept their recordings dated and filed for at least a month before returning them to head office or a monitoring company. Major companies often shipped their used security recording tapes to a central point where some poor Joe on a little more than minimum wage had to burn the tapes to disc before erasing them and shipping them back to the stores. Georgina knew that many of these poor bastards often sold the more salacious clips to cable TV to supplement their income.

Rankin walked to the checkout. The sight of her sheriff's uniform bringing a momentary loosening of the bowels to the girl sitting behind the till and scanner.

"I need to speak to your manager," Rankin said.

The girl flushed red. "Okay." She leaned down and grappling under the counter pressed a silent alarm three times. There was a secret code used in all the *Two-For* stores to attract attention or inform other members of staff of certain situations. Four rings meant armed hold-up. The girl hoped that she had not inadvertently set a calamitous chain of events in motion by pressing one too many times.

Georgina watched what she thought was a child approaching. The *child* turned out to be the store manager and while she was little more than nineteen she had the misfortune of looking much younger.

"Can I help you?" Her badge clearly read Clare Tipitzski, manager. Her mouth ruminated as she chewed gum, giving the distinct impression that everything was a hassle. Clare looked at Sheriff Rankin's badge. "Oh, you're the guys who want to see the tapes. Follow me." She walked to the middle of the store turning only once to check whether the sheriff and Georgina had followed. Georgina sidestepped a women with a shopping trolley and a mission. The rows of goods were a plethora of color and temptation to consumers with large markers indicating every bargain the *Two-For* retail group sold. Georgina watched Tipitzski punch a code into a pad and enter an anonymous looking door, the sheriff followed. Inside the room a row of monitors played the images relayed from the cameras in real time. A large server hummed quietly crunching information and relaying it back to a bank of computers where DVD burners were permanently storing all the recorded information.

"We used to be all tape but 'bout eight months ago some guy from Phoenix came in and installed this state of the art system." Tipitzski sounded genuinely proud. "They're goin' in all the *Two-For* stores but we wuz the fourteenth and the third in the state of Texas to get one."

"Impressive." Sheriff Rankin leaned closer to the monitors and looked at the quality of the image.

"Pick the hairs out of a piece of snot, these babies are a high definition, multi-angle, multi-zoom robbers' nightmare."

"We need the discs for …"

"I know, between last Tuesday and Thursday."

"To start with," Georgina added.

"Security sure has come on a long way since the days of a store guard with a baton," Sheriff Rankin said.

"I took the liberty of burning you copies of the days in question." Tipitzski handed Georgina four disks.

"Is that it?"

"They're four gig, compressed. There is even a searchable menu if you install the software on this disk. Nothing too fancy, just time shifts and various parameters such as lone shopper, male, female, youths, etc. The software scans the film for markers that are encoded at the time of recording. That's Bob's job."

A man in his forties sat behind a bank of screens partially hidden from view by the top of the monitor shelf. A hand appeared from behind the desk and waved.

"Hi."

"That's Bob," Tipitzski said. "He works a double-shift with another tech-guard, between them they cover the store when it is open. The system goes auto during the small hours."

Leroy stood in the sun just looking at the shambles of a trailer home. "Caroline Dark just disappeared."

"Yep, vanished of the face of the earth. Like a fuckin' ghost." Sutherland stood beside him. Sweat rolled down his back. It felt as though every pore in his body was open and leaking water. His shirt clung to his back as though it was desperate for attention, every now and then a small breeze would turn the dampness to a cooling but uncomfortable moment of relief from the heat.

"Got to go shake hands with god," Sutherland said.

"Huh?" Leroy turned.

"I need a piss. What is it you guys say over here … oh yeah, drain the lizard." Sutherland laughed and headed for the cover of an overgrown bush.

Leroy wondered how a person could just vanish from the face of the earth as though they never existed, how it was that nobody left behind did not care enough to make a fuss ... not even her daughter, Susan.

"Susan?"

"Sorry?" Sutherland leaned backwards from the bush. The sound of liquid splashing against the foliage in the solitary emptiness of the vacant lot seemed magnified.

"Susan?" Leroy repeated. "Where was Susan in all of this?"

"You really haven't read my book." Sutherland sounded genuinely hurt. He zipped his fly and walked back to Leroy who was peering under the trailer. A network of plumbing and drainage criss-crossed the chassis of the mobile home. Sutherland's shoes stopped inches from Leroy's face. Leroy noticed the droplets of water lying on the surface of the writer's shoes and knew that the bushes had offered privacy but little protection. Leroy reached inside his pocket and took out a torch. He switched it on and illuminated underneath the trailer. The light pierced the gloom, scything through dry air that even on the brightest of days did not get exposed to daylight.

"So, educate me?" Leroy said.

"She was handed into a police precinct a few miles west of here. Some old lady found Susan abandoned in a store with a note pinned to her coat, written by her mother, apparently. Sound familiar?"

"There was no note in the evidence box." Leroy stood. He swayed unsteadily as the blood rushed to his head.

"There was fuck all in the evidence box, but that is the story. Whether it is a myth or not is another thing."

Leroy looked at the British writer and wondered how many other nuggets of information he had that he was keeping to himself. "So, this old lady?"

"Maggot food a long time ago. She handed Susan over to the authorities and they passed her on to Stevie Anderson, who being the kind hearted caring person that he is raised her."

"Anderson was her father?"

"In all but name."

This information sent Leroy's mind spinning. "So who is the real father?"

"Birth certificate says Bobby Oates though no one ever questioned the paternity. Subject to a DNA test and obviously a comparison I guess it's not really a moot point."

"And Bobby Oates was Caroline's squeeze." Leroy turned and started walking back to his car.

"Is that it?" Sutherland called after the detective.

The engine was roaring to life before Leroy stopped to answer. "Might just have an epilogue for your book."

Plumes of red dust were kicked into the air as the tires of Leroy's car spun and the journalist watched the Chrysler rental screech away.

Georgina's motel room was getting crowded. Barbara Dace hovered behind her watching impatiently as the laptop computer booted up. Sheriff Rankin was pouring some cooled cokes from the machine outside the door. The faint red glow emitted from the buzzing drink dispenser provided a warm calming effect at night but for now in the heat of day Georgina was grateful for the contents inside rather than the aesthetic outer-glow. She placed the security DVD into the drive and waited for the software installation options to appear on the screen. Once the software was installed Georgina clicked on the pad and watched the screen divide into equal sized squares and within each square was an image from a camera inside and outside the *Two-For* drugstore.

"My God," Barbara said.

"Big brother is alive and well and living in the US of A," Georgina quipped.

A search box at the bottom of the screen opened up a variety of options. Georgina looked over her shoulder at the sheriff. "What you say we begin our search on the day after the murder?"

"You rulin' out premeditated murder then?" Rankin said.

"This is a hunch, crime of passion, call it what you want but let's say the murderer was cleaning up after the event. I dunno, maybe it was something that got out of hand. We know from the body that Paris Thorne had been dead for between fourteen and twenty-eight hours before her body was found that gives our hero plenty of time to think about disposal." Georgina typed the date in the box. The computer thought about the demand for a few milliseconds and the images changed.

"Can you search for lone males?" Barbara asked.

"Let's see." Georgina typed the request in the box. Her fingers navigated the keyboard swiftly. The program bleated its disdain at the order. "Doesn't like it."

"Maybe it can't discern male from female."

Georgina typed in *lone shopper*. A list of times appeared on the screen in an instant. She placed the cursor over one of the timed results and noticed it was a link to the appropriate section of film and clicked. The image changed. "Cool." She quickly ran through the other timed intervals bringing up one image after another until the screen was filled with single shoppers.

"This is concentrating on the checkout area but we have access to a further five cameras if need be," Georgina said. The bright screen taunted Georgina like a boxer taking jabs at an opponent then dancing out of the way, she still had a compressed sensation inside her head. The feeling was constantly moving back and forth, never settling only stopping to plunge a needle through her temporal lobe or moving swiftly to her cerebellum briefly disrupting her motor skills as her fingers clumsily clashed on the wrong keys on the keyboard. Georgina blinked hoping the pain would go away before anyone noticed. Sheriff Rankin rested her hand on Georgina's shoulder near the base of her neck. Georgina felt the sheriff's fingers press firmly near her nape, once again she felt the flow of warmth from the sheriff's fingers as though warm water was running through them to her neck and upward to her brain. The sensation felt incredibly relaxing.

"The third box down, on the right," Rankin said.

Georgina looked at the image and double clicked the box. The image enlarged. "Female." Georgina continued to scan through the footage, clicking and enlarging an image every now and then knowing full well that Paris Thorne's murderer in all probability was not on the security films.

The music was playing though a speaker hidden somewhere in the room. Susan recognized it, she could tell it was her own voice, she even knew that it was her new album but she did not care, it sounded pleasant enough and filled the questioning void in her head with something other than worry, anxiety or even fear. Slowly the feeling had returned to her limbs, little by little. Millions of tiny impulses lit up a network of nerve endings with sensations and worked their way from the extremities toward her heart until she had the strength to move. The numbness inside her mind would evaporate soon; confusion would be sure to follow but for now Susan Dark was sublimely ignorant of her predicament. Her eyes moved slowly around the room capturing everything in minute detail. A strip of wallpaper just to the right of her was torn, mustering all the effort she could manage Susan raised her arm and peeled the paper back revealing a plain underside with a scribble of biro. Someone had taken the time to write their name and below the signature was another squiggle, this time though the writing was less legible. The signature was that of her grandmother, the blotchy ink mark underneath was the mark of a three-year-old child ... her mother? She fought to regain control over her senses, using all of her might to open her eyes and turn her head to view the vista laid out in front of her. This was a dream, a surreal nightmare. Susan knew the room from photographs and from a strange sense of having been there before, even the light aroma of pine mingled with a musty sweet odor, which she now knew to be the scent of sex smelled familiar. The room was exactly as she remembered it from the photographs.

# Chapter 17 Close Encounters of the Wrong Kind

Sunday May 18, 2003

The night was drawing in when Leroy finally stopped his car at the motel. He could see the light in Georgina's room. He waited in the car for a few minutes to collect his thoughts and see if there was any silhouetted movement from Georgina inside the motel room. The windshield of his rental was littered with the corpses of suicidal flies. Red and green splurges of goo peppered the glass in a hotchpotch of indifferent insect genocide. Leroy looked at the colorful carnage; there would be no investigations into the deaths, no mourning period by close family members of the flies, no wondering why this dreadful fate had happened to loved ones. There was nothing to be envied about having lived a life and not being missed. Caroline Dark had left a legacy of music and family behind as had Amy Dark, this was a situation Susan Dark could be facing and the truth was that even though they had made a mark of some sort, nobody cared, nobody except Leroy and the darkened figure of Georgina O'Neil, who had walked to the window and pulled the heavy but worn curtain to one side to peer into the approaching darkness. Her eyes immediately picked Leroy out as he sat alone with his thoughts. She waved to him and beckoned him into her room.

The walk from the car to the motel room was short but Leroy felt tired and in need of a drink. Stevie Anderson's email terminating his employment failed to dampen Leroy's enthusiasm to find Susan but the claustrophobic weather front hovering over Texas and the panoramic vistas made Leroy yearn for the comfort of a concrete cityscape and cooler weather. Leroy turned and looked at the endless horizon. Out here it was easy to be anonymous, to be no one to be nothing but a memory, it was no wonder the theme of so many country songs was one of melancholy. He knocked on Georgina's door.

Leroy's laptop computer was filtering information from the Internet. Georgina had been waiting anxiously for Leroy's return as the hours between his departure to Wink Winkler and his return were filled with information overload. The security DVD search had proven futile. Georgina had continued to scan the disk for a few more hours after the sheriff had departed but to no avail. The bleach had been purchased by a frail old lady. Georgina accessed the cameras outside the store and followed the woman as far as the recorded information would allow but there was nothing suspicious. The disk was still in the drive but Georgina had long since moved on. The reason for her concern lay in the contents of the email from Stevie Anderson terminating Leroy's employment. Her hand was on the door handle as Leroy knocked.

"So, when were you going to tell me?" Georgina thrust the email into Leroy's hand.

Leroy automatically took hold of the email as he entered the room. He scanned over it, instantly knowing what it was. "It's irrelevant."

Georgina stepped back and closed the door behind the detective. "How?"

"Susan Dark is still missing. Ain't gonna matter an ounce whether Anderson pays or not."

Georgina knew Leroy was right, the investigation never was about money, it was about many things but money barely came into the frame. "What about this record launch he's holding, shouldn't we be there?"

Leroy opened the small refrigerator and pulled a beer from the cool box. He popped the top in a wall mounted opener above the fridge and sipped, enjoying the feeling as the dust was peeled away from the back of his throat by the cold amber liquid. Leroy searched inside his jacket with his free hand and threw two tickets back to Washington on the bed. "Where's Keller and Dace?"

"She had a call and they both disappeared about an hour ago."

"Good, maybe we can shake them for a few days. Too much baggage on this case."

For a second Georgina wondered if that was a veiled reference to her but Leroy followed it up by saying. "Finally lost Sutherland. I'm really not sure about his agenda. He's not exactly forthcoming with information."

"His agenda is his own, he's a journalist. A short hop from a jackal."

"Yeah, but there's something about him …" Leroy left the sentence unfinished. "So, are we okay?"

Georgina smiled. "We are always going to be okay. Be good to head home."

"Yeah, can't wait until tomorrow."

The phone rang with indignant urgency, its trilling sound startling Georgina. She lifted the receiver and answered. The conversation was brief.

"Something has just been delivered to the reception."

There was nothing resembling rain in the air, not even the threat of increased humidity looked possible to conjure clouds to bring in much needed relief to the achingly dry Texan soil. Georgina left trails of dust billowing in the air as she walked the short hop to the reception. Tyrone was waiting. He seemed to be on permanent duty. No matter what time of day or night Georgina had wandered through the greeting area Tyrone was there, above and beyond the call of duty, looking impeccable but exceedingly overweight. If fat was a feminist issue then Tyrone had chosen to ignore the fact. On seeing Georgina approaching he pushed himself from his seat behind the desk. He took a tissue from a box on the countertop and wiped a bead of sweat from his brow, screwed the tissue into a tight ball and tossed it with seasoned skill into a waiting basket. The tissue sailed past a dog-eared copy of William Goldman's *Adventures in the Screen Trade*, which Tyrone always read in companion with the *Guerilla Film Makers Handbook*. If Georgina had ventured closer to his desk in the middle of the night she may have read the latest draft to his *blockbuster* movie or at least seen a neatly stacked pile of paper, which was the host to twenty-seven rejection slips from various production companies around the world. But Tyrone was on his feet with an innocuous white envelope in his manicured fingers.

"Miss O'Neil."

Georgina looked first at Tyrone and acknowledged his presence, which was more than three-quarters of his regular clientele ever did and then at the slim white envelope in his chubby fingers. She recognized the FBI frank mark.

"Courier just delivered it … must be important, I thought. So I called you straight away." Tyrone said. This was in fact a lie. Tyrone had spent three minutes holding the envelope up to the brightest light he could find to read the contents and a further minute contemplating steaming the gummed seal open with his electric kettle but decided against doing so on remembering that not only was it a felony but opening FBI secured mail also carried a mandatory jail sentence. But five minutes in the scheme of things could not be important, could it … could it?

He watched her appreciatively from the far corner of the reception. She hadn't noticed him when she came in. Fisher Sutherland took the opportunity to slink back into the shadows to observe her. A feeling was growing inside Sutherland that needed quenching, as physical as thirst and as strong as desire, in a way it was desire but for Fisher the feeling was driven by a chemical imbalance that he never recognized nor had the want to diagnose even if he did. As Georgina took the envelope Fisher Sutherland made his move.

Leroy sat back on the bed and closed his eyes but promised himself that it would only be for a minute. Wearied by the day's traveling he fell into a fast and deep sleep. Dreams approached like stabbing waspish vapors, teasing his subconscious before wrestling the final threads of cognizant thought into submission. His dreams began a slow subversion into something unpleasant, lurid and uncontrollable. Leroy could not begin to guess where the nightmare began but its vivid detail was compelling. There was a director inside his head organizing his thoughts, his very perception of life and leading them on to a perverse road. The sweat that formed on his brow had little to do with the inefficient air-conditioning system and the vice like grip that forced the direction of his sub-conscious mind was relentless and unforgiving, it would not allow him to wake.

He touched her shoulder.

"Jesus, Fisher, you scared the life out of me."

*That'd be a first,* Fisher thought. He stepped back smiling. "Sorry."

He held a bottle of Laphroaig whisky. His hand gently rocked the bottle from side to side. "Forty-year-old … shame to drink it on my own."

Georgina looked at the label. It was indeed a forty-year vintage whisky. She reached forward and took the bottle, reading the label and spinning it around to read the detail on the back. "You are, of course, joking."

"I never joke about whisky."

"But, but this must have cost a fortune … and you want to drink it?"

"What else is it for?" Sutherland sounded genuinely dumbfounded. "So I would appreciate company tonight when I open it."

"Christ, open it! I think I would just sit and look at it."

"I know it deserves reverence but it also deserves a palate that appreciates the finest whisky money can buy." Sutherland pulled out his room key and dangled it.

Georgina held the bottle as though it were a newborn child. "Okay, but on one condition."

"What?"

"I want to open it."

Sutherland smiled. "Sure."

Georgina was going to tell Leroy, that was her intention but as she and Sutherland walked past her motel room and headed for Sutherland's room she found that she did not stop. She knew that the moment she stopped her nerve would give out and tonight she wanted so much just to do something frivolous. She told herself *it's no big deal, its only sex,* but it was a big deal. She could remember clearly the last time she had sex even though it was a long time ago. The frantic fumbling, tearing at clothes, the lack of foreplay, the animalistic passion that burned with the intensity of a firework and sadly lasted just about as long. Georgina wanted to erase that memory with something new, something fresh and hopefully better. Adrenaline surged through her, preparing the way, excitement that had little to do with tasting a forty-year-old Scotch.

"You seem lost."

"Huh … no, no. I am er … just thinking," Georgina said.

"Well, here we are." Sutherland stopped by the door to his room. The key slid straight into the slot and turned, popping the door open in an instant, revealing the journalist's temporary domain.

"It's not home but it has all the creature comforts," Sutherland said entering first. He placed the whisky on the bed. The deed was not lost on Georgina. "I'll just wash the glasses, you can open the bottle." Sutherland wandered into the bathroom, picking up two tumblers on the way.

If she was going to leave now was her chance, the thought crossed Georgina's mind and but did not stop to collect baggage, it just moved on out of her head. She closed the door and sat on the bed. Sutherland called from the bathroom.

"Make yourself at home, I'll just be a moment."

The sound of glass clinking and water running came from the bathroom. Georgina felt a surge of warmth filling her chest that had nothing to do with the consumption of whisky. The bottle still lay on the bed unopened. Georgina's hand went to her chest to quell her heart. The beating from within threatened to rip her chest apart. Her fingers felt cold, devoid of blood, which was racing to other places. Yet she was far from cold. She breathed deeply, trying to control the sense of expectation. Georgina opened the three buttons that secured her blouse and she pulled it open, thankful that she was wearing one of her better bras. She grabbed the bottle and sat back on the bed propping herself against the pillows which she stacked against the headboard of the bed. The question "What the hell am I doing?" raced through her head but she couldn't deny the excitement she felt or the longing for physical contact. She wanted it to be with Leroy but it had been so long since she was close to a man that a practice run was called for. She answered her question. "It's only sex."

Fisher Sutherland walked in holding the glasses. "Here we are …" His voice faltered on seeing Georgina.

For a moment she feared that she had misread the situation. Fisher's response appeared to be one of complete shock.

"Fuck …"

Georgina shifted on the bed, trying to remember how to be sexy, pushing her breasts forward. "I hope so," she said. She knew she blushed. Georgina was also aware that being sexy was something that could not be achieved by trying. She just felt awkward and in that moment the combination of awkward and blushing made her irresistible to Sutherland. He moved forward, his knee was on the bed between her thighs, his arms swooped around her back and he pulled her closer to him. His mouth found hers.

# Chapter 18 Burned out, Zoned in

Fortune's End Trailer Park
Sunday May 18, 2003

"You know they never found her body." Sheriff Mary T Rankin shone her torch into the blackened hulk of Caroline Dark's trailer home. The smell of burned plastic and wood hung in the air in scorched clumps of pollution. The sheriff tried to keep her feet dry but it was a near impossible task in the confined space. The fire tenders had only just left and the deluge of water aimed at the prefabricated building had little time to drain the surplus.

Barbara Dace followed the sheriff into the fire-ravaged building. "And your point is?"

"No point, just an observation. They say that people can't just disappear into thin air but in my experience it is one of the simplest of things to do."

Dace felt her journalist's instinct kick in. "You think she is still alive." It wasn't a question.

"Let's just say I have a more open mind than most people."

"Based on?"

The sheriff turned and shone the torch upwards, directing the light against her own features. "I know when people are dead." Sheriff Rankin closed her eyes and breathed deeply for a second. "People have died here in the past. One person, a male, mid-thirties but ..." Rankin turned her head slightly. She was trying to tune into a wavelength.

Dace felt a cold chill touch her spine.

"You feel it too, don't you?" Rankin said. "I get no sense of Caroline lingering here but ..." There was another pause and Barbara began to think that she was party to a cheap clairvoyant charade. The sort of party trick exposed on cable TV on a nightly basis. Were the pauses just for effect? Barbara could not deny the prickling of the hairs on her neck. "But I know there is a link between Paris Thorne's murder and this place."

"How?" Dace's voice left her mouth in a cold vapor as the temperature inside the shell of the building fell with the cool night air mixing with the water-sodden walls and floors.

"Because she told me."

The hairs on Barbara Dace's neck now stood rigid. Rankin turned her torch beam to one of the blackened and scorched walls.

"She told you?"

"Well I guess shown would be a better description. It's a little known fact but the dead can't talk … well, the dead people I see can't anyway. Guess they can't take their voice box with them."

The light from the sheriff's torch scanned the darkened walls. Dace was now convinced the officer was not playing with a full pack. She stood in a puddle and felt the water soak through her shoe. "Damn." Barbara Dace stepped over the molten remains of a chair. The seat covering looked skeletal. "And she is here now?" Dace said, trying to forget the feeling of dampness invading her toes.

An icebox stood against a wall, the once resplendent white finish stripped away by the flames and now covered with blackened carbon. Sheriff Rankin leaned forward and sniffed. "The fire started here. I can smell accelerant, probably gasoline. And yes, she is here." The sheriff looked back at Dace. "Standing right by your side. She's pointing to the cooler."

Dace looked to her left. She could see nothing. Barbara tentatively reached out and felt nothing. "This was arson. But why?"

The sheriff turned her attention back to the icebox. "I have no idea. She knows … Paris Thorne knows." Rankin was looking to the right of Barbara Dace. The sheriff's eyes focused in the dim light of the burned out pyre that was once the home to a country and western singer and now the link between abduction and a murder. Rankin took hold of the handle on the icebox door and gave it a tug. The seal had perished in the fire but somehow the magnetic grip maintained between the door and the body of the cooler. It opened with a sigh and the smell of trapped air and multiplying bacteria shot out filling her nostrils with putrefied air. Her torch now investigated the darkened corners of the cooler. The small recess made even more obscure by the growth of black mold that appeared to be spreading from a jar of undetermined contents though the label read "pickles" and had been handwritten at some point in history.

"God, I hope that's a pickle," Dace said, looking over the sheriff's shoulder.

The torch beam was focused on a long, rounded black object sitting in the brown liquid inside the jar. Rankin snapped on a pair of latex gloves and grabbed the jar, being careful not to spill the contents.

Dace took a step back, her feet sloshing in the cold water. "Oh, you can't be serious."

Rankin twisted the lid. "Here take a hold of this." She offered Dace the torch. "And keep it pointed at the rim of the jar. I don't wanna get this shit down my uniform. Lord only knows what it is."

Dace took the torch and directed it to the jar. Keeping her hands as still as she could manage Rankin unscrewed the lid further until it freed itself from the jar.

"Phew, sure smells like death," Rankin said. Carefully she inserted her fingers into the brown liquid inside the jar.

"Oh, you can't be serious." Dace repeated not hiding her disgust.

Rankin's fingers closed on the slimy object. Even with the latex barrier the sheriff could feel the soft skin of the thing in her fingers. Whatever it was she was feeling had long since passed its sell-by date. She pulled the jar away allowing the object to drip the brown liquid back into the jar. Rankin looked up.

"Jesus." She stammered and stepped back keeping a hold of her slimy prize. Paris Thorne stood in front of the sheriff looking deep into her eyes. "Don't do that, you near gave me a heart attack." The sheriff made a shooing motion with her hands. "Give me space."

Dace moved back.

"Not you. My friendly neighborhood Casper. Barbara let's get a little more light on this."

The reporter edged forward. All steely reserve now fading like the batteries in the sheriff's torch.

"My Lord," Rankin said. "It is a finger."

Dace turned her head as her stomach retched. "Sorry."

# Chapter 19 Whisky chaser

Sunday May 18, 2003

Sutherland tasted the whisky but it wasn't out of the tumbler. Georgina took a swig and then poured the best part of two hundred bucks worth between her breasts and down her stomach where it met Sutherland's eager tongue.

Leroy turned. There was a chill in the room but he was too tired, too past caring to get up and turn the air-conditioning off. He sank deeper into his dreams and further below the quilt.

Darkness ... Someone touched her face. This time she could feel the warmth of fingers caressing her skin and she could hear her mother singing. Susan Dark was once again a child. Nothing made sense except the confusion. In a strange way the disorder of her situation was slowly beginning to fuse together. Susan's lips moved and her brain sought the words to string the sentence together but no sound escaped. It was as though somebody had a stranglehold over her voice. She wanted to ask why she felt so calm. She wanted to ask so many questions but most of all she wanted to ask how could it be that she could feel her mother's touch against her skin. A tear fell from the corner of her eye, lost forever in the dark. Susan breathed in a scent from the hand that caressed her face. A memory. Warmth filled her body once more, a comforting feeling oozed through her veins bringing sleep, the carrier of dreams, the solace of darkness.

"I don't care ... I need a full forensics team down here." Rankin was sitting in her car. The smell of burned wood was still in her nose. She lifted her arm and sniffed the sleeve of her shirt, the smell had impregnated her clothes. She knew it would be in her hair too. "Damn." The finger was sitting on the dashboard, sealed inside a plastic evidence bag. Rankin picked the bag up and held it against the vanity light in the open glove box.

"It's gross. Do ya think it belongs to Paris Thorne?" Dace asked. She was sitting in the back of the car, cell phone in hand, as she punched a number in.

"It's pretty degraded. Decomp makes it look older than a few days but we have no way of knowing what it has been subjected too."

"What about Paris?"

The sheriff looked across at the reporter.

"You know, did she give you any indication it was her finger." Dace felt stupid asking the question.

"She led me to it."

Dace wanted to say it was the call from the firefighters that led them to it but held her tongue. She hit the call key and finally her phone connected.

The radio receiver in Rankin's car kicked into life simultaneously.

"I'll take this outside," Dace said and opened the door.

Rankin pressed the receive button on the side of the hand piece and said, "Go ahead."

The voice at the other end of the radio spoke. "You will have to sit tight until a CSI unit becomes available. Over."

"Well how long in the heck is that goin' to be?" Rankin replied.

"Be with you in an hour …" The signal on the radio jumped and crackled. "Three max."

Dace stepped out of the car and pressed the cell phone to her ear. "John, you got to get back on a flight and get down here, things are starting to happen."

John Keller was asleep when the phone rang. He was barely awake when he answered it. "You're kidding me. I only got home …" he looked at his watch. "Three and a half hours ago."

"I know, but things are getting interesting. I got a sheriff who sees more dead people than Haley Joel Osment, a finger in a pickle jar and somebody trying to cover their tracks with a serious case of arson."

The phone line went dead. Barbara knew John Keller was on his way. She sat back in the car.

"What do we do now?" Barbara asked.

"We wait … but not in here. I'm curious." Rankin stepped out of the car.

Dace called after her. "What about?"

"Everything, it's in my nature." The sheriff shone her torch into the blackened hole that once housed a door and entered.

The sleep that had come after the passion of sex had swept over Georgina quickly; it was a warm and comforting embrace that she did little to resist. Now, in the middle of the night, she had been woken by the sound of water running. The lights in the room were still on and instantly Georgina saw that Sutherland was not there in the bed beside her. She had fallen asleep in his arms but she did not feel him leave. The whisky probably played its part in keeping her cocooned from reality in more ways than one. The reality of her moment of madness knocked loudly as her foot brushed against the expensive but empty bottle of whisky. Her clothes lay scattered around the bed, Sutherland's were gone. Georgina swung her legs around the bed and stepped onto something cold. The letter she had taken delivery of remained unopened under her bare foot. Georgina bent down and picked it up. As she leaned forward she could see the naked figure of Fisher Sutherland standing in the shower. Georgina opened the letter. Her finger ran along the seal breaking the gummed contact. She pulled out a single crisp, white sheet of paper and instantly saw the seal of the FBI on the head of the letter. A brief note was printed below.

*Re; Your request for phone numbers dialed by Miss Susan Dark from her hotel. It would appear the phone company only faxed through the first page of outgoing and incoming calls due to an error. Please find enclosed a second page. Also as requested are the numbers made and received by Paris Thorne on the day of her disappearance.*

*Hope this is not the cause of any major inconvenience.*

    *Kelly Amos*

Georgina looked inside the envelope. Folded at the bottom was a further two pieces of paper. She pulled out both sheets and opened them. Quickly scanning between the two pages Georgina noticed one number that matched. Georgina looked for her cell phone on the floor. She lifted her blouse and skirt and found the small phone bundled in the clothes. The sound of singing came from the bathroom. Georgina looked through the gap in the door and saw Sutherland's frosted outline still behind the shower panel. Opening the cell phone she dialed the first number on the list and waited. There was no area code to locate the call. She dialed and waited while the signal bounced around satellites and network receivers. The singing inside the shower stopped, quickly followed by the sound of running water. Georgina looked up again into the bathroom. Fisher Sutherland was no longer in the shower. Finally the call connected. Georgina could hear the phone at the other end of the line begin to ring and a split second later she heard it all too clearly as the sound of Fisher Sutherland's cell phone rang in the bathroom. His voice echoed in her ear.

"Hello."

A cold sweat filled every inch of Georgina's bones.

It was there, shouting banging, waiting. The noise, the dreadful din, came as a blessed relief to Leroy LaPortiere dragging him from a nightmare that he could not wake himself from. Paralyzed with fear he could only watch as his ex-girlfriend's body was pulled from a mortuary silo in the coroner's office and her lifeless eyes stared directly into his. The dream came every night now, there was no peace. No escape. The knocking on the door made Leroy open his eyes. Georgina's shouting woke him. In a cold sweat Leroy staggered to the door.

"Comin'." He glanced at the watch on his wrist. It was ten to one in the morning. He had only meant to close his eyes for ten minutes. Confused, Leroy scanned the room. The banging at the door once again drew his attention.

"Hang on." He fumbled with the handle before finally opening the door.

Georgina fell through the door and collapsed on the floor. She was clutching her clothes in front of her and sat huddled on the floor in her underwear.

Fisher Sutherland walked from the bathroom holding the cell phone. The display gave no clue to the identity of the caller but in her haste to leave Georgina had dropped Paris Thorne's call sheet and his number was clearly visible. It was time to leave.

The pressure inside her head felt as though her brain was being compressed, slowly squeezed as though trapped between the jaws of a vice with the handle being turned. Georgina felt her head would simply pop open. She looked up at Leroy. The smell of whisky emanated from her body, from her mouth, from her skin.

"Where the hell have you been?"

*Hell*, the word resonated inside Georgina's head. Hell was going to be the place she would send herself when the pain finally subsided. Hell, would be the hours she would spend remonstrating with herself for being so foolish. But for now she was drunk, confused, in pain and not ashamed to say a little afraid.

"I need the bathroom, I think I'm going to be sick." She got to her feet and staggered to the bathroom, dropping her bundled clothes to the floor. The retching that came from within had little to do with the consumed whisky. She retched and vomited in the hope of expelling Fisher Sutherland. The taste of him was engrained on her tongue, the image of the things they done together burned a deeper and more foul aftertaste in her mind. As she tried to steady herself over the toilet bowl Georgina managed to say:

"It's him … it's Sutherland."

The sound of a car screeching away from the parking lot confirmed Leroy's worst fear. He just managed to catch Sutherland's taillights disappearing in the distance. Leroy ran to his rental but Sutherland had seen to the tires with his knife. The knife was still embedded in the sidewall of the front passenger tire. Leroy pulled the knife slowly from deflated rubber, using the corner of his shirt and stormed back inside the small motel room. The bright light inside the room exposed the dried blood that had pooled near the hilt as the journalist had pressed the knife down on the knuckles of the dead girl with a sickening crack until each digit was severed. Sutherland had kept Paris Thorne's blood on the knife as a souvenir of the night. The lab would report back trace amounts of Sutherland's DNA in the form of saliva from the blade but for now all Leroy could do was look at the weapon with anger.

The hospital was filled with the usual miscreants of drama and accident. Georgina sat quietly awaiting her turn to see the nurse. Leroy sat close by but there was a distance between them that could not be measured in feet and inches. Sitting opposite, on a bucket seat that was bolted to the floor, sat a smartly dressed man wearing a light summer business suit. He would have looked perfectly at home sitting in the waiting lounge of any high-flying international bank or airport departure lounge save for the four inch gash running from his hairline on his forehead to just above his eye. The passage of blood from the wound stopped halfway down his jacket. The man held a piece of gauze to his head that was soaked red. He took it away every now and then and turned it, to find an area that was not so saturated in his blood.

"Still no sign?"

Leroy looked at Georgina. "Haven't heard my phone ring."

"It's been nearly three hours. Guess he's clean away."

Leroy didn't respond. He stood. Stretching the effects of confinement from his legs, Leroy took a couple of paces forward and took a look out at the night sky. "Be dawn soon. Not so easy to hide in the light."

A speaker above Leroy's head crackled into life and a dismembered voice called Georgina's name. She stood and as she walked past Leroy he caught her arm with his fingers. "I can come in if you want. You know that don't you?"

Georgina waited a couple of beats before answering. "Thanks." As she walked away she hoped he never saw the tears falling from her eyes.


The forensics team had just arrived when the call came through the radio that a suspect in the Paris Thorne murder was heading down the highway, if he stayed on course then he'd have to pass Sheriff Rankin. Tonight might just be her night after all. Barbara Dace clung to the dash with both hands firmly locked on the plastic fascia as Sheriff Rankin hit the gas pedal and accelerated toward the oncoming vehicle of Fisher Sutherland.

"Sheriff, I know you see dead people all the time … it's just that I don't want the next one you see to be me."

"Relax, Ms. Dace. I never killed anybody that didn't deserve it and only then it was with Nancy." The sheriff patted her holster.

"Your gun is called Nancy?"

"Yep, named her after America's first lady, Nancy Reagan." The sheriff smiled and Barbara Dace had no idea if her leg was being pulled but she wondered silently to herself if the shotgun secured in its mount inside the car was called Chuck, after Charlton Heston. "Two things you should know about me, Barbara. One, I am the worst person in this part of Texas to piss off and two, contrary to popular belief, I have a sense of irony and humor." The sheriff accelerated harder on the gas and Barbara began to feel her body mass being pushed back into the seat. "But they pale into insignificance in comparison to my sense of justice. Like it or not, Barbara, my journey out here tonight was prompted by the ghost of Paris Thorne. Now, I believe that … you may not, that's your prerogative."

"What do I know, I have trouble picking up the Fox network on cable." Dace wanted to close her eyes and blank out the sight of the road speeding by. She also wished that John was with her. She trusted his driving, more than her own. Dace found her foot pressing into the footwell of the vehicle, pressing down on an imaginary brake pedal. The radio cackled some garbled message that Dace figured was harder to translate than any message from beyond the grave but Rankin picked up the handset and said "copy."

"He is less than five minutes away." Rankin snapped the catch of her holster. "Things may get a little hairy."

It was Rankin's smile that made Barbara Dace very worried.

Georgina recognized the forensic rape kit. She had often sat in on examinations of rape victims and seen the kit used by doctors and occasionally CSI's. The small box contained everything needed to collect "evidence". Often Georgina had witnessed the shocking after-effects of rape on women and occasionally men but never did she envisage herself being the recipient of the contents of the small yellow box placed on the table in front of her.

"If you would just pop behind the screen and put on the gown on the bed." The CSI officer said.

Gown … The gown was a paper sheet with sleeves and to describe it as an item of clothing was embellishing it to say the least.

"I know the drill." Georgina opened her small clutch bag and was about to fish out her FBI identity card when she remembered that here she was over a thousand miles from home and a civilian.

"Stand on the sheet of paper provided as you undress and place your clothes in the plastic bags." The forensics officer pretended not to have heard Georgina or chose simply to ignore her. "You can have a nurse present or your friend." Georgina shook her head. "Call me when you are ready?" She handed Georgina five plastic bags each marked with bold lettering. Underwear, shoes, shirt/blouse, pants/skirt, jacket. Georgina took the bags and headed behind the partition. Inside the examination area there was a bed that looked unforgiving and imposing. Leg stirrups sat out from the bed frame at angles, taking the occupant's legs apart to allow internal examinations. Georgina felt the small hairs on the back of her neck stand. She placed the waiting sheet of paper on the floor, stood on it and began to undress. The gown was cold and distinctly uncomfortable against her bare skin. Georgina neatly folded her clothing and placed each item in the correct bag before slipping the plastic nylon tie around the bag. She signed a slip of paper that accompanied each bag before pulling the tie firmly closed. The plastic bunched up, snapping out the world from within, chasing out the air but trapping every fiber, every hair and any element of transferable evidence that Georgina may have unwittingly collected from Fisher Sutherland. "I'm ready."

The forensics officer came round the partition and entered. Georgina was still standing on the paper as instructed. "Good." The forensics officer said. She was carrying the tiny yellow box, which she placed on the bed. There was a defined pop as the box was opened. "Firstly, I want to check your body for telltale signs, evidence such as hairs or semen. These checks are simple, though they may cause you distress so please do not be afraid to tell me if you feel uncomfortable with any of the procedures. They are necessary."

Georgina wanted to stop the officer mid-flow. She had heard the speech so many times.

"Please take off your gown."

Georgina slipped the gown of her shoulders and laid it on the bed. For the next seven minutes she stared ahead at the blank wall, while the forensics officer examined her body in minute detail. Her hair was combed and falling hairs collected on small sheets of white paper. Her skin was examined with a UV light, occasionally the officer would take a cotton swab and wipe an area of her body, her thighs, her arm, her right breast. A small metal scoop was run under each fingernail and the matter collected in individually plastic bags numbered one to five left and one to five right. The same procedure was carried out on her toenails.

"Did your assailant try to have anal sex with you or did he at any stage attempt penetration from behind." The officer spoke as though she was reading a shopping list.

Georgina was going to shake her head but she remembered the night so clearly, even though she was extremely drunk for most of it. "Yes." Her voice quivered. Though she was in no mood to divulge the exact details of her night with Fisher Sutherland.

"Could you please part your legs, placing your feet about the width of the paper sheet and bend forward. This is going to be uncomfortable but the collection of evidence here today …"

"I know. Just get it over with." Georgina snapped. She bent forward, knowing full well that sperm evidence can survive for up to 65 hours in the rectum.

Leroy waited in the reception. The night had been a busy one for the doctors at the hospital with what seemed like a never-ending trail of misery. He wondered how on earth the doctors managed to remain so upbeat and cheerful. Georgina had been gone a little over half an hour when the forensic officer came over to him.

"You have Miss O'Neil's clothes?"

Leroy stood. Georgina's running sweats were lost among the frame of the big man. He held them tenderly but possessively with her trainers on top. "Yeah."

"Follow me."

The officer had turned and was walking with purpose toward one of the evidence collecting cubicles. Leroy quickly followed.

He didn't expect to find Georgina crying. Leroy didn't quite know what to expect but he was shocked by the sight that confronted him.

"It's the shock." The officer that had examined Georgina said. "You the boyfriend?"

Georgina was sitting on the bed. Her head was bowed and she was gently sobbing. The gown, which made no attempt at modesty, was open. Leroy sat on the bed next to her and gently pulled the open sides of the gown together across her exposed chest, stomach and legs. "C'mon, let's get you dressed and home."

Home, the word resonated deep within Georgina. He put his arm around her and pulled Georgina's body close to his. He wanted to berate her, to say "you fool, you fool." But truth was she might have inadvertently cracked the case wide open.


Words spewed out of the radio as though they had been through a blender. Fragments, splintered in the airwaves by the oppressive cloud cover. This time Rankin struggled to interpret the message.

"Say again." Her car was still speeding down the highway and she wore a look of concentration that bunched the lines in her forehead.

More crackle.

Barbara had not relinquished her grip on the dash since Rankin's speedometer read one hundred and five miles an hour. Her eyes were fixed ahead, searching the darkness for the sign of Fisher Sutherland's on-coming vehicle. But only the night lay ahead.

Rankin looked down to the radio as though it would help her interpret the garbled language filtering through the speaker.

"... make ... assailant's car ..." The speaker hissed. The sound of static electricity being grinded followed and then a moment of clarity. "A silver BMW. License plate ..."

Rankin looked imploringly at the radio. "Damn you, you son of a bitch."

"… 276 … be passing you anytime …"

Rankin looked back to the road. Dace wanted her to slow down but kept quiet. At least there was nothing to hit, even if she lost control of the wheel it would probably take a mile or so before the car would make contact with anything other than red Texan soil.

"Where the hell are you?" Rankin whispered. A mile or so ahead there was the faintest of glows brightening the dark landscape. Rankin took one hand off the steering wheel and did something that put Barbara Dace into complete panic. Sheriff Mary T Rankin killed the lights on her car. The world or what little Barbara Dace could see of it disappeared.

"Trust me."

Barbara didn't think it could but her grip on the dash tightened even further. She felt peristalsis in her stomach and was not embarrassed by the fact that at that particular moment she let out the anguished yelp of a wounded puppy. Breathing deeply to calm her nerves, Barbara said, "I wouldn't even trust a bat out here tonight."

The sheriff smiled that unnerving smile once more and headed toward the growing light a mile down the road. Dace had the picture of a modern day joust in her mind. No horse just horsepower and two tons of thundering metal charging toward one another. Rankin wound her window down. The noise of air buffeting off the chassis of the car fought with the roar of the straining engine. Dace remembered the Space Mountain ride at Disney, the experience of hurtling through total darkness was the same but at Uncle Walt's she knew everything was in control. Everyone was safe. Somewhere ahead, it was impossible to tell how far, a secondary noise added to the cacophony. Rankin pulled the gun from her holster and somehow managed to keep her arm steady. The gun was her lance, the car her stead and rushing toward them was the black knight. Barbara Dace was screaming inside her head for the sheriff to stop the car. She hated the ride and now wanted to get off but just like Disney, once on the ride you are committed for the duration, come heaven … come hell.

"You can move if you want. Get up walk around. Tell me what you see … what you remember. Do you know where you are?"

The voice woke Susan Dark from her sleep. She constantly seemed to be asleep. The dreadful feeling of apathy would not leave her. Her limbs were heavy, at times they were numb and then the tingling of sensation as blood worked its way around her body.

"You can move your arms and legs. Open your eyes."

Susan's eyes snapped open and a world of harsh bright light hurt them. She blinked rapidly, trying to adjust to the glare. There was no focus yet but slowly that came. Susan sat up. Time was abnormally slow. Susan lifted her arm and gently peeled back a loose strand of wallpaper. Her grandmother's name was there, so was her mother's name. The walls began to move, slowly closing in on her and then ceased. The bed she sat on changed from the 1970's divan to a wrought iron bedstead.

"It will soon be over, Susan." A voice in the ether whispered softly.

She felt the presence of a body on the bed with her. The warmth of a beating heart and the comforting smell of family. Susan looked down to her side and lying on the bedstead was a child in the arms of an older woman. An older woman whom she recognized. Susan could see her grandmother cradling her mother, singing her a lullaby. At the foot of the bed was a silhouetted figure. A three dimensional shadow, standing ominously waiting. Susan could make no distinction, she could see now defining features to this black mass that she knew in her heart was evil. As surely as a heart beats then this form of darkness was truly malevolent. It needed no words to speak, it did not have to carry out any actions, its existence was pure, its intentions were focused on one purpose. White eyes bore from this entity, eyes that were fixed. Though devoid of detail, Susan knew the mission that drove the corruption with such relish. She stared death in the face and she recognized him. There were no secrets any more. Susan's grandmother sang as death approached. The sweet sound of a mother's lullaby. Now she knew the truth and she knew that everyone had got it wrong.

"Time for a quick photograph. Just hold this newspaper?"

Susan was still in too much of a stupor to argue or even properly think about what she was being asked to do and carried out her instructions to the letter.

Over eighty miles away Fisher Sutherland had escaped to a place of familiar sanctuary. He looked back at the buzzing neon sign of the Teenarosa Motel and was relieved that Elijah Fintall still could be bought so cheaply. Elijah instantly recognized Fisher from before and he thought he recognized the girl he had with him in his car from somewhere, but he couldn't put his finger on it. Not that he really cared. He glanced at the young woman holding the baby once more. The four one hundred dollar bills being waved under his nose though bought amnesia.

"A room for three … number 11."

Elijah was going to haggle but something stopped him. A gut instinct. He reached behind and swiped the number 11 key with the large fob from the hook.

"Enjoy your night, sir," Elijah said.

Fisher took the key and smiled back. "Oh, we will."

When he arrived at the car, Fisher popped the trunk and grabbed his holdall and a small travelling case. He slammed the trunk shut and walked around to the passenger side of the car and opened the door.

"All booked."

His female companion stepped out of the car awkwardly holding a tiny infant and breathed the dry air. "What would daddy say?"

Fisher laughed. "Oh, I think he'd be quite pissed." Changing tack, he asked, "Are you ready for your close up?"

Now it was Paris Thorne who was laughing.

Georgina was asleep. Leroy watched her, afraid now to let her out of his sight. He sat in a chair close to her bed and watched the rise and fall of her chest. It had a comforting and hypnotic effect but Leroy was too strung out to feel sleepy, he felt calmed, though that may have been more from the effects of finishing the last miniature bottle of Vodka from the cooler. He listened to the night's adventures unfurling through a small set of headphones attached to a police scanner. It was hard to remain impassive but the drink helped. Soon, he hoped he would be packing his suitcase and heading home. He was not sure if he would find Susan Dark or even if she was still alive but the main suspect was being hunted down on I-34 with little possibility of evading the sheriff.

Fisher Sutherland checked once more in the mirror. He smiled happy that at first glance even he did not recognize the image that stared back. Every scrap of hair from his head lay in the basin of the motel room. He rubbed his hands over his newly bald pate. The sensation alien to his touch. A search inside the rucksack produced a Polaroid camera. Sutherland walked into the main room and pulled the brightly patterned curtains plunging the room into temporary darkness, he enjoyed the safety of shadows. The comfort of darkness filled him with excitement. Paris Thorne was sitting on the bed awake.

"What are we going to do with that?" She nodded with her head toward the baby wrapped in a bundle of sheets. "It'll be hungry soon."

"We don't need it anymore. Go to a department store. Find the rest rooms and leave it. Someone will find it." Fisher said. He threw her a copy of the Washington Post. "Let's do this."

Paris sat on the edge of the bed holding the newspaper. Sutherland fired off two Polaroids in quick succession and tossed the camera to Paris Thorne. "Now a passport photo of me."

Sutherland walked back into the small bathroom still waving the photograph. He placed it on the countertop and picked out a scalpel from his holdall and set about cutting his photo down to a passport sized image. With the tip of the scalpel, Sutherland separated the laminate covering on the ID he had chosen then he skillfully removed the old photograph. A journey to the bag again yielded a glue stick, which he used to stick the new photo to the ID. He pulled the laminate free from the card. One final trip to the rucksack produced a small laminating machine. He found a socket in the main room, plugged it in and waited for the mini rollers inside the machine to heat up before placing the card inside a laminate pouch and re-sealing it. "Remember," he called through to Paris "lose the kid. There will be a small envelope waiting in a PO Box number 4566 in Crownsville post office. All the ID you need is here." Fisher threw a small envelope with more forged ID's this time with picture of Paris Thorne and a fake name.

"Irene Fuller?" Paris said after looking at the forged documents.

"Inside the large envelope you collect, there will be two smaller manila envelopes, handwritten by you know who. Put one of the photos I have just taken of you in each envelope along with the one already in there and seal it. Don't use your tongue and handle the envelope with latex gloves at all times. Then deliver one to Stevie Anderson's mailbox by hand before 10:00 a.m. in the morning. You can post the other one to …"

"Daddy." Came back the reply.

Sutherland stepped out of the bathroom. "Let's go. We got a lot of driving to do."

Paris picked up the baby and for a moment they looked like the perfect family.

Rankin turned the steering wheel slightly. "Hold on, the road shifts to the left here."

Dace wondered how the sheriff could see anything. Her eyes had been adjusted to the dark for equally as long and yet still she could not see. She tried to keep control of her breathing but truth was Barbara Dace was scared, scared like she had never been before.

The car lurched violently and the texture of the road surface changed dramatically. Dace was bounced up and down as the sheriff fought with the wheel.

"Damn … sorry." Rankin offered an apology and as she said it, the car was back on asphalt. "Misjudged that."

Dace swallowed the paella she had for dinner some hours earlier, though this time it did not taste as nice. She didn't want to vomit but life is far from perfect.

Somehow Rankin kept control of the car with one hand and her unwavering left arm remained stoically holding the pistol out of the side window. Dace didn't want to check the speedometer but found her eyes pulling like magnets to the needle as it rose above one hundred miles an hour once more.

"Jesus, where is he?" Rankin said, peering into the darkness.

The answer appeared in a frightening flash of metal. Fisher Sutherland's car leaped from the dark, a mass of lethal rage. Rankin's heart rate raised just ten beats per minute above normal. She steadied her arm with the pistol and took aim at the on-coming vehicle, now less than twenty yards away. She squeezed the trigger and the deafening boom of the gun firing exploded in the confines of the car. The bullet raced from the barrel, a blinding flash of heat and power, lighting a trail in the darkness all the way to the windshield of Fisher Sutherland's car. The sheriff watched the windshield explode into a shattering mass of fractured glass. Whether she hit Sutherland or not was of no concern now, there was no way the driver could travel further at that speed in the dark. Rankin had not counted on the vehicle changing direction though at the last second. She watched helplessly as the BMW began its unstoppable approach toward a head-on collision. Barbara Dace heard the word "Sorry" escape the sheriff's lips before the lights on Sutherland's vehicle lit up like a Christmas tree, blinding them both. The next ten seconds were filled with the sound of metal tearing, glass breaking and rubber squealing like a banshee being slaughtered. Dace closed her eyes and hoped that God existed and that if he did, he would see her plight and take mercy on her soul. The two cars imploded into each other and began a dance in the desert. Locked in an embrace of twisted metal, the cars span one hundred and eighty degrees before parting and executing a flourishing display of vehicular gymnastics. The sheriff's car flipped over and span on its roof like an epileptic breakdancer. While Sutherland's BMW rolled like a dice flipped down the crap table. The sky was briefly lit as the car burst into flames and turned seven times before finally coming to rest on its tires in the sand. The ear shattering explosion of noise faded as both cars came to a halt followed by the screaming sound of silence. Sutherland's car was engulfed in fire.

The radio crackled a garbled message from the darkened confines of the twisted shell of the sheriff's car.

"Sheriff, do not approach Fisher Sutherland's car … copy. Do NOT approach." The voice of the radio controller sounded eerie in the silent heart of the desert, it crackled once more. "Sheriff, Sutherland has hijacked another vehicle and is holding a baby as hostage. We lost him on the interstate. He is forcing the mother to drive the BMW in your direction. Repeat, do not engage the on-coming vehicle … repeat, do not engage the on-coming vehicle …"

The message was a fog of white noise to the sheriff as she hung upside down from her seatbelt.


Making only one stop and that was to leave the baby in the restrooms of an all night grocery store, Fisher and Paris drove from Talinha to Dallas Fort Worth and using their fake ID's booked tickets individually and boarded the flight to Ronald Reagan National Airport in Washington DC. They just made it in time for the last flight of the night.

# Chapter 20 There will be Consequences

Monday May 19

Like it or not, the sun had risen and Leroy peered through eyes that refused to believe that another night had been stolen away. The consequence of sleeping another night in a chair designed only for sitting on and even then for only sitting for short periods, was resoundingly brought home to him by the sharp pain in his neck. He must have drifted off to sleep with the police scanner crackling away in his headphones, oblivious to the drama of the night. Georgina was still asleep, no more than three feet away. She stirred in the bed and moved, some inner sense picking up on the activity around her. Georgina peered from under the sanctuary of the duvet.

"Morning."

Leroy was standing by the window now, looking out on the day. "Sure is. How you feelin'?"

It was too early to answer that question honestly. "My head is throbbing." Georgina's voice was croaky, as though she had spent an evening in a smoky bar, inhaling a thousand cigarettes.

"You want some Tylenol and a cup of coffee?"

"Yeah, that would be good."

Leroy picked up the phone and dialed zero. It would nearly have been as quick to walk to the reception and place an order but Leroy didn't want to leave Georgina alone for a minute today.

"You're disappointed in me."

Leroy looked at Georgina. "I care for you. It worries me when you put yourself in harm's way. If I was to judge people on the results of a one night stand then I'd have to start psychoanalyzing myself and believe me that is not a pretty thought."

Georgina heard the words "I care for you." She could not remember the last time she knew someone cared for her, someone other than her father. She knew she had hurt Leroy, probably far deeper than she would ever want to admit and maybe deeper than she wanted to allow. The knock at the door saved her from answering. Leroy pulled the door open, expecting to see one of the motel staff holding a tray with two coffees and a pack of headache tablets but was confronted by John Keller, Barbara Dace's right hand. Keller looked tired, his complexion looked unhealthily ashen and there appeared to be an urgency within that would not remain bottled up for long.

Keller did not wait to be invited into the room. He breezed past Leroy and headed for the TV. Keller paid no attention to Georgina. He barely recognized her presence in the room. Leroy threw Georgina one of his tee shirts, which she caught and pulled on. She moved out of the bed at a rate only a few moments before she would have thought impossible but Keller was generating adrenaline and it was infectious.

"I've just come from the hospital. I take it you haven't heard." Keller spoke so fast Leroy had to concentrate to decipher.

"Heard what?" Georgina said.

Keller turned channels a couple of times before settling on the news channel. "Barbara's been in a bad accident. Happened late last night." Keller spoke between announcements from the news anchor. "It's been all over the news."

A film report on the TV screen showed a car sitting on its roof in the middle of the road. The camera panned to the left to the remains of a burned out BMW. Just inside the open mouth of the car where the windshield used to sit was the outline of a figure draped in a black shroud. As the camera panned back, police tape became evident, securing the scene from contamination and keeping the media at bay.

"Tell me that is Sutherland?" Leroy said.

Keller faced the detective. "Abi Pritchard, single mother, aged twenty-four. Mother to Reece Pritchard aged eight months, currently missing."

Georgina moved closer to the television set, drawn in by the familiar scene of carnage and her too familiar proximity to its core.

"What happened?" Leroy asked

"It's too early to know. Rumor has it that Miss Pritchard was handcuffed to the steering wheel. Barbara is conscious and in a stable condition. She's lucky, escaped with a broken collar bone."

Georgina moved back from the screen, allowing her eyes to focus on the scene. As the sheriff's car came into view once more, Georgina tilted her head to one side. "The sheriff?"

"Miraculous escape." Rankin's voice came from near the open door. The sheriff entered the room.

Georgina felt something cold touch her spine and she shivered an involuntary shudder.

"You feel that too," Rankin said. The sheriff looked at Georgina.

Keller sat on the bed. He didn't know if it was exhaustion or shock but he too felt the presence of something enter the room with the sheriff.

"Fisher Sutherland is out of the county by now. Mr. LaPortiere, I am counting on you to bring justice to Abi Pritchard and I mean Texan style." Rankin patted her holster as if further confirmation of her intentions were needed. "I can't chase this scum cross border … but you can."

# Part Two
# Country

# Chapter 21 In Transit

Tuesday May 20

The forest had come alive over the past few months. Leaves had grown from tiny buds on branches, unfurling from tiny dark green balls as they took nourishment from the sky and the roots deep below ground. Now the branches of the trees fought for space with each other as they climbed evermore toward the sun. The wooded stick arms locked together, fusing under a blanket of green foliage, blocking the natural daylight from entering the verdant environment below. The path that was once a muddy trek, which highlighted the route to the wooden cabin, was now covered in wild grass. Soon all traces of the passage to the cabin would be eliminated, wiped out by Mother Nature. Soon, only the keen senses of the nocturnal nightlife would be able to detect the trace of a human hiding deep in the forest. The cabin stood alone as the only monument to man's incursion in the woodland for one hundred square miles. It was the perfect hiding place. A retreat where time was kept at bay. The generator chugged like an enthusiastic metronome drinking gasoline in exchange for electricity. The lights shone brightly at night enticing giant moths with their silent siren song. The power from the generator ran through wiring to speakers placed in all the rooms of the wooden building. And through the speakers came the voices of Amy Dark, Caroline Dark and Susan Dark singing their own enchanting songs. He never grew tired of hearing their voices singing no matter how many times the CD's were played. The same could not be said of Susan Dark though. She was tired of hearing her own voice. She had even tired of her mother's voice singing in her ears. The voice so close that at times Susan thought she could feel the warm brush of air from her mother's lips caress her ears with lullabies of sadness. Susan moved on the bed. Today everything seemed a little more real. She had woken with complete feeling in her arms and legs but lay still on the bed for a while as the fug of recollection fought for dominance in her brain. A mirror had been brought into the room; at least Susan had no memory of one being there before … before. She tried to sit up. While her limbs had sensation restored they felt weak. There was the scent of cinnamon in the air, a warm inviting fragrance that hinted at the promise of home baking. For some reason or another it was a smell that reminded her of her mother or was it just that Caroline Dark was singing 'Sweet, is the mystery of life.' It was a song Susan knew well, having learned the lyrics for her *Dark Family Album*. Susan finally managed to sit upright. She shuffled along the side of the bed until her reflection became apparent in the mirror. Someone was staring back at Susan from the world behind the glass. At first she thought the person was an imposter until she understood who it was staring back at her.

Leroy made sure that Georgina took an Alprazolam tablet before the flight. Sitting in the departure lounge Georgina cradled a cup of warm milk in one hand and the small, 0.5mg tablet in the other.

"What a wreck." Georgina held the tablet between her thumb and forefinger, rolling it gently, studying the embossed manufacturer's logo for a second while she contemplated releasing herself to the mercy of the narcotic. "How long before these puppies kick in?"

"Don't worry, you'll be on the flight and settled before they take hold." Leroy held back the smile of comfort and reassurance, having abandoned those feelings of failure and self-doubt. He felt as though he had failed to protect Georgina when she was vulnerable. Instead he let his own emotions guide events and dictate the future, with Georgina an innocent bystander to his own susceptible state of mind. Here he was chasing ghosts in Texas when what he should have been doing was spending some of his injury compensation and moving on from losing Lia. Lia, herself, now just a ghost in his memory. Georgina swallowed the tablet with a swig of hot milk. The warm liquid ran a trail down the side of her lips reviving memories of an act of intimacy that had a dire consequence. The ripple effect seemed to play an increasing part in Leroy and Georgina's lives. Georgina wiped her lips and wondered about butterflies flapping their wings. She was living in a world where chaos theory had evolved to a frightening new scale and she knew deep down in her heart that a hurricane was coming.

Stevie Anderson wandered down to his mailbox on the ground floor of his apartment block and as was his daily habit opened the metal box housed within the walls of the building. There was nothing special about the envelope, nothing that would indicate that the contents would play an irrevocable part in his life. It was anonymous in more ways than one. The handwriting on the front would have given him a clue had he been paying attention and had his memory been fully engaged. But it was Tuesday morning and as usual he was on his way to the gym. The onset of age did not deter this routine. His mind was engaged elsewhere for the moment, mostly with the memory of Lori, his thirty-six-year-old lover lying naked in his bed. He picked the solitary piece of mail out of the box and headed through the lobby to his waiting car. This was the very last act of routine that Stevie Anderson would enjoy that day. Anderson put the car in drive and pulled away from the sidewalk. He threw the letter on the passenger seat, its anonymity disguising the importance of the contents. Anderson looked down at it briefly before fixing his attention on the road. The drive to the gym was short but as far as Anderson was concerned running was meant for treadmills. He had no desire to mix with people on the street. His cell phone rang. The short trill of the phone cut out the CD player.

Anderson spoke."Talk to me."

There was a crackle and hiss of atmospherics before a female voice cut through the interference. Anderson recognized the voice immediately even though he had not heard her speak for twenty-five years.

"Did you get the letter?"

Anderson looked down at the envelope once more. Time seemed to stop. Now he recognized the handwriting. Stevie Anderson felt a tightness across his chest, a constriction, as though somebody had wrapped a belt around his ribs and was pulling it taut. He felt his heart skip a beat but not in that good way when you are talking to a lover or about to do something ultimately daring. He continued staring at the envelope but the writing was blurring. A cold beaded sweat had formed on his forehead. The blast of the horn from the on-coming vehicle should have made him avert his eyes. His throat constricted but he was still able to say "Caroline?" before his car folded neatly into the front of an on-coming truck. Anderson remembered hearing the small explosion of the air bag as it deployed and feeling it cushion his forward motion as his body moved toward the windshield and then the strangest thing, he felt the embrace of total darkness as his body shut down. One by one the systems controlling Stevie Anderson's body were closed down. The sense of smell was the first to go, though his brain clearly registered the sharp smell of cordite from the airbags, then his sense of touch, he could see that he had a grip on the steering wheel but his arms felt heavy and numb. The crunching crashing sound of his car still rang in his ears but the music on the CD began to fade away as though someone had taken the player and speakers from the car and was running away. The bitter taste of copper filled his mouth and Anderson coughed a red plume of blood onto the inflated airbag from a busted nose but the flavor began to mellow. Anderson's last thought was that he had closed his eyes but in fact they were wide open, staring at the impaled front of the truck he had collided with.

"Careful … careful now." The accent was thick Brooklyn and miles away from home. The rescue tender was only feet away from the wreckage of Stevie Anderson's Buick. The firefighter with the Brooklyn accent was coordinating the rescue, making sure the pneumatic cutters were placed in the correct position near the broken windshield. Washington DC was in the middle of a heat wave and a three-mile jam caused by Anderson's carelessness was threatening to gridlock the city. 38th Street NW and Rodman Street NW had already ground to a painful halt, but Anderson didn't care. He would not have cared much had he been conscious but his current condition led to sublime ignorance. The giant jaws of the hydraulic cutter ate the metal struts holding the roof of the car with ease.

"C'mon boys, the sooner we get this off the more chance we have of saving this guy." Brooklyn spoke again. His job as team leader and all-round good guy was perfectly matched to his personality.

The roof came off. Anderson was slumped over the wheel unconscious but remarkably unscathed apart from a broken nose. Brooklyn's large hands reached in and felt Anderson's neck for a pulse.

"He's alive," Brooklyn shouted. He withdrew from the car and cracked his hands together like thunder. "Let's get to it." The firefighter stepped back and allowed the paramedics to start their work.

Leroy loved the sight of Dulles International airport at sunset, never more so than today. He walked slowly with Georgina to the economy green parking lot and sought out his Toyota Avalon XL. The effects of the Alprazolam were slow to wear off but the fresh air, though warm, helped to clear her head.

"Home," Georgina said the word with relish. There was a clarity filtering through her mind that had been absent for the past few days. Georgina did not know whether she was fooling herself or if it was just the after effects of the sedative fooling her but items of thought were becoming compartmentalized. As though she was garnering her thoughts and placing them in a box and then labeling each box. It was an efficiency of thought that had eluded her since the onset of her headaches.

"You okay?" Leroy asked. He slowed his walking pace, allowing Georgina to catch up the four paces she had fallen behind. "Or just checkin' out my ass." Leroy felt the momentary relief of the pressurized environment they had been living in too and welcomed the prospect of the drive to Portmorion and the sanctuary of the place that he too had come to know as home. Right now he fancied sinking into a hot tub filled with whatever lotions were to hand and zoning out for a couple of hours with a good book and a better Scotch. Leroy held out an arm and scooped Georgina along. He allowed his arm to fall around her waist and to casual observers they would have appeared as lovers. The irony would have cut both of them in half. The car came into view too soon and any chance that the intimacy between them could develop was lost. Leroy pressed the door lock on his key fob and the reassuring shunt of metal confirmed that the doors were open.

"Checkin' out your ass," Georgina said as she opened the passenger door. Then she laughed. She made herself comfortable in the seat before pulling the seatbelt and snapping it securely closed. Georgina heard the trunk slam shut as Leroy stored their bags. She had picked up a copy of the *Washington Post* from a newspaper vending machine in the airport. Holding the paper felt like home. Georgina unfolded the edition as Leroy buckled in and started the engine. Sometimes the simple comforts of life come from the most unexpected sources and sometimes the things that we associate with safety and reassurance, can be unsettling.

Stevie Anderson was not the headline story but he still made front page and was pleased to still be thought of as important enough to herald some headlines. His heart pulsed with a regularity that pleased the doctors and pissed off the senior partners of his record label. A prolonged stay in hospital was a costly affair and as many on the board were thankful that he made a miraculous recovery as there were those who wished he had died. The two-faces of corporate humanity exercised itself in the form of a "get well soon, you old bastard" card and Lori Deane, the thirty-six-year-old eye candy that graced his bed and kept Pfizer's share price rising amongst other things. Lori managed to squeeze an emotive tear from her left eye, the prospect of her meal ticket pegging out before he had changed his will genuinely made her feel sad. When the doctors were not around she would take Anderson's hand and slip it between her legs and whisper sweet filthy nothings into his ear. Lori's bedside manner would kill or cure Stevie, either way she hoped to put a smile on his face.

"We're not going home."

"We're not?"

Georgina shook her head and placed the newspaper in Leroy's lap. Leroy pulled the Toyota to a halt at the next set of reds. Georgina tapped on the relevant section of the paper. Leroy read the headline. *Record producer in crash*.

"No, we're going to the …"

"Montgomery General." Leroy finished the sentence and swung a sharp right. The rush hour was over but the roads began to back up a little as Leroy's Toyota neared the hospital. The sun was all but set and city lights made DC sparkle, a bus pulled to the side of the road, stopping to let passengers off and pick up a fresh load of commuters. Life in the city never stopped. Leroy pulled out round the bus. The hospital was just a couple of blocks away when he saw her … Lia.

"That was Lia."

Georgina turned her head. "Where?"

Leroy was already slowing the car down and signaling to pull over. "There." He glanced over his shoulder and looked for the slim black lady wearing the white long coat with matching white pants. She joined the throng of people boarding the bus and was consumed amid a mass of bodies as one more little fish in the shoal. Leroy was out of the car and running along the sidewalk, trying his best to avoid the pedestrians.

"Lia." He called out, not caring that his cry was met with a mass of faces that found his desperation humorous. "Lia."

The lady in white was gone. Leroy stopped jogging and stared intently down the street, hoping to catch a glimpse of her once more. He knew it was her. He could recognize Lia's walk from a hundred yards and even though darkness was descending Leroy was certain that he had seen his ex-girlfriend. The bus pulled away from the curb. Something made Leroy turn and look at the faces on the bus. One of the faces turned and looked directly into his eyes.

"Leroy." A voice calling out jolted him. Brought Leroy back to the land of the living and pain. "Leroy." Georgina called out once more.

Leroy's eyes followed the bus. Lia was staring directly at him but there was no sense of recognition from her. The more Leroy looked at her the more he began to realize that she was looking past him. Her gaze was fixed somewhere in another life. Leroy shouted at the top of his voice in the vain hope that it would pierce the discordant melee of the city, that somehow his voice would rise about the decibels of noise pollution and pierce the thickened safety glass of the traveling bus. Lia turned her head away and the bus pulled out of sight.

"Leroy." Georgina was next to Leroy now. "You okay?"

"It was her ... it was Lia."

Georgina put her arm around Leroy's waist. It was her turn to be the comforter. "I know."

The Toyota turned onto Prince Philip Drive. Georgina was driving. Leroy sat next to her, his mind following the bus.

"It was her." He repeated.

Familiar signs for MGH appeared. Georgina had been to the hospital both as a visitor and patient in the past and to be honest she was not keen on either experience. Tonight, she was going in the hope of interviewing the man who hired them to find Susan Dark. She looked at the clock on the dash. It was a little after 8:00 p.m. "We got half an hour, unless he is in ICU."

Leroy did not answer.

"You better snap out of it, Leroy. I need you focused."

"It was her."

"Okay, I believe you. It was Lia. You know she is staying in DC, so I guess, yes, it was Lia that you saw. Now can you put it to the back of your mind, for me, huh?"

"I'm being an ass."

"No, Leroy, you are being human. I am being the insensitive ass. But, I do need you focused."

Leroy shifted in his seat. "Georgina?"

"Yeah, what?"

"Do you er ... think of me ... in that way?"

"What way?" Georgina kept her eyes on the road. She could see the hospital just ahead.

"You know?"

Georgina tilted her head as though lost in thought for a moment. "We're here." She pulled the car to a halt in a parking bay.

"You never answered my question?"

"Leroy, you are still in love with Lia. It's obvious."

"No. I am still mourning losing Lia."

They sat in silence for a long minute.

"We better go in. Visiting finishes soon." Georgina broke the awkward silence.

The nurse walked quickly. She was almost as sterile as the environment she worked in. Her feet made no sound, though they sped along the corridors assuredly. "You have ten minutes." She stopped at a door and pushed it open. Norman Frusco pushed past her. The nurse coughed as a wave of spent cigarettes followed the police captain like Pigpen's black cloud in Peanuts. Barbara Dace was sitting up in bed. The sight of her lover brought a smile to her face.

"Hey, you." Dace looked ten years younger when she smiled.

Frusco leaned forward and kissed her lips. Dace breathed in the smell of cigarettes and ash as though they were an intoxicating perfume and in many ways they were.

"You had me worried," Frusco said.

The room was adorned with flowers and get well cards.

"Don't worry about me. I am just an attention junkie. They say I can leave tomorrow. Hey, it's only a busted collar bone."

"And severe concussion."

Dace lay back on her bed. "Maybe it knocked some sense into this old head."

Frusco looked at her. His hand reached out and grabbed her good hand and he squeezed hard. "I don't want to lose you. It's supposed to be me that has the dangerous job."

The nurse that showed Norman into the room appeared at the door. "You got three minutes to say your goodbyes."

Barbara pulled the sheet back and stepped out of the bed.

"Where are you going?"

"Come on, Norman, let's take a walk. I could do with some fresh air. I'll see you out."

"You know you can't get rid of me that easily."

Barbara hugged the aging, overweight, balding detective. "Good." She pulled on her robe. "I can escort you to the elevator."

"Barbara, I mean it. I don't want to lose you."

"You got a cigarette, Norman?"

# Chapter 22 Who are You?

Susan Dark stared at the ceiling. The ceiling was somewhere above her. This much she was aware of. Some days were good and she had a grasp of some kind of semblance of what it used to be like to be alive and then on other days, days such as today, she would stare like a zombie at nothing. The dreams were the worst though. The nightmares. Seeing her mother's face, staring back at her with the same death-like gaze. Eyes open but mind gagged. To pass the time she had counted the wooden slats that covered the ceiling. There were sixty-seven. She had lost count of the times she had counted the individual wooden slats. Sometimes she would lose count halfway through or she would simply fade into nothingness. It was not sleep; it was a warm but empty feeling of vagueness. There was a man there sometimes. Susan would hear voices talking. They would soon be drowned out though by her singing or the sound of her mother's voice. The lullabies sent her into a hypnotic trance. Her mother and grandmother would sing to her. They would sing into her ear. In those moments Susan felt deep joy.

Tuesday May 20

The doors of the elevator pinged, announcing its arrival. The fourth floor of the hospital was as sterile in its décor as it was in terms of aseptic appeal. Only magnolia freaks would have found the internal blandness something to get excited about. Though spacious and bright, Georgina found the atmosphere claustrophobic. Her phobia of hospitals was just short of that of her fear of flying.

"I hate these places." Georgina looked up at Leroy surprised by his candid admission but feeling slightly more at ease knowing she had an ally by her side. "Why are they always hotter than a Florida heatwave?"

"I think they pre-bake the old folk before they shuffle off, makes the cremation easier."

"Oh, that is just gross."

Leroy laughed. It was days since he could remember laughing and yet here he was doing just that in the place he liked least.

The private rooms led off the corridor that stretched out ahead of them. A floor receptionist sat behind the main desk that occupied the center space opposite the elevator. Leroy met the disapproving gaze of the receptionist who made a point of looking at the clock to her left.

"We're nearly on borrowed time," Leroy said.

Georgina walked purposefully to the reception desk. "We're always on borrowed time."

The words filtered through the haze. Soft, gentle voices singing in pure sweet tones. Songs her mother used to sing. Susan Dark stirred from the depths of her drug induced slumber. She wanted to wake, to feel the rush of living once more but for the past few days Susan had felt as though she was viewing the world from a distant place. At times she drew nearer to reality. Sounds, smells and occasionally glimpses of places and people she knew reminded her of the fabric of a life once lived. Her mother was singing in her ear. The voice soft and gentle: another memory from a far and distant place. Susan could no longer recollect what was actual memory and what was the fabricated ideal of her mother. It was easy for her to forge memories, to align moments of her life with the recordings her mother made or with images from the TV specials and the one movie that seemed to be constantly played on cable. Susan had constructed an image of her mother that was defined by the media rather than their time—albeit, very short time—together. She started to sing along with the voice inside her head.

His left foot dragged along the ground, continually wearing the heel of his shoe at an uneven pace. His immobility was the result of a shattered femur when he was four years old. But Grant Frolan bore no grudges. His father was right to punish him. His world was small, incredibly small; in fact it did not exist beyond the realms of the forest. He had been to the edges, the very periphery on many occasions and seen the makings of men. He had witnessed the mad rushing sputum of life being propelled in an endless charge of lunacy. Often he had stood and watched from the quiet boundary of trees and returned to the inner sanctum of peace where only he and God survived.

"I have made you."

Grant looked up and caught the fixed stare of God.

"I have made you." The voice repeated.

Grant felt the tremulous fear of being in the presence of greatness. A blue aura surrounded God.

"I have made you in my likeness and you shall bring unto me many great and wonderful blessings."

Grant's father, Gil Frolan, held a worn copy of the Bible. Inside were many pages describing in full detail the wondrous miracles of his father. It was written for everyone in the world to see. It was the only book Grant Frolan had ever read.

"The time will soon be upon us. Soon, a new chapter will begin and you will be ready to fulfill the prophecy."

Grant sat on a wooden chair in the spartanly furnished room. The walls of his small bedroom were equally bare with no home comforts on display except for a hand constructed wooden bed frame and headboard. To the side of the bed was a second chair; it was equally basic in its construction and finish. The only difference being that a table lamp sat on the seat offering nighttime light so Grant could continue his Bible studies. His father moved further into the room. The light inside the small cell-like room was bright, exposing every corner. A plume of smoke arrived seconds before Gil Frolan. The record producer was holding a tray with a hypodermic syringe.

"It's time, son."

Stevie Anderson was awake when Leroy and Georgina entered the private room. Lori Deane was sitting by his side. Lori pulled into herself, her defensive body language an immediate red flag, which Leroy and Georgina both noticed. Lori clutched an envelope to her chest.

"We've already told you guys all we know," Lori snapped.

"And who do you think *we guys* are?" Leroy answered

"I can smell po-lice. Let's just call it a sixth sense."

Georgina smiled and wondered two things. The first being whether their demeanor was that obvious and the second whether the girl sitting by Stevie Anderson's bed was ever actually in possession of any of the other five senses.

"Then you won't mind repeating everything you told my colleagues." Leroy was happy to let her believe that he was still a badge.

Lori made a tussing sound that clearly displayed her displeasure. "My fiancé is tired. He is not a well man."

"It's okay Lori … I know Mr. LaPortiere. I have been expecting him." Stevie Anderson still possessed a bright strength that shone through his eyes, even though his skin pallor was clearly that of a man who was unwell. Stevie leaned forward and extended his hand. "Leroy."

Leroy met the firm handshake but noted the coolness of Anderson's body temperature.

"Honey?" Anderson looked at Lori. "Give us five minutes."

Lori stood and made the tussing sound again. She barged past Leroy. Leroy nodded with his head to Georgina and she followed the walking Barbie out of the private room.

"I take it this visit will be added to your expenses."

Leroy pulled up a chair and sat next to Stevie Anderson.

"So what, I'm still on a retainer?"

"There are things I haven't told the police."

Leroy waited. He liked revelations when they did not impact on his private life, even more so if they came from a rich employer. To some people, people like Stevie Anderson, knowledge is power, but to Leroy it was a tool to be used wisely.

Anderson pulled himself upright in the bed. He did not like being perceived as weak. "There are things I know that I have no desire to take to the grave with me."

*Great*, Leroy thought, *a deathbed confession.* "Do I look like a priest?"

"Hear me out."

"Why should I. You fired me via email three days ago, remember?"

"Things have changed."

"So you said."

The room was hot the way hospital rooms are, and the curtains hung limply like deflated lungs against a window that was locked tighter than a bank vault. Leroy sat back in the seat pressing the small of his back into the curve of the plastic seat so that he stretched his spine and instantly gained an inch in height. He hoped that Anderson hadn't noticed the trickle of sweat that ran down the side of his head. The last thing Leroy wanted to do was display any sign of discomfort or weakness in front of a man who thought little of sacking him mid-investigation and, to add insult to injury, via email. Anderson shifted to his left, the movement caused the tiny pulsing green blip on the monitor above his head to become erratic.

"Damn little bastards," Anderson said. "Can't even take a piss without them letting the world know." He shifted a little further in the bed and reached to the drawer in the bedside cabinet. "As you will come to learn, I may be a lot of things, things that sitting here right now, I am not altogether proud of." Anderson handed Leroy a bunch of papers. Inside the papers were two photographs. "I'm no fool, Mr. LaPortiere, I am heading to the dark country and there are people who will dance on my grave when I am gone."

Leroy looked at the photographs.

"Call it my redemption song." Anderson took a deep breath as his lungs fought to expand. His complexion paled a little further and his big hand clenched into a fist which he thumped against his sternum. The machine bleeped its irritation. "You can be sure that if I have received these then Randolph Thorne would have received them too."

The content of the two photos were surreal. Leroy looked at them unsure of their validity. The photos showed identically staged images. A woman sitting on a bed in a wooden cabin, holding identical copies of the Washington Post. Leroy looked closer, the papers had yesterday's date, that is what made the picture in his left hand all the more surreal. The photographs could have been doctored. But the pose both women adopted made the photograph appear genuine. The washed-out tone of their skin and the faraway look in the eyes of Susan Dark and Paris Thorne confirmed something to Leroy that was only learned through the experience gained from being a detective. Leroy looked up and caught the gaze of Stevie Anderson his employer.

Leroy was relieved that Susan Dark was alive but all that escaped his lips was "Paris Thorne's alive ... I don't get it."

Anderson had sat back in the bed and was supported by the pillows and it was clear the ravages of the past day had caught up with him. Leroy could not tell if Anderson was waiting to speak while he composed his thoughts or whether he was just composing enough strength to speak. Finally Anderson broke his silence.

"I don't know what has happened ... it's all gone terribly wrong."

Georgina found Lori Deane waiting in line for a coffee in the hospital cafeteria. Lori Deane was a clash of bright gaudy color in a room filled with monochromatic people whose minds were distracted by the welfare of sick relatives and friends. Georgina watched Lori take a seat before joining her at the table.

"I won't ask if you mind as you obviously do." Georgina pulled the chair away from the table. The steel legs protested, sending a squeal of displeasure through the cafeteria and making most of the patrons look accusingly at her.

"What-ev-ver." Lori rattled a spoon around the large china mug which looked like it held a quart of coffee.

"In my opinion people who don't like police are either hiding something or have been victims of injustice." Georgina stared at Lori. "Which are you?"

Lori stared back. Neither woman willing to break the intense eye contact first.

"I know what you're thinking." Lori broke the stalemate.

"Enlighten me?" Georgina took a sip from her coffee and suddenly realized how hungry she was. She picked up the sugar dispenser from the table and poured two heaped spoonfuls into the brown milky liquid.

"Gold digger."

Georgina didn't say anything but it was true, Lori Deane did know what she was thinking.

"Jeez Louise, I get it all the time." Lori expelled a heavyweight sigh. "So what? A seventy-two-year-old man gets regular booty and I get something that he can't take to the grave."

"Money."

"Christ, and people say I'm dumb." Lori scooped froth from the top of her cappuccino and sucked it from the spoon. "Hell, Stevie gives me all the money I need."

"So?"

"Inheritance and I'm talking long term."

"The record company?"

Lori laughed. It was a genuine reaction. "He's good. I mean, I knew he was good but man you guys really know nothing."

"As I said, enlighten me."

Lori drank from the large coffee mug. She spent a moment looking around the other faces in the cafeteria. "I've said enough. You want more, subpoena me." Lori stood. "I'm going back now to be with the man whose money I love."

Georgina watched Lori leave the cafeteria.

# Chapter 23 Found and Lost

Tuesday May 20

Fisher knew the route, even in the dark. He drove the Gran Torino as far as he could before parking it off-road and away from prying eyes. He would need it later. Paris sat sleeping next to him. He gently shook her awake.

"We're here."

The rest of the journey had to be made on foot, it was better that way. Fisher did not want to advertise their arrival. Light was fading and night was coming at a quicker pace than he could walk. The darkening conditions were not conducive to jogging or running, there were too many tree roots. The last thing Fisher or Paris wanted was a sprained or broken ankle. The forest was beginning to waken with the sound of rustling branches and the odd crack of wood as heavier mammals started their nocturnal search for food. Tonight there would be another mammal hunting in the woods. Fisher already knew where his game lay. He looked as deeply into the dense forest as he could. Within ten minutes any degree of light would be snuffed out by an opaque blanket of darkness. Home was not far away. They quickened their pace, his timing could not have been better. Fisher was just ahead of the darkness but he was bringing something very black with him. His tortured soul.

"Drive me out to the sea." Georgina needed to see the vast open expanse of water. A week in landlocked Texas left her feeling claustrophobic, even with its wide-open vistas.

"You feel it too, huh?" Leroy said. He was driving the Toyota. Leroy stretched and shrugged his shoulders as though shaking chains from them. Leroy thought about his meeting with Anderson and realized how powerless he actually was when devoid of his badge. The other thing he noticed was how blurred the line between being on the right side of the law was becoming. The distinction between being a detective and a mercenary was only his employer's ability to pay. "We need to talk about the case."

Leroy headed the car out of town toward Portmorion.

"It'll be dark by the time we get there. I love the sea at night. So peaceful." Georgina voice had a tired quality to it. It had been a long day.

"I take it that means we'll talk about the case in the morning."

"You know, Leroy, I can't remember the last time I had a normal conversation, let alone a normal life. Just for now, just for tonight can we not talk shop?"

"Yeah, I'm feelin' it too."

The bright city lights gave way to the burbs and the suburbs eventually made way for the countryside. The road out to the sea was light on traffic with only the occasional vehicle passing and as the road snaked toward the coast, the horizon ahead had a perfect setting sun seemingly dropping into the sea. The car began its climb and a scattering of lights appeared in the hills looking down on the bay. Home was close but for Georgina the sea was closer.

"Look at that sunset," Leroy said, breaking the silence.

There was less than half the sun left on the horizon as it sank below the line, seemingly into the sea. It was burning a fiery purple, looking more like some strange planet from a science fiction movie. Silver rivulets of sea glistened against the dying light.

"The world is a wondrous place."

"A truly fucked-up but wondrous place." Leroy slowed the car at the top of the climb and took a sharp left. A stone wall thirty feet ahead was the only barrier between them and a one hundred foot drop to a watery grave. Georgina pressed the small rocker button inset on the door and the side window glided down. The gentle buzz of the electric motor soon gave way to the sound of the sea breaking against the rocks below. The sound was soothing. Each subsequent break of water acting as a masseur easing away the tension Georgina felt.

"It's hypnotic, I could sleep."

"How are you?" Leroy watched the sun falling off the edge of the earth and the all-consuming darkness of the night approach.

"Big question."

Had the light been better inside the car Leroy would have noticed the lines around Georgina's eyes had deepened. "I'm fine," she lied. The pressure inside her head had returned. The slow throbbing pain had been building all day and Georgina felt incredibly tired. "I think I'm ready for a normal life."

"Huh, normal ... what's that?" Leroy opened the car door and walked to the stone wall. A safety rail had been installed to keep the curious and suicidal at bay. Georgina followed Leroy out of the car and joined him to watch the dying embers of the day.

"You know, watching TV in the evening, reading the papers in bed in the morning, not worrying about people you don't even know and definitely not putting my life on the line for a stranger. One who might not even appreciate the sacrifice."

Leroy studied Georgina's face in the dying light. "You mean, *me* time. Amen to that."

"Leroy?"

"Yeah."

"Would you like a little 'me time?'"

"Do you mean me time or you time?"

Georgina moved closer to Leroy. Her hands reached for his face and she guided him to her lips. "I mean, me time."

# Part Three
## Dark Country

# Chapter 24 So it Begins

Tuesday May 20

The old man was sitting on the decking looking out at the night. He loved the completeness of the dark. Tonight though the very thing he loved would be the death of him. Gil Frolan took a long drag on a hand rolled cigarette and let smoke filled his lungs. Frolan's capacity to inhale was severely reduced during the past decade due to increasing bronchial problems and a build-up of tarry fluid. The onset of emphysema would claim his life within eighteen months but Fisher Sutherland would get there first. Frolan closed his eyes and listened to the sound of the forest. Gil leaned forward on his chair and peered into the darkness. There was nothing to be seen. He took another suck on the cigarette that was permanently attached to his dried lips and sat back. The smoke began its journey in through his mouth, rushing down his throat, giving him a soothing feeling. He could feel his lungs absorb the smoke and diffuse into his bloodstream, it felt so good.

Fisher Sutherland could see the orange glow from the tip of Gil Frolan's cigarette from the cover of the trees, the old man's habit a beacon that would be the death of him. He sat for a while, contemplating his next move. Fisher knew the old man would be an easy kill, hardly any challenge at all, the thrill would be the son. He ran his hands over his shaved head feeling the stubble of the tiny hairs forcing their way through. It was nearly time. Fisher pulled open the rucksack, his hand immediately fell upon the item he was searching for. The knife was from his collection of hunting blades, each having their own unique function. Tonight's weapon of choice was a Gerber Gut Hook hunting knife. Fisher withdrew the knife from the leather pouch. He had the choice of three blades which could be swapped at the push of a button. He lay the blades on the ground. His hand hovered over the drop point blade briefly but he decided on the saw and gut hook. Fisher wasn't fazed by blood or violence. Fisher wasn't even fazed about getting caught, though he knew now was not his time. He picked up the saw and gut hook and slipped it into the lacquered pear wood handle. The blade snapped into place with a healthy click. Fisher ran his finger around the curve of the vicious hook then along the serrated teeth. Tiny pricks of blood rushed through the lacerated dermis. Fisher smiled. He looked toward the orange glow of Gil Frolan's cigarette, knowing that the real prey was waiting inside. Short of setting out a welcome mat and a buffet for his arrival every other aspect of Fisher's arrival had been set out and planned, he even had the invitation in his bag, a letter from Grant Frolan. A letter to a journalist, someone Fisher once knew. Fisher "knew" a lot of people. He placed the remaining blades back in his rucksack, pulled the drawstring and slipped the bag onto his back. The moon slipped behind the cover of turbulent clouds, Fisher knew the time was right. He stood.

"Wait here." He said to Paris.

The knife felt comfortable in his hand, it was nothing more than a lethal extension. He walked into the dark with purpose.

Susan's eyes were open, fixed at the ceiling but focusing somewhere else. Her mind was fighting the frustration of the daily battle against the shackles of the drugs that were used to subdue her. Selective thoughts filtered through the complex network of neurons, some connected, sparking the recognition of memory, others stopped at a wall of confusion looking to latch onto any remote anamnesis. Noise crackled through the ether, at first it was nothing more than a discordant cacophony of white noise. Susan concentrated, there was the spark she had been looking for. The recognition of a life awakened by the sound of her mother singing to her. Susan could feel the sense of empowerment return to her as she began to gain control of her thought processes and slowly the fusion of signals from her brain started to connect with the nerve endings running from her spinal cord. She felt a rush of excitement.

The light was burning. Grant Frolan was supposed to turn the lights out but he liked to watch. Voyeurism was a minor misdemeanor in the grand scheme of things where Grant and Gil Frolan were concerned. Grant opened a pale blue note book and flipped through a few pages until he found the page he was looking for. At the top of the paper was the date written in neat script by his father, underneath was the itinerary of procedures that he had to carry out. Grant ran his finger down the list, his nail bitten to the quick, and stopped at a diagram. He studied the clock on the wall for a long moment. You could almost hear the cogs inside his mind clunking over as he tried to read the hands. No matter how many times in the day he would look at a watch or clock the challenge was always the same. He decided that the time on the wall matched the diagram that his father had drawn. Next to the drawing of the clock was the familiar image of a syringe. Grant placed the book back on the third shelf of a coarse grain wooden homemade wall unit. It was time to medicate the house guest. It was time but tonight he had other plans.

The rocking chair swayed back and forth as Gil Frolan enjoyed the last draw on a cigarette before using the dying embers to ignite the next one and keep the chain connected. If there was no such a thing as perpetual motion, Gil Frolan's constant nicotine habit was a close running contender that might just challenge the laws of physics. Fisher Sutherland moved toward the continual orange glow of Frolan's cigarette. His approach from the left of the elderly record producer was shielded by a blanket of opaque night. Fisher clutched the wooden handled knife, his mind clearly intent only on one goal and that was running the serrated blade of his knife across the soft fleshy skin between Gil Frolan's chin and collar bone. He was so close to the old man now that he could smell the exhaled smoke from Frolan's lungs. Sutherland crept toward the wooden partition and dropped closer to the ground, using the barrier between them as a shield. Plumes of gray smoke wafted above Fisher's head. There was an entrance to the decking area about three yards from where Gil Frolan sat rocking on his chair. Fisher moved silently toward the gap and peered along the decking. The old man was oblivious. Fisher straightened to his full length and ran up the decking. Before Gil could even begin to register what was happening and more horrifically what was about to happen, Fisher was on top of him staring the old man in the eyes.

"Wha ..."

The blade flashed with lightning speed in Fisher's skilled hands. He was no surgeon though. The skill he deployed showed the proven dexterity of a hunter. The teeth of the blade ripped the skin on Frolan's throat with ease. Fisher could feel the warm life blood pour over his hand but he had not finished yet. The gutting hook on the blade stuttered briefly on the old man's windpipe but it showed little resistance as Fisher gave a quick yank severing Frolan's larynx, stopping him from screaming in mid-track. Fisher Sutherland stepped back to view his work. The gaping hole in Gil Frolan's throat was a perverse black void exhaling the last whispers of smoke which were chased from his failing lungs by the blood rapidly filling them. Frolan's mouth drooped open and the cigarette hung limply. The orange glow at the tip slowly extinguished fading to gray and then black.

Paris watched from a distance feeling excited by what the night was bringing.

Social graces were not high on the list of Grant Frolan's personal traits, though his pappy had always taught him to knock before entering a room. Much like Pavlov's dogs this skill was duly engrained upon Grant's memory like most learning achievements, through pain and repetition. Pain being the prize for not obeying his father's orders. Though Grant had the ability to watch Susan at will, he stopped at the closed entrance and composed himself before raising his clubby fist to rap on the door. As his hand was about to make contact with the door, a noise from outside the wooden hut caught his attention. His head turned to the side allowing his ear to focus on the sound. There it was again, a scraping sound.

"Darned rodents." Grant said to nobody in particular.

As he began to turn his attention back to the door a heavier thump stopped Grant in his tracks. He walked up the wooden hall toward the front door.

"Pa?"

His cadence slowed as he approached the door. This time a much louder thump rattled the door in its frame. It was quickly followed by another loud bang of equal violence. This time the wood inside the cabin splintered. Grant approached carefully. Something was protruding through the wooden surface, it glistened against the light.

"Pa?" Grant's voice rose. It had an edge of cautious trepidation.

There was a final bang impacting on the door. Once more the wood fractured, directly to the left of the first puncture. Grant could feel the muscles in his stomach begin to betray him. He waited a full minute as still and as quiet as a statue, before making a tentative step forward and grabbing the handle to the door. His open palm enveloped the rounded knob. On closer inspection Grant could see that the shiny objects protruding through the door appeared to be the tips of a crossbow bolt. After another full minute, Grant finally mustered up enough courage to twist the door knob. The door popped backwards, feeling heavier than usual. The weight pushing Grant back. Grant let go of the handle and let the door swing freely. The sight that greeted him, made Grant stagger and fall to his knees in disbelief. His father's body was impaled on the door with three crossbow bolts. As Grant kneeled trying to comprehend the image, he was barely aware of the figure of Fisher Sutherland standing in the void created by the open door.

Grant finally looked up at Fisher. His pupils wide, the black eating outwards consuming the color. The gut hook knife was still in Sutherland's hand, blood ran around the curve of the hook and fell back to the floor, collecting in a tiny pool. Grant Frolan's eyes mirrored over with a layer of tears. Restrained emotion fought its way to the surface of Frolan's psyche. He studied Fisher Sutherland for a long moment.

"Thank you." Grant Frolan allowed a hysterical smile to spread across his gnarled features, followed by a rush of tears of happiness.

Paris Thorne stepped from the darkness.

"We have a new patient to medicate, Grant," Fisher said.

"Be gentle with me," Paris said.

Georgina's head was resting against the head restraint of the passenger seat. Her eyes were closed and occasionally her head would flop from side to side as Leroy turned a bend. The night was down, covering the land in a silent black shroud. Light pockets of hope were being extinguished as another day was snuffed out. All Leroy wanted was a long soak in the tub and the chance to wash away the grime from his mind. Georgina's cell phone rang, it was sitting in the can holder down in the console. He pounced on the phone before the second ring could wake Georgina.

"Yeah." Leroy's voice was low.

The voice on the other end of the line was familiar, though unexpected.

"Help me." Susan's voice was weak but instantly recognizable even though it was the first time Leroy had actually spoken to her.

Leroy automatically slowed the car. Georgina's home was less than a mile away. The sound of Susan's voice excited and at the same time filled Leroy with trepidation. "Susan?" Leroy kept his voice low and calm.

"Good, I see I have your attention."

This time it was another voice Leroy recognized. Fisher Sutherland. Leroy was aware of the car slowing further and pressed a little harder on the gas.

"Listen carefully, I am not about to repeat a solitary vowel or consonant."

"You have my undivided attention," Leroy said.

Georgina stirred in the seat. She moved slightly, her body fighting against the onset of a dream.

The sign for Portmorion was on the bend in the road about fifty yards ahead. The sea was to his left, like a vast sheet of quiet but foreboding glass, ripples of moonlight reflected on the crest of each tiny wave like a billion lights reaching for the stars, but home was so close.

"I want you to hand the phone to your partner." Sutherland's voice sounded dry.

Leroy looked at Georgina briefly. She looked peaceful.

"I'll give you five seconds ... four seconds ... three ..."

Leroy rocked Georgina's shoulder. Her eyes snapped open struggling to focus.

"Huh!" Georgina studied the phone being thrust under her nose.

"Sutherland," Leroy said.

Georgina held the phone to her ear while she tried to gain her bearings. "Hello?"

"Hmmm ... Georgina."

Georgina had the repugnant image of Fisher Sutherland making love to her burned into her mind, it was an image that she was going to have to deal with for the rest of her life. She looked to her side at Leroy who was mouthing, "He's got Susan."

Those three words suddenly sharpened Georgina's mind and in an instant she felt incredibly focused.

"Do you like country?" Sutherland rasped. Georgina now pictured his face turning into the head of a snake with a forked tongue protruding. "Time for a trip into the dark country, Georgie."

"Tell me we are going to meet, Fisher. I'm dying to see you again."

"What an appropriate choice of words," Fisher said. "Go to the I-695 and then take the 95 south. I'll call you then."

The phone went dead. Georgina was left holding the phone to her ear.

"How ..."

Leroy slowly brought the car to a halt. Georgina closed the phone.

"How did he know where we are?"

"He's got your number," Leroy said "Satellite tracking, there's a million different ways."

Leroy swung the car around and headed toward the I-695. Home was going to have to wait.

"Don't fuss, Norman ... Just give me the information." Barbara Dace moved impatiently from one foot to the other. They were standing outside Frusco's hotel room. John Keller was outside the hotel in the parking lot by the open door to his Shogun. His kit was loaded in the back in a variety of bags. Camera, lighting, battery packs, chargers, stands, the whole portable TV news team condensed in a bite-sized package.

Captain Norman Frusco passed a thick document folder to the woman who shared his bed. "It's my job."

Dace allowed her hand to grasp Norman's as he passed the folder. "I know."

"Be careful. Anderson is an unknown quantity."

"What do we know?"

Norman took the cigarette from Barbara's mouth and placed it between his lips. His tongue could taste the scent of his lover. He inhaled and placed the cigarette back between Barbara's waiting lips. "Rumors, lies and half-truths."

"Great," Dace said.

"We've put away people on less," Norman said with a mischievous smile. Barbara did not know whether he was telling the truth but enjoyed the sense of irony. "I do know though that Amy, Caroline and Susan Dark met someone they trusted."

Barbara raised her hand as though in self-defense. "I know, I know. I'll be careful."

"Yeah, and look after John."

Barbara stubbed the remainder of the cigarette out under her shoe, leaned forward and kissed Norman Frusco with a passion seldom seen in people half her age. "Bastard."

The sound of a phone ringing caught her attention. Barbara listened to John Keller who was calling from the parking lot.

"Looks like I gotta go," Barbara said.

"I mean it. I don't want any more trips to hospital. You were lucky."

Barbara put on her best New Yoike accent. "Nag, nag, nag."

As she walked away Frusco patted her butt. Barbara was determined not to turn around and look at him, otherwise she wouldn't get into the car with Keller and drive through the night into the unknown.

# Chapter 25 Being Gary Morris

*Fortune's End Trailer Park, Wink Winkler, Texas*
*July 4, 1978*

*Gary Morris lathered the soap until it was a froth of foam. He used the side of his fist to wipe the misted mirror. The razor glided over his skin clearing a smooth path free from beard. Every now and then he would look up and peer out of the window in the small kitchen area. The view across the trailer park was what interested him, more precisely, the rusting trailer opposite. Morris finished shaving and wiped the remnants of soap from his face with a towel that had a slightly musty smell. He had been waiting for five days for the perfect opportunity to catch Caroline Dark alone but he was there, Bobby Oates, Caroline's boyfriend. Gary Morris had therefore decided to take matters into his own hands.*

*Morris slipped his white cotton shirt on over his vest. He had the physique of a man who looked after himself. His arms, while not overtly large or overdeveloped had definition and looked tanned against the brilliant white of the short sleeve shirt. The end of the sleeve of his shirt just covered a tattoo. The drawing, now not as defined as it once was, but still legible and disturbing enough when uncovered depicted in graphic detail a stiletto knife piercing the eye of a wolf cub and a single word inscribed below. "Tender."*

*The sound of a door closing caught Morris's attention. He looked through the small window and saw Bobby Oates leaving the small trailer home.*

*Oates was sweating and unshaven. Black stubble fought for space on his chin. His hair was long, greasy and lank but for the best part hidden under the brim of a cowboy hat. He walked straight to the silver blue 1976 Pontiac Firebird Trans Am coupe, yanked the door open, and jumped into the driver's seat, slamming the door behind him and screeching away. There was a sense of violent disturbance that affected the very air parting to make way for the gas guzzling car. Bobby Oates wasn't coming back.*

*Morris kept a discreet distance but did not want to let the Firebird race away. The roads were long and straight offering no place to* hide. Morris could tell though by the way Oates drove that the only time he would check his rear view would be to check that whatever poor dumb son-of-a-bitch that was unfortunate enough to get in his path was dead. The country opened out, wide expanses of land that seemed to stretch forever became the only vista apart from the road ahead. Ninety-three miles out of Wink Winkler, Morris pressed his foot down on the gas pedal and accelerated past the Firebird. He briefly looked in at Oates as Morris's 1972 Ford Torino GT fought to gain the horsepower to make the maneuver look natural. The Torino slugged on with Morris's foot almost pushing the pedal through the footwell. Over the rise of a hill Morris yanked on the parking brake and the Torino turned to the side, blocking both lanes of the highway. Gary Morris looked down the road at the natural area shelter behind a large advertising billboard.

Within a minute, Bobby Oates's Firebird appeared. The car barely recognized the obstruction but swerved at the last minute, hitting the rough ground by the strip of asphalt. Dust exploded in the air. Oates fought with the steering wheel and pressed sharply on the brake as soon as the car was back on the road. Oates drove a further ten yards before curiosity overpowered him and he pulled his car to a halt. The Firebird sat quietly for a moment as the occupant, Bobby Oates, gathered his thoughts.

Morris watched Oates leave the car. Even from a distance Morris could see the look of sheer bewilderment on Oates face. Oates walked toward the Torino, the car was hogging both lanes of the highway. Morris knew Oates was an opportunist, why else would he be hanging with Caroline Dark?

Oates opened the door to the car. He could see the key still engaged in the ignition lock. Oates stopped by the open door and glanced around checking that the coast was clear ... oh yes, he was an opportunist.

Gary Morris waited until Oates had committed himself and was sitting inside his car. He wondered how long it would be until Bobby Oates could smell the stench of blood. He didn't want to give Oates too long though. Morris made his move. The only thing set on his mind was murder.

Oates sat in the driver's seat. His hands gripped the leather bound steering wheel. His nose twitched, Oates's mind raced for confirmation of the heavy stench inside the confines of the vehicle. Pulling his hands from the steering wheel he noticed they were wet. Slowly he turned the palms of his hands toward him and saw they were crimson and sticky with the residue of drying blood.

"What the hell is this?"

Morris sat bolt upright from the cover of the footwell behind Oates's seat.

"Your hell, Mr. Oates." Morris locked one arm around Oates and used his left hand to hook the gutting knife into the soft fleshy part of Bobby Oates's throat. Morris pulled hard as though landing a big fish. Resistance was futile.

The billboard offered the perfect cover for him to tidy up. After parking his Torino, Morris strolled back to Oates's Firebird and reversed it, stopping ten feet behind his car. Morris stripped to his boxers, carefully folding the clothes he was wearing, placing them inside his car. He then opened the driver's door of the Torino and leant in and manhandled Oates's still warm but totally lifeless body onto his shoulder. With a mighty heave, Morris lifted Oates's dead weight. He could feel the warm blood from Oates's slit throat trickle down his back as he walked to the opened trunk of Bobby Oates's Firebird.

Morris then walked back to his Torino and popped his trunk. Lying as dead as a fish in the midday sun the real Detective Gary Morris stared through milky glazed opaque eyes at the sight of his killer. The dead detective, Gary Morris, was hoisted onto the shoulders of the man who had killed him and consumed his identity. It was a short walk to Oates's car and the killer dropped the corpse into the trunk to join the body of Bobby Oates. Garry Morris's head made a nasty cracking sound as it hit the metal framework of the trunk, before the body settled into place next to his dead companion.

Fisher Sutherland rubbed his hands down his bare chest. Trails of blood smeared into the hairs on his chest matting them against his skin. He walked back to the Torino and dressed. In the forty-five minutes that he was there not one single vehicle passed. He sat for a while composing his thoughts. Sutherland looked through every piece of documentation he found on the bodies and in the cars of both men. He walked back to the Firebird and doused the interior of *the car with gasoline and leaned inside the driver's cockpit. He pushed the cigarette lighter in on the dash and waited for it to pop out. He pressed the heated lighter onto the fabric of the seat. Immediately fire took hold as it chased the vapors of gasoline. Sutherland closed the door and calmly strolled to the trunk and slammed it shut, trapping the dead occupants, to be consumed in a fiery inferno. As he drove away in the direction of Wink Winkler, Sutherland heard the explosion as the heat penetrated the thin shell of the gas tank. Sutherland aka Gary Morris smiled to himself.*

# Chapter 26 A Diner to Die For

Tuesday May 20, 2003

The I-695 seemed to go on forever. Leroy was already growing tired of it. He needed a comfort break and looked at Georgina who was once again asleep. Georgina's hand gripped the cell phone, her fingers wound so tightly around the plastic casing it was hard to imagine anyone being able to sleep like that, but the relaxed muscles on her face and the fluttering of her eyes under the closed lids confirmed that she was in another place. It had been forty minutes since the phone last rang, a sign by the side of the road indicated that the turnoff for the I-95 south was due in ten miles. Leroy's bladder was telling him he would last six, maybe seven miles. There was a diner a mile or so up the road, it wasn't a "Wendalls" like back home in Missouri, but it was good enough for a piss, a coffee and a snack. Whenever possible Leroy liked to eat before going into battle. Gallows humor told him it was like a final meal, in his line of work it was often worth humoring the dark side.

Georgina awoke as the car pulled to a halt outside the diner. "Hu ... are we there?" She tried to appear alert but was as cognizant as an eighty-year-old with Alzheimer's who was suffering from five straight days of sleep deprivation. Leroy looked out at the diner.

"We ain't anywhere. It's time for a break, that's all. You hungry?"

Georgina couldn't remember the last time she ate. "You buyin'?"

"No, George W Bush is buying. I'm putting this one on expenses."

"'Bout time that man paid for something. In that case I am famished."

The inside of the diner belied the cheesy kitsch all-American exterior. It wasn't that Leroy and Georgina were not patriotic but they knew the difference between good and bad taste. The contrast inside to the garish neon stars and stripes flag bordering the building suggested that they had somehow fallen through a portal into another world. Leroy was expecting to find a traditional 1950's diner filled with chrome and worn leatherette, but the mirrored windows hid a warm, sumptuous eatery decked out with cozy tables draped in white linen tablecloths and highly polished cutlery. Waitresses moved gracefully from table to table with a quiet professionalism.

"Am I dreaming this?" Leroy asked.

The kitchen doors opened and with them wafted the aroma of a dozen dishes. Short of having a maitre'd, Leroy could easily have believed he had walked into Eleven Madison Park, Flatiron in New York.

Leroy picked a table by the large window that looked out onto the parking lot. He remembered the mirrored windows on the outside thinking how tacky it all looked, but now he appreciated the sense of privacy the reflective opaque surface offered.

Georgina sat, pulling the chair closer to the table. She noticed for the first time the music playing in the background and looked for the speakers. One was mounted directly above them on a metal bracket.

"Spooky, eh?"

Leroy looked at Georgina. "What, the restaurant?"

"No, the fact that they are playing Susan Dark."

Leroy listened. The hairs on his arms began to rise, one by one.

"Synchronicity?"

Georgina laughed. "Must be, because I know you don't believe in coincidence." She listened to the words in the song.

*I'm all alone with you so near,*
*You'll never know how much I care,*
*I can feel every beat of your heart,*
*I'm invisible ...*

"Suddenly I'm not so hungry," Georgina said.

"We have nothing to feel guilty about." Leroy reached forward and touched Georgina's hand. Her hand remained still under his, but was cool to touch.

"You okay?"

"You know, I want a vacation. I just want to get away from this all. At times it just seems too much ... too much responsibility."

"We are going to find Susan." Leroy tried his level best to sound reassuring.

The nagging throbbing inside Georgina's head had returned. It felt as though two hands were inside her head slowly pushing inwards, squeezing her brain. For a second her vision blurred wildly out of focus. She tried not to show Leroy the discomfort she was feeling, hoping that the pressure would find a way to relieve itself other than the obvious rupturing of another vein inside her head. Georgina pinched the bridge of her nose, it sometimes helped. Leroy pushed the menu toward her.

"Come on, we gotta eat. Might not get the chance again for a while."

Georgina looked up. The room was brightening, getting lighter. Her head felt woozy.

"Come on ... concentrate." She told herself.

A waitress arrived at the table. Pad in hand, ready to take their order. Georgina realized that she couldn't read the words on the page. They were a fuzzy collection of letters, bearing no resemblance to her knowledge of the English language.

"You order, I'll er ... I'll make my mind up as you order. Too much choice that's the problem." Georgina lied. Bright car headlamps filled the parking lot. Georgina was able to follow the progress of the vehicle but could not discern any recognizable shape beyond the two orbs of bright light. Leroy's voice began to blend in with the background music as his baritone voice joined Susan Dark in a duet.

"Georgina ... Georgina. What are you ordering?"

"Sorry. Erm, I'll just have whatever you are eating."

The doors to the restaurant opened. Leroy looked instinctively to the door.

"I don't believe it," Leroy said.

Georgina tried to follow Leroy's gaze and hoped she was focusing in the right direction. A dark figure stood in the aperture where she judged the door was. Light haloed around the person.

"I'll be damned." Leroy stood and walked toward the door.

The pain inside Georgina's head ratcheted up a few notches, she closed her eyes, willing the pain to go away. She pictured her fingers entering her head and massaging the pulsating clot, pushing it away from her brain, down her spinal cord and into the larger cavities connecting to her heart where the bubble of blood dispersed. When she opened her eyes it was as though the room had snapped back into focus and color. The clarity stung her. Georgina knew it wouldn't last though, but for now the pain had vanished. She saw Leroy walking toward her and behind Leroy was the last person she expected to see.

"I have every right to leave this hospital. It was only a busted nose for Christ sakes." Anderson stared the doctor down. Unwilling to be the first to blink.

"You also have angina." Doctor Emile Ouellet shook her head. "Fine, I can't stop you, but it is against my better judgment. Here, sign the discharge papers." She thrust a clipboard at Anderson "This is totally against medical advice."

Anderson signed the papers.

Susan lay on the bed staring at the figure standing in front of her. She had more feeling and control over her body than for days and that was the problem. She had no real memory of what she had endured since this nightmare had begun, but now she was finally regaining her full senses, she wished she was drugged to the eyeballs and slumped in a sublime stupor. Grant Frolan was rubbing the crotch of his filthy jeans. His hand more than suggestive, Susan feared what would happen next. Grant moved on though, his foot dragging lazily making the image of him somehow more obscene. Susan remained rooted to the bed fearful of moving, knowing that a single movement would betray her and scupper any chance of escaping. She heard the sound of flesh slapping and dreaded to think what he was doing. Half of her wanted to turn her head and see the cause of the sound, the other half was afraid that the confirmation would be too dreadful to contemplate. Susan didn't know what was worse, feigning paralysis or being paralyzed. Slowly she turned her head ...

"Oh God." Barbara Dace held the report in her hands and couldn't really believe what she had just read. She closed the folder and felt the panicked excitement that had been missing in her work for so many years. "John, we need to get to Georgina O'Neil, yesterday."

John Keller passed the cell phone. "What's the story?"

Barbara put her hand up, cutting John as the cell connected. "C'mon, answer."

Three hundred miles and two states away the call linked with Georgina's cell phone. It rang and it rang and it rang. "Where is she?" Barbara scrolled through the address book looking for Leroy LaPortiere's cell number. She pressed the button to connect the phones and waited while the signal bounced through the air colliding with antenna and phone masts in different towns and states. This time she was met with the engaged signal. "Damn." She went back to Georgina's number. The air inside the car felt heavy. Barbara breathed deeply trying to steady the rush of excitement and nerves, the combined sensations a heady but complex mix that would have had lesser seasoned players reaching for a brown paper bag to breathe into. The connection rang again.

"O'Neil."

Barbara Dace steadied herself. She sat a little more upright, watching the dark country flash past her window as John Keller paid little regard to the speed limit.

"Where are you?" Dace asked.

"Barbara?"

"I've got news. Big news." Barbara said, opening the folder. She read the salient points to herself once more. "We have to meet."

"Barbara, now is not a good time."

"Has he been in touch?"

"Honestly, Barbara, now is not a good time."

"Has he been in touch?" Dace's voice was insistent. "Sutherland. Fisher Sutherland." She waited, listening for an answer.

"You could say that ..."

Georgina watched Leroy approach the table. The man behind Leroy walked with purpose. He carried a drawstring bag, casually slung over his shoulder. The man arrived at the table less than a second behind Leroy and slipped the bag off his shoulder. It hit the table surface with a deft thud, shaking Georgina's coffee cup. She watched the ripples spread outward on the surface of her coffee. Leroy sat beside Georgina and watched Fisher Sutherland take a seat in front of him. Sutherland pushed the black beanie off his head, revealing the stubble from his shaved head. Georgina felt a wave of revulsion fluttering through her chest.

"Georgina." Sutherland nodded recognition. His shaved head bobbing a bow of respect.

Georgina remembered the night they had spent together. She remembered the intensely pleasurable feelings she had. She felt guilt at the wild, uninhibited nature of the sex they shared and revulsion at the knowledge of the obscene acts of violence and murder this creature sitting in front of her had committed and here he was being civil, as though they were friends. What was it he expected of her? She chose to ignore his greeting.

"So when were you going to join the 95. Cos it looks to me like you're not in a hurry?" Sutherland voice had a serpentine quality that added to the revulsion Georgina felt both with him and herself.

"What's the game, Sutherland?" Leroy's question was as pointed as the look he gave the killer.

"You're not a cop now, but I guess the instinct never leaves. It's in the blood."

"Your point?" Leroy asked. He wanted to reach across the table and wipe the smug grin from Sutherland's face.

"It's in the blood." Sutherland blew a snort of air through his nose, much the way a bull does before deciding to attack.

Georgina's hand instinctively moved to her side, ready to unclip her holster.

"Talking of blood." Sutherland pushed the drawstring bag across the table.

Leroy noticed for the first time the red pooling at the base of the bag. Blood was soaking through the canvas material slowly saturating through the interwoven fabric, reaching to the bottom of the bag. Blood smeared underneath the bag on the glossy white surface. A bridge of death from the killer to the ex-cop.

"I've brought you a little present to aid your investigation."

Georgina shivered.

The slapping of flesh against flesh continued. Loose unconditioned skin and fat resonating as it collided. Little by little, Susan Dark turned her head.

"Aid our investigation?" Leroy did not bother hiding the incredulity from his voice. He was beyond sarcasm.

"Open it?" Sutherland said.

She found her eyes closing as her head turned. Slap ... slap ... slap. The tempo increased. The rhythm picked up.

"You could say I have done half your job," Sutherland said.

A waitress began walking to their table. Leroy held up his hand before she got too close.

"Give us five minutes."

The waitress turned away.

"Uh ... Uh ... Uh."

Susan slowly opened her eyes, so that at first everything was a dark blur. Grant Frolan's actions were becoming more frantic. Susan knew what she was about to see but still she felt that she had to have confirmation. It was like passing a car crash and being lured inevitably to the scene of carnage. She opened her eyes, fully and mentally prepared. She could not have been more wrong.

Leroy grabbed the bag. The weight was surprisingly heavy. He pulled it to the edge of the table, careful not to spill any blood over the edge. He opened the drawstring bag. The top of the bag spread like a flower opening to revealing a dark interior. The smell that escaped the bag was familiar to both Leroy and Georgina. Too familiar.

"Now, no looking until I'm gone." Sutherland spoke as though he was teasing a child with the excitement of a Christmas gift. Leroy pushed the bag back in revulsion.

Slap, slap, slap. "Uh ... uh ... uh ... aaarrrrrrhhhh."

Susan's eyes were fixed and focused with horror on the sight before her.

"I have to go now." Fisher stood. "I know you won't follow because you want to see Susan alive. You couldn't bear to be responsible for her death … not now, but don't worry, I will be in touch." His hand reached forward and rested on Georgina's for a split second before she pulled it away, feeling repulsed.

Grant Frolan was standing, naked from the waist down. His body thrusting rhythmically, almost with the quality of a metronome into a decapitated body. The scene of obscenity made Georgina want to retch but Frolan's face had an intoxicated appearance. At this point in time he was oblivious to her, to the room or anything in it except the body that he was entering.

"And we shared such times," Sutherland said, feigning mock hurt. "Got to go." The smile on his face was malevolent, pure evil and it was so obvious that he was enjoying every twisted second. He turned and walked out of the restaurant, stopping only to grab a waitress by the arm. "Table 54 need a few napkins, their starter was a little too bloody for their liking."

Georgina wondered whether the encounter that had just taken place was a figment of her tired mind, but the pool of blood and the heavily stained rucksack Leroy was holding confirmed to her that she was not going mad, only that she had been in the company of madness. The bright lights of Fisher Sutherland's car briefly illuminated the restaurant and added as another witness to her sanity.

"Are we not going to follow him?" Georgina asked.

Leroy was holding the bag away from him. Blood dripped from the bottom of the bag like a leaky tap, pooling by his feet.

"And risk Susan's life. Besides this is now a crime scene." Leroy flipped open his cell phone.

Georgina placed her hand on the phone. "Stop. Wait a minute." She turned her own cell phone on and quickly scrolled through the numbers, stopping at her father's name. "I have a better idea." She watched as the display read connecting to *Wynan O'Neil*.

The waitress clearly hesitated as she approached Leroy and Georgina's table.

The drive back to the forest was short, much shorter than anyone could guess. Washington DC ... Washington, Dark Country. Fisher drove under the speed limit, not because he cared about getting caught. He could deal with that the way he had dealt with that snoopy detective Gary Morris, all those years ago. No, Fisher knew it was nearing the end of days. As the trees grew taller and his journey drew nearer to an end, Sutherland recognized that now was the time to open his game plan. Forty-eight years of torture, forty-eight years of nurturing hatred had already begun to spill uncontrollably and now there was only one missing piece of the jigsaw remaining. His father. It was time for a family reunion. Fisher drove one handed while picking the number from the illuminated address book in his cell phone. His face glowed with a green tint from the phone display making his eyes appear black and sunken in his skull. Passing motorists would have paid no attention to Sutherland. His ability to go unnoticed was the reason he had managed to kill with huge success for so long. He could be nice, even described as lovable by one victim. Fisher Sutherland had many traits which one may describe as desirable in any human being and only one which made him differ from ninety-nine percent of the human race. The casual observer would call his actions the work of insanity. A trained scholar with every available piece of knowledge to the working of the human mind may have noted Fisher's ability to disassociate his actions and feelings to a primal level. Fisher's genius was that he controlled the switch and whilst these murderous actions were truly abhorrent to most, they fed an addictive nature and nurtured an ancient desire. Fisher began to sing an Amy Dark number as the cell phone connected. His voice carried a cold, toneless quality to it that would not threaten the charts but would scare the hell out of anyone unlucky enough to be within earshot.

*It's borderline, but the cryin' time is over*
*I've seen the signs within your eyes*
*It's over*
*You left me a long long time ago but*
*You're in my heart*

The sound of the phone ringing stopped Fisher dead. He listened to the trill of the ring and then the pick up at the other end.

"Hello?" Randolph Thorne answered.

Fisher breathed in savoring the moment for a second. "Daddy ..."

# Chapter 27 Echoes of Déjà Vu

*Phone Booth Four Miles South of Wink Winkler*
*June 2, 1954*

*Amy drove through the night, stopping only for one break for coffee and the use of a roadside services toilet. She wasn't sure which one was the worst experience but at the time was grateful for the opportunity of both. Washington was a long way from Texas but Amy was determined to make him listen. She didn't know what it was about her choice of lovers, but somehow the men she chose always dramatically changed their personalities after they had sex with her. The drive through the night was not the first time she had made the journey but it was the first time she had made the journey as a mother-to-be. As the hours passed, the country changed from wide open space with endless vistas to narrow roads with trees that seemed to be closing in on her. The night became darker, blacker than Amy knew could exist.*

*The bright lights of the city cast an orange hue over the tops of the trees. She gripped the steering wheel tighter, fighting the fatigue that was sweeping through her body, but determination was driving her as much as her Ford Thunderbird. The sight of the lights spurred her on, raising her adrenaline level. The tentacles of night's grip pulled back a little as the city approached and with it the trees began to become more sparse. Every now and then a building introduced itself and one by one the woods became suburbia and finally the city. Amy stopped the car at a phone booth. She opened her clutch bag and searched for change in her purse. The echo of coins rattled an uncomfortable truth, Amy had spent her last ten bucks on gas. She was tired and needed food and shelter, the bunch of quarters in her hand represented hope for the night at least. She entered the booth and dialed the only number she knew by heart.*

*"It's me ..."*

*Amy felt queasy. Dark rings under Amy's eyes told the tale of too many lost nights' sleep, a high dependency on alcohol and too few people she could actually call, let alone call "friend." She waited for an answer but was greeted with slow steady breathing down the telephone line. She hiccupped and the acidic taste of vomit stung the* back of her throat. Amy held the phone away from her mouth but kept the ear piece pressed to her ear and leaned into the corner of the booth, tilting her head down and stepping back, moving her body as far away from any predicted splatter zone. The sound of the last of her stomach's contents hitting the floor was transmitted down the line. The rancid smell of broiling vomit putrefying in the confines of the call box. She tried to wipe the moist stomach spill off the sleeve of her jacket by using the corner of the single phone book which was attached to the booth with a large steel chain. A continuous tone registered in Amy's ear and she screamed.

Amy waited in the coffee shop for over an hour, cupping a mug of stone-cold coffee. Her eyes followed every passing car in the hope that it would stop. Amy's own car was now parked in a parking lot and she did not even have enough money to retrieve it. Desperation, anxiety, confusion and fear were the bed fellows of the insane, she felt at least three of those emotions. She waited. Another hour passed and all that happened was that her coffee got colder. A waitress, looking as fried as a ten-day-old burger stood in front of her with a coffee pot in her hand.

"You want a fresh one, honey?"

Amy looked up and was greeted with a warm but tired smile.

"Hey, aren't you that singer ... Amy Dark?"

"Hell no ... I get that a lot." Amy offered her full cup of cold coffee for refill.

The waitress took the full cup without comment but noticed two things. The first was that Amy Dark's hands were shaking, the second and most obvious was that the woman sitting in front of her was indeed Amy Dark and a liar.

Amy watched the waitress walk away. She strolled with a tired gait, the heels of her flat shoes were worn heavily on one side, revealing an uneven cadence in her step. The waitress disappeared behind the counter and returned almost instantly with a fresh cup. As she poured the coffee from the jug, she couldn't help but comment.

"You sure as hell do look like her."

Amy looked at the waitress, square in the eyes.

"A hell of a lot."

Amy's eyes were tired and the waitress could see little humor in them or point in trying to progress the conversation further. A light spatter of rain hit the large sheet glass window. At first it could have been the overflow pipe above weeping, but then the black clouds above, camouflaged by the night sky, ripped open discharging their contents in a violent expression of exuberance. Amy watched what her mother once called the tears from heaven. She took the smallest of sips from the cup and continued to wait. She knew that eventually he would come.

Normally he would arrive in a little more style. The flamboyance of his wealth would mark his path, usually in the form of a chauffeur driven limo, but tonight he took the unusual step of driving himself in a cheap rental. Randolph Thorne spotted Amy Dark sitting alone in the coffee shop. He sat down in front of her. Amy looked up. She was tired. The dark rings under her eyes a betrayal of her physical and mental condition.

"You want a top up?"

Amy stared at Randolph. His presence, even when he was not trying to attract attention, was commanding.

"You've got to work on your chat-up lines, Ran." Her voice buoyed by the presence of the man who bankrolled her slide into mediocrity, compulsion and habitual alcoholism and drug abuse.

"You look like shit," he said sitting opposite her.

Amy wasn't in the least offended by Randolph Thorne's bluntness, also she knew it was true. Her breath had the acidic stench of vomit, her hair was flat with the detritus of three weeks of Texan air and smoky bars.

"Still good enough to fuck though eh, Ran?" Amy lifted her foot from her shoe and pressed her toes into Randolph's crotch. She felt him almost immediately harden. "Obviously."

"I'm sure you didn't drive through the night to feel my cock."

"Don't do yourself a mis-service, Ran. I might have." Amy pressed her foot a little firmer against what was now a full erection.

Coffee arrived courtesy of the waitress. Amy's foot remained in place. The waitress began to pour the coffee from the glass container. Black, aromatic liquid poured like oil into the waiting cups.

"I'm pregnant," Amy said.

The waitress continued filling the cup, watching it overflow in to the saucer as though she was mesmerized. Coffee flowed over the saucer, spilling onto the table.

Randolph's hand shot out with fierce direction, gripping hold of the waitress's arm forcing it back, away from the table.

"Fuck off." Thorne's voice rasped with the same ferocity as he had physically shown seconds earlier. The temperature inside the coffee shop dipped and Amy felt the wave of ice course through her veins.

"How?" Thorne continued.

"You're the bareback specialist ... you tell me?"

"And you're the one with endometriosis." Thorne's voice had an accusatory quality to it.

"Believe me, I don't need no baby. What am I supposed to say, sorry my doctor's fucked up? We have been screwing for three years without protection."

Randolph cut her short. "So what are we going to do about it?" Thorne waited a few seconds before adding. "I know a place ... it's ... discreet."

Amy looked at him. She was expecting his response. Which was more than he could say.

"If it was one, I'd say yeah. But this is twins, Ran. I've had a checkup. Two tiny fetuses, or is it feti?"

Randolph Thorne shifted a little uncomfortably on his seat and then rocked Amy with his reply. "I'll buy one from you. Give you enough money to raise the other one or do what you want with it."

"What?"

"Of course, I get first choice," Randolph said coldly.

September 24, 1954

She screamed. The pain was unbearable.

Amy looked around the room. Her eyes wide with fear. Her body felt as though it was ripping itself apart. Intense muscle spasms convulsed through her body. The doctor took an alcohol wipe and ran it across Amy's spine.

Amy's eyes widened. She felt the cold sensation as the alcohol evaporated.

"It won't be long now." The doctor said. He aimed the number twenty-seven gauge, three and a half inch needle with precisioned skill midway down her spine. The pain inside Amy blotted the moment the needle pierced her skin and sank deep inside, aiming for the spinal column. She felt a sensation of pressure and coldness enter her as the morphine started its work. The coldness swept through her body numbing the nerve endings as it travelled. The sensation in her head similar to the headaches she received when *she ate an extra cold ice cream on a summer's day. Her arms and chest grew heavy. Amy was leaning back against the stacked pillows. Her hand rested in front, close to her knees.*

*"Soon be over. You can lie down now."*

*Hands, she was not sure whose, guided her down. A wedge was placed under her right hip, though she could no longer feel any sensation, she sensed a general manipulation of her body. Amy stared at the ceiling.*

*"Can you feel that?"*

*"Feel what?" Amy raised her head and looked down to see an intravenous drip had been inserted into a catheter in her arm. The arm could have belonged to anyone. Amy felt so detached from her body. She could control her upper body to her shoulders but beyond that it was all alien.*

*"Lie back." The surgeon's voice commanding and authoritative.*

*Amy had no option but to lie back. The weight of her body felt as though it was increasing by the second.*

*The surgeon pinched a fold of skin on Amy's extended abdomen. Happy that she was feeling no sensation, he began making a small incision across her lower abdomen. Cutting carefully, he opened her womb. Baby number one was clearly evident. Had Amy lifted her head from the bed she would have seen her son for the first and only time.*

# Chapter 28 It's in the Blood

Monroe's Diner
Tuesday May 20, 2003

Leroy collected samples of blood in small plastic food containers borrowed from the kitchen and labeled them, making notes where each sample came from. Georgina used a digital camera to record each collection, marking each area with a small numbered paper napkin hastily scrawled with the numbers in black marker. Leroy opened the duffle bag, pulling the drawstrings loose. The pungent smell of warm meat and congealing blood assaulted his nostrils.

Leroy tugged gently at the wrist of his latex glove. His phone rang. "Damn." It trilled once more. "Okay, enough already." He stepped away from the bag and took the call. "LaPortiere."

Leroy listened for a moment before glancing toward Georgina. She stared at him with a puzzled look on her face before returning to collect another sample and photograph the scene. Georgina kept repeating the words Fisher Sutherland had said a few minutes earlier. "It's in the blood … it's in the blood."

Leroy turned and walked a few steps away from Georgina. She was now too engrossed to bother with Leroy's conversation. Leroy listened intently to the earpiece of the cell phone.

"Uh-huh. No, she's alright. I told you I have been keeping a close watch on her."

Fisher Sutherland knew this moment was coming. He felt more lucid and alive than he had for ages. The end was near, he knew it. Stevie Anderson and Randolph Thorne were near, he knew that too. He stood alone in the woods, almost consumed by the towering trees, an insignificant, magnificent monster. Fisher opened his mouth and screamed. The roar that raged from his throat echoed for miles.

Susan Dark knew her moment was coming. She feigned stupefaction, afraid to move until the time was right. The bigger fear though was slumped over the body next to her. Grant Frolan had fallen into a post sexual slumber. His release bringing a natural narcosis induced by endorphin release. Susan wiggled her toes and allowed her fingers to flex a little. The prospect of regaining her sense of feeling was intoxicating. She wanted to be close to her mother, to hear her mother singing another lullaby but all she could hear was screaming. The noise woke Grant Frolan. He shifted his weight from the decapitated corpse and struggled with his consciousness as his mind made the short hop from sleeping to being as lucid as he could manage. He could not be described as a complex man by any stretch of the imagination, but Grant Frolan had his secrets. Traumatised through a mind-crushing induction to fundamental Christianity, regular beatings and undiagnosed autism, Frolan's imagination and intellect were underdeveloped. His existence operated on a very base level, eat, drink, masturbate, shit and read the Bible though not always in that order and at other times all at once. Now at least he could add two other skills to his résumé, drug abuse and fornication, though he did wonder if it counted if he did it with the corpse of his father.

The night would not let go. Darkness refused to relinquish its grip and would not do so for at least another six hours. Georgina looked out of the window of the diner at the near empty parking lot. She was waiting. It was the sort of night where everyone seemed to be waiting. Leroy drank from his fifth cup of coffee that evening. Sleep was not going to be an issue, it was staying awake that presented the biggest challenge. He watched Georgina, wondering what she was withholding from him. She had not been the same since her encounter with Fisher Sutherland in the motel room in Texas and he had to be honest with himself, he did not think the same of her. His attitude to her had changed. His heart ached. Leroy realized that somewhere in this mad dark and violent world, he had fallen in love with her. Georgina remained seated at her table. A singular island adrift from the mainland, distanced and remote. She looked lost but the fact was she was slowly finding herself. The person who lived inside her head for the past few months had moved on. Georgina realized that her focus had returned. She recognized the car pulling into the parking lot.

The tires crunched on the broken asphalt surface. When Wynan O'Neil answered the phone in the middle of the night he was not surprised to receive the call from his daughter. He had been waiting for it. Wynan checked his appearance in the rear view mirror before exiting the car. It was not a long drive. Less than an hour on the road. He placed three phone calls before he left his pregnant wife alone in the bed. The first call was to the forensic team at Quantico. He was told a mobile unit would be chasing his taillights all the way to the diner. The second call logged him in to the FBI mainframe that linked Wynan to the resources and facilities of the entire network computer system. Before making the third call, Wynan packed his lightweight notebook computer in his briefcase. The computer weighed just under one kilogram and was able to connect completely securely to the network from any location in the US. Wynan O'Neil placed the computer on the passenger seat of his Saab and made the third call from his cell phone. He looked out into the dark night with a sense of excitement. He looked forward to working with his daughter again. His Georgie. Wynan scrolled through the numbers on his phone, stopping at L. He called Leroy LaPortiere before firing the ignition of the car and driving to the diner.

Leroy knew he had to work quickly. It would only be a matter of minutes before the FBI arrived. He hoped Wynan O'Neil would get there ahead of them and was relieved to see the Saab pulling up in the parking lot. Georgina sat at the table scrolling through the images on the LCD on the back of the camera. Every now and then she would stop and study an image or just stare out into space. The sight of her father leaving the confines of his car snapped Georgina's focus into sharp clarity. A parade of vehicles followed. Three SUV's with blacked out windows, each vehicle killed its headlamps before they had parked. Wynan walked to the first vehicle. Georgina watched the darkened window glide down as her father spoke with the driver. Soon he was leading a team of ten men and women toward the diner. Georgina stood and awaited her father's entrance. There were three more visitors heading down the highway who would join Leroy, Georgina, Wynan and the FBI forensic team before the next hour passed.

Wynan stopped just before the entrance to the diner. He had always taken pride in his ability to disassociate his personal feelings from his work, even when working with his daughter. Tonight though he felt different. There was a tangible bond, which he could already feel even though he was separated from Georgina by a solid door and seventeen feet of space.

Highways can sometimes be long, lonely cold places, even in the midst of a summer's day when you are alone, but on a dark night with nothing but the radio for company, on a drive through six states, it is hard to believe that you are not the only person left alive on the planet. Sheriff Mary T Rankin looked at the clock on her dashboard, it had been one hour and fifteen minutes since she had seen a car in either direction; maybe everyone was dead. She knew this could not of course be the case, her empathic senses would have been screaming. The fact was though that her empathic senses were screaming. Her heightened sensitivity drove her on, heading northwest. She knew she was getting closer.

The world seemed to stop. Fisher Sutherland looked at the writhing body of the imbecilic creature that was Grant Frolan.

"You know, we never really appreciate the moments we are truly happy. Just stop and take a deep breath and say 'I'm fuckin' happy and I know things can't get much better than this.' Strange though, we always mark the moment when we are sad, unhappy or depressed. Are you happy?"

There was no answer. But then again Grant Frolan would have had difficulty talking with his larynx protruding from the gaping wound in his throat.

"I'm fuckin' happy." Fisher looked at his hands, they looked unusually dark under the silvery glow of the moonlight. Grant Frolan's legs twitched uncontrollably, performing a perverse dance that brought a smile of amusement to Sutherland's lips.

"Yeah, I'm happy." Fisher wiped the fresh blood from the serrated blade against the flap of his jacket. A little more blood really wasn't going to make a difference. He crouched down by the twitching body of Grant Frolan.

"Here's a little philosophical puzzler for you." Fisher pulled Frolan's chubby fingers back one by one until they relinquished the grip on the Bible he carried everywhere with him. "Don't struggle now." Fisher pulled the book away from its owner. He smacked Grant Frolan hard across the face with the book, so hard that the sound echoed in the empty environment. "C'mon now Grant, keep focused. These are the important questions in life."

Frolan's face rocked to the left under the heavy impact of the Bible. As Frolan's head moved the last gasp of air rattled through the exposed larynx.

"So, where is your God now?" Sutherland said.

John Keller leaned across the small expanse inside the car and gently rocked Barbara Dace's shoulder. "We're here."

Dace opened her eyes. "I was hoping it would be morning and I would be lying in my bed or even better in Norman's."

"Is a diner's parking lot on the outskirts of DC the next best thing?"

"It doesn't come close." Barbara opened the door of the car. "Looks like we got company." She nodded toward the troop of CSI's entering the diner.

"Lab coats," Keller said.

"Good, looks like we have a crime scene. Grab your camera, John."

The short walk to the diner gave Barbara little time to think about what was happening inside the eatery. John Keller carried two bags, one with the camera and one with his portable light setup. Barbara waited at the door holding it open with her foot. She stopped John at the door before they entered.

"John, am I selfish?"

"Where the hell did that come from?"

"No, but am I? I mean how long have we worked together ... ten years?"

"Thirteen. And the answer to your question is *focused*. Although most people who don't know you think you're a selfish bitch." Keller smiled and stepped past the reporter.

Barbara nodded knowingly as she digested Keller's comments. "Focused, eh ... Hey?" She caught up with him as the room ahead unfurled before them. "Are all of your observations photographic similes?"

The room was a hive of activity. White-suited people consumed the area, moving with the efficiency of worker bees.

There was no hug; this was work. Georgina knew the boundaries. She had tried to breech them on other occasions only to be met by cold indifference. The pain of that public rejection was enough to experience once in her life, Georgina's stubbornness meant that she had to go through the procedure three times, each time the rejection was followed by a private lecture on why Wynan O'Neil, her father, retained professional distance whenever their paths crossed in the field. She allowed a smile of recognition and hoped the transference of warmth might be reciprocated. It wasn't.

"Agent O'Neil." Wynan nodded to Georgina. They were standing less than three feet from each other. Father and daughter.

"I'm a civilian at the moment, Pops." Georgina chanced her arm at expressing familiarly.

Wynan held his hand out. At first Georgina thought he was offering his hand to shake then she noticed the familiar leather wallet in his grasp. "Agent O'Neil, I would recommend addressing me as Director O'Neil while you are on duty."

Wynan allowed the briefest flicker of a smile as he handed Georgina back her badge. He turned and took a small bag from a white-suited technician. "Your weapon and holster with loaded clip and spare clip, plus cell phone, fully charged."

Georgina took the bag. Leroy made his way across the room to greet Director Wynan O'Neil.

"Hey, you got game," Leroy said noticing Georgina studying her FBI identity card.

"I always had game, Leroy. It's just that now I am back in the game."

"So, what we got here?" Director Wynan O'Neil asked.

"We got a hell of a lot of blood." Leroy pointed to the table.

"I can see."

"And a dead body in the bag," Georgina added.

"I daren't even think." Wynan walked to the drawstring bag sitting on the table. The smell of corrupt flesh reached his nostrils as he approached the table. Leroy followed.

"Our resident lunatic has left us with a souvenir of his work."

Wynan leaned forward and peered into the open bag. He caught sight of the bloodied, matted straggly hair on the decapitated head.

"How original."

"We've only taken samples of blood from around the table and what permeated through the bag," Georgina said.

Wynan beckoned a white-suited CSI and asked for a pair of long latex gloves. He took off his jacket and slowly rolled up the sleeves of his crisp white shirt. The gloves were not standard issue. Specially imported from Scandinavia, the latex gloves arrived hermetically sealed in a transparent plastic bag. He tore open the bag and reached inside retrieving the prophylactics. The gloves snugly ran the entire length of Wynan's arm to elbow joint. He took a deep breath before plunging his hands into the drawstring bag. Wynan could feel the icy touch of death as his fingers embraced the cold stiffened flesh of the severed head. The weight of a human head always surprised Wynan. Eight pounds of human hub. The entire source of being, of existence, in his hands. Wynan held the very soul of Gil Frolan. He held the head toward the light unaware that John Keller was filming him from across the room. Georgina stepped closer, compelled by the gruesome sight in her father's hands.

"Jesus, that's Gil Frolan." The close up facility on John Keller's camera made picking out the distinguishing details of the head in the FBI man's hands.

"I always remember him as taller," Barbara quipped.

Barbara Dace moved forward passing though the small team of forensic technicians. Keller followed until a human wall stepped in front of him in the shape of Leroy LaPortiere.

"John, you know you can't use any of this."

Keller lowered the camera.

"This is not the reason I called you guys here."

"This place is like a circus, Agent O'Neil. We can't have the media in here." Wynan said lowering the decapitated head onto a large white paper towel covering one of the tables to his left.

"Special dispensation, da … Director O'Neil." Georgina corrected herself. "Nothing goes out until the case is solved."

"It's been nearly fifty years in the making, we could all be dead before then." Wynan did not show any hint of sarcasm.

"Actually, I think we're on the home strait," Leroy said.

"I just love those cop hunches." This time Wynan made no attempt to hide his sarcasm.

Leroy took it in good nature. He had played second fiddle to the feds before. Just because Wynan was Georgina's father didn't alter the relationship between the professions. Georgina had her badge once more. Leroy wondered how it altered her perspective. Wynan held Georgina's gaze for a long second. He leaned forward and moved close to her ear. The hot expelled breath from his lungs teasing the micro thin downy hairs on his daughter's ear.

"Just get rid of them."

Georgina knew there was not going to be another chance to fight her cause. She walked toward the cameraman and journalist.

"They may prove useful," Leroy said.

Wynan shot Leroy an icy stare of disdain and turned his attention back to the severed head on the desk. He picked the drawstring bag up and put his hand inside once more, very slowly searching, fishing through the dark congealing blood. He pulled his hand out and placed a small sealed plastic bag filled with blood on to the table, next to the head. This he did twice more before placing the bag down. On each occasion his hand returned holding a similar bag. Three small bags of blood, no bigger than a squash ball.

"It's in the blood."

"What is?" Wynan looked up at Leroy.

"It's something Fisher Sutherland said. It's in the blood."

Wynan called out to one of his white-suited yes-men. "Take everything back to the lab. I want blood work results in an hour."

"Blood work on what?" the suit said.

"Everything. And I want it cross-referenced against every known database. Start DNA testing. I know it's going to take longer, but this is our number one priority. Who is our best serologist?"

The white suit thought for a second. "Sam Walker."

"Is he here?"

"He's a she, and no, she'll be at home." The white suit looked at his watch. "I'd guess in bed."

"Not anymore. Call her, get her in. She's on constant duty until we get results. Tell her I said so."

The white suit scuttled away reaching for his cell phone.

"Mr. LaPortiere, you have no jurisdiction here. I cannot condone any involvement you have on the case, but I also know that you are a skilled detective and undoubtedly have garnered a great deal of useful information. I know that if I have you removed my daughter will make my life hell, and I appreciate what you have done here, but don't for one moment confuse my acquiescence with acceptance." Wynan handed Leroy a card from his pocket. "On certain occasions ... rare occasions, it is necessary to recruit members of the public into temporary duty, sometimes as a consultant and sometimes something a little more. This is one of those times. This pass will give you the same access afforded to Georgina. Welcome to the FBI, Mr. LaPortiere."

Leroy took the card and looked at it. His picture had been printed on the plastic laminated card, along with an agency number.

"Now, get the fuck out of my face while the lab boys do their work. Don't worry Mr. LaPortiere, when I need you I will call." Wynan turned his attention briefly to his daughter and she thought that she saw the slightest hint of a smile before resuming his study of the severed head of Gil Frolan.

John Keller filmed Georgina approaching. She walked slowly with an air of resigned hesitation. Keller knew enough about body language to realize that privileges were about to be suspended, at least for the time being. Barbara Dace was sitting at a table and writing notes on a heavily used A5 pad.

"What d'you have to do around here to get a coffee? The service is terrible." Barbara lit up a cigarette.

Georgina sat next to her. "No more filming in here."

"No problem." Dace did not have to tell John Keller. He was already packing away his camera. He had enough footage in the bag.

"And nothing in here to be aired, not for a few days anyway."

"You're bustin' my balls, O'Neil," Dace said, playing the hoary old hack to perfection.

"I would say you don't have them, but then again, I'm not so sure." Georgina touched Barbara's arm. It was a genuine show of respect and affection.

Barbara passed the lit cigarette to her cameraman and lit herself another. "Looks like country music has got its dark side, after all."

"Always had. There's enough tragedy here to write a double album."

Barbara nodded toward the decapitated head that Georgina's father was studying. "Gil Frolan."

"Yep."

"He produced three generations of Darks."

"Yep."

"So you don't think a music critic is responsible." Barbara allowed a devilish little smile to creep onto her lips.

"Try not to get into my father's face Barbara, and for God's sake be discreet." Georgina showed Barbara her newly restored badge to emphasize the point. "Hour by hour the rules are changing."

Leroy appeared at the table and tapped Georgina on the shoulder. "Your father wants you."

"Don't piss my father off and you get to keep your scoop." Georgina stood and walked back with Leroy toward the window and her father. "So, you an' my old man getting on?" She said to Leroy.

"Yeah, you could say that we've been bonding."

"What you talking about?"

Leroy flashed the plastic FBI temporary ID card. "I'm a paid up Fed now. Genuine G-Man."

Georgina knew why her father had taken this unusual step, though to be fair to Leroy he was a damn fine detective and a benefit to any homicide or kidnapping case.

The blood dripped slowly now. The relative heat of the restaurant was eating what little oxygen remained in the sticky scarlet substance turning it to an oxidized brown color. Drip … drip … drip. The gathering pool below the severed head collected and grouped unenthusiastically like a group of volunteer sewerage inspectors on a wet Saturday afternoon. Georgina looked closely at the ragged flesh where the neck used to connect with the rest of Gil Frolan's body.

"You see these marks?" Georgina used the tip of her pen, pressing against the torn skin. "Whilst this looks like the head had been hacked off in a random fashion, there is a repetitive nature to the incisions. This indicates that a blade…" Georgina stopped for a moment and made a quick measurement using her pen as a rule "… approximately, five to six inches was used. The strength to have carried out such an act using such a relatively small knife would have been great. The way the skin is cut also indicates that perhaps a hunting knife was used. You know the sort that has a hook end. I think they are used for gutting prey. Also, the head was severed post mortem." Georgina placed the head back on the table. "Phew it's heavy. A man's wisdom is not gauged by the weight of his brain, nor the years he has walked the earth."

"So say Confucius?"

"No, so say me. This dumb son of a bitch lived to what … seventy something? And he ends up having his head cut off by some knife wielding maniac with something to prove."

"We all have something to prove," Leroy said. He tried consciously not to look at Georgina's father, but she caught his eyes briefly flicker in Wynan O'Neil's direction.

Sheriff Mary T Rankin stopped at the crossroads. It was the darkest place on earth. There was no light anywhere apart from the beam from her headlamps. If she turned those out she would disappear. Mary closed her eyes and waited for a sign. A message from somewhere telling her whether to turn right, left or continue on a straight path. Her cell phone rang. It was the sign she had been waiting for.

"Mary T," she answered. The sheriff spoke first. "Which way, now, Georgina?"

The tiny hairs on the back of Georgina's neck stood to attention.

"I'm not even going to ask," Georgina said. "If you are so good you won't need my help."

"Oh, I'll find him. It's just that I want to be of help to you and Leroy. My parlor tricks impress, but often they are not as efficient as a GPS system or directions from a colleague."

"I'll tell you where we are, but you are way out of your jurisdiction."

"Consultancy only … not hands-on, I promise."

"I've no idea why the hell I even rang you."

"Because I wanted you too. Georgina, I can see where this son of a bitch is. He's surrounded by trees and he is in a very dark place right now. I can lead you to him if you get me within a couple of miles of this rat bastard. Right to his front door."

Georgina didn't know what compelled her to ring Sheriff Mary T Rankin when she did. A notion, a gut feeling. Maybe it was the slow pounding in her head, which was returning. Georgina knew one thing to be true though, the sheriff had helped Georgina twice before. Once to relieve the pain inside her and once to track the man she was now chasing. Mary T had the scent of the man in her nostrils, how either the sheriff or Georgina chose to interpret those skills was an individual and personal choice.

"Where are you now?"

"Fifteen miles south of DC heading north. The I-95 is about …" The sheriff looked down at the map on the passenger seat. "… three miles from here."

Georgina was impressed. Rankin was close. Very close.

"I'm at a junction close to joining the Interstate if I take the next left."

"Which exit route?"

"Close to the 619 turnpike and Prince William Forest Park."

"Jeez, Louise, you're close." Georgina felt an involuntary shudder pass through her body. A mini seismic wave.

The sheriff sitting in the car at the crossroads also felt the sensation, though she was more attuned to what it was. "Did you feel that, Georgina?"

Georgina didn't answer. The sheriff's voice came through the earpiece of her cell phone. Plugging directly to the neuro-receptors in Georgina's brain.

"I know you felt that. It's the world shifting. Only a few of us can feel it. It happens at times of great importance. Not always world importance. These things can be portents. You have to trust me and believe that something is happening that is shifting the balance of our world. Yours and mine." Rankin's voice trailed off.

"There's a diner on the I-95. Glitzy Americana, called Monroe's." Georgina felt her body tremble from the feet up. The dull pain was probing inside her head once more. She closed her cell phone and whispered. "Not now."

Susan hoped upon hope that it would be the fat slovenly retard that would serve dinner and not the rakish but powerful man with the dull but mad looking eyes. She shook her head, what a choice. The mere fact that she could shake her head though filled her with confidence. The retard had forgotten to top up the immobilizing drug cocktail, which she was being fed. The room was quiet now that Grant Frolan was gone. The pungent smell of his body sweat was slowly dissipating or maybe it was just being overpowered by the new odor of corruption from the rotting carcass a little more than ten feet away. Susan dared not to look, but occasionally she felt overpowered by curiosity and she stared at the headless body of the old, naked man sprawled on her mother's bed. Everything was so surreal. The sheer madness of it, made Susan believe that she may be losing her mind. What was real? What wasn't? Was the dead man a figment of her mind corrupted? The stench of decomposition confirmed her sanity. Yet Susan took no pleasure in knowing she had not lost her mind, in many ways that would have been the lesser of two evils. Susan started to sing in the vain hope of transporting her mind to a more pleasant place. Her voice whisper quiet and trembling with fatigue and fear of being caught.

*Sweet little child, sweet little child*
*You know that your mammy is watching*
*You smile*
*My little angel with black eyes*
*Your mammy is watching you cry.*

# Chapter 29 Into the Darkness

Tuesday May 20, 2003

Stevie Anderson kept looking at the cell phone in the holder on the dash. Waiting for the LCD screen to silently scream notice of an incoming call only added to the anxiety he had been feeling. The envelope that caused him to crash had filled him with a sense of unease, which even now Stevie Anderson could not shift. He switched CD's on the multi-changer. Somewhere in the trunk of the car mechanical grabs worked silently, efficiently changing the disks. A second later Giacomo Puccini's *Madame Butterfly* filled the confines of his rental. Trees lined the road, closing in on either side, adding to the sense of impending danger. Anderson's senses were on hyper alert. The prescribed drugs in his system to regulate his heartbeat worked hard to keep the rhythm regular and constant. Though the air-conditioning was on full blast and the clock on the dash read a little after 10:00 p.m, Stevie Anderson wiped a rolling trickle of sweat away from his brow. The darkness continued for mile after mile, with the only relief from the opaque landscape coming from the white light of the rental's headlamps. Anderson felt a raw compulsion to keep driving south. He was driven by an acute instinct, but knew that it was only at the end of the cell phone that he would find any true answers. The colored screen lit a fraction of a second before the ring tone announced the incoming call. The phone diverted through the Bluetooth headset sitting in Stevie Anderson's left ear. Anderson's speed momentarily dropped as he waited for the caller to speak.

"How long have I been asleep?"

Georgina didn't look at her watch. "Thirty minutes."

"Sorry."

"It was a good use of time." Georgina smiled briefly at Leroy, before retuning her gaze outside the window of the diner.

Activity had dropped to a minimum, now only a small team of working forensics remained in the restaurant. Wynan O'Neil headed that team. He concentrated his efforts at the table where Fisher Sutherland had met Georgina and Leroy earlier in the evening, but he seemed to be working solely through his cell phone. Making his way from the table, Wynan strolled with purpose toward Georgina and Leroy who were sitting a couple of tables away. Georgina looked up, briefly at the man who was her father, then at the man who wore the detached demeanor of a director of the FBI.

"Our boy's on the move," Wynan said. "He just used his cell phone. The signal places him about thirty miles from here."

"Any news from the lab yet?" Georgina asked.

Wynan shook his head. "Nothing yet."

"This cell phone signal," Leroy asked "how are you tracking that?"

"We know the number of his cell phone from your encounter with Sutherland at the motel, and can track him to the nearest half mile radius by monitoring the signal it omits every time he connects. Nearly as good as GPS and a total infringement on civil rights, therefore we use it all the time. It's how the CIA manages to track down Al-Qaeda and various Iraqi generals who have escaped *justice*."

Leroy instinctively held the cell phone that was in his jacket pocket.

"Each time it is tuned on it sends a unique signal to a transmitter/receiver," Wynan continued. "We know for a fact that Sutherland's phone is now thirty miles due southeast from here. We can grid it up, but basically he's heading out toward Black Lake Memorial Park. We also know that he has contacted three other cell phones. Phone companies are very cooperative with information in cases such as these. We know for instance that he has contacted an unregistered cell phone, probably a pay as you call credit phone. He has also called Stevie Anderson on his cell phone." Wynan watched Leroy's face for a reaction. "Of course you know Mr. Anderson, and he has also called your friends the mobile roving reporters."

Georgina's eyes peered through the darkness outside the diner window to the parking lot and noticed Barbara Dace's car had gone.

Leroy's cell phone vibrated in his hand. The silent alert told him of an incoming call. Wynan held his finger to the small earpiece plugged discreetly inside his ear and listened intently for a couple of seconds before speaking. "Oh, and the unregistered cell phone … I'd answer it before Fisher Sutherland hangs up."

Leroy pulled the small Nokia handset out and gave it to Wynan O'Neil's daughter.

There had been no movement inside the house for over an hour. The paralyzing fear Susan felt most of the time was only equal to the immobility that kept her restrained without the need for shackles. A feeling of warmth spread throughout her limbs now though, and little by little her confidence grew. She risked trying to raise her leg, slowly the limb rose from the bed under her control. Her heart pounded with anxiety and excitement. The stench of corruption in the room was unbearable and with the return of sensation in her limbs came the stupefying realization that all of her senses had been heightened. Susan placed a shaky foot on the ground, unsure whether gravity would play any cruel tricks on her. She swung her other leg around and shifted her weight to test whether they would bear the load. Susan didn't know whether it was the adrenaline kicking in, but she surprised herself by standing with ease. Slowly she shuffled toward the door, one small step at a time. She would not win any friends if it were a runway show for a fashion house, but there was no one to impress save for the headless body of Gil Frolan and he was past caring. Another step on the wooden floor and she was almost within reach of the door. The excitement and the adrenaline now turned to light-headed wooziness and for a brief moment Susan thought she was about to pass out. She stopped and composed herself, drawing in a large lungful of air. That experience alone nearly made her retch, as the air was quite fetid. The light in the room dipping caught Susan's attention. At first she thought it was her senses battling with the stress, but with the dip came a reduction in sound from outside the building, and Susan was aware for the first time of the constant drone of a generator. With the door handle just a solitary step away the power cut and Susan was plunged into total darkness.

Leroy was glad to be outside the stifling confines of the diner; though the air was heavy it beat the enclosing atmosphere of death inside. Georgina stood next to him feeling equally relieved.

"Phew, must be eighty still." The air clung to Georgina's body like a wet blanket. The parking lot was virtually empty, though it was hard to see the dark recesses where the reduced street lighting didn't reach.

"Summer ain't gonna end fast." Leroy wiped his face with a paper napkin, lifted from one of the diner's tables as he left. "Radio says it's gonna reach a hundred and twelve tomorrow."

A set of car headlamps lit the entrance to the parking lot. Georgina and Leroy followed it in. Leroy's hand instinctively hovered over the handle of his revolver, self-preservation being an instinct that was usually on high alert most times with the detective. Georgina tried to peer through the harsh glare.

"Visitors?" Leroy said.

"Sheriff Rankin," Georgina replied.

She tried to blink away the burning white spots indelibly burned on her corneas from Rankin's car.

Leroy felt the tension ease from his arm as he released the grip on the handle of his pistol. He watched the sheriff park the car. Georgina grabbed hold of his arm and he escorted her to the vehicle.

His eyes adjusted to the dark as quickly as many of the night creatures in the forest. Fisher Sutherland was a hunter though; a prowler watching his quarry.

Susan Dark stumbled forward, hands outstretched, still blind by the sudden shock of darkness. Fascinated, Sutherland studied the singer, knowing that soon the answers would be known and with it the freedom and recognition he had longed for, for so long. Susan moved forward, barely perceptibly in the dark. She reached out and touched nothing but black empty space, it was as though someone had stolen the universe and she was in a dream, some part of a strange experiment. Fisher watched.

# Chapter 30 A Trip into the Dark Country

Tuesday 20 May

The night was darker than usual, the car headlights seemingly unable to penetrate the opacity that was closing in around the car. Stevie Anderson felt the tightness across his chest once more. He slowed the car down and looked for a suitable place to park. Trees lined the road for what appeared to be endless miles adding to the omnipresent oppressiveness of the night. There was no reflection from the headlights of following vehicles in his rear view, so Anderson applied a little extra pressure to the brake pedal and brought the car to a halt. A bead of sweat confirmed both the closeness of the night and his elevated body temperature. Anderson wiped the sweat away using the cuff of his Armani shirt. He looked at the interior temperature and noted that the air conditioner was working at a reasonable fifty-four fahrenheit. Pressing an inset button on the armrest the side window gently lowered accompanied by an efficient electrical whir. Anderson pressed the button on his radio/CD player and muted the sound of Puccini's *Madame Butterfly*. Pure silence greeted him. He opened the refrigerated glove box and took a bottle of lemon-flavored water out. Twisting the cap there was a satisfying fizz, which only served to heighten Anderson's thirst. He reached behind to find his jacket hanging on the hook inset in the handgrip above the passenger door and fumbled blindly through his pockets until his fingers gripped a small box of aspirin. The tightness in his chest remained constant. Anderson knew it was elevated stress and ipso facto, angina, but he was less than surprised that his past was coming back to haunt him. He popped an aspirin under his tongue and hoped it would work a little magic. His phone rang. Anderson pressed the switch on the steering wheel and waited for the caller to identify himself through the car's speakers before answering. But there was no talking voice just the sound of Caroline Dark singing. Anderson had been present at every single recording ever made of the Dark trinity and knew this was a new song, one he had never heard her sing. One that by rights she should not even know. The song "Love is a Mystery" was one of the new tracks on Susan Dark's CD. The hairs on the back of Anderson's neck rose and his heart danced an arrhythmia of confusion. The line went dead bringing nothing but an uncomfortable silence. Stevie Anderson looked at the screen of his cell phone in the hope of seeing a number he would recognize, but there was just a string of random numbers that told him it was a cell phone. A text message arrived. Anderson reached forward and grabbed the phone. He opened the message.

"Wanna find me ..."

As he was reading the message his phone bleeped again, another message. Anderson scrolled through until he found the new message and opened it. This time they were map coordinates. And a simple note, "Can't wait for this family reunion."

Anderson switched on his GPS navigation system and punched the map coordinates in. He waited while the computer searched for first his location and secondly for the final destination. Anderson knew it would be hell.

He sat for a while looking at the digital map. Stevie Anderson knew the actual journey would not be so easy. His heart began to regulate and Anderson noticed he no longer felt so hot. He started the ignition of the car, quickly looked in the rear view and pulled away. He knew the destination and knew it well. He didn't need the guidance of the robotic tour guide but the detached female voice of the GPS informed him to continue driving for eight point two miles.

Barbara Dace and John Keller watched the meeting of the sheriff, O'Neil and LaPortiere from the comfort of darkness and with more than a little curiosity. She wondered what the Texan sheriff, a Missouri ex-police detective and a nomadic east coast FBI agent were going to do next and was a little surprised to see the trio head toward a black SUV.

"Get ready, John," Dace said. "Looks like it's show time."

Keller adjusted his slouched position behind the driver's seat and stretched out, straightening his arms and locking his fingers together in an embrace that shifted the weary gremlins from within. He watched the red taillights of the black SUV glow with life.

Barbara Dace shifted position in the seat slightly. Her collar bone still throbbed slightly and the restriction of the sling did little to ease the pain. "They'll know we're following, so you don't have to worry about being seen." Dace looked out of the side window at the eternal blackness and said, "Where are we going on this dark night?" Her voice was almost a whisper.

"That sheriff gives me the heebie-jeebies," Keller said. He felt icy fingers play a minuet on his spine.

"Tell me about it." Dace stared ahead at the taillights of the SUV. "Don't let them get away now."

"On it." Keller shifted gear and pressed down on the gas pedal.

The car followed at a discreet distance. Nothing too obtrusive. This was how Dace and Keller were going to have to play it now. John Keller leaned forward slightly in his seat and depressed the cigarette lighter. Though partially immobile from her broken collar bone, Dace had partnered Keller long enough to have a couple of cigarettes waiting.

"So, what do you think that whole gruesome episode was about in the diner?"

"Gil Frolan … man," Keller said exasperated or maybe it was just the fact that he was exhaling a plume of smoke. "I mean I don't like country, but he was like the Colonel Tom Parker of the industry."

"Frolan's head," he continued. "Damn shame we can't use it."

"Not even with pixilation," Dace sighed. "You *don't* like country? How can you not like country?"

Keller shrugged his shoulders. "I don't like apple pie either."

Barbara laughed. "You're a freak."

Three hundred feet away the red taillights grew dimmer in the blackness. Keller pressed down on the gas pedal once more to rein in the distance. It was as though he was fishing and had a line caught on a giant marlin, but this marlin was a black SUV. Slowly Keller reeled in the distance, determined not to let his fish get away. Keller sucked hard on the cigarette between his lips; concentration was etched on his face.

Dace watched the road ahead with equal concentration. Both Dace and Keller equally oblivious to to the vehicle trailing behind them. The road stretched ahead for miles in the enveloping night, any turns or gradients seemingly lost in the darkness and the gentle undulation of the landscape. The trees the only changing variables in the unrelenting bleakness and sterility. Add light, and a sunny day and the drive would be breathtaking, but here in the consuming muggy heat and the dark it was a thousand miles away from happiness. Dace could feel a tangible sense of foreboding. She had a sixth sense that this night would see a climax to events in Washington.

Georgina's ring tone on her cell phone was "Precious" by Depeché Mode. Her eclectic music taste no longer a surprise to Leroy. Georgina pressed "answer" before Dave Gahn began his vocal. Her voice was quiet, almost respectful of the night.

"O'Neil."

The phone signal struggled with the isolation of the countryside. Trees neither making good conductors nor springboards for telephone communications. It was Georgina's father, Wynan O'Neil.

"Georgie." Wynan for once allowing himself to be father, mentor and superior. "Preliminary tests have come back from the lab on the blood work taken from the diner.

"That's quick."

"These results are very basic tests, but good enough to make some assumptions ..." Georgina's father's voice crackled and fought to retain hold of the air stream carrying the signal to her ear.

Leroy continued to drive but with his mind now engaged on the conversation next to him.

"... thirteen alleles in common ..."

Georgina pressed the phone closer to her head as she struggled to capture her father's words against the ambient noise of the vehicle cruising through the DC country.

"... definitely relat ..."

"You're breaking up," Georgina said. "Repeat." The signal dropped. "Damn." Georgina stared at the handset in the hope that it would show signs of life. The signal strength icon was blank.

"There's nothing but the sound of lost souls out here in the ether." Sheriff Rankin leaned forward.

"Well, if you can get one to call direct to my father I'd appreciate it," Georgina said. She wasn't being curt, but had a genuine hope in her voice that Rankin not only recognized but had heard before.

"I'll see what I can do."

Leroy shot Georgina a glance which didn't need explaining and he fought with all of his will power to stop following through with a hand gesture indicating in no uncertain terms that he thought Rankin was cuckoo.

Rankin was all too aware of skepticism. She was after all still a law enforcement officer at heart.

The black night drifted past with no sense of ending. Leroy looked at the clock in the dashboard. It was fifteen minutes from midnight. Time was almost going backwards. Two vehicles behind their black SUV remained at a discreet distance, unseen and unheard.

She moved forward. Her perception of distance skewed. Her senses numbed but no longer shackled by the chains of drugs. Someone *was* in the room with her in the dark, but now she was alone. She was sure of that. Susan Dark felt the walls for a light switch and then flailed her arms in a swooping motion hoping to hit a cord attached to a switch, and then as if by magic the room became illuminated. The bright flashing, harsh flickering, fluorescent tube above her head danced in a series of epileptic movements, each of which would expose a new vision of horror in the room. Her instinct for survival was kicking in now and amazingly she felt a surge of energy coursing through her body. Adrenaline began to engage with the receptors in her brain. Clarity of thought began to communicate with the motor skills that had lain dormant for she didn't know how long. Her overriding thought now was on her freedom. Susan began to think a little more clinically and this helped her focus on the carnage in the room. One body was hanging from a cross beam. Lynched through the arms with a chain from a pulley mechanism used for winching car engines from the bodies of vehicles. The corpse was wearing dungarees and would not have looked out of place in a garage workshop, but for the one shortcoming of being decapitated. The second body, again headless, lying half-naked over a gurney close to the bed she had spent so long incarcerated on in a drugged oblivion. This was the body of a thinner man. She looked around the room for the door. Her vision settled on the handle of the door. Was it too much to ask for that it would be open?

Fisher Sutherland no longer cared. All the days of his life had come to this one night in the country. Soon everybody would know why he acted as he had, why he had done the terrible things, and he knew people would understand. He sat on the wooden porch in the chair once occupied by Gil Frolan and rocked gently back and forth waiting for the party to begin. His guests would all arrive in due course and then of course the fun would begin, but for now he enjoyed the solitude knowing full well that this was the calm before the storm. He felt devoid of any tangible emotion though a sense of expectation dwelt somewhere in the recesses of what was human in him. Briefly, Fisher pondered on the fact that retribution and revenge may not bring the satisfaction he craved as he realized that this notion was of course mad. Fisher breathed in the hot country air knowing that animals could smell the scent of blood that lingered on him. He envied that heightened sense and breathed a little deeper. The blood was his sense of triumph. For Fisher this was like the coming sunrise. Victory was inevitable no matter what the outcome. He purposely left the doors unlocked and no longer cared that Susan Dark was slowly making her break for freedom. In time people would come to see that he was the real hero, even Susan.

Stevie Anderson was ahead of the trailing pack by ten minutes. He knew he had to finish what had been started nearly fifty years ago. He picked up his cell phone and scrolled through the received numbers. His eyes darted from the road to the illuminated display and back again. Not that it mattered, the only thing he would possibly hit would be a deer with insomnia or a buck rabbit blinded in the beam of his headlamps. Anderson could have taken both hands off the wheel and jumped in the back seat and had a sleep for the past half hour and not needed to shift the wheel an inch either way.

The tightness across his chest left him feeling drained and the notion of closing his eyes for a minute seemed comforting. He found the number he was looking for and dialed. Anderson slowed the car and took a sharp left off the main road onto a dirt trail. The car scraped through bushes and trailing branches from the overhanging trees. The cell phone connected with a digital hook-up. Anderson knew he had to be quick, the cell phone signal would drop within a mile. His speed now less than fifteen miles an hour due to the rough nature of the terrain and his overriding need to make one final call.

"Angel, it's me."

"Try your old man once more," Leroy asked Georgina. His eyes never left the road. A solid no overtaking line indicated a change in the road conditions if not the straightness. The incline on the road increased sharply and seemed to climb for miles toward the dark starry sky. The car engine protested only slightly at the rise. The surrounding trees obliged by reaching toward each other and blocking out the cloud peppered sky. Georgina pressed the redial on her cell phone.

Georgina focused on the phone and the voice of her father. She felt tired of this mad life she had chosen and wanted nothing more than to hop in the driving seat, turn the car around and head for home. Her head pounded, the thumping dull ache that she knew so well. It was the kind of pain the doctors told her to be aware of.

"Georgina, I need you to listen carefully." Wynan's voice brought distraction and comforting relief all be it for a few seconds. "The blood work came back."

"Are you still there?" Wynan's voice sounded flat in his office. It was like the night had robbed the life from his voice.

"Still here." Georgina's voice bounced back almost instantaneously.

"I was trying to tell you earlier. The bag that Fisher Sutherland brought to the diner had four different blood samples. The real surprise is that Sutherland and Thorne share the same DNA. The serologist thinks we are having our chain yanked, though that does not account for the other three bags which as yet have unidentified human blood and all seemingly related."

Georgina listened intently. Her fading optimism was taking another pounding. "Thorne is Sutherland's biological father?"

"We are still testing the blood that was sealed in the plastic bags inside the holdall and obviously cross-referencing with that of Gil Frolan. Seems that whoever done this to Frolan also done him a favor. Although we don't have his body yet, tests have proven advanced stages of cancer. Apparently, he was lucky to be alive."

"I wouldn't like to see him on an unlucky day." Georgina's gallows humor was not lost on her father who allowed himself a wry smile.

Georgina looked at Sheriff Mary T Rankin. Rankin sat upright, her eyes clear and focused. She pointed her finger ahead and said:

"Three hundred yards up the road there is a right turn. Go slowly, cos it is a dirt road, barely wide enough to get a car down."

Georgina nodded to Leroy, who immediately set the car rolling slowly toward their final destination. Georgina spoke quickly not knowing how long the reception on the phone would last. "Can you give me coordinates?" She asked Leroy.

"Don't worry we are tracking you by GPS," Wynan said. Then he added "Be careful. We have a back-up vehicle on the way with a team to assist."

"Okay. I gotta go." Georgina closed the cellular phone.

Susan Dark sat for almost twenty minutes before deciding to make a move. Fisher Sutherland spent that time sitting on the porch, seemingly without a care in the world. Occasionally he would cock his ear and tilt his head, the way a hunting dog might, if it thought it heard prey. Susan watched silently from a small opening in the door. All that stood between her and freedom was a deranged and psychotic killer sitting in a rocking chair on the porch. Fisher took the knife from the holster he had strapped to his leg and looked at the blade in the moonlight. Then he did something quite unexpected; he placed the blade against his tongue and slowly licked it clean from the dried blood on the stainless steel surface. Happy that it was clean after inspecting it once more, Fisher Sutherland slid the knife back into the holster strapped to his calf. He looked around and stared straight into the small gap in the door frame and for a moment locked eyes with Susan. Or at least she thought he did. He could not have known she was there though, but still she darted back into the darkness within the cabin. The smell of pine and birch tree used to construct the cabin was still heavy in the air and whether her senses were heightened or if it was just the result of plain fear, Susan Dark became extremely aware of all of her senses. She tentatively pressed forward to the gap once more. Fisher Sutherland was gone. Susan waited a further five minutes before daring to move again.

Fisher Sutherland knew she was there, he knew she had escaped. His job was almost finished. He bent down and picked up hunting crossbow and bolts that he found inside the cabin. He knew Gil Frolan used the weapon to kill deer and a host of other animals trying to live the quiet life in the woods. He also knew that Anderson would be arriving soon. He could hear the earthy throttle of Anderson's car and somewhere in the distance were two or maybe three trailing vehicles. Fisher knew the location of Anderson and Frolan's tree climbing stands, where they used to sit for hours stalking their prey. The padded seat platforms were anchored high up in various trees within a short vicinity of each other with rope ladders giving easy access. Fisher Sutherland had so far managed to find seven. He had already plotted out the route that Anderson would take and had relocated three of the climbing stands to ensure a clear shot and some guaranteed fun would be had before moving in for a close and personal kill. He climbed one of the short ladders and positioned himself in the seat, making sure he was comfortable and at ease with the crossbow. He took a bolt and lined up the sight. Fisher Sutherland pulled back on the string to get a feel of the weight of the crossbow and then engaged the bolt. He did not fire a shot, instead choosing to run with the thrill on a live human subject. One would be along any minute.

Barbara Dace punched in a number on her cell phone and waited for the connection.

"Who ya calling?" John Keller asked, not taking his eyes from the taillights of the car carrying Georgina O'Neil, Leroy LaPortiere and Sheriff Mary T Rankin.

"Who'd ya think?" Dace replied.

Before Keller had a chance to answer, Dace spoke again. "Randolph … Randolph Thorne? It's Barbara Dace. You wanted the heads up on Paris's killer. Well, we're close. I have to call now because I am not sure the cell will keep a signal out here."

Keller couldn't hear the media magnate's reply but his mind filled in the blanks.

"Twelve miles out of DC heading toward the Cedarville State Forest. Yep, we're heading into the forest. Yes … close to Black Lake."

Keller watched the car ahead slow and turn sharply off-road onto a dirt track. "Hold tight."

The car bounced in protest to the rough, undulating surface. Dace gripped the hand bar above her head and kept the phone glued to her ear with her free hand. "We've just turned off onto a dirt track road." She looked at the GPS display and using the touch screen navigated onto the map coordinate's page. "I'll give you the longitude and latitude for a map reading if you hold on a second … Latitude is 38.87765 and Longitude reads 77.018419."

"It's okay; I know exactly where you are." Randolph Thorne's distinctive deep voice came back to her through the cell phone.

The connection to the phone severed. Dace looked at the phone display. There was still a signal.

Thirty yards behind them a black SUV with black tinted windows followed. The headlamps on the SUV were extinguished making it impossible to be seen in Keller's rear view mirror. The driver of the SUV was driving wearing a sophisticated pair of PVS-7 night vision goggles strapped to a head mount on a military style helmet. Randolph Thorne was similarly dressed but held a 5.56mm G36K carbine submachine gun. It was evident that he did not intend hunting his prey with any real finesse.

The road, such as it was, narrowed, eventually coming to a halt one mile from the cabin. Anderson killed the engine and waited. A text message arrived on his cell phone.

"Walk 1 mile northeast ... mind your step."

Anderson grunted and began the walk to the cabin. The night air was warm with humidity high making his clothes almost instantly stick to his body. The slight temperature he still ran did not help make the trail to his destination any easier. Sweat soon began to drip from Anderson's brow. Stevie Anderson knew he would have to watch his footing; breaking a leg out here in the dark could be a matter of life and death.

She stumbled out into the night. Confused as to what had happened during the last few months of life and why it had happened. Was she the victim of some cruel hoax or was it just that fate and history had entwined in a slow dance and was doing no more than repeating the same cruel destiny that had beset her mother and her grandmother. Susan Dark thought about many things as she slowly and silently made her way through the black countryside, her sense of despair was shielded by a rush of optimism now that she was free. She stopped walking for a moment and waited by a tree. She could not escape the feeling of being watched and did not know if it was just the remnants of memory from her imprisonment. Less than fifteen feet away, Fisher Sutherland sat in his deer-hunting stand some ten feet above the ground. Fisher looked through the night sight, steadied his crossbow and aimed the arrow tip at the center of Susan Dark's head. His hand could feel the pressure of the strain on the trigger as it fought a battle with the tension. A part of him—the sadistic, psychotic part—wanted to release the bolt and let it fly silently through the dark to kill its prey, but for the moment the sane rational part of the conflict raging in his brain retained control over his motor functions and his common sense. He let Susan walk on and silently bade goodbye to her ... for now.

# Chapter 31 Family Reunion

The Teenarosa Motel, Talinha, Texas
09:03 a.m. July 26, 1958

*Jonah Fintall lay in the dust. The earth around his body reddened by the out-flowing of the vital liquid that once kept him alive. His body had finally stopped small spasmodic twitching some two and a half minutes from when the first bullet had entered his head shredding the cerebellum, before decimating the temporal lobe and searing a path through the frontal lobe. The bullet's path continued before shattering the bone of the skull at his forehead and exiting through the thinnest layer of skin. The shell itself would be found two days later and over three hundred yards away, by a deputy from Talinha County Police, who now found himself in the unfortunate position of having obtained a promotion due to the demise of Officer Mike Reynolds. But for now Jonah Fintall was sublimely ignorant of the finer details of his murder and would remain so forever more. A trail of footsteps led from the body back to the motel room containing the body of Amy Dark. The impression of a booted foot in the dusty red soil continued the trail into the room and through the small dwelling to the bathroom. Sitting in the bath was Caroline Dark aged three years and ten months. Upon seeing the man enter the room her eyes lit up. Recognition brought a smile to the small child's face.*

*"Dada?" Caroline opened up her arms to receive a hug and be welcomed into an embrace.*

*Randolph Thorne brushed the dust from the sleeves of his black cotton shirt and lifted the little girl. His arms were rock solid and for a moment it appeared as though his little girl would become lost in his hold. He swept his hair back from his eyes, using his fingers so he could look into the eyes of his little girl.*

*"Close your eyes now, Peaches," he said. His southern drawl almost sounded lazy, but to the ears of the child in his arms it was soporific.*

*Caroline Dark did as asked by her father and instantly closed her eyes as though this was all part of a huge game. The reality was though that Randolph Thorne didn't want his daughter having a memory stored that would corrupt her. Thorne held the back of*

Caroline's head burying her face in his black cotton shirt. He looked at the body of Amy Dark. The fight and the anger, the sadness and the betrayal were all gone now. All that was left was the shell of someone he used to know and love. As he walked he felt Caroline's head turn and he could see her arm reach out as she whispered.

"Mommy."

Thorne quickened his step. He felt angry that Caroline had looked at the body of her mother against his express wishes. "Mommy's sleeping, Peaches. Don't wake her." His hands covered the little girl's eyes. "Ssh."

Blowflies had begun their morning feast, searching for any entrance into Amy Dark's body. The warmth of the air had already quickened the onset of rigor mortis. The damp and the dark areas producing the best feeding and laying grounds for the flies and their eggs. The first fly, a lone female arrived a mere ten minutes after Amy had stopped breathing. It had nestled within the nasal cavity of Amy Dark and began to lay the first of over a hundred eggs. Other flies followed, some choosing the corners of her eyes as a nesting ground for their larvae.

As Thorne passed he paid no attention to the incessant buzzing or the odor of his lover's decomposing body, seven hours had passed since her last breath. He took a swipe at a fly that landed on his daughter's hair. He was upset that Caroline was present during her mother's demise. She should have been miles away with him at the time of her death. He had planned it all so differently with Stevie Anderson. He was more than upset to receive the call from Anderson informing him that he had decided to bring their plan forward by a week. The plan had now gone to hell. Stevie Anderson was now more than four states away and Randolph Thorne was as many states from a perfect alibi. The scene outside the motel room was no more fit for a child than that inside. Thorne kept his hand securely placed over the eyes of Caroline Dark and he hurried his pace as he made his way to his 1957 Buick Century. He cursed the fact that the car offered little sanctuary from the sight of carnage lying in the red soil.

"Let's play a game, honey," Thorne said. "You gotta keep your eyes closed till I tell you."

"Like hide and go seek." Caroline's voice was almost as small as she was.

"Yeah, like hide and go seek," Thorne said.

"Is Mommy gonna try and find us?"

Randolph Thorne gripped the steering wheel tightly. Dark thoughts ran through his mind.

A boy, exactly the same age as Caroline Dark, sat on the rear seat of the Buick. He had watched the whole bizarre Greek tragedy unfurl before his eyes. He had witnessed the deaths of the policeman and the fat man. The boy laughed when he saw the fat man fall. His mind unable to interpret the true consequences of the violence playing out before him, but the scene was like a magnet to his once innocent eyes. Fisher's fascination with the visceral scene would stay with him until his own last breath. They say monsters are not born they are created, if that is true Fisher at least knew the time and date he was created.

Fisher watched the little girl, who was now curled into a fetal ball on the seat next to him, enthralled by everything that was happening.

"Look after your little sister, Fisher," Randolph Thorne said.

Fisher had unquestioning faith in his father and of every word that spilled through the man's malevolent lips. If Randolph Thorne said this girl was his sister, Fisher was prepared to believe it.

The sun was high in the sky now, with the heat searing. Just the few minutes waiting in the car had started to redden Fisher's pale skin. The acceleration of the car began to cool the boy down. He enjoyed feeling the breeze rushing against his face in the open top car. His unfashionably long hair flowed in the air current. His mind raced almost as quickly as the car which was now tearing down the freeway.

Fortune's End Trailer Park, Wink Winkler
July 26, 1978

The boy becomes the man, and history has the awful habit of repeating itself. The echoes of which will keep reverberating long past this day. Fisher excelled in patience. He had lived for this day since he was a child. He had fixated on what was now a glamorized version of events twenty years ago. He was blooded, there were bodies waiting to be discovered in many states in America and there would be many more. The preparation had taken years. The Teenarosa Motel was a run-down tourist trap when he found it. Room 11 had lain dormant for twenty years since Jonah Fintall's *face impacted on the dry red soil, yet still the scent of death hung in the air. It was a smell Fisher knew well. He reveled in it. Fisher had paid the greedy son, Elijah, two hundred dollars to rent the room for three days. The motel was now a time capsule hidden in the heart of the Texan desert. Traffic had long since stopped, ever since the freeway by-passed the motel cutting its vital arterial supply of commerce. Fortunately Jonah Fintall never had to witness the slow decline of the motel. In many senses it died with him that hot day in 1958. Fisher watched dusk turn the sky blood red as the sun set fire to the landscape. He prepared the room for its guest before leaving for the drive to the Fortune's End Trailer Park and a date with his sister.*

# Chapter 32 Let's Go A-Hunting

Wednesday May 21, 2003

"It's this way." Sheriff Mary T Rankin's voice sounded breathless in the dark.

"This is mad," Georgina said to no one, but loud enough for it to be heard. They had left the car when the trail ran out over a mile back and had been stumbling blindly in the woods since. Every now and then she would stop and listen, sure that they were being followed.

"You okay?" Leroy asked.

"Think I'm getting spooked out here. You think she's tuning into the dead?"

"Man, I don't care if she's tuning into CNN, as long as we are heading in the right direction."

"But that's just it. That's the madness of this." Georgina looked up. Her vision cutting through the endless vista of darkness. "Did you see that?"

"What?" Leroy tried to follow Georgina's gaze.

"A light." Georgina pointed to a clump of trees ahead of her. "There it is again."

This time Leroy saw the dim glow of an LED light. It was hard to tell how far away the light was in the woods.

"Coincidence?"

"Yeah, like a light out here in the middle of nowhere," Georgina said.

A fluorescent glow now emanated from the undefined point in the woods.

"It's a cell phone." Rankin whispered. "Three hundred yards ahead."

Almost as soon as she had spoken the light disappeared as though engulfed by the all-consuming darkness.

"Follow me." Sheriff Rankin broke into a slow trot, which in the blackness of the woods seemed suicidal or at least the shortest route to the hospital.

"She must have the night vision of a cat," Leroy said.

Rankin didn't see the tree root, disproving Leroy almost instantly, and she vanished from view followed by a soft yelp and a hard thump.

Georgina looked at Leroy and could not help but laugh.

"You okay?" Georgina said through her now suppressed laugh.

No reply came back.

"Sheriff?" Leroy's voice was low as though he sensed an omnipresent danger.

Still no reply. Once more the LED light appeared in the near distance, followed quickly by a brighter phosphorescent glow. Georgina reached inside her pocket and produced a small Maglite torch. She turned it on and suddenly felt extremely vulnerable. The bright beam cut through the black forest and acted as a guidance system straight back to her hand.

"What you doing?" Leroy said. His voice hard.

Georgina lowered the beam and concentrated it on the area thirty foot in front of her. She expected to see the Sheriff on the floor holding her ankle. She saw nothing but tree roots, leaves and overgrown vegetation.

"Turn the light out," Leroy whispered. "My spider sense is tingling."

"You see something?"

"I'm just getting a bad vibe."

A low moaning came from close to where the LED light source was emanating. It was a guttural sound, almost as though it came from an animal.

"This way," Georgina said. She moved slowly forward, keeping the beam of the torch concentrated about one foot ahead of her feet.

Leroy grabbed hold of her arm. "I'd feel a hell of a lot better if you turned that off."

"Okay." She extinguished the light.

The darkness poured over them like thick black paint.

A whooshing sound close to Leroy's face, too close to his face, made Leroy stop in his tracks.

"What the fu ..." His hand automatically went to his face and he felt dampness. "The torch, the torch," Leroy said. His voice unusually panicked.

Georgina instantly reacted and shone the torch on his face. A large gash on his cheek exposed raw flesh. Though only a few millimeters apart the wound bled ferociously. Leroy could see

Georgina pale even in the dull light. It was almost as though the blood was running from her.

Leroy looked at his blood-soaked hands. "You got a tissue or something."

"There's a first aid box in the car."

Leroy looked back to the darkness from where they had come. "Man, that's a mile away."

"Jesus, what's going on?" Georgina said. The frustration in her voice could not hide the worry she felt. "Wait a minute." Georgina took her jacket off. She then grabbed hold of the bottom of the white cotton vest she was wearing and lifted it over her head. "Don't get no ideas," she said trying to make light of the moment. She handed the warm item of clothing to Leroy. He put it to his face. It smelled of her. The fragrance was unmistakable, warm and somehow comforting. Leroy grabbed Georgina's hand that was holding the torch and gently guided her through a three hundred and sixty degree sweep of the immediate vicinity. He was looking for signs of a sharp low hanging branch or even an animal that might have caused the wound to his face. He was also looking for Sheriff Mary T Rankin. Neither were evident. The stinging sensation in his face and blood soaking into Georgina's vest confirmed he was not imagining what was happening. Leroy's finger pushed softly against Georgina's index finger, applying pressure to the on/off switch on the torch and darkness engulfed them once more. The all-consuming heat still clung unmercifully around them like a neoprene suit dipped in hot tar. Georgina didn't want to put her jacket back on as a relief from the sweltering night heat but the thought of running through the woods in her bra and skirt seemed ridiculous. She reluctantly put the jacket back on.

"The sheriff?"

Leroy held the cotton shirt to his face. "She can't be far." Once more the light that first attracted their attention appeared, though this time a little stronger. This time it was accompanied by a short tone.

"Cell phone. 'Bout thirty feet away," Leroy said. He grabbed hold of Georgina's arm and pointed it in the direction of the noise.

Slowly and carefully they moved toward the light. As they moved closer, there was another short beep and the outline of the person holding the phone was illuminated. As they neared, Georgina's own cell phone rang. The shock of the sudden outburst of sound almost stopping her heart. She quickly pounced on the phone and answered it, silencing any further outburst.

Susan Dark stopped running. There was nothing in her head now except pain and the uncomfortable echo of silence. She no longer knew which direction the cabin was in or indeed how far she had run. All she wanted to do now was collapse and curl into a ball. Her heart pounded in her head, its thump, thump, thumping a ringing endorsement of the fact that she was alive. The drugs which had held her captive for so long were now a distant memory for her body if not her mind. Everything was so dark, Susan barely knew which way was up. She no longer felt as though she was being pursued. She didn't know why but the sense of being hunted was gone. Her instinct for survival ran deeper than a gut feeling though and for now she decided to keep moving, slowly, quietly but with purpose even if she didn't know where she was going.

A gargled gurgling greeted Georgina. She listened carefully as they approached the illuminated figure by the tree.

"Great, in the middle of all this shit I get a pervert," Georgina said "Hello?"

As they drew closer to the light source it became clear who was calling her.

"My God," was all Leroy said upon seeing the figure attached to the tree with a crossbow bolt impaled through his forearm. As they drew nearer Georgina once again turned on her torch. The small penlight beam lit up the area as though it was a floodlight and the extent of the horror of the situation became much more transparent.

Stevie Anderson was pinned to the tree with more than one bolt. The one through his arm secured him to the tree. Somehow he managed to retain a grip on his cell phone. The whiteness on his knuckles confirmed that this was an involuntary action, a spasm brought about through pain. How he had managed to dial was a mystery.

As Georgina neared she shone the torch directly into Susan Dark's manager's face. It was only then that she knew why Anderson was making such a strange noise. The crossbow bolt had passed through Stevie Anderson's mouth with the blade protruding through the back of his neck. It was hard to discern if his mouth had been open at the time when the arrow hit him, not that it really mattered. All Georgina and Leroy saw was the fact that the lower part of his face was decimated by the sheer power and force of its entry. He made a low mewing noise, which could have been an attempt at communication, though it could easily have been nothing more than abject pain. The light from his phone died, the phone still remained in his hand as though glued.

Stevie Anderson stared at his impaled arm and made a guttural noise.

"Nurrrh."

And then the phone rang.

Georgina looked at Leroy and then at Anderson's hand. Anderson slowly uncurled his fingers. It was clear that this small action caused him immense pain. The muted scream echoed in the darkness. The phone rang again and in that moment even through all the pain and the horror Stevie Anderson wished he had chosen a different ring tone than "Crazy" by Patsy Cline. Anderson found black humor in the fact that it could have been worse if he had chosen "Little Arrows" by Leapy Lee. Georgina gently prized the phone out of Anderson's hand and answered it.

"Hello?"

"Not far now, Georgina. Three hundred yards straight ahead then turn directly right and I'll be waiting a further four hundred yards away. You have two minutes."

"Sutherland." Georgina recognized the voice on the end of the line. The phone went dead.

For a moment Leroy forgot about the wound to his own face and looked at Anderson, at a loss as to what he could do to ease the man's burden. If it was an animal the quick and humane thing would be to place the muzzle of his pistol to the man's temple and squeeze off a round. Anderson's eyes appeared to be imploring him to do something similar. Instead Leroy grabbed hold of his cell phone and scrolled through the list of names, stopping at Wynan O'Neil.

"I'm calling your father. We need help out here," Leroy said.

"There's some weird shit happening out here that's for sure." Georgina looked around. This time she did not hesitate to use the torch. There was nothing, nothing but trees and darkness. "Where the fuck did the sheriff go?"

Anderson's groaning brought her attention back to the tall music manager. Lesser men would be dead by now. The bolt which filled Anderson's permanently opened mouth made him look like a bizarre version of Jacob Marley from the old Charles Dickens's tale, *A Christmas Carol*. Though the temperature was still in the late seventies, Georgina felt a shudder. The whole scene was so macabre.

"O'Neil?"

Leroy's voice caught Georgina's attention. She looked over at her partner to find him talking on the cell phone.

"We're gonna need some help out here."

Wynan O'Neil took the call just as the full blood work results were pinged to him via email. He opened the email and read it while talking to Leroy LaPortiere. "I already have back-up in the vicinity." O'Neil paused as he re-read the message on the screen. "This doesn't make sense."

Leroy pulled the bloodied vest away from his jaw. The blood was clotting now. The flow slowing down. "Damn right it doesn't."

Their voices were intimate in the stillness of the night. The distance separating them seemingly nothing but a breath of air.

"How's Georgie holding up?"

Wynan's question caught Leroy off guard. "We're gonna need a paramedic out here."

Wynan dared not ask the question he needed the answer for.

Realizing the ramifications of what he had just divulged, Leroy quickly followed up with. "Georgina's okay. But we've got a situation here." Leroy looked at Georgina's questioning face. He waved a placating hand at Georgina.

"A paramedic team is on the way." Wynan spoke as he continued reading the LCD computer screen. His mind now settled back on the job at hand knowing his daughter was safe, for now. "The blood work is in on Sutherland's goody bag."

"And?"

"If the answer is in here, it's well-hidden." Wynan scrolled down the page. "I think we have a hell of a lot of contamination. Four donors, three of them are clearly related."

This time the sound of Georgina's cell phone ringing interrupted. Georgina quickly answered it. "Yes."

It was Fisher Sutherland. "Tell your boyfriend to get a move on or he gets another one of Cupid's arrows, only this time it won't be a graze. Look at his heart, quite prophetic really."

Georgina looked at Leroy's chest. There was a small red glowing dot directed on it.

"You have ten to start moving. Nine … eight … seven …"

Leroy though still talking to Georgina's father was now tending Stevie Anderson's injuries. He felt Georgina pulling at his arm, pulling him away from the impaled record manager.

"C'mon we have to move."

"What." Leroy shrugged Georgina off.

"No time to fucking argue, Leroy. We have to move now." The urgency in her voice resonated deep into the woods. She pulled at him again this time off-balancing him. The big man swayed sideways and crashed to the ground. At first Georgina feared the worst and wondered if she heard the flight of Leroy's silent assassin.

"Jesus!" Leroy dropped his phone in the confusion, and scrabbled around on all fours looking for it.

Georgina was happy to hear Leroy's protestations. But she didn't wait. She grabbed at him once more and dragged him as best as she could. "The fucker's got you in his aim." Georgina spat, and pressed hard at the red dot still trained on Leroy's chest. "Let's move it. He's calling the shots ... literally."

Leroy briefly brushed at the red mark. He didn't know why. "What about Anderson?"

"Help is on its way. Move it, Leroy. Otherwise you're next."

"My phone," Leroy said getting to his feet.

Georgina shone her torch in the area where Leroy had tumbled and found the phone or what was left of it. The carbon steel head of an arrow had shattered the cell phone, breaking it into tiny fragments.

"Time to go," Georgina said.

Leroy didn't need telling a third time. He was now running, following Georgina, as she headed toward her destination. Occasionally Leroy would look down to check that the marker was not following him. He was more than relieved to see that it wasn't.

As she ran, the blinding and crushing pain returned to her head. Even in the darkness Georgina could see that her vision had suddenly become blurred. The vice like grip inside her head had come back, this time without any warning. No mild nagging headache, no pressure around the sinuses, nothing. Her legs wobbled slightly and threatened to fall out from under her, but she was determined to keep her stride and not let on to Leroy that she felt vulnerable. As Georgina's vision began to falter she became aware that what was dark was now becoming light. It was almost as though she was seeing the world in reverse, in a negative form. The pain threatened to overwhelm her and with it a feeling of nausea.

Bile rose from her stomach. Reflux acids fought with the motion as her body carried on moving forward until she could no longer hold it down and she stopped dead in her tracks. She stopped running so quickly that Leroy collided with her. The impact sent her sprawling to the ground where she vomited.

# Chapter 33 Final Report

Wednesday May 21, 2003

As John Keller pulled the black SUV to a halt in a clearing in the woods another smaller SUV pulled in directly behind. The occupants of this car moved quicker and with a greater sense of urgency. Two of them were out of the car and heading toward Dace before Keller had the engine turned off. The sight of the black suited men approaching unsettled her.

"John, we got company." Dace took the portable GPS tracking device from the dashboard and glanced at it quickly before slipping it in her coat pocket.

The familiar figure of Randolph Thorne emerging only slightly eased Dace's concern. The two men that were leading stepped to one side and adopted a proactive security stance. Thorne tapped the side window of the SUV. The noise amplified among the silence of the setting. Dace pressed a button and the window lowered with an electrical whir.

"Where are they?" Thorne's voice was sonorous, echoing off the confines of the vehicle's interior.

"A mile or so into the woods," Dace replied. She nodded forward with her head, indicating directly ahead.

"Paris is alive." Thorne threw the Polaroid at Dace. Not hiding his anger. "You know, it all ends here. Tonight," Thorne said. "Where's the tracking device?"

Dace's hand instinctively went to her coat pocket. It was a natural reaction that betrayed her. She hoped against hope that Thorne hadn't seen. But the man knew more and saw more than most people who walk the earth. Thorne didn't ask a second time.

"You know that show I promised? Well, I guarantee you'll have hours of network air-time."

Dace looked blankly at Randolph Thorne. She couldn't quite understand why she was staring down the barrel of a silencer. She saw the flash and for a moment felt a searing burning heat followed by the smell of scorched tissue. The noise inside her head was phenomenal, and though this all lasted for a fraction of a second it was a lifetime to Barbara Dace. As she slumped forward, Randolph Thorne steadied his aim and fired off a second round this time clean through John Keller's forehead. Thorne knew they were both kill shots. It was not the first time he had dispatched people this way. Thorne reached in and took the small GPS device from Barbara Dace's pocket. He turned to his guards.

"Clear this mess away." Thorne looked at the screen and headed into the woods alone. As he walked a bright orange flare engulfed the black SUV containing the bodies of Barbara Dace and John Keller. Briefly Randolph Thorne became a black silhouette against a blazing inferno of flames. He was Dante raging against his own fiery hell and the rage inside his heart was burning harsher than the fire consuming the vehicle.

The light from the burning car invaded even the darkest part of the forest. Susan Dark felt vulnerable from the glow it cast. People were near but she had no idea if they were good people or bad people. Her ability to trust was already shattered beyond normal comprehension and no amount of self-help books or therapy was going to put that right quickly. She decided that her best choice was to move away from the light and head further into the woods. Susan got to her feet and began her walk. Her limbs felt drained of energy now that the sudden rush of adrenaline had burned off. Lactic acid had accumulated in her leg muscles making them feel heavy and leaden, but her instinct for survival kept them moving. She had no idea where she was going and even less of when this nightmare was going to end. She kept walking.

Wynan O'Neil felt uneasy and it wasn't just because his daughter was involved. This was an instinctual gut feeling that he had which he always listened too when in the field. He picked up a phone. He dialed the number he needed from memory. After two short trills it was answered.

"Miller?"

"Yeah."

The connection was far from good. The voice coming through the ether distorted and metallic.

O'Neil continued. "Have you made contact with Agent O'Neil and LaPortiere yet?" Wynan was now feeling distinctly edgy and was moving around the large office space as he talked.

"They're close by." The robotic answer came back. "The reading from LaPortiere's ID card is strong. Can't be more than a couple of hundred yards away."

"Make contact as quick as you can and get back to me ASAP."

It was a question and the line going dead confirmed O'Neil's intent to Miller. If only life was that simple though. Fisher Sutherland stepped away from FBI Agent Miller and over the body of his partner, Agent Browning who was lying prostrate by Miller's feet. The cross bolt through the back of Browning's head told its own story.

"Good. Now my part of the bargain. I said I'd let you live. Though to be honest you'll soon understand what a bad decision that was."

Miller watched the red laser light from the crossbow travel up his body. Briefly there was a blinding red light in his right eye as the light burned his retina. Not that it mattered, the red light was the last thing Miller would ever see out of that eye. The crossbow bolt followed decimating the eyeball. The bolt's journey through his eye missed Miller's brain but carried on through his skull, traveling at such speed that it carried the two hundred and twenty pound man backwards impaling him on the bark of a cedar tree directly behind him. Sutherland had kept his promise, Miller was still alive. The pain and the fear were unbearable though. Miller cried like a baby until he passed out. Sutherland watched with the curiosity of a child, taking his time to enjoy the moment. He neared the body of Miller. The weight of his body pulling down against the crossbow bolt and the ever enlarging wound in his head. Fisher Sutherland prized the GPS tracker from Miller's hand and studied the display. He assumed rightly that the bright green blip was Agents O'Neil and LaPortiere and reloading the crossbow with a fresh bolt headed toward the signal.

Georgina took a moment to catch her breath. She finally stropped retching when the contents of her stomach were depleted. The light inside her head was blinding. It was as though a torch was being shone straight in front of her eyes, but there was no torch and there was no light. She studied the outline of Leroy LaPortiere. A matter of only seconds had passed since they collided but time was taking on a strange reality for Georgina.

"I knew it was too soon. I shouldn't have pushed you." Leroy's voice was filled with concern.

"I'll be alright."

"You are a bad liar."

Georgina thought she was a rather good liar. She had hid her headaches and slow debilitation well enough. Even from her father and the medical experts monitoring her. "Don't fret. I really am okay. Probably that pizza back at the dinner."

"Don't remind me." Leroy looked around the darkened woods. "Where the fuck is Rankin?"

Georgina's vision was still affected. The feeling of pressure inside her head slightly eased now that she had been sick but this odd optical illusion which turned light into dark and dark into light still altered her vision. Through the light, bright trees she could see a patch of solid darkness about three hundred feet to her right. "Follow me." Georgina got to her feet a little unsteadily. She unclipped her service revolver from her holster and gripped the weapon tightly and headed for the darkness.

"What the hell can you see?" Leroy jogged after Georgina.

The wound across LaPortiere's cheek was now congealed, but the detective didn't relinquish the makeshift bandage, choosing to clench it in his hand as he jogged.


Randolph Thorne moved with purpose. He knew his destination and finally after seventy-two years on planet Earth he knew his fate. Everything that mattered to him was condensed into a microcosm of life and death that would culminate within the next hour. His two assistants kept up with him but could feel the toll of the pace in the heat. Thorne was sweating, his breathing a little labored but he was not going to stop until he reached his final destination, even if that meant killing his only son. The irony of having created the monster far from lost on him but now wasn't a time for self-loathing, recrimination or introspection; those things would be a far sweeter pill after cold blooded revenge. His pace increased. His direction set and his mind determined. He held the submachine gun in front as he marched, willing to cut down anything in his path.

"Sir, shouldn't we slow down. We could be heading straight into a trap?" The taller of his two assistants called out.

"Of course we are, but Paris needs me," came the terse reply from Thorne. "We're close, keep up."

The two assistants increased their pace and each made sure in turn that the safety catch was released on their weapons. Thorne's breathing finally began to succumb to the humidity. Maybe it was the excitement or the knowledge that years of secrecy were about to come to an end. If his assistants knew exactly what was going on in

Randolph Thorne's mind they would have abandoned the quest. Thorne pushed on.

Susan Dark could see the light from the cabin. It was nearer than she wished but all the time she could turn her head and see it behind her she knew she was heading in the right direction. It didn't matter which direction as long as it was away. A song came to her as she moved cautiously onwards. A song her mother sang. "Lonesome, as I am" but the song was not inside her head, it came to her through the trees. The song was in the air, it was real. At least she thought it was real. Briefly, Susan turned back to look at the cabin. Suddenly the voice was close, Susan could almost feel the words. She stopped and listened. Her mother's voice carried through the still air. Susan stood, hypnotized by the voice as though she was being called by a siren's song. Susan's gaze followed the line from which the voice was coming. From behind a cedar tree a figure emerged. The sweet voice of her mother coming from the lips of the woman who looked so familiar but oddly, very different. Susan was transfixed.

As they neared the light glowing from the cabin, Leroy and Georgina instinctively began to slow down. Thoughts of being followed or pursued diminished as the reason for running through the woods in the early hours of the morning overtook any idea of self-protection. Forming in Leroy's mind was a plan to free Susan Dark if this was where she truly was. Georgina's head was still filled with pain. The pressure behind her eyes made it feel as though they were going to pop out of their sockets. Georgina caught her breath by a tree no more than thirty feet from the now clearly visible cabin. Her vision was still distorted, though she was in no mind to let Leroy know how distorted it actually was. She hoped this strange negative world she was seeing through her eyes would soon revert.

"You okay?" Leroy's voice was a little breathy. The humidity was clearly having an effect. "You'd think after years of living in Missouri I'd be used to this."

"You'd think," Georgina said with a hint of sarcasm. She tried to focus on the cabin. The light spilling out from the porch made it a little easier for her to define certain objects, a chair, a hammock and an open door. "You think Sutherland's here?"

"I hope so." Leroy patted his holster and put his hand to the congealed blood on his jaw.

"How is that?" Georgina asked.

"Think your vest is ruined. Finally stopped bleeding though," Leroy said.

"Good." Georgina was genuinely pleased and concern showed in her voice.

A silhouetted figure briefly walked past the window closest to the door.

"Someone's home."

"Plan?" Georgina asked.

She hoped Leroy was about to say "wait for back up and let them go in first." But she got: "He knows we're coming. Christ's sake he invited us. He's not concerned about us bringing in reinforcements, either that or he knows they won't arrive in time. That means whatever is going down is going down very soon. So, we storm in now while he has the advantage, or we sit it out and wait to see exactly what is going down."

"What about Susan?"

"It's not about Susan. She's the lure," Leroy said scanning the building.

The decision to wait or act though was taken from them with the arrival of Randolph Thorne and his two cronies.

# Chapter 34 Reborn in a Mystery

*Room 11, The Teenarosa Motel, Talinha, Texas*
*Saturday July 29, 1978*

*He promised the pain would go away and in a way it did. Caroline Dark woke to a new world. Her hands went to the back of her neck, she felt the cool touch of her skin, almost clammy and her fingers pushed out to touch her hair. She had no idea of how much time had passed. The stranger promised her that the world of pain that she had experienced for so long would disappear. That Caroline Dark would be dead. The stranger was true to his word. She didn't know where she was, all that Caroline did know was that she was in a room, sitting on a bed and a newspaper was by her side. The paper was open on the obituary page and she was looking at a picture of herself. A picture incidentally that she hated. Sitting on the bed next to the newspaper was an envelope. As Caroline reached for it she realized how groggy she felt. Obviously whatever drug she had been given was still making its way out of her body. She picked the envelope up. Neat handwriting suggested somebody who was in control of their thoughts at least at the time of writing. The envelope felt heavy, there was more than just a letter inside. Caroline hesitated before opening the seal. She paused for a moment and took a deep breath, then she watched almost as though she was a witness, as her fingers automatically ripped the gummed flap sealing the document holder. She pulled a standard folded piece of paper out, and with it something wrapped inside. As she unfolded the paper she saw the familiar black skinned book which was a passport and a driver's license. She allowed them to fall onto the bed along with two keys. Caroline turned her attention back to the letter, hoping to find some answers.*

Dear Caroline,

How does it feel to be dead? Don't worry, you will feel a little groggy now, but believe me you will feel great very soon. Death, you will find, becomes you. You will come to understand why I had to kill Caroline Dark and you will realize that it is the best thing that could possibly have happened to you. If you have not already looked, you will find a new passport and driving license; a new you if you like. There are also two keys and pinned to this letter are directions to a locker in Hereford in Deaf Smith County. Follow the directions to the letter and you can begin a brand new life. Celebrate your death because today is your birthday.

*Caroline looked down at the bed. Her fingers hovered over the passport and driver's license. She flipped the passport open and was surprised to see her face staring back.*

*A photograph of Caroline was so expertly inserted that questions would never be asked. Caroline didn't recognize the name under the image though. The driver's license was equally impressive. She hadn't seen many forgeries in her life, but Caroline had seen many real documents such as these and even in her slightly groggy state of mind was unsure if they were real or not. She continued reading the page of neatly scripted copy.*

It's time for a completely fresh start. Leave everything of Caroline Dark behind and you can have that happy life you so long for, one denied to your mother. To give you this life you have a forfeit which I know will be painful. You will need time to sink into your new life. Time to absorb your new self, to build your new life and we both know Susan was never a planned part of your future. The only way I can make this work for you is to convince the people who want you dead that you are indeed dead. And in many ways Caroline, you are. This is the last time I will use your old name. Don't worry about Susan. I will make sure that she is well looked after.

Good luck with your second life.

*Caroline flipped the sheet of paper and found a second sheet stapled to the back of the letter with road directions to Hereford. Gingerly she got to her feet. For a second or two she swayed unsteadily. It was still dark outside the window. She had no idea of the time elapsed except to ironically think that it felt like a lifetime. That somehow seemed apt. Memories of this room came flooding back to Caroline, a real sense of having been there before haunted her, it was much stronger than déjà vu. She turned and instinctively walked to the bathroom, knowing it was there, though in a two room motel this was no great surprise. As she passed the bed an image formed in her head of her mother lying on the bed. A ghost from the furthest corner of her mind. Caroline reached out to touch the vision* but it began to fade and as it faded she realized that it was not her mother's image she was looking at but her own.

Caroline walked on through to the bathroom. Strands from her memory were reaching out to touch her ... whispers. Everything was so familiar. She ran a bath and though the enamel was yellowed and stained it looked inviting and comfortable. It took a while for the water to run clear and even longer for an electric boiler to kick into life somewhere in the cellar of the main building adjacent to the small block of motel rooms, but once it did Caroline could think of nothing else but sinking in the hot water and washing away the ghosts of her life. As she walked past a mirror another piece of the jigsaw fell into place. Her long auburn hair had been cut. Not just cut, but dyed into a lighter color and styled. She stopped in her tracks and spent time looking at this new face, getting acquainted with it. In her mind she introduced herself. "Hello".

It took Caroline another hour before she had gathered her thoughts and her meager belongings together. She walked to the door and looked briefly back at the scene of her death. The room was tired, neglected and in need of a makeover. All that was Caroline Dark had died in the bed that was now nothing more than a collection of rumpled sheets on a worn out mattress. She didn't dwell too long before opening the door. Outside darkness had fallen. Caroline had no idea how long had passed. Hours, days, weeks, months ... all sense of time was lost and somehow irrelevant. A 1973 Ford Pinto sat waiting outside the motel room. Caroline looked at the two keys in her hand and for the first time in a long while allowed herself a smile.

# Chapter 35 Darkness Comes

Wednesday May 21, 2003

"Wait." Leroy pulled Georgina back. His voice was insistent.

Georgina immediately halted. Her peripheral vision was almost non-existent and it wasn't until she followed Leroy's arm pointing to his right that she saw Randolph Thorne and his minders. Though what she actually saw was a blurred outline. All definition was gone.

"Randolph Thorne, what the hell is he doing here?" Leroy's voice was a whisper in Georgina's ear. Leroy noticed the heavy artillery the media magnet was holding, "And he is packing some serious motherfucking weapons."

Georgina wanted to tell Leroy that she was half-blind that all she could see was shapes and even then she was seeing them in negative form. She knew she was a handicap and that not only was she endangering her own life but his as well. The pain came searing inside her head once more. She closed her eyes and saw a firework display behind her shut eyelids. Georgina could not help but emit a low groan. She tried to stifle the noise but the pain was so intense. Her hand shot out and gripped Leroy's arm just to steady herself. Her vice-like grip told Leroy all he needed to know.

"Ahhh-fuck," Georgina said breathing in at the same time. She winced and then shivered as the pain throbbed inside her head, threatening to explode. Georgina rested back against the bark of a tree and slowly slid down to her haunches. "I'll be alright in a moment." Her voice low but etched with pain.

"Why didn't you tell me the headaches were back?"

"This is the worst in a long, long time. It'll go in a minute." Georgina's stomach contents threatened once more to rise and betray her. She sucked in the warm night air. Leroy joined her at her level, all the time keeping an eye on Randolph Thorne and his cronies. He watched them pass only ten feet away. He had the power in his hands to end this madness and was sorely tempted to draw his firearm and challenge the men, but he knew how this would likely end. He continued watching them walk to the wooden cabin about thirty feet away.

Randolph Thorne stopped. Darkness gathered around him. His two men stood a few paces back like anxious hyenas straining on a leash. They surveyed the territory, scanning the blackness for anything malevolent but could see nothing in the all-consuming night. The only light was that which was emanating from the wooden cabin a few feet away. The woods were silent but if Thorne listened carefully he would have heard the gentle chug of a generator powering the cabin, but he already knew this. He needed no maps, no tracking devices, hell; he didn't even need the welcoming cell phone call from Fisher Sutherland. Thorne looked at the cabin. He knew the layout intimately, he knew where Susan would have been kept, and he knew where Grant and Gil Frolan would have spent hours reading the Bible. He'd make them pay if they had any part in taking Paris, he promised himself. That most definitely was never the plan. He even knew where Stevie Anderson kept his stash of whisky, Viagra and porn. All of this knowledge wearied Randolph Thorne. All he wanted to do now was kill every single one of them, rescue his daughter and go home to a peaceful night's sleep. What was left of it.

Thorne checked the gun in his hands. The safety catch was off. His finger stroked the trigger, pushing against the cold metal, knowing exactly how much pressure was needed to fire off a round. He turned to face his jackals. Without speaking he ordered them to the right and left of the building, by pointing the muzzle of the gun. The two men scampered off running as silently as they could. Thorne watched them disappear into the darkness. He looked up, trying to locate the moon. Nothing.

Thorne heard a muffled sound followed by a thud. "Silly bastard's fallen over," he said to himself.

Thorne could not see the towering henchman felled by the silent velocity of a crossbow bolt. The sharpened tungsten tip of the arrow ripped through the flimsy shirt material and shattered the man's breastbone before severing the aortic artery, traveling through his body and finally exiting out through his exploded ribs. The man fell never to rise. Thorne walked on cautiously.


The pain was easing now. Georgina blinked a few times and pressed her fingers deep into the sides of her temples.

"We should call again for back-up," Leroy said. There was no sign of help coming. He looked back in the direction from which they had come. A faint orange glow filled the sky. It was too early for sunrise. "Try your cell phone again."

Georgina pressed the green button to access the last number dialed. She pushed the button to call, the phone lit to signify life and waited for a moment with the phone pressed to her ear.

"Nothing … no signal … nada." Georgina looked at the screen. There were no bars. "No surprise. We're in the ass of nowhere."

"We're on our own then. We gotta get inside as quickly as possible. As soon as Thorne is inside count to ten and then we go in."

Georgina looked up and saw the silhouetted man approaching the cabin. All she could see was an outline but the definition was improving. She got to her feet and made a good show of doing so without betraying the pain and debilitating dizziness she felt. If there was one thing she did not need in her life now it was confrontation or action of any sort. Thorne was almost on the threshold of the cabin Georgina drew a deep breath and smiled at Leroy.

"Ten … nine … eight …"

Leroy looked at the cabin and whispered, "no time for heroes and no time for cowards", and heard Georgina's slow countdown.

"Three … two … one."

And they were running.

# Chapter 36 Sweet Dreams

Wednesday May 21, 2003

It was almost as if the cabin in the woods had waited for tonight. Worlds were going to collide and collapse and by the time daylight broke nothing would be the same again. Randolph Thorne scanned the long corridor inside the cabin. He waited a couple of seconds hoping to see the arrival of his men. After a minute he knew they would not be coming to his aide. Slowly, tentatively he edged his way along, sticking close to the wall. His semi-automatic gun was held in front, safety catch off. The sound of music suddenly blaring out of speakers placed around the cabin rocked Thorne back on his heels and this time the composure crumbled and a spray of bullets spewed out of the semiautomatic weapon splintering wood and burying deep into the walls. Thorne's heart threatened to rip out of his chest and for the first time that night he questioned his sanity in trying to obtain closure of a decision he took nearly fifty years ago. As he waited for his pulse to return to normal, Thorne's mind began to process the information it was receiving. The song was familiar, as were the voices. It was Caroline and Susan Dark singing a duet from Susan's latest CD. The song was the old Patsy Cline classic, "Sweet Dreams".

Leroy's hand was on the door about to push it open when the sound of bullets firing from a gun made him dive toward Georgina pushing her to the ground. Georgina's head struck the wooden decking sending a rainbow of colors dancing in front of her eyes. Music filled the air and the whole scene was surreal. Georgina lay for a moment too stunned to think.

"You okay?" Leroy's voice close to her ear.

"Most fun I've had in the dark in ages," Georgina lied. She rubbed her forehead and felt a tiny swelling from a bump against the unforgiving wooden decking. She was thankful that it wasn't concrete at least. Her ears were still ringing with the echo of semi-automatic gun fire and the sound of Caroline and Susan Dark duetting on "Sweet Dreams". And then just as suddenly silence and darkness. Georgina instantly panicked thinking that her auditory senses were now failing her as well as her eyesight until Leroy spoke.

"What the … stay here a moment."

Georgina felt a little pressure on her back as Leroy carefully got to his feet. She didn't need persuading to stay put. The old Georgina would have been on her feet arguing with Leroy that there was no way that she'd let him enter the cabin on his own. She waited alone in perfect blackness for what seemed an eternity, devoid of sight and with no sound, not even the cry of night creatures going about their nightly duties. It was as though the world had stopped. When Leroy did not return after five minutes of slowly counting to three hundred, Georgina unclipped her holster and felt the comforting grip of the cold metallic handle of her revolver embrace her palm. She got to her feet and felt her way along the wooden shack to the door, using her fingers as her eyes. The door was open. Though there was no light or sound to indicate life inside. Another burst of semi-automatic gunfire was so loud and sudden that Georgina felt her bowels would betray her. Her heart thumped madly and she wanted to get the hell out of the building instead of venturing deeper, which was what she knew she must do. This was no longer a case of bravery or even stupidity but the only option. The muggy heat of the night somehow made the darkness feel even more claustrophobic than normal. More gunfire and now Georgina could not help but let an automatic yelp escape from her lips as a response. She didn't want to die here tonight.

"You must stay here."

"Who are you?" Susan asked. She sensed more than familiarity with the woman who emerged from nowhere in the woods.

"It doesn't matter. All that matters is that we keep you safe."

Susan looked around and thought "who is we?" They walked together for what seemed to be miles through the darkened woods until they came to a clearing and then a road and finally an old American car. Susan had no idea what make the car was except that it looked like a classic American car. The sort that she had seen in old photos. They waited in the car. Susan studied the woman who had pulled her from the forest. The police uniform gave her reassurance but there was more to it than just a uniform. Susan felt a sense of familiarity with the woman that was for now unspoken but as definite and unseen as the air she was breathing.

Mary T Rankin placed her hand delicately on Susan's shoulder. "Hush now."

The sense of déjà vu became a moment in life confirmed with the physical touch of the sheriff's hand on Susan Dark's shoulder. Susan looked long and hard into Mary T Rankin's eyes hoping for a flicker of recognition but nothing was forthcoming, except the foggy sense of frustration. The sheriff began to hum. At first quietly. The tune was instantly recognizable to Susan.

"What are we waiting for?" Susan asked, impatient to get moving and leave the nightmare of the woods behind her.

"A new day." The sheriff continued humming. Rankin looked at the old analogue clock set in the dash. "Don't worry, it's coming. We'll be gone soon." Now she began to quietly sing. The words so familiar to Susan.

*Lonesome as I am,*
*I still don't need no man.*
*My life's a travelling sham*
*To be lonesome as I am.*

Rankin stopped singing and a deathly awkward silence hung in the air like the Washington heat wave.

"You never asked." Susan finally broke the silence.

"Asked what?"

"Anything. You're the sheriff. Aren't you curious?" Susan said. "About what happened to me?" Susan wound the window down and the sound of the forest entered the car. Night insects singing the last of their song before the coming dawn and somewhere in the distance the sound of a raging fire cracking trees and consuming everything in its path.

"You were taken and held hostage for over six months. Undoubtedly drugged and held against your will." Rankin placed a comforting hand on Susan's arm. It felt warm, genuine and an action of concern.

"And then let go … for no apparent reason," Susan said, almost wistfully. "Who are we waiting for?"

"Oh, there *was* a reason …" Mary said.

Randolph Thorne edged carefully forward. The loud music blast and now sudden and complete darkness had left him disorientated.

"You know, I thought this would be more fun, more of a challenge." The voice came out of the darkness.

"Fisher?"

Wynan O'Neil tried dialing the number for a third time. The trees passed by in a blur, exposed under the headlights of his car. The speakers inset in the door panel and the dashboard projected the sound of his call trying to connect with the phone of his daughter. The sound was almost as desperate as he was. At least that's how it sounded to Wynan. He pushed his foot down on the gas pedal eager to reach his destination. Behind a cavalcade of five black SUV's followed smoothly, swiftly and silently. The speakers inside his car told Wynan what he didn't really want to know as they relayed a message that his call had been forwarded to a voice messaging system. This time he allowed the message to end, deciding to leave a message, just in the hope that Georgina might be out of signal briefly.

"Georgie, it's Wynan." He didn't know why he introduced himself. He was certain his daughter would recognize his voice from the utterance of the first syllable. "I'm a couple of miles away. Be with you soon. Hang tight."

Somewhere directly above Wynan's car a helicopter followed the progress of the vehicles. The pilot could see what Wynan could not. The glowing orange radiance of what she first thought was sunrise but a quick check on her cockpit instrumentation indicated that unless the sun was rising in the northwest this morning that it was a fire. The glow from its source so bright in the perfect darkness. The helicopter raced on ahead but the pilot took a moment to relay the message.

"Delta alpha Charlie; we have a fire approximately two miles northwest. We have a densely grown forest with little or no chance to set down but I can guide you through."

The glow was a pin in the map for the pilot but she knew unless there was a clearing there was no way she'd be able to set down.

The voice cut through on Wynan O'Neil's speakers. He looked up through the panoramic blackened sunroof to the sky and could see the beam from the helicopter cutting through the sky, scything a path for him to follow. He could now see the fire or the glow from the dry burning trees and somehow that made his sense of anxiety worse. The GPS reading from the chips embedded in Georgina and Leroy's warrant cards showed him to be a little less than two miles away. Agents Browning and Miller were closer, their readings static, having been still for over thirty minutes now. Wynan O'Neil feared the worse. His daughter's reading at least showed some movement.

"Delta alpha Charlie, there is a sharp left turn approximately three hundred yards on your left. Partially hidden dirt road. Confirm. I'll guide you in."

O'Neil began to slow the car. He glanced in his rear view to make sure the following parties were hitting the brakes. They were a suitable distance and evenly spaced. Wynan suddenly saw the break in the trees and indicated the left turn to the following group. The tires hit the dirt road and the suspension bounced against the undulating and unforgiving surface. The sky appeared much brighter, the orange glow confirming the chopper pilot's previous message. It wasn't long before O'Neil saw Barbara Dace and John Keller's blacked out shell of their SUV and Stevie Anderson's car. Another SUV, Randolph Thorne's vehicle, had been taken in the ravages of the fire. The flames still licking the paintwork of all the vehicles. The small clearing in the woods was beginning to resemble a car lot of burned cars. O'Neil waited for the five back-up cars to arrive before thinking about venturing further into the densely, burning, forested darkness ahead. The tractor beam of the powerful lantern underneath the helicopter guided a path. O'Neil looked into the woods knowing that their way forward would not be so clear; the light would not cut a swathe through the woods. Each of the FBI cars pulled to a halt, killing their lights almost immediately. O'Neil stayed in his car for a moment, collecting his thoughts and composing himself before opening the door to the oppressive heat and uncertainty of the night.

"Fisher?" Randolph Thorne's voice was controlled and measured. There was no hint of fear. "Where is she?"

"Safe … for now."

"Good."

"You brought yourself a whole hunting party." A noise from above briefly caught Sutherland's attention. "A whole damn party."

They stood silently in the darkened cabin.

Leroy could smell the gasoline. He knew the generator was near but he was blind. His fingers were his eyes as he searched for a switch in the opaque outbuilding. His leg could feel the heat from the powerful motor used to light the building. Leroy crouched down and fumbled in the vain hope of finding something recognizable, not that he was an expert or even knew what the hell he was looking for. He found the core pipe housing the electric cables and followed it upwards to a junction box. The box was open. Leroy found what he hoped was the main rocker switch which (he hoped) acted as the circuit breaker to the generator. He didn't wait to question his actions. His forefinger and thumb gripped the switch and he flicked it up. There was a short pause. It was almost as though the machine connected to the wires feeding into it was pondering the consequences of his action. The pause was brief and the generator fired into life almost instantly flooding the room with light. The sudden burst of light momentarily blinded Leroy. He waited a second for the purple swirls and flashes to stop dancing before his pupils finally adjusted. Shapes formed and the sight of familiar objects began to register in his brain. Sitting dead still in a rocking chair was the headless body of one of Randolph Thorne's henchmen. Before he could take in any of the horror inside the small outbuilding a round of gunfire set his pulse racing. Leroy looked around for the opening where he had entered the building and was confronted by a second body, sitting slumped in a corner with one leg impossibly bent underneath his large frame. With the sound of gunfire still reverberating in his brain, Leroy quickened his pace toward the door.

The sudden burst of light had caught Georgina by surprise. The gun that she held in front of her was still emitting a trail of blue smoke. Her hand was clearly shaking. She lowered her arm for a second to allow herself time to gather her thoughts and surroundings, now they were both bathed in light, and she cursed silently for being so scared. Her vision though still blurry was clearly restoring. Georgina tried to blink away the fuzziness in her vision but everything still had a soft undefined edge. Georgina tried to focus her mind if she could not sharpen her vision and she thought about Susan, hoping that she was close and unharmed. The idea that someone was relying on her spurred Georgina on and she allayed the creeping notions of fear which had temporarily paralyzed her. Somewhere from the back of her mind her training and experience was pushing its way through the fog. Her fingers pressed hard into her temples and she briefly closed her eyes. Now when she opened them clarity had returned and with it a renewed sense of confidence. It was as though all of her senses had been heightened. Georgina pushed away from the wall she was resting against and looked down the long corridor. A door was open with light spilling through the frame flooding the corridor.

"Follow me. We don't have long," Fisher said. He turned and walked a few paces to a door and stopped. "You'll appreciate this."

Randolph Thorne could have shot Sutherland in the back but it wasn't that easy for him. The prospect of what lay in the room was the real reason he was there. Besides, Thorne felt a sense of resignation. This was the end game, all of his chips were on the table and the last card had been dealt and right now Randolph didn't know if he had an ace up his sleeve or a joker, but either way he was committed to play. Thorne had to admit to himself that he was excited and intrigued by whatever it was he was going to see inside the room. He entered. The wood built walls had been covered with Sheetrock and papered. A large metal framed bed occupied a large part of the room and another door led off from the far wall. Thorne knew what the room represented. That it was supposed to recreate the motel room back in Talinha in 1958. The curtain on the faux window, the bedding, the grimy wallpaper, every detail was how it should be. Right down to the body in the bed covered by urine-stained sheets.

# Chapter 37 Return of the Family Man

Wednesday May 21, 2003

Wynan O'Neil stopped in his tracks. The vibrating of his cell phone felt almost in sync with his racing heart. He could see the body of Stevie Anderson impaled by crossbow bolts to a tree by his arm, hand and mouth. He knew nothing could be done for the man, even from a distance of thirty feet. The phone vibrated again and Wynan raised his hands to halt the following team of FBI agents. His eyes darted around the wooded enclave. Occasional beams of light from the million watt halogen tractor lamp circling overhead would pick out areas less densely populated with trees. In a way it was comforting knowing the helicopter was there a few hundred feet about his head. Wynan answered the phone, what he didn't expect to hear was his wife, Cally, on the other end. He knew it must be an emergency, she never called.

"It's started." Her voice was slightly breathless, with an edge of excitement and panic. "My waters have just broken."

As Wynan received news of a life entering the world he had reached the body of one which had just left. Stevie Anderson died a painful and unquestionably horrific death. Blood pools around the body told of a story of a prolonged fight while suffering.

"I promise no matter where I am or what I'm doing I'll drop it to be by your side for the birth. Nothing is more important to me."

Wynan heard his own voice relayed through the cell phone. He clearly remembered the pact and making the recording into a digital voice recorder on the day they found out Cally was pregnant. She must have been holding the device—a standard MP3 recorder—to the phone.

"You're sure?"

"If I ain't, I got the worst incontinence you ever seen ..." Cally took an audible breath in. "Contractions are every twelve minutes, but they're beginning to be real mothers. Pardon the pun. You're gonna be here, aren't you Wynan?"

"Of course."

"You on your way now, then."

"As soon as I am off the phone. A promise is a promise."

"I won't need the ambulance or medics then. You can drive me straight there."

"Hold tight. I'll be home soon,"

"How long is soon, cos the baby is in the driving seat here, Wynan."

Within the hour," Wynan lied.

"You take care and be home soon. I love you, Wynan."

O'Neil listened to some dead air for a second before closing the phone. He quickly dialed a number from the stored numbers. "I need an ambulance out to 22 Forgolia Ridge Mont ... yeah DC. My wife's in labor. Contractions are twelve minutes apart. Her attending physician is Dr. Ray Collins at the Grainbank Memorial ... Wynan O'Neil ... Yes, Cally." O'Neil closed his phone and looked at the scene of carnage in front of him, never once doubting the world he was bringing new life into. The glowing embers of the burned-out cars still glowed while the neighboring trees which had erupted into flames still burned brightly spreading to the trees close by. O'Neil turned to his waiting men and women. "Make sure the firefighters get here soon otherwise this is gonna spread in these dry conditions." The order was not aimed at any singular person with responsibility, yet Wynan knew it would be acted upon by the appropriate person. He began walking again and for the first time could see a glow from the lights in the cabin. His pace quickened to a jog; the light from the helicopter above helping to guide his way as much as the flames from the burning trees and scrubland.

Leroy made it to the door. His heart was pounding and sweat from the oppressive heat soaked his shirt. He briefly scanned the area looking for Georgina but knew she would not have waited for him. She'd be inside. He wiped beads of sweat from his forehead with his arm, allowing the cotton shirt to wipe away the perspiration. Leroy felt as though he was a mouse pulling at a big lump of cheese set on a trap. He knew the lure was too great and that in reality he had no option but to enter the building. He took a breath and as he did saw the approaching helicopter soaring through the skies above the trees. Hell and help was coming at the same time, though he wasn't sure which would arrive first. Leroy didn't have time to allow the choice to be made for him and without pausing for another breath he entered the cabin. Leroy noticed the dried blood which had soaked into the wood grain on the front door and puncture marks which had splintered the surface where a sharp object had penetrated deep into the door. Inside, the stark bareness of the cabin told another story of depravation. A blood stained copy of the Bible lay in the middle of the floor in the corridor. Congealed almost jellified lumps of fatty blood sat on the upturned pages slowly drying. Had he looked further outside he would have seen the remains of Grant Frolan slumped in a rocking chair. A bare bulb hung from a socket lighting the hall. Leroy looked carefully to his left and right down the long corridor which stretched a total distance of over twenty-five feet. There were lots of rooms leading off which were ideal hiding places, but only one with light flooding the hall. Leroy instinctively walked toward the light. As he drew closer he began to hear voices. Both of them male, the sound of conversation. The voices were low at first, seemingly quite distant but as he nervously moved forward it was clear this was no idle conversation passing the time of day, and then suddenly a third voice entered the conversation, one which Leroy knew well and instantly from the tone in her voice.

"Drop your weapons and turn to face the wall."

"What the fuck are you doing?" Leroy said in a low voice to no one but himself. His heart was pumping heavily once more as adrenaline started to surge through him again. The sound of two different rapports of gunfire only quickened this process. Leroy stumbled into the room with his revolver drawn, only to be confronted by a set of steps leading to a lower hidden level in the cabin. The smell of gunpowder from a discharged gun mixed with the raw wood in the cabin producing a burned smell in the air. His strategy—what there was of it—was shot to hell and he hoped that was not going to be the condition of Georgina when he entered the room at the foot of the stairs.

Georgina watched the two men closely for what seemed an eternity. They were so absorbed in each other that at first neither noticed her. She could feel sweat running into the corners of her eyes. The salty substance stinging them, making her blink and with each blink acting like a cleansing agent her focus became slightly clearer. Her mind was telling her to quietly turn while still unseen and run, but she felt the words come trailing out of her mouth almost like an involuntary reaction.

"Drop your weapons and turn to face the wall."

The man directly in front of her finally turned his attention to her and looked up, straight into her eyes.

"Oh, this is interesting," Fisher Sutherland said without any sense of melodrama. He turned his head slightly to look at the splintered wood next to his head where Georgina had fired her warning shot.

"Put your weapons down, turn and face the wall," Georgina repeated. She tried to steady her hand and hoped that neither man could see how much it was shaking. Georgina had never in her professional life felt so vulnerable.

Randolph Thorne was standing over a king-sized bed. The body of a young woman clearly defined underneath a thin cotton sheet. Thorne pulled the sheet back exposing the deathly white features of Paris Thorne and her staring open eyes. Tears rolled down his face, falling from his cheeks and hitting the sheet. "I'm too late." His shoulders shook with an involuntary shudder.

"I'm not gonna turn and I'm not gonna drop my weapon," Fisher said.

Georgina tried to understand what was going on in the room. She wiped sweat from her eyes on the arm of her jacket. She watched Randolph Thorne lift his arm. And though Georgina could see this tragedy unfurl in front of her there was little she could do to stop it. The media tycoon opened his mouth and placed the muzzle of his G36K 5.56mm Heckler & Koch inside.

Georgina shouted, "No."

There was a short burst of gunfire followed by mayhem. Georgina watched in horror as Randolph Thorne's head juddered with the force of a raft of bullets as they shredded his brain and skull turning the back of his head to nothing more than a large opening housing nothing but air. Thorne fell forward and slumped over the body of his daughter.

The sound of semi-automatic gunfire hastened Leroy's progress. Throwing caution to the wind he now took two steps at a time and found himself running down a much shorter corridor. There was only one light visible and Georgina's voice confirmed how close he was to her.

"Stand still."

"I can't do that. You know I've got to go. Either I walk out now or I use this," Fisher replied.

The crossbow was leveled squarely at Georgina's head. Georgina noticed how cool the man looked. Not a bead of sweat and a rock-steady hand.

Leroy could not disguise the sound of his entrance. Driven by fear for Georgina, his haste had signaled his arrival long before he was at the open doorway. Georgina turned for the briefest of seconds to see Leroy, as she turned back Fisher Sutherland had moved. He had readjusted his aim to the left.

"Leroy," Georgina screamed and dived to her left.

The bolt left the crossbow and before Georgina could fire a round from her pistol Sutherland was running. She looked at Sutherland's back as he ran but knew her partner would have been in the line of fire. She also knew Leroy would stop Sutherland in his tracks and expected to hear the sound of his pistol but nothing came except the echo of Fisher Sutherland's heels as they made an unhindered exit. Georgina got to her feet and made her way to the door. Leroy was sitting slumped against the wall in the corridor. He looked up and smiled.

"Lucky the bastard is a shit shot. He nicked me again."

Leroy's hands were pressed into his stomach. Blood oozed between his fingers.

"Oh, Leroy."

"I'll be alright. Just call it in."

Even in the darkened light, Georgina could see a clammy pallor to Leroy's skin. Georgina fumbled for her cell phone and cursed the lack of signal.

"I gotta go back out for a signal." She couldn't hide the concern from her voice.

"Don't worry I ain't going nowhere." Leroy winked.

Georgina stood. "I'll be back in a moment."

"Hey, Georgie?"

Georgina was already halfway up the stairs. "Yeah."

"Be careful."

She ran up the stairs. She knew Sutherland was gone. There was no way, even if he was insane, that he would lie in wait. Georgina ran. She ran as though her life depended on it, before she knew it she was out in the open air. The bright orange glow made it look as though the sky was on fire and the heat felt so oppressive. The trees crackled. Georgina looked at her phone, still no signal. She ran toward the sweltering heat and from the depth of darkness at the base of the trees she heard a familiar voice calling her name.

Wynan O'Neil was within one hundred feet of the cabin when he saw his daughter emerge, running from the wooden structure. The beam from the helicopter overhead picked her out. Behind the forest had, as he had feared, become a raging inferno and the sound of trees exploding under the fierce heat was terrifying. In the distance there was the approaching sound of the fire tender's alarm sounding as it raced to the woods. Wynan shouted to his men not to shoot and hoped they heard. He called Georgina's name. She sprinted the last few feet to her father.

"Leroy's been shot. We need emergency evacuation, now. There's at least another three possibly four bodies, maybe more." Her voice was breathless and for the first time Georgina noticed the trees on fire.

Wynan used his short wave radio to communicate with the circling helicopter. "We need help in here. We're getting pretty strung-out. We need a medi-vac and a clear way out." Wynan turned and looked at the raging inferno eating the trees. "Over."

"What the hell happened?" Georgina said, catching her breath.

"Another trail of bodies and a burned out SUV," Wynan said looking at the burning woods.

In the distance there was the sound of another explosion. Georgina flinched. "Sounds like the fire is spreading back. We got about five vehicles back there."

"We got to get to Leroy. He needs help fast."

"What about Sutherland?"

"He's gone. Didn't you see him come out|?"

Wynan shook his head.

"The man's like a ghost," Georgina said. She grabbed her father's hand and pulled him in the direction of the cabin. "C'mon, Leroy needs us."

Wynan broke into a trot. He knew now wasn't the time to mention the fact that Georgina was going to have a little brother or sister but something compelled him to mention it.

"Cally's in labor."

"She's gonna be pissed then."

"Why?"

"You know you made that pact. God knows she played it enough times whenever I was round for dinner. Let's hope it's a long labor."

They reached the door and stopped for a moment for the group of trailing FBI men and women to catch up. The fire was now only a couple of hundred feet away and consuming trees quickly. The sky to their left was bright orange while to their right there was still perfect darkness. Wynan O'Neil grouped his men and women for a final briefing before battle. His flock gathered listening with expectant ears.

"Agent's Whitmore, Marsh and Sandford, I need you to check the out-building to my right." The three agents turned their heads and studied the compact structure. "Elvirez and Clay check the immediate perimeter." A hispanic and a black agent, one male, one female nodded. "And Carter, Macklin and Scott follow me. Remember I hate heroes, they usually cost the department money with funerals, body bags and disability pensions."

Georgina hadn't waited for the speech, she was already heading down the stairs in the inner sanctum when she heard her father following. She was relieved to see Leroy turn to greet her with a smile.

"Thought you forgot about me."

Georgina kneeled beside him. Her hand touched his face, her fingers lightly touching his skin, which now felt cool but clammy.

"Never." Georgina could feel something damp underneath her knees and when she looked down she realized that she was in a pool of Leroy's blood. "Help is on the way."

"Hey, you found your old man," Leroy said looking up to see Wynan approaching with two men and a woman in tow. "Have you got any drugs, sir, because this is starting to sting a little?" Leroy said. "Forgive me if I don't get up and shake hands." Leroy hands were still pressed in around the area of the protruding bolt in his stomach. He tried to feign a smile.

Wynan could not help but feel selfish relief that it was not his daughter lying there wounded. "The paramedics will be here soon."

"Sir?" A female voice came from within the room. "We've got a live one in here."

"Help will be on its way very soon, Leroy." Wynan reassured the detective. He side-stepped Leroy's out-stretched legs and entered the room with Agent Scott and the newly found victim. Sprawled across the bed with most of his face missing was the corpse of Randolph Thorne. Agent Lana Scott, slightly over-weight, sharply intelligent and surprisingly fit and agile had already documented the condition of the room upon entering with her compact digital camera. She had also rolled Randolph Thorne's body off the body in bed and managed to extract Thorne's ID, which without a face was now vital for identification.

Agent Scott tended the body of Paris Thorne under that of the lifeless frame of Randolph Thorne. "She's not dead ... pulse is weak and thready." Scott threw Randolph Thorne's wallet with his ID to Wynan.

He caught it without blinking. "I know who it is. Randolph Thorne."

"The media magnet?" Scott replied.

And I know who that is," Wynan O'Neil said. "Paris Thorne. Which is really odd considering she had an autopsy a few weeks back."

O'Neil's shortwave radio crackled. "Sir, the fire is about thirty feet away."

"Any sign of the medics?"

"No."

"Well they better be here soon. We've got two down here in mighty poor shape. Is that Agent Whitmore?"

"Marsh, sir." A female voice came back through the small handset.

"I want you to get back on the radio and get me an ETA and then find Macklin and head out. This place is going to hell and I am not in the mood to lose any more men tonight. That's an order."

"The rate of the fire approaching, I'd say you have less than two minutes to get out of there, sir."

"Noted." Wynan looked around the room. "Agent Scott, grab those sheets and any blankets and towels you can find and quickly soak them in water."

"But the evidence, sir?"

"This place will be nothing more than a pile of cinders in thirty minutes barring a miracle. Our evidence is there." Wynan said pointing to Paris Thorne. "Quickly, Scott."

"Sir."

Agent Scott pulled the sheet from the bed and in the process sent Randolph Thorne's body tumbling to the floor. There was a cupboard to the side of the bed. A large brown single wardrobe. She opened the door. A solitary duvet cover was sitting in the otherwise empty wardrobe. Scott grabbed it and left the room with purpose in her step.

"Georgina?" Wynan shouted into the corridor.

Georgina came running in.

"You think we can move Leroy?"

"I'll be alright."

Wynan and Georgina turned to find Leroy swaying unsteadily on his feet.

"You sure?" Wynan asked.

"Hell, I ain't gonna run the one hundred meters but I can make it up a few stairs."

Wynan O'Neil was not so sure and they were not in the position to take chances. "Georgina, you help Leroy. Agent Scott and I will carry Miss Thorne." He took a pocket knife from his jacket and walked over to the body. He rolled Randolph Thorne's body onto its back and grabbing an arm turned it so the hand was splayed. "You and I know who this is and I know we have his ID but pathology and the courts are going to need something more for a positive identification for the death certificate."

Agent Scott came back into the room holding a bundle of dripping sheets and duvet cover. Her own clothes were soaked as she held them to her chest. "Sir, we gotta go. I can hear the fire above."

"So much for the paramedics and firefighters." Wynan turned to Scott. "I need you to document this with your camera. Start filming or shooting or whatever you got in that wee camera of yours."

Scott placed the dripping sheets and blankets on the bed. Paris Thorne had not stirred an inch and everyone in the room knew there was not a damned thing that could be done to make her predicament any better. Scott took her camera out of her pocket.

"There is a movie function on here … somewhere." Scott twiddled with the camera's functions. "There, got it." Scott began filming Wynan O'Neil.

"As soon as I introduce you, start to make your way out of here. We can't afford to wait." Wynan told Georgina. "Unfortunately, Scott, you'll have to wait with me and Carter. Has that thing got sound?"

Scott nodded and the camera moved with her.

"The purpose of this film is to document evidential crime scene we are going to lose to fire. I am FBI director Wynan O'Neil, badge number 477431. With me are Agents Georgina O'Neil, Lana Scott, Paul Carter—where the hell is Carter?"

"Finishing a sweep of the lower part of the building, sir."

"Okay and finally we have Special Agent La Portiere."

Scott moved the camera around the room trying to locate each person before concentrating back on Wynan O'Neil and the dead body of Randolph Thorne.

Wynan held Randolph Thorne's ID to the small camera for a long moment and said "We obtained this ID from this body." O'Neil allowed the camera to focus on the now faceless body of Randolph

Thorne. Wynan looked up and saw his daughter wrapping Leroy and herself in one of the wet sheets, ensuring they were both covered from the head down before supporting Leroy as they made their way upstairs. She gave her father a glance and mouthed, "Be careful," before turning and heading up. Wynan O'Neil continued to the camera, not missing a beat. He turned Randolph Thorne's hand over so the palm was facing upwards and straightened the dead man's fingers. He looked at each ensuring that there was a legible fingerprint to be had. The FBI director chose the main and index fingers. He placed the knife against the crease of the knuckle and pressed down applying his weight against the length of the blade. There was a sickening crunch as the finger severed. Wynan repeated the process with the other finger. Agent Scott sucked in air and prayed that she wouldn't hurl. Wynan picked an evidence bag from his inside pocket, his hand returned to the pocket and he pulled out a plastic tie, both items were numbered. O'Neil offered them to the camera to be recorded and Agent Scott duly obliged. O'Neil's radio crackled.

"Sir, Agent Marsh. The fire is within ten feet of the house. If you do not get out within the next minute, there will be no way out."

Wynan O'Neil dropped the fingers in the bag and sealed the bag. Ideally each item should have been bagged separately but there wasn't time. He nodded to Agent Scott indicating that he had finished. "We're on our way up. You should see Agents LaPortiere and O'Neil any moment."

"Sir."

Wynan O'Neil stood. "Grab those wet sheets, Scott. Where's Carter?"

As soon as he said it Agent Carter appeared at the door frame. "Sir, I have carried out a full sweep of the lower floor and it's clean."

"Give me a hand here. We've got to get this body out of here." O'Neil said pointing to Paris Thorne's body. It was impossible to tell if Paris was alive or dead. There was no detectable movement of her chest rising and falling. Agent Scott helped Agent Carter wrap the body in one of the wet sheets, covering her from head to toe. As she did so she obtained a faint pulse reading from the carotid artery. It was weak but steady.

"Let's move it," O'Neil said, anxious that time was running away from them. There was one flimsy sheet left on the bed to somehow cover each of the three agents left in the room. Wynan O'Neil hoped that the fire had not yet made it to the cabin. He threw Paris Thorne over his shoulder in an ungainly fireman's lift.

Each step Leroy took was agonizing and slow. He felt incredibly weak and could not get warm even though the temperature inside the cabin was over eighty degrees fahrenheit. Georgina looked at him with more than a little concern in her eyes. They had made it to the fifth step and looking up, Leroy was faced with what now looked like climbing Mount Rushmore. There was another eight steps to go and with each subsequent step Leroy would lose more blood, feel weaker and lean even more heavily on Georgina. The sound of an explosion outside rocked the cabin and plunged it into darkness.

"Great," Georgina said sardonically.

"The fire must have reached the generator," Leroy said, thankful for the adrenaline rush the explosion gave him. The noise and the added danger gave him a strong mental picture to focus on. He took the next three steps with renewed vigor. The top of the stairs and a short walk to safety seemed perilously close. As they drew closer they could feel a rise in temperature. The fire must be upon the cabin. The sound of glass breaking confirmed Georgina's worst fear.

"C'mon Leroy, we can't stop." She tightened her grip around his waist, careful not to disrupt the crossbow bolt embedded in her partner's stomach. "Only a few more stairs and we're there." Sweat covered Georgina from head to toe. The effort of helping Leroy combined with the searing heat and heart pumping fear causing her to perspire heavily. Leroy took another step then stopped.

Agents Scott, Carter and Wynan O'Neil were now at the foot of the stairs. O'Neil looked up and could see the slow progress his daughter had made. His own journey was far from easy, though Paris Thorne only weighed about one hundred and thirty-three pounds her weight was multiplied by being unconscious and hampered the progress of Wynan O'Neil and Carter with its lack of rigidity. Paris Thorne's muscles were totally relaxed and handling the body was like lifting a large bag of potatoes.

"Are you okay?" Wynan shouted up the stairs to his daughter.

"We'll make it." Georgina's voice sounded strained.

The fire had taken hold of the forest burning with a ferocity that was awesome in its destruction and indiscriminant in its direction or choice of target. Coupled with the speed of its movement the fire was going to be impossible to contain. Firefighters stood at the periphery of the inferno which was now almost a mile from the cabin in every direction but the impact their hoses were having on the fire was like pissing on the fires of hell. A decision was made to send air support to quell the fire or at least stop it from spreading further. Three large Boeing aircraft flew past unloading gallons of dyed water to smother the fire with little impact at first, save for painting the ground in a wet blood red coating.

Fisher Sutherland walked slowly to the car. He now hoped the FBI and the other law enforcement officers at the cabin would do their job or this would just be a case of revenge. Behind him the forest burned bright orange casting him as a black silhouette against a raging sky. Sheriff Mary T Rankin watched his slow unhurried approach. The fact that he made it out of the cabin meant their work was now finished. Years of planning, pain and uncertainty had come to an end and now they would all be free to live the lives that had been denied them. The ghosts of their lives were finally laid to rest. Rankin allowed herself a brief smile of satisfaction and breathed deeply savoring the moment.

"There is nothing to fear now," Rankin said to Susan.

"What the hell is going on?" Susan asked. She was mentally and physically exhausted but that was nothing compared with the sense of dislocation and confusion.

Rankin fired up the V8 engine. The healthy roar of the engine preparing to flex its muscles reverberated inside the vehicle.

"You're not a sheriff, are you?" Susan asked. The tiredness in her voice was now replaced with more of a resigned acceptance to her fate.

"Oh, I most definitely am. One hundred percent bona fide." Rankin smiled a reassuring smile. "I am duty bound to serve and protect and that is just what I have done. No one is ever gonna harm you or anyone else in our family."

"Our?"

Before Rankin could answer the car door opened and Fisher Sutherland entered. "It's done." He sat in the empty passenger seat in the front of the vehicle.

"It's over?" Rankin asked

"It's over." Sutherland paused for a moment and then looking at Susan said. "Have you introduced yourself?"

"Not yet, I was waiting for you." The sheriff replied. "Though deep down I think she already knows."

"Susan Dark, meet Caroline Dark … your mother."

Susan passed out.

Sutherland looked at the sheriff seated next to him. "Nope, she didn't know."

Sheriff Rankin looked at the fire encroaching the cabin, its flames reaching like fiery tendrils grasping onto branches of trees and seemingly leaping to the next combustible spot.

"and the fire?" she asked.

Sutherland watched the flames dancing as they licked the extremities of the cabin almost obscenely. "She'll be fine. There's enough bodies in there to make sure of that."

Rankin put the car into drive and after a brief spin of the tires to gain traction they pulled away and headed out of the forest and away from the consuming fire that was now eating acres of woodland.

For the last two stairs the heat was almost unbearable. Leroy and Georgina were huddled under the protective embrace of a sodden sheet. The air was getting thinner and it became more difficult to breathe. Georgina could feel Leroy rapidly weaken. A lack of oxygen was the last thing his body needed now. Leroy had closed his eyes and was now just willing his body to carry on step by step. Part of him wanted desperately to stop and sit down. The very thought seemed so comforting.

"Another couple of feet, Leroy and we'll be out of here." Georgina said. But she wondered what hell they would be entering. She could hear the approaching steps of her father.

"Is everything okay?" Wynan's voice was labored as he carried the dead weight of Paris Thorne in a firefighter's lift, her body was wrapped in a soaking shroud of a duvet cover to protect her. Every now and then he stopped to readjust his grip on Paris Thorne's ankles, ensuring that they all made it out of the building as quickly and safely as possible.

"Peachy." Leroy's voice rasped back a reply. The effort of talking nearly causing him to black out and a decision he instantly regretted. He sucked in what air he could and moved a leaden foot forward. Step by painful step they approached the door. All thoughts of the investigation now vanquished from their minds and concentrated only on one thing, survival. The front door creaked and bulged under pressure from the ravages of the flames eating it from the outside in. A worrying amber glow lit the gaps around the door where there should have been nothing but darkness. From above came the sound of thunder and for a moment Leroy thought that he had died and was suffering his fate for the rest of eternity. The door ahead looked like the entry to hell.

"You gonna make it, Leroy?" Georgina asked, more out of desperation than hope. She knew he was in a bad way. She was expecting a quip in reply but was greeted with silence. "C'mon Leroy, don't flake out on me now. A few more steps, we've got to keep moving." For the briefest second the full weight of Leroy slumped and it was all Georgina could do to remain upright holding him up. The door ahead appeared to pulsate under the pressure of the fire pushing against it. She looked to her right, down the long corridor hoping to see an alternative exit.

"Gotta move, Georgie." It was Wynan, her father, right behind her on the last step.

"I know."

The hall was illuminated with a threatening, living orange glow which moved and changed hue. The noise from the approaching fire now almost deafening and petrifying at the same time. The roar from above increased and with it followed an almighty thud as a cargo plane seconded by the firefighting department unleashed its contents directly onto the small cabin. Everything became dark and quiet.

They burst through the door bringing with them the fury and mayhem of hell. Flames still licked at the surface of the door, now swung open and rocked off one hinge. Bright halogen lamps cut swathes through the smoky darkness and behind them came verbal commands, not panicked but clear, functional and urgent. Names were being called. Georgina heard her own name. It was as though she was being evacuated from a strange planet. The weight of Leroy seemed to increase in those final moments as her strength finally began to give out. Maybe it was the thought of rescue which, like a tap, suddenly shut off her adrenaline the only thing driving her forward. Georgina's father stepped past her. He was no longer carrying the body of Paris Thorne.

"We've got a two minute window. Look lively." The alien voice inside her head belonged to a stranger in a firefighting suit and breathing apparatus.

The world outside the open door appeared quiet, resolute. Georgina knew this to be the work of a trickster, the fire had not disappeared it was merely holding its breath.

"We need two stretchers for evac," Wynan said as he grabbed the arm of a firefighter leading them to Paris Thorne and Leroy LaPortiere.

A team of eight firefighters entered the cabin and within a minute were feeding oxygen to Georgina, Wynan, Carter and Scott. Before the second minute had begun Leroy and Paris were on stretchers and everybody was being guided out of the building with breathing apparatus held or worn. To her left Georgina could feel a wall of heat, it was as though she had opened an oven door which had been left on heat. She briefly glanced at the wall of fire, a vast pulsating monster eating everything in its path. To her right was their small window of opportunity—a clear path leading to two armor plated rescue vehicles. Debris and evidence of mangled forestation evident in the metallic tracks of the tank-like vehicles. Above came the sound of a large aircraft on its way to deliver another payload to drench the fire in what was clearly a lost cause. Georgina watched as Leroy and Paris Thorne were placed on gurneys inside the closest rescue vehicle. There was no time for anything other than prompt evacuation. She felt herself being guided toward a second armored rescue vehicle in a manner that more than suggested that the option was not open for debate. The plane above was now a few hundred feet away and flying so low that it was frighteningly surreal.

"Let's move it. That plane is going to unload whether we are inside the RV or outside." A voice behind a mask with breathing apparatus said.

Inside the RV it was very basic and cramped, two lines of padded bucket seats with six seats in each line. Georgina shuffled along a few seats and buckled herself in. Her father, Carter and Scott were next, quickly followed by four of the firefighters. The door to the RV was shut and the vehicle's diesel engine roared as the drive engaged gears and started to move the heavy beast. Within seconds the RV was hit with a mighty thud as a wall of dyed water from the cargo plane above was unloaded. The driver seemed totally unfazed and didn't even pass comment. The RV trundled through the forest following its route in, taking them away from the fire. Georgina peered through the driver's window, the small slot no more than twelve inches deep by thirty wide. With the fire behind them and the sky ahead looking brighter she knew the sun was finally rising on a new day. The RV trundled on until it finally broke free from the forest into a clearing and the even surface of the asphalt road. Wynan leaned forward and smiled.

"Cally's gonna be mighty pissed." His cell phone rang. Wynan reached inside his pocket and answered the call. He listened intently to whoever it was on the other side of the line. Wynan looked up at his daughter, catching her eyes. He only uttered one solemn word. "Okay." And closed the phone.

# Chapter 38 Requiem

Wednesday May 21, 2003
Eleven Hours Later

Georgina woke. The room was dark even though it was the middle of the afternoon. The blackout curtains worked perfectly but they did not shut out the pain. Leroy was dead. The phone was ringing off the hook and it was only now that the confusion of noise in her head made any sense. She reached to the side table and picked up her phone. Her voice was horse, the vocal chords strained from breathing too much smoke and sobbing.

"Hello."

"Cally asked if you would like to come and meet your new sister."

Georgina instantly recognized her father's voice. She sniffed and swallowed hoping to lubricate and clear her throat. "Of course."

"I'll come round and pick you up on the way."

"Dad …"

"Yeah?"

"Can we see Leroy after?"

"Of course."

Georgina placed the phone handset back in the docking station. The house felt empty. Georgina walked down the hall past Leroy's closed bedroom. She had purposely pulled the door closed as soon as she got in and wasn't sure if she'd ever get the courage to open it again. How she'd be able to face seeing his dead body in the mortuary was a mystery and one she put to the back of her mind as she prepared to get ready for her father's visit. She made a cup of tea and sat for a while just cradling the mug, her mind not functioning, just numbed by the events of the previous day.

Georgina washed and dressed. She had not had the luxury of quiet time to herself for what seemed like days. The clock in the kitchen ticked loudly. The rhythmical sound hypnotic and sending Georgina into a calmer state which lasted a full minute before her door buzzer shattered the temporary peace. She stood to answer knowing it would be her father on the other side of the door. Somehow she also knew that she needed the noise in her mind to allow her escape from thinking too deeply about Leroy. She didn't invite her father in;

instead she stepped out into the daylight and the continued sweltering heat.

"Let's go."

"You okay, Georgie?" Wynan asked. He could not hide the deep concern that only a father could have.

"No." How else could she answer.

In a rare moment of father and daughter closeness Wynan's hand embraced Georgina's and she became his child once more. The strength and protection was there in his grip sending out the message that nothing could harm her while he was with her. If only life was so simple. The drive to the hospital took twenty minutes. Georgina chatted about everything except Leroy. She asked her father if she could see a picture of her new sister. Wynan obliged by handing her his cell phone.

"Cally sent a couple of images over this morning and there's about forty I took earlier this morning." Wynan allowed himself a small laugh.

"Only forty?" Georgina took the phone and began scrolling through the images of the wrinkled pink bundled that weighed eight pounds and eight ounces.

"Music?"

Georgina turned to her father. "Yeah." She knew what he was trying to do and thanked him for it. The gentle sound of Diana Krall drizzled through the speakers, like honey. It was easy listening jazz that was inoffensive and hung in the air like the scent of blossom on a summer's day. Georgina scrolled through the images on the phone's display, each subsequent shot portrayed a new life that was filled with innocence and hope. Georgina felt sorry for her already.

Georgina looked up at her father. "We never even found Susan."

Wynan didn't answer. Their destination cutting short a moment of reflection. Wynan pulled into the large hospital parking lot. Georgina had become so absorbed by the images that time had flown past and with it the twelve miles to the large municipal building. The elevator took them to the fifth floor which was the maternity ward. Cally was out of bed and walking, which surprised both Wynan and Georgina.

"Get me out of this place it's driving me crazy," Cally said. "You're a director of the FBI, flash a badge or something … arrest me." She leaned forward and kissed Wynan lightly on the lips.

Georgina was expecting "hello" or at least a smile but on reflection shouldn't have been surprised by Cally's reaction. In the distance came the sound of new lungs being stretched, filling the air with cries of anguish, horrified at being exposed to this strange new world.

"You wanna see your sister?" Cally said to Georgina.

"Half-sister," Georgina said. She didn't know why and regretted being so churlish the moment her lips stopped moving.

Cally raised an eyebrow and shrugged off the barbed response. "Follow me."

Georgina could see from her father's eyes that he was disappointed with her aggression, though nothing was said.

And there she was. Lying in a cot. A small living human being.

And there he was. Lying on a slab. Cold as the steel table he was on. Perfectly dead. Leroy LaPortiere neither looked at peace or in glory; he was vacant, devoid of spirit and soul. There was no hint of an afterlife, only the confirmation of the end of this one. His brown skin looked darker when drained of life. The bluish tinge of death matched the cold and unforgiving touch of his skin. Georgina watched him for some time. It was almost as if she expected him to suddenly exhale and get up off the table laughing. But the joke was most definitely on him this time.

"You bastard, Leroy." Was all Georgina could bring herself to say.

# Chapter 39 The Sound of Silence

Friday May 30, 2003

It was supposed to rain at funerals, but the heat wave dragged on. Georgina longed for a break in the weather and a return to normal temperatures. Somehow it didn't seem right dressing up in black on such a sunny day. The flight to Missouri was as horrendous as she thought it would be. Her fear of flying would never be conquered and it was only the thought of spending two days behind the wheel on the journey south that swayed her opinion. Her father had sat next to her and would make the return flight with her the following morning. But for now she just sat in the church awaiting the final chapter on Leroy's life. As she waited for the proceedings to begin she watched strangers filter past in various states of grief, all of them touched by Leroy's life in some way. Georgina watched to see if Lia would show. She waited to see if somehow someone had managed to get the message to her in Washington that her ex-lover had been killed. Maybe they had and she chose not to attend, maybe Lia had moved on too. The days following his death had been a mixture of painful sorrow and tiny moments of joy as Georgina held her baby sister for the first time. Time is a healer so they say but for Georgina it merely allowed time for reflection. What had she achieved? Her health was worse than it had ever been in her life. Her one true friend was lying cold in a wooden box about to be lowered into freshly dug earth, her career … she laughed at the notion of the word career, was in tatters with another failed case to blotch her CV, not that it mattered. Georgina knew her decision to leave the FBI would be made for her if she didn't choose to resign, especially as her father had dropped a bombshell on the flight down to Missouri that he was opting for early retirement. He said the failed case did not affect his decision. It was true he had stored enough money to comfortably see him through to the end of his days. This was time he wanted to spend with Cally and little "Natalie-Jean O'Neil" as her sister was to be christened. Any protection their relationship afforded would be gone, but she did not in the least begrudge her father his decision. She actually felt envious and jealous that her new wee sister would get all the attention she longed for all of her life, and so would Cally. It was bittersweet. Mourners filed by the open coffin. Georgina joined the end of the queue and shuffled her way to the pristine oak casket. Wynan remained seated confirming his position as one of support for his daughter and respect for the detective rather than sorrow. He wanted to be back home with his wife and baby and used his retirement as a bargaining chip to accompany Georgina on this trip to the southern state. Even at her most illogical Cally could not argue against such a deal. Georgina reached the coffin and looked at Leroy for one last time. But this was actually looking at a representation of him by a stranger. Leroy was lost under a layer of funeral cosmetics whose purpose it appeared was to breathe life into a corpse. There was no honesty in this type of death or showcasing of his body. In a way she would rather have remembered him as he was in the mortuary at the hospital. Georgina stood for a moment lost in her own private thoughts and memories. The friend that she loved was gone even though the body was within touching distance. She had no desire to touch Leroy's body for one last time. What was the point, there would be no connection now that his life force was gone. It was not as if she could shake him awake or whisper to him all the things left unsaid.

The funeral moved outside, into the heat of the day. Georgina felt as though she was partaking in a play; a theatrical production. There had been music and speeches and there had certainly been drama with the two great gods of theatre "tragedy and laughter" slugging it out for position as favorite. Georgina wondered if Leroy actually told anyone of his final wishes. This was the step by step handbook of mourning, nothing more or less than a cliché of grief. Georgina hoped there was an alternative.

The coffin was carried for what seemed like a mile in a slow procession through fields of headstones until finally they came to Leroy's final resting place. They gathered round the freshly dug hole. Mounds of earth were placed to one side. Georgina watched her father take position next to her. His hand once more slipped into hers and felt reassuring. Leroy's brothers and sister and their husbands, wives and children all stood in complete silence as the eulogy was read. The voice a memory from another time. Georgina looked up to see a grieving Captain Norman Frusco. The balding, squat policeman was looking shorter as though crushed by the world. Within four hours he and Georgina would be attending another two funerals, those of Barbara Dace and John Keller whose bodies were eventually found and identified when the fire burned itself out. It was going to be an extremely long day.

# Chapter 40 Destiny and a Twenty-Two Pound Bag

Wednesday June 4

The letter was waiting in her mailbox when Georgina arrived home. It was mid-afternoon on a Wednesday, though the importance of days had really lost their relevance, mostly they all blurred into an endless stream of consciousness or sleep. The buff manila envelope looked pretty innocuous but the local postmark and federal stamp betrayed its real intention. This was not the first invitation to a disciplinary meeting she had received or been the focus of. The fact that Georgina planned to tender her resignation would not make her immune from any decision found at the tribunal though and attendance was not optional. She slid the envelope open. The sharp edge of the paper cut Georgina's index finger causing her to flinch. Blood smeared along the envelope dropping onto the starch white papers. Papers which demanded her attendance the following Tuesday at 8:00 a.m. Georgina wanted closure, not just on the case but on this shitty chapter of her life. There was nothing redeeming … no that was a lie. There was a lot of redeeming factors, meeting Leroy, seeing her sister for the first time and the fact that she felt closer to her father than for a number of years. Yet still she would be happy to close the book and walk away from it all. What there was, was just not enough. The throbbing pain behind her temples returned. A slow pounding pressure seeking release. A second envelope in the small pile offered hope.

*Dear Ms. O'Neil,*

*After a period of review and on the basis of results from MRI, CT scans and blood work passed to us by your consultant at Maryland, I am pleased to inform you that Dr. Peter Jacobson will see you at his New York practice on Tuesday June 10 at 10:30 a.m. If you cannot make this appointment or need to reschedule please be aware that Dr. Jacobson is in extreme demand as one of the most eminent oncologists in the world and has a full diary for eighteen months with little room to rebook.*

Georgina appreciated the frankness of the letter if not the lack of notice. She looked at the date on the postmark. Why had it taken two weeks to get to her from New York? There was a signature at the bottom of the letter, clearly signed by an assistant; at least the phone number was legible. The disciplinary board would have to wait. Georgina picked up the phone and dialed the physician's office to confirm and then booked a single rail ticket to New York's Grand Central Station and a room at the Old Georgian on 42nd West and 35th Street.

08:04 a.m. Tuesday June 10

"In her absence we can only surmise that Agent Georgina O'Neil is happy for us to proceed with this review." Senior Director, Agent Ruth Henry-Osborne took a deep breath which translated itself as a weary sigh through the small microphone on the desk in front of her. She gave one final glance around the large room in the hope that Georgina would appear. "The case for review dates back to October of last year and the incidents related to the kidnapping and murder of Missouri State Detective Rick Montoya and the subsequent kidnapping and successful release of his wife and child. This review has already been delayed due to the ill health of Ms. O'Neil and she had been temporarily suspended from duties dependent on the outcome and findings of this review."

"Senior Director, if I may interject for a second." Director Daniel Martin cut in politely. "It would appear that Agent O'Neil's status was reversed by Director Wynan O'Neil."

"Her father?" Henry-Osborne looked over the rim of her glasses directly into Martin's eyes.

"I have a written statement explaining the reasons behind his decision and the events following her reinstatement. Wynan is waiting outside and prepared to give his statement."

"It would be interesting to hear what he has to say. Maybe he knows the whereabouts of Agent O'Neil." She nodded to an agent sitting by the double doors leading to the room.

Wynan was sitting in the long corridor collecting his thoughts. The white noise of office life collected around him in an ambient drone filtering down to a background buzz. Wynan had tried calling Georgina numerous times and had left three voicemails of increasing urgency. The third voicemail finally prompted a response. It was just as the FBI agent was walking toward Wynan that his cell phone rang. He looked at the display and could see a digital image of his daughter.

"Georgina, where the hell are you?" Wynan's voice was low, forceful and direct.

There was a short pause before Georgina answered. She sounded tired. "New York." Georgina did not offer a further explanation. "I just wanted you to know that I am alright." Georgina was lying on her bed on the eleventh floor of the hotel. The curtains were pulled back offering a view of the Empire State building.

"I know you haven't forgotten the review and I also know that whatever reason is keeping you from being here must be important. If it is what I think it is, then I should be there with you too."

"I'll be alright, Dad."

"You know, sometimes it doesn't hurt to ask for help or say I am afraid. But I guess I am as much to blame. I have raised you to be tough, to be independent … to be distant." The FBI agent reached Wynan and stood waiting impatiently. Wynan raised his hand in acknowledgment. "I gotta go, hon."

"I didn't want to put you in an awkward situation, Dad."

"I know. I love you too." Wynan closed the phone and looked up at the young agent waiting for him.

"Sir, they'd like to see you now."

It was a crystal clear blue sky day and everything had a clarity and sharpness to it. The buildings were more defined, the people in the street were moving about their daily work with what on the surface appeared to be no trouble or problems, even the air seemed cleaner. Georgina felt like the tourist which in part she was. The buzzing cacophony of traffic both human and mechanical did nothing to spoil her rose tinted assessment. Georgina had purchased a bus ticket from a street vendor and hopped on one of the open top busses operating in the city. She made her way to the upper deck and sat right at the back. Georgina had over two hours before her due appointment time. She wanted to kill time and be with people, even if they were strangers. It was 8:20 a.m. and still too early for anyone but serious tourists of which Georgina counted six other people. Three sets of couples, each of them in their forties or fifties, all of them lost within the splendor of their own adventures. Georgina envied them the purity of their endeavors. She wished that she was there only as a tourist, she needed the help and support of a friend … of Leroy. She envied the people on the bus their partners too and the simplicity of their moment in New York. Her mind kept replaying the incidents at the cabin, trying to figure out what had really happened. None of it made sense. Where was Susan Dark? Was she ever there? What happened to Sheriff Rankin? How did Fisher Sutherland escape? And most importantly what was the bloody point in it all? Blood … the answer is in the blood. Her thoughts returned to what Sutherland had said in that surreal meeting in the diner, "The answer is in the blood." What did he mean? Trace returned some matches but nothing which conclusively tied it all together. The whole thing was a mess and made the incidents in Turtle Island appear as clear cut as an Agatha Christie novel. The low pounding in her head returned, reminding Georgina why she was in New York. "The answer is in the blood." The thought kept returning to her like a tennis ball in a rally. Her stop approached. Time to alight. Somewhere in the background of the cacophony of thoughts and noise inside her head was the sound of the tour guide imparting the history of New York. Georgina made her way down the bus. She pressed the bell to make sure the driver would stop and took the fourteen or so steps down to the lower deck. While she waited for the view of the Flatiron Building to appear at 175 5th Avenue, Georgina scanned the inside of the bus, looking at the passengers. There were only five downstairs, two couples and a man in his mid to late thirties. Georgina waited for the bus to come to a halt. The walk was less than five minutes. Life was in full flow in the street, hustle and bustle and the chance to slip into comforting anonymity. She watched the bus she had been sitting on for the past two hours whoosh by carrying its cargo of passengers to enlightenment. Georgina's journey ends here outside the clinic of Dr. Peter Jacobson. She opened the clear glass door and entered the building.

Wednesday July 2

Susan Dark sat on a park bench. A tune ran through her head but she resisted the urge to hum it. Six weeks had passed since those lost months in the woods. She had read about the devastating fire in the papers and online on a daily basis for the best part of three weeks before the story began to fade to be replaced by news of the world recession and foreign wars. She was secretly pleased for the world's miseries and that they could somehow make her problems fade away. She studied an attractive, confident young woman walking toward her carrying a brightly colored tote bag. This young woman drew closer to her and eventually sat next to her on the park bench. Paris Thorne looked the picture of health. Thorne placed the brightly colored bag next to Susan. Susan noticed the missing index finger on the young woman's left hand—a small sacrifice about which Susan would never know the full story.

"For a while I thought that idiot boy, Frolan, had given me an overdose," Paris said. She sat for a while just enjoying the breeze and the warmth of the sun on her face. "But he hadn't. I could see the whole thing. It was worth a near death experience. Worth every penny or should I say dollar. All seven million of them."

Susan turned and looked at the young woman. "You can't choose your families."

Paris squeezed Susan's thigh. "But you can choose your friends." With that she rose and left without picking up the bag. Susan sat for a while and then happy that no one was looking, reached inside her jacket pulled out a small travel luggage scale. She hooked the curved metal arms under the handle and lifted the bag. It took quite a bit of effort while sitting down but the bottom of the bag cleared the seat and air was placed between then. Susan looked at the digital display. It read twenty-two pounds. She smiled and began to sing *Lonesome as I am*. Susan waited a further five minutes, spending the time watching the quiet serenity of the park and singing to herself before picking up the bag and leaving.

Susan walked back to the waiting car. It was exactly as she was told it would be and had expected. There were no surprises. She kept looking down at the bag and resisted the temptation to run. She felt the giddy excitement of a young child being presented with a new puppy. Susan opened the passenger door of the Gran Torino and sat.

"Did it go as planned?" A voice from the rear of the vehicle.

"Without fault or deviation." Susan replied. She passed the tote bag to her mother in the back of the car.

"Wow, it's lighter than I thought it would be."

Susan looked at her. Seriousness engrained in her eyes. "It's twenty-two pounds. I weighed it."

"And the pick up tomorrow?"

Susan passed Caroline Dark/Mary T Rankin a folded piece of paper. Mary opened it read the contents and passed the note to Fisher Thorne in the driver seat.

"Another town, another state, another bag."

"And another million." Fisher smiled. He put the car in drive. "Four down, three to go."

Wynan O'Neil sat at his desk. His office felt empty, stripped of the human trappings of life, personal mementoes, photos, and artifacts. All those items of life now packed neatly in three cardboard boxes. Someone he didn't know who worked in facilities would deliver them to his home in a day or so. Early retirement, the thought a year ago would have sent a cold chill down his spine but now the notion not only appealed it was positively attractive. He was independently wealthy, his pension secured and he had a young wife and new daughter, so closing this chapter on his life was easy. He knew the exciting part lay ahead. A short walk to the elevator and a ride to the fifth floor for a meeting with HR would finalize everything bar a round of farewell drinks and parties. One folder remained on his desk, his last case, Susan Dark; it would be good to finish his career tying up the loose ends but there were so many and there just was no time left. Sometimes you have to know when to quit. Nearly being trapped in the fire was a close enough call. Wynan opened the folder. There was yet another report from the pathology lab. The word "URGENT" was marked in bold red capital letters. Wynan flipped the folder open. Other keywords stood out as his eyes scanned the report. "Cross contamination, re-test, lab error." The nature of the way the blood samples were presented posed difficulties and it was hardly surprising there was some cross contamination. Extrapolating clean, uncontaminated samples to test would have been a nightmare. All the same, Wynan did not expect to read "lab error" in the report. Somehow with a scientific procedure, all of those elements of luck you need in the field become obsolete as you work to a set of strict guidelines. Not that for a moment he thought the lab guys were perfect ... who is? He closed the folder without reading on. It was not the first unsolved case he had worked on but it would be the last. There were over 100,000 unsolved homicide cases at the FBI that this could get lost in. As dedicated as he was, Wynan just knew he did not have the time left at the bureau to work on it. He had other pressing matters such as raising his daughter. His knew his replacement would be so full of ambition and eagerness to impress that he or she would relish a challenge like the Susan Dark case. Wynan thought about his wife, his new daughter and Georgina, and somehow solving a case where the victim was thought to be alive somehow did not rate that high in his list of priorities. His phone rang. Apart from the folder and his computer it was the only other item on his desk.

"O'Neil."

"Sir, we'd like you back for the summary."

O'Neil looked at his watch. Six weeks had passed since he left the review. Thirteen minutes was the quickest time he knew of for his peers to come to any decision in a disciplinary matter. Over six years was the longest. This case was anything but special in their eyes. So it was neither a good sign nor bad. Wynan O'Neil straightened the Susan Dark case folder and stood. He briefly looked around the room, before taking his jacket off the hanger on the coat stand, putting the jacket on and catching the elevator to the thirteenth floor.

Six weeks in New York had failed to give Georgina any real closure on either the case or the loss of Leroy.

Dr. Peter Jacobson stood six feet seven inches in his socks. In another life he would have been a basketball player or a jock of some sort, had he chosen to skip a life of academia and science. He dominated the office. He actually dominated most rooms. Jacobson had a full head of natural bleach blonde hair which sat comfortably with his chiseled Scandinavian heritage and unnervingly blue eyes which sat behind expensive designer glasses.

"You know," Jacobson began. "This is remarkable. With many people there is no choice when they walk in this office. Most have a small percentage life expectancy." Jacobson smiled an expensive smile. Crystalline white porcelain veneers flashed. "But you, my dear, you do. Since your last CAT scan these aneurisms have literally moved closer to the surface of your brain. Remarkable. I have seen them spread and multiply and yes I have seen them move, often burrowing deeper but rarely, if ever, have I seen them become more accessible." Jacobson passed the digital print to Georgina. She took the sturdy piece of paper from the doctor and studied the colorful three dimensional series of images of her brain. Hot spots flashed in vibrant warm colors. It was clear to see the seven individual swollen sacs of fluid which were the cause of her problems.

"I suggest we operate today," Jacobson said.

"And what are the chances?"

"Mortality?"

Georgina nodded.

"We all die. But your chances have just improved by around forty percent."

Georgina looked at Jacobson. Based on his previous calculations and those of other eminent specialists her survival rate had just more than doubled.

"We can't afford to wait," Jacobson said.

"Okay."

"Is there anyone you would like to contact before …"

"No. They have enough to deal with." Georgina handed Jacobson a folded paper. "Just in case."

"Georgina, your father really should be told." Jacobson was now sitting a couple of feet from her. He reached his large hands out and held Georgina's hand for a second. His eyes smiled warmth.

"If I die then I would have saved him days of anxiety. If I live I promise you can tell him as soon as I am functioning normally." Georgina spoke of herself as though she were a machine.

Jacobson nodded. "Okay, it's a deal. We operate this afternoon."

Georgina spent the remainder of the morning settling into the comfortable room which was hopefully going to be home for at least the next fortnight. She had a small case which she managed to fill with a number of items she knew she would never need but reminded her of home, which she hoped would aid the convalescence period. The side-effects from the operation were as serious as they could get. Death, paralysis, blindness, deafness, loss of long-term memory, loss of short-term memory. She had to accept that today would be the last day she would be the person she was whatever the outcome of the operation. Georgina looked at some photos and with a black permanent marker wrote on the back of each one the relationship she had with the person in the image and whether she liked them or not. Loss of long-term or short-term memory was one thing but forgiveness through malfunction was another. She looked at a picture of her father proudly holding her new sister, Natalie-Jean. He was embracing Cally. Georgina laughed, a small outburst, whether it was pre-operation nerves or something else she didn't know. A random dark thought entered her head. "What if I end up blind with permanent memory loss?" She looked around the room and the contents of her case and all her photographs and said. "Then none of this will matter."

The TV was on in the background. Georgina had found a news channel and somehow through the cacophony of thoughts and white noise running through her head she heard a name she recognized. Her attention caught, she looked up to see a picture of Paris Thorne. She tuned in mentally.

"… just inherited the Thorne Media empire worth an estimated $4.2 billion. It appears now that the recent demise of her father, Randolph Thorne, was brought about as part of an audacious rescue attempt to free his kidnapped daughter, who was previously thought to have been murdered. Sources close to the investigation have revealed that the successful rescue of Paris Thorne was not without further tragedy to the world of media with the deaths of MRTV's veteran reporter Barbara Dace and her long-time cameraman John Keller both of whom are believed to have been executed before perishing in the fire which swept through Cedarville State Forest. Paris Thorne seems to be putting this all behind her and was on the red carpet last night at the premier of the new Aarron Haart movie with a new beau in tow. United through grief, tragedy and loss Ms. Thorne's latest squeeze is Brett Anderson, grandson of the music management company's founder looking after the still missing Susan Dark. Brett also lost his grandfather in the event in the Cedarville State Forest tragedy at the end of May. Curiouser and curiouser. Moving on to other news …"

A nurse appeared at her door with a small aluminum trolley filled with meds of one sort or another. "Time for your pre-med."

Georgina sat on the corner of the bed and took a small plastic container from the nurse and a cup filled with water. She swallowed two innocent looking capsules drowned in a swig of water.

"I'll pop back in ten minutes then we'll go down to the operating theatre." The nurse took the plastic cup from Georgina and continued her round.

Georgina stood and took a deep breath. "Ten minutes," she said to herself. She walked to the window and pulled back the blinds. Dappled daylight streamed through the slats. The day was still glorious. Georgina blinked away the stinging light. Purple spots danced behind her eyelids. She went over and over the Susan Dark case in her mind and began to doubt what she thought was real, what was convenient and what now looked like something more sinister. She remembered again what Fisher Sutherland had said in the diner, "It's in the blood." As she thought about all of the associated and disassociated family ties she could see that he was right. The slow pounding throb of pressure and pain returned to her head. Georgina tried to focus on the buildings opposite, looking for confirmation of life still going on outside this sterile world she was locked in. The heartbeat of the city pulsed.

"It's time."

Georgina turned to find the nurse standing, waiting with a wheelchair by her side. "Was that ten minutes?"

The nurse looked at her watch. "Fifteen." She looked closely at Georgina. "Are you ready?"

Georgina wiped her face and looked at her palms. They glistened with salty tears but she felt calm. "It's a beautiful day."

"One of the best."

Georgina sat in the wheelchair and was taken to the elevator. As they glided down the elevator shaft to the third floor where the operating room resided Georgina thought about Leroy and how right now she could do with his strength, support and comfort. The elevator slowed and came to a halt. A red neon declared this to be the final destination. After a brief musical ping the doors parted and Georgina entered a more functional element of the building, pushed by the nurse. She didn't know if the drugs had made her too chilled or relaxed to find words but she didn't speak and the nurse respected her silence. The nurse turned and pushing her back against one of the double swing doors wheeled Georgina in. As she swung around to face the waiting operating theatre Georgina could see the operating table.

"Let's help you onto the table," Nurse Batten said, reaching out and offering her arm for support.

Georgina stood. At first she thought she could make it on her own. The table was only a few feet away and climbing onto it should have been easy considering it was on a lowered pneumatic setting. But after less than a second of standing grabbed the nurse's arm and allowed herself to be guided. She lay on the table and looking up wondered if this was to be the last view she would have in life, an operating theatre light.

"You're going to feel a slight scratch in the back of your hand. It's just the catheter going in for the anesthetic."

Georgina closed her eyes. She had no fear of needles or of the minor discomfort of the insertion of the catheter she just no longer wished to look at the ceiling. The catheter went in.

"Now, I'm just going to place some monitoring pads."

Georgina felt a cool gel being applied to her chest and temples and a little pressure as Nurse Batten stuck the monitoring pads to her. The door to the operating theatre opened and Georgina could hear two voices talking; one male, one female. She recognized Peter Jacobson.

"Hello, Georgina." Jacobson's voice. "In a moment you'll be going to sleep. There is nothing to worry about. You will feel a warm sensation and then just drift off and when you wake everything will be fine."

"I'm ready."

"Georgina, begin counting back from ten," Jacobsen said and nodded to Nurse Batten. She began to administer thiopental.

In her mind Georgina began to count from ten. As she said it she saw a picture of Leroy. Nine ... she saw her father. Eight ... everything was fading. Systems shutting down.

Jacobson looked at the monitors capturing data from Georgina. "Nurse, time for the muscle relaxant." Jacobson watched the effects closely on the monitor, waiting until he was sure that Georgina was under. "Ventilate the patient." Jacobson waited for another minute then leaned forward and whispered, "Welcome to the dark country, Georgina."